CRUEL
MAGIC

Cruel Magic

A VICTORIAN FAERIE TALE

E.B. WHEELER

Rowan Ridge
Press

ISBN: 978-1-7360411-6-1

First printing: August 2022

Published by Rowan Ridge Press, Utah

Cover design by Lauren Makena

Cover and interior design © Rowan Ridge Press

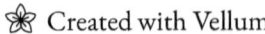 Created with Vellum

For my fellow spinal cord injury warriors

Chapter One

Smile.

Never contradict your betters.

Move gracefully.

Do not draw attention to yourself.

Cassandra repeated The Rules to herself as she finished her last letter. She had to make her first visit to the village of Drixton to post the letters—and meet her new neighbors—and The Rules would help her avoid social blundering. As long as she could remember them all.

The pencil in her left hand trembled with fatigue, but she signed the letter and grinned in triumph at the proper handwriting free of any smudges. Her schoolmaster had warned her not to use her left hand—the devil was on the left, he'd said —but what could he expect her to do now? Despite the autumn sunlight streaming into the garden and warming her silk dress, her crippled right hand was stiff and cold.

Useless.

She fumbled with an envelope, trying to hold it open with

the curled up fingers of her damaged right hand so she could slip the letter inside. After a couple of attempts, she huffed and jammed the paper in, frowning at the crumpled letter. She wanted to pound her good fist on the writing slope in her lap, but a young lady didn't do such things. She'd been forced to add her own rules to her mother's list.

Ignore people who stare or laugh at you.
Do not hit people with your cane, even if they deserve it.
Pretend to be normal.

She set her writing slope beside her on the garden bench and shook out her aching fingers. What a chore! But her mother's six older sisters each demanded a weekly report on their family, especially the state of her mother's health during these last few weeks of her pregnancy. At least this was something Cassandra could still do for her family. She fanned herself with the envelope, perfuming the autumn air with the smell of fresh paper and ink.

A breeze grabbed the papers from her writing slope. Cassandra fumbled after them, groaning when they landed like ungainly white birds in an elderberry bush on the far side of the herb garden. The paths were gravel. They looked deceptively neat and inviting, but Cassandra had already turned her ankle once strolling there.

She rose to her feet. The steel bars of the brace on her right leg jabbed at a raw spot under her fine wool stocking. The brace raised blisters if she wasn't careful, but it let her go without her cane, and she had practiced walking over the past months until her limp barely showed. That was on solid surfaces, though, not the treacherous shifting of gravel.

Sophie, her older sister, strolled over, her spotless white parasol tilted to shade her face. She wore the latest fashion, the wide overskirt of her bright blue dress gathered into a bustle that set off her tiny waist, and her honey-blonde hair arranged in neat curls.

"Cassie, what are you..." Sophie spotted the papers. "Oh, for pity's sake."

She minced over to the elderberry bush and plucked the papers free. The gravel barely crunched under her soft shoes.

She handed the papers back to Cassandra. "Are you ready to go inside? You're going to be shockingly freckled."

"No, I'm not. Not ready to go inside, I mean." Cassandra probably would develop freckles, but she loved the fresh, spicy scent of the garden. "I need to address these letters, and the light is better out here."

Sophie caught another piece of paper that tried to flutter off the writing slope. "You don't have to keep yourself so busy. We can afford leisure now. And especially for you—"

"You can stop treating me like I'm fragile." Cassandra cradled the papers against her chest with her good arm. "I'm not an invalid anymore."

Sophie gave an exasperated sigh, and Cassandra braced herself for an older sister lecture.

Beth, the local girl they'd hired as a maid, hurried over to them before Sophie could begin. Wisps of brown hair escaped from beneath the maid's crooked cap, and she clutched a bound sketchbook. "Have you seen Miss Charlotte? She was on the front porch, drawing, and I just ducked inside for a moment..."

Sophie and Cassandra shared a worried look. Charlotte was their youngest sister, just four years old.

"You lost Lottie?" Sophie asked.

Beth nodded, her chin trembling on the verge of tears.

Cassandra stepped in before Sophie could vent her frustration on the maid. "She likes to play hide-and-go-seek."

"Yes, miss," Beth said. "Nancy and Miss Georgina are

searching the house, but there's no sign of her."

Nancy, the family nurse, and their sister Georgina would know the best places to look indoors, but Cassandra frowned at the vast grounds of their father's new estate. "She could be anywhere if she's out here."

Sophie, wide-eyed, scanned the empty garden paths. "Beth, you and I will search the lane."

"I'll help." Cassandra set her papers aside.

"We'll be faster without..." Sophie glanced at Cassandra's right leg and grimaced. "Why don't you help them look inside? Beth, you go up that way, and I'll head toward the village."

Beth handed the sketchbook to Cassandra and dashed off, and Sophie bustled away before Cassandra could protest.

"Help inside," Cassandra muttered, glaring at the two-story stone house towering behind her. If Lottie was just playing hide-and-go-seek in there, she wasn't in any danger, but outside was another matter. Their father's new estate stretched away from the house, the orderly garden giving way to straight rows of orchard trees and finally the wild woodlands beyond.

"Lottie!" Cassandra set the sketchbook aside and picked her way down the gravel path.

A lone crow uttered a raspy caw, but otherwise, a still, empty quiet filled the garden. Would Lottie have wandered into the orchards? Cassandra glanced at the house. She could move faster with her cane, but she didn't want to waste time going back for it. Not when Lottie might be frightened or hurt. She reached the orchard and limped past trees weighed down with red apples awaiting the harvest.

A fluttering shape on a low branch caught her eye. She hurried over and tore it free. A long, blue ribbon like the ones tied on the ends of Lottie's braids.

Cassandra clutched the ribbon. "Lottie, dear! Where are

you?"

Faintly, on the edge of the orchard, the murmur of a stream broke the quiet. Lottie would like to see the water. She might fall in. A terrible fear coiled in Cassandra's stomach, turning to stone.

She followed the sound, pushing her leg harder, ignoring the blister stinging under the brace. Her right foot dragged despite the iron support bars, and her toes caught on the uneven ground. Her good leg buckled, and she stumbled to her hands and knees, the taste of dust filling her nose and mouth. She brushed off her skinned hands and staggered back to her feet. How could she help her sister when she couldn't even walk across the orchard without tripping?

"Lottie, dear, come to me!"

The deep quiet of the woods seemed to swallow her words. But beneath the song of birds, the mocking burble of the water rolled on.

"Lottie!"

Cassandra dragged her right leg along, her right hand curled into a tight fist. Tall grass and the occasional rowan or alder tree crowded the edge of the stream, but Cassandra fought her way along, scanning the water for any sign of Lottie. The thin branches of a wild rose snatched at her skirts, holding her back as she pushed closer to the bank.

The water ran deep and fast through a narrow channel. In its murky shadows, the reflection of river rocks rippled into the shape of a dark castle. The stream's mocking voice burbled over the rocks and echoed back her call.

Lottie. Lottie. Lottie.

Cassandra leaned over, trying to see deeper. Distorted faces replaced the slippery brown backs of trout.

Come to me.

Chapter Two

The distant sound of the church bells rolled over the trees, and Cassandra shook her head and took a step back from the murmuring waters. Her fears were making her imagination run wild.

"Get back!"

Cassandra looked up to see a curly-haired young man barreling toward her from the woods on the other side of the stream. He snapped through the brush and leapt the water, landing next to her. Without even a moment to catch his balance, he grabbed Cassandra and swung her clear of the stream bank and the brush. She nearly tumbled again, but the young man's grip kept her upright.

Cassandra wrenched herself free, stumbling back. "What do you think you're doing?"

He moved to block her view of the woods. He looked about eighteen—her own age—tall and broad-shouldered, with a brown suit that spoke of someone who was comfortably situated but not wealthy. His necktie was loose, its end shoved rather hastily into the top of his waistcoat, and his respectable bowler hat tried—but failed—to keep his wild, curly brown hair contained.

"I'm saving you from yourself," he said. "Stay away from the water."

"I have to find my sister." Cassandra dodged around him, but he grabbed her arm. "Let go of me!"

"I can't do that." He smiled a little, almost a smirk, like this was a game.

Cassandra jerked her arm free, tempted to slap him for interfering with her search for Lottie. He was trespassing, and despite his respectable clothing, he appeared oblivious to how improper it was for her to be alone with him.

"Henry, she's not enchanted," said a male voice from behind them.

Cassandra's breath caught, and she glanced over her shoulder, finding herself outnumbered. Another young man walked toward them. He had the black hair and brown skin of a Sikh or Hindu, though his face was clean-shaven and he wore a conservative dark suit with an immaculate cravat.

She backed away from them both. "No, I'm not enchanted or charmed or amused by whatever games you're playing at. My little sister's lost, and you're wasting my time."

The two young men exchanged a worried glance, and the curly-haired one—Henry—looked back at her, his blue eyes all seriousness now. "You think she went in the water?"

Cassandra caught a sob, forced it down, tried not to be sick. She wanted nothing to do with arrogant, silly young men—she shouldn't even be talking to them—but Lottie needed help. "I don't know. I found her ribbon in the orchard. She's only four."

"Domin, you'll search along the stream?" Henry asked his companion.

The dark-skinned young man, Domin, nodded and jogged into the brush, slipping easily through the branches that had held Cassandra back.

"If she's near the water, Domin will find her," Henry said. "We'll check the woods."

And he walked off, not bothering to see if Cassandra was following. She limped after him, clinging to the blue ribbon and gritting her teeth as her right leg spasmed in protest of their pace.

Henry kept his eyes on the ground, pointing out the occasional small footprint. Cassandra's wariness of him eased— a little—since he took the hunt for Lottie seriously and kept a respectful distance. He guided them to a narrow stream crossing and paused.

"She went over here and followed the deer trail."

Tears of relief stung Cassandra's eyes. The woods, untamed as they were, still had to be safer than the water. She hesitated, then took an uncertain step onto the soft, damp stream bed, her exhausted right leg tightening and twisting inward against the brace. Her balance wavered. Henry stepped across the stream and reached a hand back for her. She surrendered and accepted his help, just to cross the water. His steady touch gave her a jolt of warmth and reassurance, but she pulled her hand away quickly.

"What's the girl's name?" Henry asked over his shoulder as he led them into the shadows of the ancient oaks and birches.

"Lottie," Cassandra whispered. Then she called, "Lottie, dear!"

The trees felt too close, as if they did not welcome intruders. They threatened to swallow the narrow path back into the dense green shade of the woods. And yet, something about the wildness eased the strain in her mind. The Rules didn't matter as much here, only finding her sister.

Cassandra took a deep breath. "Lottie!"

"Cassie?" a small voice called.

Cassandra gasped in relief. "Lottie! Where are you?"

"I'm here, in the tree."

Cassandra gave a stuttery laugh and limped past Henry, following Lottie's voice. "The woods are full of trees, dearest."

She came around a bend and saw Lottie high up the Y-shaped trunk of a rowan tree, among the sprays of reddening berries. Cassandra stepped toward her sister, but the little girl was staring farther down the path, where a creature stood watching them.

A white stag.

Its antlers towered overhead, the many points seeming to pierce the sky. Cassandra gasped. This was no docile storybook creature, but a wild thing, those magnificent, deadly antlers only a few short bounds from Lottie.

Cassandra limped forward to put herself between the stag and her sister.

The stag hopped to the side, its back leg almost buckling. A trickle of red trailed down its limb from a ragged hole: a wound from a hunter's careless shot. The stag watched the girls as though measuring them with its dark eyes—proud but wary. Then it made its slow way down the path, past them and to Henry, who stood on the trail.

The stag paused for a moment to study Henry. It lowered its great horned head as if bowing in greeting then pressed on into the woods.

Lottie and Cassandra exchanged a look of wide-eyed awe. Cassandra reached up for Lottie, but the girl shook her head.

"I can't get down. I don't know where to step."

Cassandra studied the tree. "Maybe if you put your foot—"

But Henry made a running leap at the tree and grabbed one of the branches, pulling himself up near Lottie and grinning down at Cassandra from his perch.

He turned to Lottie. "I'll lower you down to your sister, Miss Lottie. How does that sound?"

Lottie nodded. Henry reached out, and the little girl took his hand, allowing him to pull her away from the trunk. He shifted, lowering Lottie to Cassandra while he kept himself balanced in the tree. Cassandra snatched her sister into her arms, staggering under her weight. She let Lottie's hair tickle her nose and breathed in the scent of lavender soap.

"Never run into the woods! What were you thinking?" Cassandra wanted to shake her sister, but she was hugging her too tightly.

"I was following the fairy, but then I got scared."

Cassandra scoffed at her sister's stories and let Lottie slide to the ground, taking a firm grip on her hand. Henry jumped down and straightened the satchel slung over his shoulder. Cassandra cut off her impulse to shower him with thanks when she caught the self-satisfied turn of his lips.

She straightened and granted him a formal, "Thank you for your help, Mr..."

"Stewart. Henry Stewart. I'm glad I could be of assistance after all." He gave her a mischievous smile that was altogether too familiar, like he was inviting her to be part of a private joke.

She almost smiled in response but quickly schooled her expression. Though his accent was cultured, his careless attitude and recklessness belonged more to the wild woods than a civilized drawing-room. Besides, the Ashbys hadn't mentioned him, and her father's well-bred friends had been very precise about whom Cassandra and her sisters should consider appropriate companions.

She returned a formal nod. "I'm Cassandra Weaver, and this is Charlotte."

Lottie gave a pretty curtsey and smiled shyly at Henry, who grinned back at her.

A snap sounded from the trail where the stag had watched them. They all turned to see a gentleman with a hunting rifle approach on the deer trail. He wore a brown plaid coat and trousers, an ensemble which would have been hideous if it wasn't so fashionable. A thin brown mustache perched over his frowning mouth. His eyes narrowed when he saw Henry and the girls standing in his way.

"Where's the stag?" he asked. His voice bore the polish of West End London. Of someone who was used to commanding and being obeyed.

Cassandra pointed into the woods. Away from the direction that the stag had taken.

"Are you sure about that?" he asked.

Cassandra nodded firmly.

The man fixed his cold gaze on Cassandra. "I hope you're not interfering with my business. It could be dangerous."

"What, a wounded deer?" Cassandra asked, trying to hide her unease at the man's scrutiny.

"There's much more than deer to be frightened of out here." He smiled grimly. "Besides, it's already crippled. You're only prolonging its misery by leaving it alive."

Cassandra's skin turned chilly then flushed hot. Was her weakness so obvious? She looked down.

"We told you what you wanted to know, Rushford," Henry said, stepping up to the hunter. "And you're not on the Ashbys' land anymore. You could have shot someone."

"Don't worry, Stewart, I always hit my mark."

"That wounded stag says otherwise."

Rushford narrowed his eyes. He bobbed his head in a mocking sort of bow and strode off in the direction Cassandra had pointed.

When he was gone, Lottie squeezed Cassandra's hand. "I'm glad you lied to him. Don't worry, I won't tell Momma that you fibbed."

Cassandra flushed and laughed. "Thank you, dear."

"May I escort you out of the woods?" Henry smiled down at Lottie. "It's not a place for young ladies. Some people say they're haunted."

"By what?" Lottie asked.

"I wouldn't want to frighten you," he said to Lottie, but he gave Cassandra a teasing grin.

Cassandra raised an eyebrow. "Don't worry. The Weaver girls aren't prone to fainting."

"Nancy, our nursemaid, tells all sorts of scary stories about goblins and elves," Lottie said.

"The Fay aren't kind, then, helping children and shoemakers?" Henry's voice had a bitter edge.

"Not at all!" Cassandra said. "They're monsters, luring travelers to their deaths and kidnapping children." She gave her sister a stern look. "You'd think that would be enough to keep Lottie from trying to chase them."

"Indeed." Henry looked thoughtful, but Cassandra was sure he was still teasing them. He turned back to Lottie. "And what was the fairy like that you saw?"

"Pretty, with wings. But it was mean like in Nancy's stories."

"How so?"

"It bit me when I wouldn't follow it. See?" She held out her chubby hand, and Cassandra was surprised to see two tiny pricks of fresh blood on her thumb. "It stings."

Henry's brow furrowed in concern. "I'm sure it does. May I see it?"

He glanced at Cassandra, who nodded her permission.

Henry knelt and touched Lottie's hand, then jerked back as if he had been shocked. Cassandra leaned closer, trying to see what had alarmed him. With a deep breath, he turned Lottie's hand over and studied it, his frown deepening. He reached for the satchel slung over his shoulder. "I was out gathering elderberry. It's good for drawing out all kinds of infection. Since this injury is fresh, I think we're treating it in time."

"Did something actually bite her? Is she in danger?"

He applied some deep purple elderberry pulp and sat watching Lottie for a few long moments.

Her eyes widened. "It doesn't sting anymore."

Henry smiled. "No danger at all." He gave Lottie a warning look. "Just don't follow any more fairies. They're not to be trusted."

Lottie nodded seriously.

"Just to be sure..." Henry drew out a small paper envelope with some herbs in it and handed it to Cassandra. "Purple deadnettle tea. Add a bit of sugar and it won't taste too bad."

"Thank you," Cassandra said. "You seem to know about the woods and all these plants. It must be interesting. I mean, to me it's like walking through a... a strange poem."

She bit her lip to cut off her silly rambling. Henry's eyes were bright with amusement. She did tend to talk too much, but he didn't have to laugh at her.

He led them back down the deer trail, constantly scanning the trees. Probably looking for his friend Domin. Cassandra followed, keeping a tight grip on Lottie's hand. She wanted to ask if there was anything growing wild around her that could cure the palsy in her right limbs—something the city doctors hadn't tried—but that would acknowledge her flaw. Henry must have noticed it, but he hadn't acted awkward about it. Obnoxious and presumptuous, but that was surprisingly refreshing after being pitied or ignored. Bringing it up would transform her from proper young lady to invalid. She said nothing.

They exited the woods and crossed the stream, and Cassandra felt the weight of The Rules close around her again. She was suddenly aware of her dirty, torn dress. And she had wandered off unescorted with a strange young man. At least she had her sister back, and Henry Stewart, for all his devil-may-care self-assurance, didn't seem like the type to gossip about her. Or even remember her once she was out of sight.

He bid them farewell, and Cassandra made a stiff curtsey—grateful but distant, all that was proper. She led Lottie back to the garden, where a stray piece of paper flapped from a tangle of overgrown mint. Cassandra limped past it, guiding her sister inside and leaving her abandoned writing slope for another time. She wouldn't admit it aloud—especially not to Sophie—but her muscles trembled with exhaustion after the long walk. She was still broken. She might always be. Not good enough. Not perfect enough. But she could hide it.

Do not draw attention to yourself. Pretend to be normal.

She delivered Lottie to Nancy and her worried sisters in the drawing-room, and they flocked around the little girl.

"Lottie!"

"Where were you?"

"Never do that again!"

Cassandra hobbled to the stiff-backed wooden armchair to strip off her brace. The blister had burst and stuck to her stocking, but she carefully peeled the knitted wool away from her skin and propped her foot on a velvet-cushioned ottoman. Pain crawled over her leg like hundreds of ants biting her. She tried not to think about it. Or about the woods or hunters chasing white stags or arrogant young men with teasing smiles. Only then did she realize that Henry Stewart had never answered her question about what had injured Lottie.

Chapter Three

"Are you certain you're ready for this?" Sophie asked.

Cassandra tied on her bonnet. Her fingers trembled a little, but she met Sophie's eyes. "It will be easier with fewer people watching me. If today goes well, then I won't be as nervous for the Harvest Festival."

"Are you taking your cane, then?"

Cassandra glanced at the polished cherrywood stick sitting by the door, then shook her head. Sophie shrugged but looked relieved. A little limp didn't stand out like a cane did. Cassandra arranged her letters in a basket. She looped it over her crippled right arm to disguise her weakness. Ready to play the part of the perfect young lady, she followed Sophie outside.

The roses growing around the porch were blooming one last time, sweetening the air in defiance of the coming frosts.

Cassandra leaned heavily on the rail going down the stairs to the lawn. This was just a short shopping trip for some ribbon and silk flowers. She could do this.

As they made their way down the dirt lane to the village,

Sophie glanced at Cassandra occasionally, her eyes troubled.

"You're not hurting too much?" Sophie asked.

"No," Cassandra said truthfully, warmed by her sister's concern.

"And you'll remember not to ramble on or say anything foolish?"

Cassandra rolled her eyes. "Of course. I'll behave." At least Sophie treated her much as she had before the fever. She risked a quick glance up at a goldfinch gliding free in the sunlight. "I enjoy being outdoors. I think I'd like to learn to garden."

"I suppose that would be acceptable. Many fine ladies garden. As long as you don't get dirt under your fingernails."

Cassandra squinted through the gaps in the hedgerow, catching glimpses of songbirds flitting through the lacy shade of the woods beyond. She wanted dirt under her fingernails. She wanted the warm scent of soil and tangy herbs and life. She wanted to stroll under the canopies of the ancient oaks spreading their branches over the woods like the protective arms of a mother, a place that didn't care for The Rules.

She slowed, admiring the reds and golds frosting the tops of the trees. But beneath the inviting shade, Cassandra caught a glimpse of a deeper blackness lurking. Something older than roads and villages, the shadows of childhood fears lurking under beds and in the backs of wardrobes. Yet she didn't want to flee from the darkness. She wanted to step closer. To feel more of the excitement making her mouth go dry and stirring her heartbeat.

"Cassie?" Sophie asked.

The village church bell rang out, and its silvery tones called Cassandra back to the present. She'd been reading too much melodramatic poetry. She smiled at her imagination and caught up with her sister.

Before long, the hedgerow fell back to make way for thatched cottages. The top of the church's bell tower poked above the trees. The sisters came around a bend to the main square of Drixton: shops with wooden signs swinging in the breeze, a two-story inn, and an old stone church all clustered around a village green as if the buildings were wary of the woods beyond the hedgerows.

Two ladies in bonnets gazed in shop windows, and a group of men gossiped about London on the village green. Only a few people to impress. This would be a perfect test of The Rules. Cassandra forced her shoulders to relax.

"Oh, look, it's the Miss Weavers!" a female voice called.

The sisters turned to see a figure riding sidesaddle. Miss Elizabeth Ashby. Her older brother Robert trailed behind on his chestnut gelding. They were the children of Sir Walter Ashby, a friend of their father. Sir Walter was the very person who had convinced their father to move to Drixton.

Elizabeth waved. "Yoo-hoo!"

She pulled her palomino mare to a stop beside them and smiled down. A tiny red hat that matched her riding gown topped her glossy black hair. Her eyes widened as she took in the sisters. "The both of you didn't *walk* here."

Sophie and Cassandra exchanged a quick glance.

"Yes," Sophie said. "We wanted the exercise."

"You ought to ride," Elizabeth said. "It's much *better* exercise and far more fitting for your station now."

Cassandra fought to keep her face neutral. Even if her father could afford to stable riding horses for his oldest daughters, she liked to feel the ground beneath her feet. But arguing was against The Rules, so she forced a smile. Beside her, Sophie did the same.

Robert cleared his throat. "I think the walk must have

agreed with the Miss Weavers." His gaze lingered on Sophie. "They look lovely."

Elizabeth giggled and rolled her eyes. "Well, of course they do. Anyone can see their dresses are the latest thing."

Cassandra watched Robert. She doubted Sophie's fashion sense made the least difference to him. Or, perhaps it did. Not long ago, the sisters had only been the daughters of a shopkeeper, and Robert Ashby would hardly have given them a second glance. Their family's new wealth gave them new opportunities, and Cassandra couldn't ruin this for Sophie.

"What brings you to Drixton this afternoon?" Sophie asked the Ashbys.

"The Harvest Festival. We're overseeing the decorations," Elizabeth said. "Father says we must see that it's done correctly. You're coming to the Harvest Ball next week, of course."

Robert gave Sophie a hopeful look.

"Of course," Sophie said with a quick glance at Robert through her eyelashes.

"I'm so glad. Come see what we've done so far!" Elizabeth unhooked her leg to dismount, forcing Robert to hurry down from his horse and catch her.

Elizabeth, chattering like a starling, led Sophie away, and Robert, with the horses, followed close behind, trying to get in a word to Sophie. Cassandra watched them go. The muscles in her right leg spasmed, and she winced. She couldn't keep up with their pace. What was she supposed to do now?

She limped over to the inn to drop off her letters for the mail cart. The railways didn't even run to Drixton, so the cart had to take the village's letters to meet the train.

Cassandra glanced around at the shops lining the street. There could be little harm in shopping alone when her sister was so close. One sign showed a serpent twined around a chalice for an apothecary or pharmacy. Probably the closest Drixton had to a physician. Sir Walter extolled the health benefits of country living, and Henry Stewart's talk of elderberry and teas made Cassandra curious about what new remedies the countryside might offer for her weakness. Not that she had been thinking of Henry Stewart. She had pushed him out of her mind every time his teasing grin sprung to her memory.

When she limped closer to the apothecary shop, Cassandra noticed something odd in the window nook. Tendrils of frost uncurled across the glass like the opening fronds of a fern. She gaped in wonder. How was it done? It was beautiful, almost like magic.

She pushed the shop door open, and the bell overhead rang.

The pungent scents of thyme, oregano, and other herbs rolled around her. An empty counter sat to her right, and on the left, shelves of glass bottles filled with tinctures and dried plants lined the wall. The slanted light from the window played over the bottles and made them glimmer.

Henry Stewart stood in the window nook, his finger on the glass and a halo of ice spreading away from his touch.

Cassandra gave a start and stepped back. The basket on her arm banged against the shelf, tipping over several bottles.

She gasped and scrambled to catch them, but her right arm was too stiff and slow, and she was tangled with her basket. The bottles rolled across the shelf like truant children fleeing school. Henry vaulted the counter and grabbed the bottles before any could crash to the floor.

So much for moving gracefully. Or not drawing attention to herself.

Henry righted the bottles and grinned, his curly hair even more mussed than before. "If you wanted my attention, there are easier ways to get it, you know."

"What!" Cassandra's face burned. "No, I wasn't. You see, I mean, I was just shopping with my sister. We were going to pick up ribbons and silk flowers. Not that I expect to find them in here."

Don't gibber on like an idiot!

She added that to The Rules and clamped her mouth shut.

Henry glanced around. "Ah, so you've lost another sister, have you? Or is it the same one?"

"No!" She saw the laughter in his eyes. "Oh, it's monstrous of you to tease me!"

"Monstrous, is it?" He grew more serious. "Then I'm sorry. But your eyes flash quite charmingly when you're angry."

Cassandra's face flamed red again. Was she supposed to thank him or to slap him? The Rules were woefully unclear.

Henry grinned. "Now, what *did* bring you into the shop today?"

She couldn't find the words to talk about her affliction. She'd been expecting to talk to a wizened old man, not a young, handsome... No, her tongue felt tied in knots. He had to be an apprentice or the shop owner's son. Only, his accent was far too refined for a shopkeeper. He didn't belong behind the counter. And she did. Drixton was all mixed up. Her right hand curled up more tightly at the wrist.

"I just..." she stammered, "I mean, in the city, it seems like we had only weeds. I didn't know... Well, I suppose I *knew* there were so many kinds of plants, but it was hard to imagine. I wanted to see..." *Stop rambling!* Her gaze flitted behind Henry to the nook. "Your window! It's lovely. How did you do it?" She limped toward the counter to admire the icy designs on the glass.

"Ah, yes, I was experimenting with, um, saltpeter," he said.

The shop bell rang again.

"Saltpeter?" a familiar male voice asked from the doorway. Sir Walter Ashby. "Is *that* what happened to your window? Thought it must be something like that."

Henry straightened to attention. So, he *could* be serious.

"Yes, Sir Walter," he said.

Sir Walter Ashby strode into the shop and lifted his monocle to examine the window. "We should speak of this some time. Saltpeter," Sir Walter said again as though tasting the word. "Very interesting. Good to see young people dabbling in science. You'll make an excellent physician someday."

"Thank you, sir." Henry beamed.

Cassandra studied him. Physician. So, maybe Henry was a younger son of some gentry family. But why send him to a forgotten little village like Drixton for training? Unless he had been banished there to keep him out of trouble. He seemed the troublesome sort.

The shop bell rang again, and Mr. Rushford entered, wrinkling his nose like he had stumbled into a goat barn, his thin mustache climbing almost into his nostrils. This time, the hunter wore gray-checked trousers with a drab green coat. Only a little better than the plaid. Next to Sir Walter's conservative black suit and comfortably round form, Mr. Rushford looked like a tall, gaudy weed.

"Ah, Rushford!" Sir Walter exclaimed. "Young Stewart here has been experimenting with saltpeter. Thought you might enjoy chatting with each other sometime about the astounding possibilities of science."

Rushford and Henry exchanged a look of mutual loathing.

"But for now," Sir Walter said, "I'm here to check on Miss Cassandra. Your sister lost track of you."

"I'm sorry to have worried anyone," Cassandra said. "I was just doing some shopping."

"Not much in *here* for you, anyway." Rushford studied Cassandra with a critical eye, making her feel as if she were a butterfly trapped under glass with a pin held just over her heart. "Half of these 'medicines' will do you more harm than good. Hawthorn berry! Bah! Perhaps someday the *real* sciences will offer you a real cure." He smirked at Henry, who kept his expression impassive.

"Maybe. Maybe," Sir Walter said. "But leave the poor girl alone. We don't want anything about her changed."

Cassandra smiled shyly at Sir Walter. If only her parents felt the same way.

A thin, old man came in through the back entrance, shoulder bent under the weight of a doctor's satchel. He looked like the apothecary Cassandra had imagined.

"Mr. Tanner!" Sir Walter's voice overfilled the room, and the apothecary gave a start. "I was hoping to see you while I was in town."

"Of course, Sir Walter." Mr. Tanner set his satchel down with a weary smile. "What can I do for you?"

"I've had some tenants complaining to me of a strange affliction in their cattle," Sir Walter said. "The animals take sick suddenly and die. Rushford hasn't yet diagnosed the problem, but the farmers claim it's elf-shot. What do you make of that?"

Mr. Tanner shook his head, making his thin, combed-over hair flap like a wheat field in a storm. "I don't know as much about animals, but sounds like they've gotten into some poisonous plants. You know how these country folk are. Quick to blame things on superstitions."

Cassandra listened with interest, but she caught Henry's expression, which had gone several shades paler.

"Superstition. Of course, of course." Sir Walter polished his monocle on his waistcoat. "I'll tell them to rotate their fields.

Any suggestions on how to help the animals that are already ill?"

"Purple deadnettle tea," Henry said. Everyone turned to him, and he hurried on. "And a syrup of elderberries. It might help flush out the poisons."

Cassandra raised an eyebrow. Just what he had given Lottie.

Mr. Tanner shrugged. "It's just an old folk remedy, but I don't see the harm."

"Ha!" Rushford said. "I'll find out what's really behind their troubles. And speaking of that," he turned back to Mr. Tanner. "Those chemicals I ordered?"

Mr. Tanner hesitated. "Some of them came in. You realize they can be dangerous. Oil of vitriol is highly acidic. It causes severe burns."

Rushford smirked. "Anything can be dangerous if used incorrectly. And anything can be wondrous in the proper hands. Think of electricity! A deadly power when wild, like lightning, but when tamed, it may someday perform all types of miracles for us."

Mr. Tanner shook his head. "I don't know about that."

"I have already built machines that harness just a fraction of its potential." Rushford placed a small stack of coins on the counter with a dull thunk. "This should cover the cost of the chemicals. After all, it's almost Michaelmas. Time to settle all accounts, am I right?"

He said it with a smile that made the room feel colder. Cassandra shrank away from him.

Sir Walter glanced at her. "You'll be wanting to get back to your sister, Miss Cassandra. Good day to you, Tanner, Stewart."

Chapter Four

Henry watched Cassandra limp out of the apothecary shop on Sir Walter's arm. He sensed a good deal of cleverness behind her proper formality. Interesting girl.

"Henry, see if you can find Mr. Rushford's order," Mr. Tanner said.

"And bring along some of that saltpeter as well," Rushford added with a smirk.

Henry nodded to Mr. Tanner and ignored Rushford. He headed for the back room. Rushford didn't need any vitriol—he had plenty of his own. But Henry had to find out if the Fay were spreading elf-shot through Drixton. He had thought little Lottie Weaver was an isolated case, but if the Fay were killing cattle too...

Henry grabbed his hat and continued outside to the small garden behind the shop. Mr. Tanner would wonder what happened to him, but Henry could say he'd been called away on an emergency. It was even partly true.

"Domin?" he called.

No sign of his friend. Technically, Domin worked for Mr. Tanner, too, but most of the time, the old apothecary seemed to forget about him. Domin certainly didn't complain about that.

Henry jogged out of the village toward the old woods.

A tangled hedgerow thick with rowans and elderberries followed the wooded hills at the edge of the town fields. It formed the border between the cultivated order of human civilization and the wildness of an older world that answered to its own laws. The hedgerow should have been enough to keep any wandering Faerie creatures in the oldest parts of the wood and away from the village. But people were forgetting the hedgerow and what it had once protected them from. In some places, it had grown thin.

Behind Henry, the church bells sounded the hour. He relaxed a little at the familiar sound. The Seelie Court of the Fay would play tricks on humans—even harm those who offended them—but the Unseelie Fay could not unleash their cruel magic on the village as long as the church bells rang.

Henry followed the hedgerow and paused to study the branches of an old oak stretching over the barrier. The quickest way in. He grabbed the lowest branch of the oak to pull himself up.

"You're going to fall."

Henry twisted to see Domin watching him, arms folded and a frown creasing his dark features.

"Have I ever mentioned how much I appreciate your confidence in me?" Henry swung up to the next branch. "Are you coming?"

"Someone will have to bury you when you slip and break your neck. *Why* are you climbing the hedgerow?"

Henry scooted over against the tree trunk. "That little girl may not be the only elf-shot victim in the village."

"And you believe it's your duty to fix every problem the Fay cause."

"No one else will. No one else can."

"Some problems are out of your hands. If the Fay are passing through, you would be wiser to wait them out at Telesm's sanctuary."

Henry swung around the trunk to a thick branch hanging over the old woods. "Lucky for Drixton that I'm not wise, then."

"Henry!" Domin growled. He paced at the bottom of the tree. "It's the Seelie Fay. They're unlikely to do any serious harm to humans, but if they catch you—"

"That little girl would have died if I hadn't caught it in time." He saw Domin's hesitation and pressed his point. "I need to see what they're doing here. Make sure they *are* just passing through. I'll be careful." He grinned. "But I'm less likely to get caught if you help me search."

Domin glared at Henry. "Very well."

Henry tried to hide his smile. "You look to the south; I'll go north."

Domin nodded. He studied the hedgerow for a moment, then threaded his way through it without so much as snagging his shirt.

"Show-off!" Henry called.

He dropped into the shade of the old woods and took a moment to open himself to the energy of the trees around him. Not that they ever had answers for human problems, but the sweet, musty scent of green breathed promises of freedom. The slow pulse of the woods thrummed through Henry: the heartbeat of ancient trees. He sank into the quiet hum of warm energy.

Yet something was wrong. A sour note in the symphony, a

screaming trumpet among the angel voices of a string quartet. The discordant buzzing grew into a pressure in his ears. A prickle itched between his shoulder blades. The threads of magic throughout his body tensed in recognition. The Seelie Fay were near. Not some tiny, winged pixie, but a creature much more powerful—one that drew strength from the cycles of life and death woven into the natural world.

Henry drew his iron dagger and slunk forward among the trees. The energy pressed against him, alive with power from a time when people did not know of gaslights or locked doors but sat huddled around fires at night, telling stories to ward off the darkness always hovering on the edges. The trees welcomed the presence, acknowledging its reign over the ever-shortening days.

Henry paused at the edge of a blackened patch of ground. It did not look burned. It was withered as though an early frost had swept a path through the grasses and trees, sucking life and green from the branches. He followed the barren trail a short distance. It blasted through the protection of the hedgerow, opening a way for the wildness of the old woods to creep into Drixton. Henry knew the beast that did this. He could not have it near the village.

"Pooka?" he called.

The pooka was there, in the shadows of the withered hedgerow, wearing the guise of a black mare with golden eyes. She stood perfectly still, making no effort to change form or speak. Strange.

Different, bitter magic crept around Henry, leaving a metallic taste in his mouth like blood. The bright buzz of life turned to sharp edges of black and gray. Unseelie magic, fed by human suffering and strife. At least the pooka, whose breath brought the touch of autumn's decay, was still part of the Seelie Court. Her eyes rolled in terror at the approach of some Unseelie creature. Her muscles quivered as though she fought invisible restraints. Henry tightened his grip on the dagger.

"Henry Stewart," said a familiar voice. "What a pleasure to find you here."

Henry whirled to face Douglas Fitzhugh. The Unseelie elf was dressed like a dandy, with a black top-hat, walking cane, and a gold fob chain dangling from his waistcoat. He grinned at Henry, who took a step back. Where Fitzhugh was, the Dark Lady—Queen of the Unseelie Fay—wasn't far behind.

"What are you doing here?" Henry asked.

Fitzhugh produced a silver snuff box and took a pinch. "Really, Henry, is that any way to greet an old friend?" He offered the snuff.

Henry shook his head.

Fitzhugh flipped the box shut. "Very well, a potential ally then. You couldn't have been happy to find the Seelie Court here." He gestured toward the town. "A clever place to hide, by the by, but so very dull."

"Then why are you here?"

"I'm here for the hunt."

Henry backed away. "I'm not returning with you."

Fitzhugh chuckled. "Last I heard, the earth revolves around the sun, Henry—not you. This is much bigger than your tiff with the Lady of the Woods. There's an end coming. An end, and a new beginning, and you can play a part in it. We have a common enemy, you and I." He held up his hand to show off a coiled lock of long black hairs.

"Those are the pooka's?" Henry glanced at the creature. By holding her hair, Fitzhugh could put her under a geas—a magical compulsion. He controlled her powers now.

"Yes." Fitzhugh played with the hairs, holding them up in

the light. "What do you say, Henry? Should we have a little fun with the villagers? Liven up their dull lives?"

"No."

"Oh, I see. They've befriended you, have they? Invited you to their tea parties and balls and musical evenings. No?" Fitzhugh leaned closer. "They never will. And what does it matter? You were made to rule over them. Given your talents and your bloodline—"

"That's in the past. It's not important anymore."

Fitzhugh chuckled. "It will always be important. You cannot escape what you are. You can wander and hide until boredom or loneliness drives you back into the arms of the Seelie Court. Or you can ally yourself with my Dark Lady now. She will help you unlock and control powers you have yet to dream of. No more hiding. No more lies."

As Fitzhugh spoke, Unseelie magic coiled around Henry, searching for his weaknesses: something to feed on. It was like mistletoe, sending roots into the tiniest cracks and sucking life from its host. The very touch of Unseelie magic was laced with blood. It echoed with suffering in the bitterness of night, when dawn is too far away and hope dies with each tick of the clock. It would make Henry powerful enough to defeat an army of Seelie Fay if he embraced it. It would make him truly and forever a monster, and prove how unworthy he was.

"You must have something more in mind for a pooka than teasing a few villagers." Henry drew energy into his hands from the woods, calling on the warmth reflecting off the orange leaves and the afternoon light breaking through the clouds.

"Perhaps." The elf's eyes narrowed. "What are you doing?"

Henry lunged and wrapped his fingers around the hairs. The elf pushed him back, but Henry forced the heat out of his hands. The black locks twisted like snakes and smoldered into ash. Fitzhugh hissed and released them. The acrid smell of burning hair wafted around them. The pooka whinnied triumphantly and galloped away, leaving a trail of dead grass behind her.

Fitzhugh snarled and made a grasping gesture, tearing at the cords of Faerie magic woven into Henry's being. Pain crushed the breath from Henry's lungs. He twisted, but he had no way to fight the elf's hold. His vision went dark. He fell to his knees, his nose full of the smell of earth and blood.

The pressure dissolved. Henry curled up, fighting like a broken bellows to suck in enough air.

Domin stood in front of him, one hand clutching Fitzhugh's throat. The Unseelie elf's elbows jerked as he tried to break free. Domin released him with a shove that sent him sprawling on the ground. Fitzhugh staggered to his feet and spat.

"I didn't know you had a pet, Henry. You'd better keep him on a leash or he might turn on you."

The ache was fading from Henry's lungs, but the pounding in his head made it impossible to do anything but glare.

Fitzhugh smirked. "You're idiots, both of you, dabbling in a game you don't understand." He glanced at the blues and purples bruising the western horizon. "But darkness is coming soon. And the church bell won't protect the village forever."

Fitzhugh gave them a mock bow and sauntered deeper into the woods.

"What do you think he wants from the village?" Henry asked.

Domin stared in the direction Fitzhugh had gone, his eyes narrow. "I don't know."

"If we could warn people..." Henry shook his head. "Most of them wouldn't listen."

"Is that why you feel free to use magic in the shop? In the middle of town?"

Henry shrugged, not meeting Domin's accusing gaze. "No one believes it's magic."

Domin shook his head. "Sometimes I think you want people to catch you."

"Of course not," Henry said. They might run him out of town if they knew. He'd have to start all over again. Unless they accepted him.

Unlikely.

Domin gave him a searching look. "The Fay are far more likely to notice you before any of the humans do. And I know you don't want that."

Henry had to agree. But he didn't have to admit that Domin was right. Again. "Very well. But now we know the Seelie and the Unseelie Fay are lurking around Drixton. I don't think they're after me, so what do they want here?"

This time, Domin had no reply.

Chapter Five

"What a perfect day!" Sophie exclaimed when she and Cassandra arrived home from the village.

Cassandra muttered something that sounded like agreement. She peeked into the drawing room. Her three youngest sisters worked on their embroidery under the watchful eye of Nancy, their white-haired nurse. Lottie rushed over to hug Cassandra and Sophie then trotted back to the sofa. Jane, age twelve, sat with the perfect poise of someone hoping her parents would let her out into society soon. Lillian, who was a couple of years behind Jane, stuck her tongue out between her teeth as she tried to thread her needle.

"Where's Georgina?" Cassandra asked.

"Out in the garden, painting, of course," Nancy said.

"By herself?" Cassandra asked, but Nancy was distracted by Lillian dropping her needle on the sofa.

It made Cassandra uneasy to think of one of her sisters out there alone with the woods so close. It was probably because she was used to the city, but there was something about the shadows lurking under the trees that felt like a threat. She unpinned her bonnet and went to the back door, but Sophie caught up with her.

"You did well today," Sophie said. "I want you to know how I admire your patience with everything that's happened to you."

Cassandra expected to meet a sarcastic look from her sister, but Sophie seemed sincere. She hadn't seen Cassandra floundering in the apothecary's shop, though. Cassandra shrugged. It wasn't truly patience if she didn't have a choice. If she could make her body whole and unbroken again, she would do it in a moment.

"Just keep working at it." Sophie squeezed her arm and bustled back down the corridor.

Cassandra rested her forehead against the door and shut her eyes against the sting of tears. It had been a year since the fever stole the strength from the right side of her body. She would be "working at it" for the rest of her life and might never be good enough. She rubbed her eyes and limped outside to see her sister's painting.

Georgina stood with her back to the house, her long brown hair caught up in a tangled bun. As Cassandra watched, Georgina stepped back, brush poised to attack any flaws. She'd captured the mysterious look of the woods, adding a crooked stone tower rising from the trees. Cassandra imagined a storybook enchanter keeping his prisoners there and wondered if her sister felt a little trapped too.

"I like it," Cassandra said when Georgina finally blinked and emerged from her work.

Georgina watched her closely when she spoke. She'd become so practiced at reading lips that few people realized the fever had left her almost completely deaf.

"Thank you," Georgina said a little too loudly. "It's so

beautiful here that maybe it doesn't need any embellishment, but the ruins seemed to fit. Besides," she said, dropping into an overly prim-and-proper voice, "by staying busy, I am able to maintain good cheer in the face of my afflictions. It's very commendable of me."

Cassandra laughed. "Sophie's been talking to you, too?"

"I'm afraid she wants to smother me in a saintly image."

"I think she means well, and maybe it helps her feel less guilty that it was us and not her. Sometimes, though, I worry that if I don't act cheerful..."

"They'll turn their backs on us," Georgina finished quietly. "We're going to have to hide behind our smiles the rest of our lives."

"Maybe things will be different, here in the country," Cassandra said with forced optimism. "Maybe as they get to know us, they'll accept us."

"People are people no matter where you go," Georgina said much too bitterly for someone only sixteen. She cleaned her brushes and put them away.

Cassandra felt the same melancholy threatening to weigh her down. She forced it away and picked up one of the wooden mallets her younger sisters had left leaning against a tree. "Come, Sophie wouldn't object to a game of croquet."

"Can we explore the woods instead?" Georgina asked, sounding more like her old self.

"The woods?" Cassandra glanced at the trees beyond the edge of the cultivated land. The branches reached out as though beckoning, hungry.

"Or just walk through the orchard?" Georgina said. "So I can watch how the light moves through the trees? If your leg isn't hurting too much."

Cassandra still felt uneasy, but she shook it off. Silly. This was their home now; they were safe here. "Very well."

Georgina took Cassandra's arm and guided her forward. Cassandra kept the croquet mallet in her other hand as a makeshift crutch. She glanced again at the shadowy trees across the stream.

"You don't like the woods?" Georgina gave her a curious look.

"I don't know if it's safe. I've heard they're haunted."

"I could almost believe in ghosts here." Georgina shivered. "The only time I was ever afraid of spirits in the city was when we were sick. I thought I heard things—voices—even after ..." She drew a deep breath and touched her ear.

"It was the fever." Cassandra squeezed her sister's arm, though a chill rushed up her spine at her own memories of the hot, sweating delirium.

Georgina nodded, then a thoughtful look came over her face. "Where did you hear the woods are haunted? We haven't met anyone yet except the Ashbys and their stuffy friends, and I can't imagine *them* talking about anything that interesting."

Cassandra fidgeted with the croquet mallet, unable to meet her sister's eyes.

"Cassie! You're keeping secrets! Please tell me."

"If you must know, I met someone near the woods the other day when we lost Lottie. A young man."

Georgina exclaimed in disbelief. "You managed to meet someone with Sophie always watching? Was he handsome?"

"Georgie!" Cassandra paused, remembering Henry's smile. "Well, yes, he was. But he knew it. I mean, he's arrogant... and more than a little odd."

"But handsome." Georgina sighed and smiled dreamily.

Cassandra chuckled.

They strolled through the orchard in companionable silence. As they neared the stream that bordered the woods, the hairs on the back of Cassandra's neck rose. She stopped to scan the trees and brambles. The darkness in the woods was watching. Waiting.

"What is it?" Georgina asked.

Cassandra's mouth went dry. "The birds. They've stopped singing."

Georgina cocked an ear, straining to hear, then shook her head. Cassandra listened, but only an occasional rustle broke the silence. Something moving closer. Perhaps the stag had returned.

Georgina's arm tightened against hers, and her sister pointed. A large, black shape prowled through the dappled shade.

Cassandra backed away. This was a threat more dangerous than the stag. It was probably wise not to show fear to a wild animal, but she pulled Georgina farther from the stream.

Something crashed through the brush.

"Run!" Cassandra pushed Georgina ahead, stumbling over her weak foot. She risked a glance back. A massive black dog closed the distance between them. They would never make it to the house.

She caught Georgina's hand and dragged her toward the closest tree. Their fingertips barely brushed the rough bark of the lowest limb. Cassandra boosted her sister to the branch and grabbed her discarded croquet mallet.

"Cassie!" Georgina screamed. "Someone help!"

The huge dog leaped for Cassandra. She swung the mallet, connecting with the animal's head. The wooden handle snapped, and she stumbled to the ground. The beast shook its head and snarled. Cassandra tossed the broken mallet aside. She needed something stronger.

A knee-high metal croquet stake jutted out of the ground nearby. Cassandra rolled over and wrapped her hands around the stake to yank it free. The dog lunged, and she jabbed the stake forward.

Her blow caught the beast in the chest. The impact jarred her arm, but the dog yelped and twisted away. She scrambled to her feet, the brace pinching her leg. The dog growled—a deep rumble that resonated behind Cassandra's racing heart—as drool trickled from its jaws. Through the haze of fear, she thought its eyes glowed red.

It darted for her weak leg but stopped short with a snarl. Cassandra stepped forward and swung the stake. The beast recoiled, teeth bared. Georgina whimpered, and the creature's eyes locked on her. It bolted around Cassandra to the tree, jaws snapping after Georgina's skirts as it clawed the trunk. Georgina shrieked and kicked out. The dog caught her boot, yanking her to the ground with a crash.

Cassandra smashed the metal stake down on the animal's head, and it released Georgina's foot. The creature lowered its head, ears flat and teeth flashing. Cassandra's hands shook as she lifted the stake.

A deafening crack tore through the air, and the dog's body jerked. Cassandra gasped and stumbled back. Another boom sounded from the direction of the lane, and splinters exploded from the tree next to the creature. It snarled, hesitating between the sisters and its new assailant. Cassandra didn't dare take her eyes off the dog, but she heard footsteps racing toward them. Hefting the stake in her trembling hands, she edged closer to Georgina.

Another blast blistered Cassandra's ears and filled her nose with the sour smell of gunsmoke. Blood oozed down the dog's side like dark treacle from a broken pot, but the creature paced, muscles tight under its black fur.

A young man in a broad-brimmed hat and duster rushed past Cassandra, his revolver trained on the pacing dog.

The animal circled away, closing in on Georgina. Cassandra raised the stake, and the dog lowered its head and stepped back.

The young man placed himself between the dog and the girls.

"What's that pole made of, miss?"

"What?" Cassandra's ears buzzed.

The dog lurched forward. The young man cocked his gun and fired again. A sulfurous white cloud rolled around him. The creature faltered.

"That thing in your hands," the young man said. "The beast doesn't like it. What's it made of?"

She stared at the rust peeking through the stripes of red, blue, and yellow paint. "Iron?"

"Interesting idea. Cover me."

He stepped back to holster his revolver and pulled a short, double-barrel shotgun from under his coat. Cassandra swallowed hard and brandished the stake. As the young man reached into the bag slung across his chest, the dog lunged. She slammed the stake into its neck like a spear. The dog staggered aside. She raised the stake again, knees trembling.

"Get behind me." The young man lifted his gun.

She stumbled back as the shotgun's hammer clicked and its first barrel roared. The beast snarled and crumpled to the ground, struggling to rise on its mutilated leg. The stranger jumped forward and pulled the other trigger. The creature jerked under the blast before finally lying still.

"Georgina!" Cassandra sank to her sister's side.

Georgina eased herself up, cradling her arm. Cassandra supported her, relieved that her sister could move and that her head wasn't bleeding from the fall.

"Are either of y'all hurt?" The young man replaced his gun under his coat and knelt next to them.

Cassandra caught her sister's gaze. "Georgie, how badly are you injured?"

"I landed on my arm." Georgina gulped, and tears cut a path down her dirty face. "I thought that dog was going to kill us."

The young man offered a white handkerchief, and Georgina's eyes widened as she gazed up at him. She whispered her thanks before wiping her face and arranging her torn dress.

Cassandra shook her head. Even if the stranger hadn't saved them, he had the sort of fair-haired good looks Georgina always swooned over. His suntanned face had made Cassandra think he was several years older than her, but up close, he didn't look much more than twenty.

"We'd best find someone to look at that arm," he said. "Is there a physician in the village?"

"There's an apothecary," Cassandra said.

"That'll do. I'll get you ladies somewhere safe, and then I'll fetch him." He grinned. "I suppose I should introduce myself. I'm Jairus Hale." He tipped his hat.

"I'm Cassandra Weaver, and this is my sister Georgina." It was against The Rules to pry, but her curiosity won out as she tried to place his accent. "Are you American?"

"From the Utah Territory. I'm touring your English countryside." He turned back to Georgina. "Can you walk?"

She shifted and the blood drained from her face. "My ankle!"

"Hmm. I imagine I can carry you. If I may?"

Georgina nodded, bouncing the tangled curls that had unwound from her bun, and Cassandra managed not to roll her eyes.

Jairus gathered Georgina in his arms and set off for the house. Before following, Cassandra glanced back at the dog. Its corpse already looked withered and dry, nothing like the massive creature that had terrorized them a few minutes before. A movement in the woods jerked her attention to the trees. Nothing else stirred, as if the forest were holding its breath. With several glances over her shoulder, Cassandra limped after Jairus.

Chapter Six

Cassandra, Jairus, and Georgina entered the house through the back door. The cook was heading downstairs to the kitchen with a tea tray. She stopped to gawk.

Jairus nodded at her. "This child is hurt. Can you fetch her mother or father?"

Georgina caught the word "child" and scowled.

"Mistress is ill," the cook said, eyes questioning Cassandra.

"We won't disturb her unless we have to," Cassandra decided. Her father was in Manchester on business, and her mother's pregnancy was difficult enough without adding to her worries. "But get Sophie, please, and ask Nancy to clear the drawing room."

The cook set the tea tray on a side table and scurried down the corridor. Cassandra directed Jairus to the drawing room as the last of her little sisters hurried up the stairs.

"Keep her calm and comfortable until I get back," he said, setting Georgina on the sofa.

"Of course." Cassandra grabbed an embroidered pillow for

her sister's foot. Sophie rushed into the room and threw her arms around Cassandra.

"What happened?" Sophie dropped to her knees next to Georgina, caressing her hair. "The cook said you were hurt."

"We were attacked by a dog, but Mr. Hale here saved us," Cassandra said.

Jairus shrugged and said to Sophie, "I heard them shouting as I happened past, but your sister was giving a pretty good account of herself before I showed up."

Cassandra looked away. She had managed to hold the dog off, but if it weren't for Jairus, she or Georgina might have been killed.

"Miss Georgina! Oh, my poor dear lamb!" Nancy bustled over to Georgina, checking her eyes and forehead. Cassandra exhaled and sat on a footstool. Nancy had always known how to take care of them. Georgina whimpered when the nurse's hand grazed her arm.

"I was just going after the apothecary," Jairus said.

"Yes." Nancy's frown deepened the wrinkles in her face. "We may need someone to set this arm."

"I'll bring him back shortly." Jairus tipped his hat to each of them and jogged out the front door.

Cassandra watched the clock tick away the minutes as Nancy and Sophie fussed over Georgina. They called for Beth, remembered she had the afternoon off, then asked the cook to bring more tea.

Sophie kept adding more pillows around Georgina until Nancy shooed her away. "Leave her be, Miss Sophie."

Sophie perched on the sofa near Cassandra. "What happened out there?"

Images from the dog attack rose before Cassandra like a half-remembered nightmare. She carefully related everything she remembered, even mentioning the part where she thought the dog's eyes glowed. As she spoke, Sophie's cheeks slowly lost their pink.

"You say Mr. Hale shot it, but it didn't stop?" she asked, her voice shaky.

Cassandra nodded.

Sophie made certain Georgina wasn't following the conversation and whispered, "Could it have been mad?"

Rabies. A death sentence. Nancy's head jerked up, and cold poured over Cassandra. "It bit her foot. I don't know if it broke through the boot."

"No! Not our Georgie!" Nancy said.

"What's going on?" Georgina asked, her gaze flitting between them as she tried to read their lips.

"Don't fret, my lamb," Nancy said, though her hands trembled. "All will be well."

She unbuttoned Georgina's shoe and checked the thick leather for punctures.

Sophie peeled off her sister's stocking and examined her swollen foot.

"The skin doesn't look punctured," she said, "but I can't be sure."

A rap sounded from the front door. Cassandra stood to answer it, but Sophie flipped Georgina's skirts back over her legs in a rustle of silk and hurried into the entryway. In a few moments, she led Jairus into the room, followed by Henry and Domin.

At the sight of the dark-skinned young man, Nancy went still and fastened her gaze on the floral rug. Cassandra glanced between her old nurse and the East Indian, confused. They'd seen people from all over the British Empire in the city, and Nancy had never reacted oddly to them before.

Henry set his bowler hat aside. He smiled a little at Cassandra, then addressed all the girls. "I'm Henry Stewart, apprentice to Mr. Tanner, the apothecary. He's visiting another patient, but I can set a broken bone."

"Mr. Stewart." Cassandra lowered her voice and approached Henry. She hoped his usual show of confidence was justified by his medical skills. "We're afraid the dog may have been mad, and it bit my sister's foot."

Concern flashed in Henry's eyes, and he turned to his companion. "Domin, will you have a look at the creature? Mr. Hale, please show him where it is."

Jairus nodded, but he kept his hand close to his revolver and gave Domin a wary look before leading the way out of the room.

"What's going on?" Georgina repeated, her voice edged with fear and frustration.

Henry studied her with a quizzical expression. "We're just going to make certain you're all right. May I look?"

She nodded, and he set down his satchel.

"Tell me what happened." Henry looked at the discarded boot then lifted Georgina's foot.

Cassandra described the attack again, though she left out the part about the glowing eyes, not wanting Henry to think she was hysterical. He listened without pausing his examination until she told him the number of times Jairus had to shoot the dog to stop it. Henry lowered Georgina's foot.

"I know it sounds strange," Cassandra said, "but it's true."

"I believe you." Henry stood and ran his hand through his curly brown hair then turned his attention back to Georgina. "The skin is bruised but not broken, so there's little chance of infection."

Footsteps in the corridor announced Jairus and Domin.

"Well?" Henry asked.

"It's gone," Domin said. His voice bore a faint accent Cassandra couldn't place.

"Gone?" Henry asked. "You're certain you killed it, Mr. Hale?"

"Absolutely." Jairus crossed his arms, and Cassandra nodded.

Henry exchanged a glance with Domin. "The constable should still know that there may be a dangerous animal at large. Mr. Hale, would you warn him?"

"Yeah, I'll do that, now that I know the ladies are safe."

"Thank you, Mr. Hale," Cassandra said.

He nodded to the girls and saw himself out. Domin waited a few heartbeats and then walked out as well.

"But Georgina's going to be all right?" Cassandra asked. "I mean, she's not..."

"Her ankle is twisted. She needs to stay off it for at least a couple of days, but she'll recover." He knelt by Georgina again and gently moved her hand and wrist. "You'll probably miss out on the Harvest Ball, Miss Georgina. I don't feel any broken bones, but your arm may be fractured. I have a sling."

He rummaged through his satchel for a rolled up piece of linen and a bottle of brown ointment, which he applied to her wrist.

Nancy took charge of the extra linen and ointment, accepting them gingerly as if Henry had offered her a snake.

Henry caught Cassandra's eyes then tilted his head toward the entryway. She blushed, realizing he wanted to speak to her alone. Entirely improper, but she was shaken. And curious.

"Um, I'll see you out, Mr. Stewart," she said.

Henry collected his hat and satchel, waiting to speak until the drawing-room door clicked shut behind them. Cassandra tried not to glance at her cane resting near the front door, hoping he didn't notice it.

"Miss Weaver, I may be overstepping my bounds, but it really would be best for you to stay away from the woods."

He was overstepping his bounds, but he didn't look arrogant about it this time. In fact, he looked apologetic. And worried.

"Very well." She let out a tired breath, all the excitement and worry of the afternoon draining away to leave her empty. "Thank you for coming." She remembered what Mr. Rushford had said about Michaelmas. "My father will settle the account once he returns."

He smiled as he donned his hat. Cassandra opened the door to find Domin waiting on the porch. Domin handed something to Henry as she swung the door around behind them.

"What's this?" Henry asked.

"A bullet from one of Mr. Hale's guns," Domin said.

Cassandra stopped the door so it was open a crack.

"It's silver," Henry said after a moment.

"There was iron shot scattered around too," Domin said.

"Mr. Hale is unusually well-armed, isn't he?" Henry murmured.

Their boots thumped down the porch steps, drowning the rest of their conversation. Cassandra let the door click shut and leaned against it. Mad dogs. Silver bullets. She wanted to hear what else Henry said about them, but that kind of curiosity was definitely against The Rules.

Chapter Seven

A distant knock sounded at the Weaver's front door. Cassandra jumped and dropped the silk flower she'd been pinning to her bonnet. More visitors. She rubbed her right leg, sore from walking up and down the stairs. Maybe this time they would forget about her.

"Cassandra?" Her mother peeked into the room. She wore her reddish-brown hair brushed back into a braid and rested a protective hand on her belly. "Go down and greet our guests."

"I've been greeting guests for the last three days."

Everyone in the village wanted to gawk at the young ladies who had survived the mad dog attack. Cassandra's father was away finishing up business with his warehouses, and her mother was in confinement. It fell to Sophie, Cassandra, and Georgie to entertain their visitors. A few farmer's wives brought practical things like fresh bread and preserves, but most of the callers made awkward conversation with Sophie while Georgie pretended to follow along and Cassandra prayed they wouldn't notice her crippled limbs and pity her.

Her mother gave her a stern look. "Sophie and Georgie aren't complaining, and Jane would love to be allowed to go down. I expect you to act like a lady." Her voice softened. "We have to make a good impression."

"Yes, Mother."

"And remember..."

"Don't interrupt. Don't ramble. Don't draw attention to myself." Cassandra kept her eyes on the fallen silk flower to hide her rebellious thoughts.

She clutched the banister on her way downstairs, trying to move gracefully under her mother's worried gaze. Her nervousness only made her right leg tighter, and she stumbled once near the bottom.

Male voices drifted from the drawing-room, and her interest perked up. Had Henry Stewart come to check on Georgie? Not that she needed his teasing. Even if it did make her eyes look... What had he said? Charming?

She limped into the drawing-room to find the Ashbys visiting. The flutters in her chest stilled. It was probably for the best that it wasn't Henry Stewart. He was only likely to irritate her.

Robert Ashby gazed at Sophie with fond concern, and Elizabeth carried on a one-sided conversation with Georgina.

Cassandra would have found an excuse to back away—surely Cook needed help with the tea?—but Sir Walter noticed her lingering and beckoned her over. He lounged in the wing chair like a king holding court. She settled primly on the edge of the sofa near him, but not too near.

He smiled at Cassandra. "I must make Lady Ashby's apologies. She was feeling under the weather."

Cassandra had met the icy Lady Ashby. It was more likely that she was feeling unwilling to sully herself by appearing in such a meager drawing-room, even for a charity visit. "I hope she's well soon."

"Thank you, child. Of course, she's just as happy as the rest of us to hear you are all safe after this shocking incident. I have Rushford combing the woods for any dangerous animals."

She thought of the poor stag, and her smile tightened. "Thank you, sir."

"I can't help feeling responsible. Your father asked me to watch out for you while he's gone, and I intend to do it."

"No one could have foreseen—"

"I'll watch more closely. You still want to go to the Harvest Festival, of course. And the ball."

"Well..." She wasn't sure she wanted to do either.

"Oh, but I have guests coming to Ashby Hall." His round face clouded with concern then brightened. "No trouble, though. No trouble. Rushford will escort you girls to the festival."

Cassandra clasped her hands together. "That's really not—"

"Oh, it's the least I can do." Sir Walter patted her shoulder, beaming at his suggestion.

Cassandra's stomach churned, but she made herself smile. Being ill might not be such a bad thing if it kept her away from Mr. Rushford. No one expected Georgina to attend the Harvest Festival on her sprained ankle.

As soon as the Ashbys left, Cassandra hurried upstairs to beg her mother for rescue.

"Of course, you must go to the Harvest Festival," her mother said. "It is very kind of Sir Walter to think of you. And this Mr. Rushford. He's respectable, is he not?"

"I suppose so," Cassandra whispered.

"Then I see nothing to object to. You can't expect Sophie to go alone, and she's very much looking forward to it. Please don't make a fuss, dear."

"Yes, Mother." Cassandra backed out of her mother's room, her heart heavy.

That Sunday, Cassandra took a little extra time adjusting her bonnet in the mirror. She wanted to look her best for the Harvest Festival. Everyone would be there, including Henry Stewart. Not that he was likely to notice how she looked, unless he was teasing her about it.

Georgina watched Cassandra and Sophie prepare, a frown creasing her forehead.

"I suppose the Harvest Festival won't be that enjoyable," Georgina said. "And Mr. Hale isn't likely to be there, is he? He hasn't even called to see if we are well."

"I don't know, dear," Cassandra said. "Maybe he's finished whatever business brought him to Drixton." Business that involved carrying guns loaded with silver bullets and iron shot.

"Humph." Georgina pouted.

Beth announced that Mr. Rushford had come for them. Cassandra took a deep breath to steel herself. She picked up her basket brimming with sweet-scented apples from the orchard to add to the display in the church. When the festival was done, the food would go to help the poor. The basket was almost too heavy for her weak right arm, but she held it close and followed Sophie out the door into the warm afternoon sun.

Mr. Rushford did not offer to carry either of their baskets. Instead, he took possession of their free arms and guided them down the lane. He didn't slow for Cassandra's limp either, instead half-dragging her toward the village.

As they walked, he stared intently, first at Sophie's head and then at Cassandra's. "Have you ever had your skulls studied?"

"Pardon?" Sophie asked.

Mr. Rushford stopped and prodded at Sophie's head. "Phrenology. I can tell so much about you by the bumps on your skull. You are stubborn, uninventive, and of below-average intelligence."

Sophie stared at him as if he'd shoved her. Cassandra scowled. If she had brought her cane, Mr. Rushford would have a new bump on *his* skull.

"You see," Rushford went on, "this is one reason we know women should never have the right to vote or hold political offices. Also why they cannot excel in the sciences and only rarely in the arts. Your brains don't have the capacity for it."

Sophie gasped in indignation.

"Would you also say that of Queen Victoria, Mr. Rushford?" Cassandra asked, forcing her voice to be sickly sweet.

"I have not had the privilege of examining her, Miss Cassandra," he said coolly. "Perhaps someday, once my experiments have proven themselves. As for you..." He reached for her head. She shrunk away, but he still had her arm. He poked her skull roughly. She squeezed her eyes shut and wished she could scream at him to stop. Rushford muttered to himself. "Interesting. Very interesting. What a pleasant combination— full of possibilities. Intelligent, for a girl, but not *too* clever. Naturally sweet-tempered and obedient. Hmm."

Cassandra tried to hold in her laugh at his misunderstanding of her "sweet" temperament and snorted instead. Mr. Rushford's science was clearly inaccurate.

"Uh, Mr. Rushford," Sophie broke in. "Aren't we late for the Harvest Festival?"

He frowned and released Cassandra's head. "Phrenology doesn't have all the answers, of course. Nothing does. But we're getting closer."

"Oh?" Sophie asked with strained politeness.

"The sciences, working together. They can tell us how to improve. Get rid of weaknesses. Identify which people have traits that make them superior to others. Do you know the story of Pygmalion?"

"We've heard it," Sophie said.

"The brilliant sculptor Pygmalion crafted the perfect woman: Galatea," Rushford went on as if she hadn't spoken. "The gods brought her to life to reward him. Science is our god now, and with the right materials, I believe we can create our own Galateas, even from crude raw material."

The way he was looking at Cassandra made her skin crawl. She wanted a cure, but she did not think Rushford would be an ideal sculptor. She and Sophie exchanged an uncomfortable look as Rushford rambled on about superior bloodlines and scientific measurements.

The sound of the church bell ringing finally overpowered Rushford's lecture. Cassandra smiled in relief. They came around a bend in the road to see the village green. Harvest wagons decorated with wreaths of braided straw lined the dirt road. Children played Blind Man's Bluff on the lawn, while the young people picnicked and the adults stood in circles gossiping.

Cassandra spotted Henry talking with his friend Domin, but Rushford whisked her past them before she could send a look pleading for help.

"Oh, there's Miss Ashby!" Sophie said. "I'm anxious to hear about their new guests. I understand one of them is a *very* handsome gentleman, Mr. Douglas Fitzhugh." She wriggled her

arm free and waved to Robert and Elizabeth, motioning for
Cassandra to come with her.

Cassandra tried to follow, but Mr. Rushford didn't
relinquish her arm.

"Mr. Rushford?" Cassandra asked.

"Miss Cassandra Weaver. You are an interesting young lady.
I would enjoy your company during the picnic so I may get to
know you better."

"Oh, but..."

"Miss Weaver!" Henry Stuart strode over and bowed with a
mischievous grin. "I hope you have not forgotten that you
promised to share your picnic with me."

"Oh!" Cassandra almost laughed in relief. "Oh, Mr.
Stewart. Of course, I had not forgotten you. You understand,
don't you, Mr. Rushford?"

Rushford looked at Henry with narrowed eyes, but
Cassandra took Henry's offered arm and let him guide her away.
For once, she was grateful for his impulsive, high-handed
manners.

"Thank you," Cassandra said under her breath.

"Rushford is a snake, and you looked like you'd had enough
of his venom."

"I had! Is that a terrible thing to say?"

"Possibly," Henry said, grinning. "Here. That basket is too
heavy for you. I'll carry it."

He took it without waiting for permission. Cassandra
pressed her lips together at his presumption. But hadn't she just
half an hour before thought Rushford rude for not taking it?

"Oh, and you'll find this worth reading." Henry dropped
her arm and rummaged in his satchel with his free hand,
bringing out a leather-bound book.

Cassandra accepted the tome hesitantly. What kind of

book did Henry Stewart think she needed to read? An etiquette guide, perhaps? She opened the soft leather cover to find page after page of beautifully illustrated plants and animals.

"You sounded interested," Henry said, "and you live right by the old woods, so I thought..." He shrugged.

"It's beautiful." She met his expectant gaze. "Thank you."

"Make good use of it," he said.

"I ... will?" she said, confused both by his thoughtfulness and his seriousness.

"Excellent. Come. Let's add your offerings to the display in the church."

He took her arm again, but at least he let her set the pace. As they walked, villagers stared and whispered, no doubt talking about the dog attack. Was it wrong for her to walk with Henry? He was not exactly a gentleman, but he was respectable enough. And he appeared oblivious to the curious glances, which helped Cassandra ignore them as well.

Henry left her in front of the church while he delivered her basket to the women organizing the harvest offerings inside. Cassandra rested her hand against the cool stone of the front archway. Her fingers brushed something rough. She looked closer to see an image of a snake coiled into a figure eight etched into the stone. The edges were fresh and sharp. She drew her hand away and wiped her fingers on her skirt. Who would deface a church?

A mousy girl about fifteen or sixteen hurried past her with a basket of turnips, glancing over her shoulder as if afraid of being seen. As the girl reached the church door, Rushford strode out. The two collided, and the girl's basket went flying, launching turnips to fly every which way like misshapen pigeons.

Cassandra scooped up a few of the fallen vegetables that landed by her feet.

Rushford sneered down at the girl and straightened his waistcoat. "Watch yourself, brat."

The girl cringed and stumbled back, tripping on the hem of her outdated, too-long dress. She fell on her backside, flipping her crinoline up to reveal a petticoat made colorful by the number of patches added to it.

Rushford snorted, and a group of choir boys chortled.

"Oh, that's Mary Leland for you," a woman nearby said to her companion.

Cassandra clutched the turnips. Didn't the girl have family or someone who would come to her defense? If anything, everyone in the church seemed to have shifted further from the girl as she struggled to get her underthings back in order. Was it wrong to help her? Better to pretend it hadn't happened? Cassandra's impulse was to throw a turnip at Rushford, but that couldn't be right either.

As Cassandra struggled to decide what The Rules said about such a situation, a vibration rumbled beneath her feet. Her ears throbbed at the low hum as it grew to fill the church and echoed out onto the green. The sound took on a musical tone, and the stained-glass windows rattled, shaking the colored light that spilled across the nave. The pipe organ groaned out a melody of cacophonous notes as if playing itself. The crowd in the church grew silent and gaped at the instrument. Several cast dark glances at Mary Leland.

Miss Leland trembled, and tears rolled down her cheeks. A thin man with graying hair hurried over and helped her to her feet, putting a fatherly arm around her shoulders and sheltering her from the stares. He glared at the crowd. His accusing eyes caught Cassandra's as he guided the girl away from the church.

Cassandra turned her attention to the stone floor, her face red with shame. Of course, she should have helped. She shouldn't need rules to tell her that.

The rumbling of the organ quieted. The villagers stared at each other in unease.

"There must be a storm moving in," Sir Walter said, coming to the church door. "It affects the pressure in these old instruments."

People nodded, but the crowd cleared out of the church. Cassandra picked up the rest of the turnips while balancing Henry's book in the crook of her arm. She brought the vegetables in with the other offerings. Henry was staring at the church organ, his expression troubled.

"What are those?" he asked when he saw the turnips.

"That girl—Mary Leland—she dropped them."

"Oh." He sounded just as exasperated over Mary as the other villagers did.

"And what's so wrong with her, then?" Cassandra asked.

Henry wrinkled his nose. He looked prepared to deliver a long list of Mary Leland's faults. No doubt he had strong opinions about clumsy, awkward girls.

Before he could speak, the church bells chimed the hour. After the first gong, a cracking sound split through the church. A horrible, off-tune clank was followed by a crash from outside. Once the echoes died, a hollow, tomb-like silence filled the church.

Henry's face turned ashen, and he dashed outside. Cassandra limped after him. The broken clapper of one of the church bells stood embedded in the lawn like a crooked spear flung from the bell tower. The villagers slowly gathered around, their expressions curious and wary.

"I've never heard of such a thing," someone whispered.

"Back luck," said another.

Henry looked like he was going to be sick.

"Mr. Stewart?" Cassandra asked quietly.

"They've broken the church bells," he whispered, more to himself than to her.

"Who has?"

His eyes narrowed. "I don't know. Yet."

He strode off without even a farewell. Perhaps it was improper to try to defend Mary Leland, but Cassandra couldn't see what the poor girl had done wrong. If being clumsy was such a sin, Cassandra was just as guilty as Mary.

Cassandra clutched Henry's book to her chest and stared up at the bell tower. One of the bells was cracked, its empty mouth gaping and tongueless. A flock of crows alighted on the tower. Their caws sounded like harsh laughter.

Cassandra wanted to be grateful that the broken bell distracted the gossips from her, but the sight of the large, black birds on the damaged bell tower left her stomach heavy with dread.

Chapter Eight

Cassandra peered around Sophie to check her hair in the dressing table mirror one last time. It had been almost a week since the Harvest Festival, and most of the village had put talk of the broken bell aside in their excitement for the Harvest Ball. Cassandra just hoped to survive the night without humiliating herself.

The younger Weaver sisters crowded in Sophie and Cassandra's room. Jane and Lillian copied Sophie's preening, adding discarded ribbons and flowers to each other's hair, while Charlotte sat on Georgina's lap to listen as she read them a story from Henry's book.

"Sophie, you look lovely." Cassandra tried to pull her older sister away. "We should be ready to meet the carriage."

"It's fashionable to arrive late." Sophie kept her eyes on the mirror as she added another rose to her hair.

"Is it fashionable to arrive after the ball is over?" Cassandra stepped around her younger sisters, lifting her blue tarlatan gown so the delicate fabric didn't snag on the stems of the flowers they were playing with. "If you're not ready when the Ashbys arrive, we'll have a long walk to the village."

"Do you think that handsome Mr. Fitzhugh, will be at the ball?"

"Why don't we go and find out?"

Cassandra didn't care much about the mysterious Mr. Fitzhugh. She wondered if Henry Stewart would attend. He wasn't likely to ask her to dance, though, after she had broken The Rules and confronted him about Mary Leland. It didn't matter.

She checked her hair in the mirror again anyway.

Georgina looked up from Henry's book. She had skipped past the main section of the book, with its notes on various plants, to the back pages, which were filled with illustrated folk tales. "These drawings are beautiful. Have you seen them, Cassie?"

Cassandra settled down carefully on the edge of the bed to look over Georgina's shoulder. Jane and Lillian gathered around the book as well.

"I remember Nancy telling us most of these stories, but there are some I haven't heard," Georgina said, flipping through pictures of goblins, trolls, banshees, pixies, and red caps. Cassandra frowned at the image of a small, human-like creature holding a hat dripping with the blood of its victim. The drawing may have been skilled, but Cassandra thought the subject a little too gruesome for the younger girls. Especially Charlotte, who tried to go back to the image of the pixies. Cassandra quickly turned the page to one labeled "Queens of Faerie."

"I didn't know there were so many," Cassandra said. She studied the pictures. Each queen was impossibly lovely and labeled with names like Titania, Lady of the Woods and Mab,

Lady of the Mountains. The drawings showed exquisite detail on their gowns and faces, as though sketched from life, with the exception of the last: a vague, unfinished figure entitled The Dark Lady.

She heard the rumble of a carriage on the drive and rose to part the lace curtains. "The carriage is here, Sophie."

"Perfect," Sophie said, giving her reflection a nod.

"Are you wearing the brooch I painted for you, Cassie?" Georgina asked. She laughed and pointed to the book. "It says here that roses keep dark creatures away."

Cassandra showed her the rose pin fastened to her bodice. "I wish you could come with us, Georgie. You're old enough to be out."

"My ankle still hurts, and the music is just a muddled mess to me," Georgina said. "It's better this way." She flinched as Jane and Lillian shoved flowers into her braids and Charlotte sprinkled the bright blue petals of Michaelmas daisies over her hair. Cassandra gave Georgina a sympathetic smile as she headed out the bedroom door.

"Miss Sophie, Miss Cassandra! Nancy's calling you," Beth said from the stairway.

Beth stared at their airy gowns with a toothy gawk. The harvest ball's open invitation meant she could have attended, too, but they couldn't spare her with their mother in her delicate condition and Nancy serving as the young ladies' chaperone.

"These came for you, miss," Beth said. She trotted up the last few steps and held out a little bouquet of white rose buds.

"Oh!" Sophie exclaimed, reaching for them.

"No, sorry," Beth said quickly. "I meant Miss Cassandra."

"They're for me?" Cassandra asked, as surprised as Sophie looked. "Who are they from?"

"I don't know. The note just said, 'For Miss Cassandra Weaver' in a gentleman's handwriting."

Cassandra took the roses, their stems bound in a simple white ribbon. "Is it right for me to wear them?"

"Well, I think we can guess who they're from." Sophie studied the bouquet, her nose wrinkled. "Mr. Rushford has shown you a great deal of attention."

"Oh." Cassandra held the flowers away.

"Then again, I did notice Henry Stewart watching you during the Harvest Service on Sunday."

"Really?" Cassandra's face warmed. Even after she had started a quarrel with him?

Both girls examined the bouquet as if hoping to find a hidden clue, then Sophie met Cassandra's eyes and shrugged. Cassandra bit her bottom lip. Mr. Rushford did not seem like the type to think of flowers.

"I'll wear them."

Sophie nodded and pinned the flowers to Cassandra's bodice. "Mr. Stewart wouldn't be a brilliant match, to be sure, but he could be acceptable when he finishes his apprenticeship. Papa and Mama won't have any objections."

Their parents would probably be happy for any interest in their damaged daughter. Cassandra had heard them weighing the benefits of taking away from her other sisters' dowries to increase her own and Georgina's portions, hoping to bribe some mercenary young men into overlooking their imperfections. Could her dowry be Henry's motivation? At least he didn't treat her like an invalid. Her stomach fluttered at the thought of dancing with him.

"He's only loaned me a book. And you saw how strange it is. I mean, it talks about how to keep fairies away and treat illnesses caused by witchcraft and magic. He seems too sensible for that kind of country nonsense."

"Hmm. I imagine he meant it to be entertaining." Sophie put a gentle hand on her arm. "Remember not to be so outspoken tonight, Cassie. Gentlemen prefer young ladies who are circumspect. They like a little mystery."

Cassandra resisted the urge to roll her eyes. She'd spent all afternoon reviewing The Rules. She was armed as well as she could be for the social battle of the ballroom.

"Girls!"

Cassandra and Sophie turned to see their mother leaning against her bedroom door frame, her long, reddish-brown hair hanging loose over her shoulder. She cradled her belly.

"Cassie..."

Cassandra held her breath, longing to hear the words she needed from her mother: *Everything will be well. You are enough.*

"At the ball tonight, please, just...Sophie, look after your sister."

Cassandra looked down, wondering again if attending the ball was a mistake. Maybe she wasn't ready. Maybe she never would be.

She didn't want to be forever hiding, though, and this was the last of the festivities before Michaelmas marked the end of the harvest season. She just had to make it through one night.

"We'll be fine, Mother," Sophie said. "Please, get some rest."

Their mother squeezed Sophie's arm fondly and hobbled back into her room.

Cassandra often saw the glances her parents exchanged over her mother's growing belly and knew their silent prayers: let the baby be a boy, let him be healthy and whole. Cassandra gripped the banister as she limped down behind Sophie.

Move carefully and gracefully. Do not draw attention to yourself. Move carefully and gracefully. Do not draw attention to yourself.

"Are you muttering to yourself?" Sophie asked.

"What? No." Cassandra pressed her lips shut to be sure.

At the bottom of the stairs, Beth caught her arm. "Begging your pardon, miss. Mr. Stewart seems like a good enough sort, but watch out for his companion, Domin. Everyone says he's a fakir: an Indian wizard."

"Beth, really! That's ridiculous." Sophie took Cassandra's other arm.

Beth leaned in and lowered her voice. "My sister's beau is in service at Ashby Hall. *He* heard that Mr. Stewart's family were gentry, and Domin came to England with them after they toured abroad. Mr. Stewart saved his life once, so even when Mr. Stewart's parents died and left him so poor he had to take up this apprenticeship, the fakir stayed with him, on account of the blood debt he owes him."

Sophie shook her head. "That's an unlikely piece of country gossip." She dragged Cassandra away.

The flutters in Cassandra's stomach multiplied. Henry worked in a shop, but there was a refinement to his speech and self-assurance to his manners above that of an apothecary's apprentice. Perhaps he was a gentleman's son. But Beth's talk of magic was silly. Domin was only another apprentice alongside Henry, not an ascetic monk with mystical powers.

Nancy smoothed her white hair and handed the girls their cloaks. She glanced at Cassandra's neglected cane, but Cassandra shook her head. Tonight, she would show everyone how well she could fit with them.

Nancy shrugged and ushered them outside. The evening chill crept around them, and Cassandra snuggled into the soft, green lambswool cloak draped over her bare arms. A footman helped the ladies into the upholstered confines of the carriage, where Lady Ashby waited with Elizabeth and a petite blonde woman.

Elizabeth motioned for the Weaver sisters to share her bench, her wide grin crinkling her nose. Nancy paled when she saw the remaining spot next to the young blonde woman and huddled into the cushioned seat as the carriage rattled forward. Cassandra watched her old nurse with concern. She seemed to be shy of strangers lately.

"How pleasant to see you tonight, girls," Lady Ashby said coolly. "Lady St. Clair, may I introduce Miss Weaver and Miss Cassandra Weaver? Girls, my guest, Amy, Lady St. Clair."

Sophie and Cassandra bowed their heads in acknowledgment. Amy smiled, showing off dimpled cheeks and perfect teeth. She looked young to be married to a titled lord, but pretty enough that it wasn't all that surprising. Cassandra suspected her of using cosmetics to achieve her porcelain-smooth skin, but if she did, she was expert at hiding it.

Lady Ashby snapped open her fan. "Tell me, Miss Weaver, is your father still concluding business at those shops of his?" She said "shops" like she was talking about something dumped out of a chamber pot.

Elizabeth frowned at her mother.

"Yes." Sophie kept her shoulders straight, but her cheeks reddened. "We expect him in another week."

Cassandra fidgeted with her reticule to avoid glaring at Lady Ashby. Her father—her whole family—had worked hard for their money, and that was the problem. No amount of polish or etiquette could make them belong with people like the Ashbys, with their old money and old blood.

"What business is your father in, Miss Weaver?" Amy asked in an overly cheerful tone.

"He deals in men's clothing," Sophie said.

"Premade clothes, aren't they?" Lady Ashby said with a smirk. "Designed to fit the common man."

Amy's eyes brightened. "Oh, yes. I've heard about that. What a brilliant way to provide up-and-coming men with suitable new clothing without the need for bespoke tailors." She cut a quick glance at Lady Ashby. "After all, we're none of us made quite as differently as we often think."

Lady Ashby narrowed her eyes and stared over Amy's head.

Cassandra gave Amy a surprised look, and the blonde woman returned a dazzling, slightly wicked smile. Cassandra smiled back and turned her attention out the window. Thatched cottages punctuated fields stacked with fresh-cut hay until the farmland gave way to clusters of stone houses and shops. For a moment, she thought she saw a dark, wolf-like shape shadowing the carriage, but when she looked again, it was gone. She shivered and huddled into her cloak. Even with Lady Ashby's sour company, the carriage was better than walking when no one knew what had become of the mad dog.

They passed the town square and the church with its silent belltower. The carriage jingled to a stop in front of the inn. The ladies disembarked into the warm light trickling out from its dusty window panes.

"You both look very nice tonight," Elizabeth Ashby said, taking the sisters' arms as soon as her mother was out of earshot. "I wish my hair would curl like yours, Miss Weaver," she added, and Sophie smiled at the covert apology for Lady Ashby's rudeness.

The sign overhead creaked, and Cassandra squinted up at it, trying to decipher the picture in the dim light. The old-fashioned calligraphy read "Queen's Head Inn," and the image, painted to look like stained glass, depicted a beautiful woman with a crown of leaves and berries.

"Which queen is that meant to be?" Cassandra asked, remembering the portraits she'd studied in school. "Certainly not Victoria or Elizabeth. Perhaps Anne Stuart?"

The last Stuart queen's story tugged at Cassandra's sympathy, the way her family shunted her aside, never certain what to do with her. Even when the whims of fate and Parliament placed her on the throne, few people had taken her seriously.

"It's Titania," Amy whispered, staring up at the image.

Cassandra squinted at the picture again. "The Faerie Queen?"

"One of them, anyway." Amy shook her head. "But it's best not to speak too much of such things, Miss Weaver."

Amy looked so serious that Cassandra forced herself to keep a straight face. People in the country were certainly more superstitious, but Lady Amy St. Clair too? She shone with London polish. Cassandra glanced up again at the beautiful woman on the sign. Maybe it wouldn't be so bad if there were magic in the world. Something to believe in besides living under the iron authority of The Rules and the faint chance of finding a husband who would stoop to accepting a crippled bride for a large enough dowry.

"Ladies, how lovely you all look! How lovely!" Sir Walter's voice boomed. He nodded a greeting to Sophie and Cassandra, but his gaze slid past them, not quite meeting their eyes. Cassandra adjusted one of the roses in her hair. Had they done something disgraceful without realizing it? Perhaps his wife had complained to him, and he was regretting his kindness to their family.

Robert Ashby, having handed his horse off to a groom, came up behind his father and grinned broadly at Sophie, who smiled shyly back. He tweaked one of Elizabeth's dark curls. "You'd best hurry inside and preen, little sister. Fitzhugh's not far behind me."

"Robert!" Elizabeth blushed to the tip of her upturned nose, but she broke out in a grin to match his.

Cassandra smiled, wondering what it would be like to have a brother. The young women exchanged their donations for dance cards at the inn's front door and headed to the ladies' dressing room. Giddy young ladies flocked around them like hungry peacocks. Cassandra hid her nervousness behind a smile and tried to catch a friendly eye, but the others couldn't stop gawking at Amy, who only took a moment to glance in the mirror before sweeping out to the ballroom.

"She looks like a fashion plate!" One girl exclaimed, staring at the door where Amy had disappeared. "I wonder how much fabric it took to make that bustle."

"More than I can afford," another girl mumbled and several heads nodded, waving the feathers and flowers in their hair like a garden ruffled by a breeze.

Cassandra scowled at a bow on her sleeve that had come untied and looked around for help. Sophie was busy adjusting the gathers on the back of Elizabeth's skirt, while Nancy held a pin box for them.

"I can tie it for you, miss," said a timid voice.

A pallid girl with huge gray eyes hovered at her side—Mary Leland. Cassandra noticed the disparaging glances the other young ladies gave her and wondered if talking to the awkward girl was somehow a faux pas.

"I can tie it for you," the girl repeated, eyes fixed on the offending bow.

Cassandra couldn't find anything wrong with accepting the offer. She remembered how it hurt to have people pretend to look right through her or act as though speaking to her was a terrible duty. As though her crippled hand and leg were somehow contagious. She nodded.

The girl's nimble fingers quickly tamed the rogue ribbon. "It won't come untied again."

"Thank you." Cassandra admired the neat bow. "I'm Cassandra Weaver."

"I know, miss," the girl said, still not meeting her gaze.

Cassandra waited until the silence became uncomfortable. "What's your name?" she prompted.

"Mary Leland," the girl whispered, as if afraid the others would overhear.

"It's a pleasure to meet you, Miss Leland," Cassandra said, and Mary finally looked at her, a hesitant smile tugging at her thin mouth.

"Come along, Cassie," Sophie called, and Cassandra followed the other young ladies with a parting wave at Mary.

They emerged into the great hall in a haze of chatter and flowers. The girls dissipated, and Nancy sailed along behind Sophie, leaving Cassandra alone. She watched dancing couples twirl past and acquaintances greet each other. No one returned her smiles, so she limped to the chairs lining the wall. As she passed a pair of young men, one of them whispered, "Cripple." Her face burned, but she sat up straight and pretended she hadn't heard.

A familiar face caught her eye, and her heartbeat stepped up to match the quick beat of the polka. Henry Stewart stood alone near the doorway, an island in the flowing river of people. He scanned the room, and she sat so straight her back could have been nailed to a board, trying *not* to look pathetic.

"Good evening, Miss Weaver," drawled a friendly voice.

Jairus Hale had traded his duster and wide-brimmed hat for a crisp black tailcoat. He looked at home in the ballroom, despite his sun-bleached hair and brightly patterned silk waistcoat, which jarred with the simple colors around him.

He swept her a bow. "Is your younger sister well?"

"Quite, thank you," Cassandra said.

He sprawled in the chair next to her. "I hope it isn't impolite to assume an acquaintance with you. I'm finding that my American manners don't always suit here."

"I've never read an etiquette book that addressed our situation," she said with a smile, "but I'm happy to see you again."

"This means you can't escape the acquaintance now." He shook his head in mock concern. "I hope I'm not making a scandal of you."

"The other girls will be jealous."

"Really?" he asked, raising his eyebrows and grinning.

He adjusted his coat, and Cassandra saw a glint of metal at his belt.

"Tell me, Mr. Hale, is it an American custom to come armed to a social occasion?"

"In some places it is. We live in dangerous times."

Cassandra frowned and scanned the room, the crowd suddenly feeling too close. Her attention fell on a group of men in casual suits whispering together as they observed the dancers. Mr. Rushford stood at their head. When he rested a hand on his hip, the bulky outline of a gun showed through his coat.

She gestured with her chin. "Are those men friends of yours, too, then?"

His eyes narrowed. "They're not the friendly type."

He looked like he would elaborate, but Sophie hurried to

Cassandra's side. She gave Jairus a dismissive glance, and he stood and excused himself with a bow.

Before Cassandra could chastise her sister for her cold manners, Sophie launched into a monologue.

"I've been looking everywhere for you. Mr. Fitzhugh is *so* handsome, and he asked after you, so he is obviously very polite as well." She clutched her dance card to her chest. "He engaged me for two dances, and Robert Ashby put himself down for two as well. At this rate my card will be full before the ball is half over." Her elated expression faded. "But if you get fatigued, I can beg off and leave early."

"I'll be fine." Cassandra twisted her card around to hide all the blank spaces. It was good to see Sophie enjoying herself, at least. She studied her sister's bright expression. "What happened to your roses?"

"Oh." Sophie patted her hair. "Mr. Fitzhugh didn't like them, so I took them out."

"But...after all that work?"

"Come on." Sophie dragged Cassandra through the crowd.

Chapter Nine

Sophie and Cassandra found Amy St. Clair and Douglas Fitzhugh standing with the Ashbys observing the dancing. Nancy stood off to the side, her face pale and her forehead creased with worry. Fitzhugh's dark hair was just untidy enough to give him a rakish look, and his blue eyes shone when he laughed at something Elizabeth said. Despite their finery, even the Ashbys looked shabby compared to him and Amy.

"But this is such a country affair," Elizabeth said, fanning herself. "It makes me miss the balls in London."

Fitzhugh grinned at Sophie. "The country does have its charms."

Sophie smiled, and Elizabeth glared at her.

Elizabeth snapped her fan shut. "I suppose it's diverting at times to mingle with the *common* folks."

Cassandra stared. Was this the same Elizabeth who had been so kind and charming just a few minutes before?

Fitzhugh smirked. "For instance, see that woman's hat? It

almost looks like a bird's nest. Or, perhaps that's exactly what it is."

Sophie and Elizabeth snickered, but the more Cassandra heard from Fitzhugh, the less handsome he became. She edged away from the group, but when she looked up, Mr. Rushford was watching her. He smiled coldly and wormed his way through the crowds toward her, like a wolf stalking a deer.

"Miss Weaver?" Henry appeared at her side.

"Mr. Stewart!" Her heart jumped into her throat as she curtseyed, and he returned a bow.

Mr. Rushford paused to frown at them from a few steps away.

Henry studied her face, as if looking for the symptoms of some illness, but he smiled when he saw the white rose buds pinned to her dress.

"Do I have you to thank for these?" she asked, touching one of the flowers.

"I thought they were appropriate for someone who likes to go wandering through poems."

Of course, he would remind her of the silly things she said. At least he didn't seem angry with her. Her stomach did strange, fluttery things at his teasing grin, and she had no idea how to respond.

"Is your sister feeling better?" he asked. "Not in too much pain?"

"Yes. I mean, no." She shook her head. "She's doing well."

A smile flickered on his lips. "Could I trouble you for a dance?"

"Of course." She wished her dance card wasn't so empty as she passed it over.

Behind them, Fitzhugh said something in French, and Sophie replied in a smug tone. Their father had insisted they learn the rudiments of the language, but when Fitzhugh addressed Cassandra, the French words jumbled together in her mind.

"Sorry, Fitzhugh," Henry took her elbow, and an electric jolt raced up her arm at his touch. "I've already engaged Miss Weaver for the next dance."

Fitzhugh gave a curt nod before turning back to the other girls, but Cassandra caught the mocking look in his eyes. She stepped a little closer to Henry.

"Thank you for rescuing me," she whispered.

"Of course. I only wish I could protect you the rest of the night." He flushed faintly. "Uh, that is, I want you to know that if you need help—with anything—you can ask."

His concern surprised her, but it didn't feel condescending as it did when Sophie hovered around her, and she liked the sensation of his gentle grip on her arm.

"Apparently, I could use French lessons," she said with a smile. "I had a tutor, but my French is atrocious."

He chuckled, and she wondered if she was saying too much again.

The master of ceremonies called out the next dance, and Henry released her elbow and offered his arm. Robert Ashby and another gentleman escorted Sophie and Elizabeth away, though the girls watched Fitzhugh over their shoulders. Cassandra puzzled over their rude behavior.

Henry led her to the floor and placed one hand on her waist for the waltz. She had waltzed before, of course, but the nearness to her partner had never made her skin feel so warm. Henry guided her expertly, his dancing decidedly elegant, reminding Cassandra of Beth's rumor that he was gentry. It made her more aware of her slightly-off-rhythm gait. If he noticed, though, he gave no indication, except that he didn't guide her through any intricate spins. She lost herself in the feel of twirling through the room with his arm around her waist.

When the dance ended, Cassandra searched for a way to keep him talking to her. And not, she admitted to herself, just to keep Mr. Rushford at bay.

"Thank you for loaning me your book." Not exactly clever conversation, but it did the trick.

"Of course." He glanced at the roses in her hair. "I trust you're finding it enlightening?"

She nodded, trying to decide if he was teasing again.

"Henry, I hope you'll not forget to dance with me," Amy called as they strolled passed her. "It seems ages since we've danced together."

"Indeed, it has been ages, but I won't forget you, Amy."

Their informality shocked Cassandra—addressing each other by first names was definitely against The Rules—but Henry's expression eased her surge of jealousy; she'd never seen a young man look so miserable at the prospect of dancing with a beautiful lady. *Was* Amy actually married, or could she be a very young widow? Before Cassandra could puzzle out their relationship, they reached Sophie, who sat with a blank expression and not even a teasing glance for her sister. Cassandra wondered if she was unwell.

Robert strolled over to Sophie and asked to sit by her. Before she could answer, Fitzhugh sauntered into view. Sophie bolted past Robert to join the flock of girls gathered around the tall, handsome man. Robert glared, and Henry offered him a sympathetic look.

"So much for circumspection and mystery," Cassandra muttered.

"What?" Henry asked.

"Nothing."

The musicians struck up another dance, scattering the group gathered around Fitzhugh. Fitzhugh pinned Cassandra with that mocking smile and made his way over to her.

"Miss Cassandra, please allow me the honor of this dance." Fitzhugh glanced at Henry. "If you're not otherwise engaged."

Cassandra wished Henry would claim the next dance as well, but he said nothing, only exchanged a barbed look with Fitzhugh.

"Well..." Cassandra hesitated. The dance was a quadrille, which was even more difficult than the waltz to execute gracefully with her weak foot, and she doubted Fitzhugh would be a forgiving partner.

Rushford stepped forward as if he would speak to Cassandra.

What was the saying about the lesser of two evils? Cassandra took Fitzhugh's offered hand. "Thank you."

Fitzhugh gave Rushford a cutting look. "Wait your turn. This one is mine."

Cassandra flinched at his possessive grip, and she caught Henry's frown as Fitzhugh led her away.

"Are those flowers from your garden, Miss Weaver?" Fitzhugh glanced at the roses in her hair, then his gaze rested on Henry's bouquet fastened to her bodice, his eyes lingering there too long.

Her skin flushed under his gaze, and she suddenly wished for a higher neckline. "Yes. Some of them, anyway. They grow all around our house. The scent is divine."

"Hmm. But with your eyes, do you think they're a flattering color? Some other flower might better bring out the green, and that would make you all the more lovely. Roses are such an common flower, after all."

Horrified at the offending flowers, Cassandra plucked one

out of her hair, scattering delicate petals on the ground. Its reek made her wild to pull the others off, but as she crushed one, she remembered Henry's book and Georgina's teasing reminder. Roses were supposed to repel dark creatures.

The room sharpened, though she hadn't been aware of her vision blurring. She stared at the bruised petals littering the floor and the many young ladies who had torn roses from their hair and dresses.

"I like roses," Cassandra said as much to herself as to Fitzhugh.

"Really?" He frowned, but the glint returned to his eyes. "Miss Weaver, it's refreshing to meet a young lady with such resilient opinions. You've given me something to think about."

Uncertain how to respond, Cassandra took her place for the quadrille, mentally reviewing the steps of the dance so she wouldn't turn in the wrong direction or trip and make a fool of herself. Henry and Amy joined their set as the music began. Fitzhugh said little else as they danced, which let Cassandra eavesdrop on the conversation between the other two.

"Some of us have been worried about you," Amy said.

"I'm fine," Henry answered.

"You look it. I think what you did was brave."

For a few measures, the movements of the dance took Cassandra too far away to hear more. Then, she was close again.

"Will you tell them where I am?" Henry's voice was low.

"Not if you don't want me to. I'm not angry, Henry. I hope we're still friends."

Cassandra didn't hear his answer, since Fitzhugh's question about how she enjoyed living in the village required a reply, but her mind remained stuck on Henry's conversation. What sort of brave act would force Henry to hide from someone? She missed one of the turns and hurriedly limped back to her place, face burning. When the music ended, Fitzhugh escorted her off the floor and left with a bow.

"What do you think you're doing?" Sophie hissed, digging her nails into Cassandra's elbow. "Stick to Mr. Stewart and leave Mr. Fitzhugh alone." Her sister smirked as she released her arm. "Though it's not as if any elegant gentleman would want a hopeless, awkward girl like you. You're such an embarrassment."

Cassandra gasped. Tears clouded her eyes. Sophie had never been intentionally cruel before. Cassandra turned away quickly, and her weak foot twisted. She stumbled and fell to her hands and knees in a heap of blue tarlatan. A group of girls standing nearby snickered behind their gloved hands. Cassandra squeezed her eyes shut, determined not to cry. Hopeless. Awkward. Just as Sophie said.

A gentle hand took her arm, and she looked up, expecting to see Nancy. Instead, Henry knelt beside her. Of all the people to witness her humiliation...but his expression was nothing but sympathetic as he helped her to her feet.

"Thank you," she whispered.

"You ought to sit," he said. "Perhaps you need something to drink? It's easy to get faint when the room is so hot."

She would rather have his company while people watched her and whispered, but it was unladylike to say that, so she nodded. "Thank you."

He left her with a bow.

"Miss Weaver, are you unwell?" Amy sat on the chair next to her, cutting off Nancy, who shrank out of the blonde lady's way. "I hope my cousin didn't offend you."

"Your cousin?" Cassandra glanced at Fitzhugh. "Oh, no. I'm fine, Lady St. Clair."

"Fitzhugh's not a good person to know, Miss Weaver. His faults spread like lice."

Cassandra squirmed on the hard, wooden seat, surprised Amy spoke so openly against her own cousin.

"How well do you know Henry Stewart?" Amy asked.

"Not well."

"He's charming company, is he not?" There was a push in Amy's voice, and she placed a hand on Cassandra's arm.

The lonely ache in Cassandra's chest swelled. Why shouldn't she confide in Amy? She was swimming in strange waters with dark things circling beneath her, and she wanted an escape to a familiar shore. She drew breath to speak, but then a thought stopped her: Amy was just as much a stranger as everyone else in the village. The room snapped into focus again.

"Mr. Stewart is a fine dancer," Cassandra managed to blurt out.

"I'm so glad to hear you say that," Amy said, releasing Cassandra's arm with a quick squeeze.

Cassandra drew back with the sense that she had just come through some sort of trial. She wanted to bury her face in her hands and disappear from the ball. Instead, she watched as Elizabeth pressed closer to Fitzhugh, and he leaned away to whisper in Sophie's ear. Elizabeth's eyes narrowed, and she cast her angry gaze around until it fell on Mary Leland. The girl sat on a chair near the wall, swaying to the rhythm of the music.

"I don't know why that Leland girl bothers to leave the house," Elizabeth said to Fitzhugh. "Just look at what she's wearing. I think she made it herself out of some old linens."

Fitzhugh chuckled, and the flock of girls around him giggled in chorus. Amy frowned at him.

Mary turned away, wiping her eyes, but her fingers weren't quick enough to catch all the tears streaking down her cheeks.

Cassandra grimaced when she saw Sophie laughing along with the others. She pushed herself up from her seat to face Elizabeth. "If she did make it herself, she's remarkably talented. Her dress is about the same color as yours, and that shade is far more flattering on her than it is on you."

She slapped a hand over her mouth, as shocked with herself as Elizabeth looked with her jaw hanging open. What had come over her?

"Indeed." Amy smirked. "She chose her colors well. Fine fabrics can be bought, but good taste cannot."

Fitzhugh again led the laughter, leaving Elizabeth crimson. Cassandra squeezed her eyes shut. This was all wrong.

She grabbed Sophie's arm and whispered, "We should go."

A female scream from the front of the inn pierced the dullness of the room. Cassandra tightened her grip on Sophie and scanned the crowd, but most of the people acted as though they hadn't heard anything.

"Excuse me," Fitzhugh said, bowing to the girls and hurrying away.

"Why did Fitzhugh have to go?" Sophie pouted.

"Didn't you hear that scream?" Cassandra asked. Was something wrong with everyone? Or was she delirious again, as she had been during the fever, and hearing voices?

Amy rested a hand on Cassandra's shoulder. "Stay here, Miss Weaver, and everything will be well."

Cassandra shook her head and tried to drag Sophie away from the crowd and back to where Nancy huddled against the wall. Everything was not well.

Chapter Ten

Jairus jogged toward the cries for help. Tension had been filling the room all evening like smoke from green wood held over a fire, but now the flames had finally caught. He turned his eyes heavenward.

"See, all I needed was a little direction."

People should have given him a wide berth, the crazy American talking to himself, but he had to fight his way through the crowd. He knew something was very wrong in Drixton as soon as he'd tracked Rushford to the village, but he still couldn't pinpoint the source. Black magic? Restless spirits? None of the supernatural threats he'd faced in the past seemed to be at work here.

He pushed through the ballroom. Sticky heat washed over him, thrusting his mind back to a bivouac on a Mississippi battlefield. He drew a deep breath, inhaling the scent of flowers and perfumes. Laughter mixed with the polka playing in the background. The war was over. He was thousands of miles from the cannons and the screams of the dying.

Near the entrance to the inn, he bumped into Douglas Fitzhugh retrieving his silver-knobbed cane from the cloakroom. Something about him raised Jairus's hackles, like the man was a mountain lion stalking in the shadows.

Fitzhugh smirked at him. "Mr. Hale, isn't it? What a delight. I've been wanting to talk to you, to ask you to teach us that American game, poker."

The hunger to hold the cards stirred in Jairus's chest, poising over his heart like a rattlesnake. "Sorry, I don't gamble."

"Oh, is that so?"

Fitzhugh glanced down at the gun in Jairus's hand. Jairus didn't remember drawing his revolver, but its smooth, familiar grip rested in his palm. A sword whispered against its sheath as Fitzhugh pulled a thin, single-edged blade from his cane.

Jairus raised his eyebrows at Fitzhugh, who responded with a grin.

They approached the entrance of the inn shoulder to shoulder. A pair of men just inside the doorway fanned a fainting woman.

"Mad dog!" one of them warned Jairus and Fitzhugh.

Jairus nodded and stepped outside, Fitzhugh still flanking him.

Fog trickled into the streets from between the buildings, and a growl rolled out of the darkness. The hairs on Jairus's arms stood on end. Jairus and Fitzhugh turned to face a black dog prowling from the shadows.

Jairus pulled his trigger, and the gunshot echoed in the street. The creature snarled and retreated. Jairus winced. He only had seven silver bullets, and he'd just wasted one. A shape emerged from the alley next to Fitzhugh. Jairus spun but took his finger from the trigger when he recognized the apothecary's apprentice, Domin.

"Fitzhugh, what's this about?" Domin demanded.

Fitzhugh turned his sword on the dark-skinned man. "That's what I'm going to find out, mongrel. Stay out of my way."

Domin didn't flinch at the insult, but pushed the sword aside and stepped up to Fitzhugh, his gaze challenging.

Something moved in the street.

"Fitzhugh! Over here!" Jairus pointed at the black dog that had reemerged from behind a merchant's wagon parked up the street.

Domin melted back into the shadows.

"There!" Fitzhugh said when another of the animals paced out in front of them.

"A third one on our left."

Jairus pulled the trigger, and the gun danced in his hand. The familiar scent of gunsmoke mingled with the fog. The animal in front of him lurched backward, caught itself, then continued its approach. As before, he couldn't do more than delay these monsters by hitting them with silver, but he didn't have his shotgun, and iron would tear the barrels of his revolvers to shreds.

Fitzhugh circled around to one side, sword ready. Jairus shot the dog to the left, flipped the hammer back, and fired at the animal closest to Fitzhugh. Both creatures jerked when the bullets slammed into them, but they didn't fall.

Fitzhugh lunged at the one nearest him. It darted away, but Fitzhugh slashed the dog's leg. The animal yelped and collapsed, and the other two dogs charged.

Jairus fired into the face of the dog on the left. It staggered, swiping at its damaged eye.

Fitzhugh's blade left a bleeding trail along the second animal's shoulder. He lunged at the creature again. It ducked

aside and grabbed his arm. With a shake of its head, it threw
Fitzhugh to the ground and sprang at him.

Jairus's gun flashed in the dark, and the beast yelped. A gray
wolf leapt over Fitzhugh and knocked the dog away from him.
The two animals tumbled to the ground, snarling and tearing at
each other's throats. Jairus blinked. He'd seen wolves, and he'd
seen werewolves, but this creature was something else entirely—
fighting with more cunning and more ferocity.

Fitzhugh snatched up his sword. The dog with the injured
leg struggled to rise, but Fitzhugh plunged his blade through
the creature's chest. He yanked his sword free as the animal
shuddered and lay still.

Jairus spun back to the dog pacing a half-circle around him.
Red glowed from its undamaged eye, while the other shone a
cloudy silver. Jairus was too close to miss. His last shot hit it in
the head. It staggered but stayed upright, backing up into
the fog.

Cold seeped into his fingers as he traded guns. This one was
only loaded with lead. It probably wouldn't even slow the
creature.

The gray wolf's opponent broke away and tore down the
street with a whimper. Jairus met the wolf's eyes, and the sense
it was sizing him up gave him goose bumps. Then the wolf
turned to race after the escaping dog.

Jairus scanned the foggy street for the last animal.
Something moved in the shadows. He snapped his gun in that
direction but didn't dare fire without a clear shot.

"A little help, Mr. Fitzhugh?" he asked, but Fitzhugh had
run up the street after the dog and the wolf. Jairus was alone
except for the small crowd gathered at the doorway of the inn.
They stood watching as though mad dog attacks were as
common as sheep shearings. Most of the guests continued

dancing. Definitely not normal behavior. He squinted into the murky night, not daring to look away even when he heard Henry Stewart's voice.

"It's dangerous, Amy. Go back."

"I might be able to help," Amy said.

"What could you possibly do?" Henry's tone mirrored Jairus's own impatience.

"Well, what are *you* planning on doing?" A smirk colored her voice.

A sudden breeze stirred to life, cutting through the fog to give Jairus a glimpse of the black creature prowling forward. He pulled the trigger. The report sounded muffled in the misty street. The breeze picked up, sweeping the fog back as the beast circled, head low and good eye fixed on Jairus.

Sir Walter and Mr. Rushford ran into the street from the inn.

"Don't let it escape. Try to take it alive," Rushford called back to his companions.

"Don't let it hurt anyone!" Sir Walter said. "Remember what's important here."

The men who'd come to the ball with Rushford circled around the creature, guns drawn. Jairus scanned their outstretched hands. As he suspected, each wore a gaudy signet ring bearing a serpent in a figure eight. One of them shot, and the animal bounded back into the shelter of the fog.

"Get it!" Rushford shouted as he dashed up the road. The other men followed, and Henry started after them.

"Mr. Stewart!" Jairus called.

Henry gave him a suspicious look but halted his pursuit. Jairus sighed. He preferred working alone, even when dealing with people he knew and trusted—and Henry was neither—but the quiet voice in the back of his mind, guided by either divinity or insanity, told him that the apothecary's apprentice could be an ally. It was awfully hard to see how, though.

"They're not likely to accomplish anything, except maybe getting themselves killed." Jairus replaced his other gun's empty chamber with an extra from his pocket. "Do you know how to shoot?"

"A little." Henry frowned as he accepted the revolver.

"You have seven shots, but the bullets are only lead. I'm out of silver," Jairus said. Henry raised an eyebrow, but Jairus pressed on. "If we can track that last creature down, we should be able to get everyone home safely."

Henry nodded, and Jairus stooped to examine the body of the dog Fitzhugh had killed. Its skin was dry and papery like a mummy left out in the sun. When Jairus touched it, it crumbled under his finger. The breeze carried the black dust into the night. He shook his head.

"Have you ever seen anything like this before?"

Henry stared at the dog a moment then shook his head. "Not exactly."

"Hmm." Jairus straightened. "Do you have any iron on you? I'm betting that's what Mr. Fitzhugh's sword was made of."

"I have a knife."

"Keep it handy," Jairus said. "I'm going to scout around. Give a holler if they head back here."

Jairus ignored Henry's scowl and jogged around the perimeter of the inn. Tails of fog twisted after him, setting him on edge. No sign of the dogs. As he circled back toward the front of the building, he heard angry voices. He slowed and edged closer, clinging to the shadows.

"You think I'm going to believe you have nothing to do with this?" Henry asked

"I said it, so, yes, I suppose I do," Fitzhugh replied.

"I know it can't be a coincidence. I'm going to find out what you're planning."

"I would advise you to stick to your own affairs. Unlike dear Amy, I won't hesitate to let certain of our friends know where you are."

"You may do that regardless of what I do."

"You're no good to us dead or locked away somewhere. My Lady's plans are going to benefit us all. We'll finally be free, Henry. No more hiding. You of all people ought to appreciate that. You may come to realize that helping us is in your best interest."

"I doubt that," Henry said.

"Be reasonable. You can't hold off the others on your own, and you shouldn't put so much faith in Domin. He's only looking out for his interests, too. At least I'm being honest about it."

"Honest!"

"You know my word is good. Stay out of my way, and I'll stay out of yours."

"You expect me to just sit back and watch people get hurt?"

Fitzhugh laughed. "I don't expect much at all of you, Henry. That way I won't be disappointed."

A cold wind gusted by, and Jairus shivered at its unnatural feel.

"Fitzhugh, Henry, what are you doing?" Domin asked. "We need to find that hound."

Jairus made a quiet retreat down a side lane and walked on. Henry Stewart had more than his fair share of secrets, perhaps dangerous ones. Still, the idea that Henry could be an ally ran through his thoughts like a ghostly whisper.

He looked heavenward. "Let's leave them out of this. I don't want their blood on my hands, too."

The wrongness that permeated the village grew thicker, wrapping itself over the streets with the fog. Jairus knew the dogs were just the beginning, but until he understood more, all he could do was keep hunting.

Chapter Eleven

Henry paced in front of the inn, Jairus's revolver in his hand. The waning moon cast a thin light through the fog and the clouds racing across the night sky—barely enough to see by. Fitzhugh and Domin were still hunting, but he suspected the black dogs were most interested in the people in the inn. Possibly Cassandra Weaver, since the creatures had targeted her and her sisters before, though what the young ladies might have done to attract this kind of attention from the Fay was beyond him.

Faerie magic gathered in the air, its pressure building around him. He sensed the effects rolling off him like water on oilcloth. What was it meant to do to people? He pushed against the energy and winced as pain lanced his chest. The latent magic woven through him repelled the influence of the Fay's glamours, but the villagers had no such protection.

Domin reappeared out of the darkness and paused, tilting his head at the gun. Henry didn't try to explain. Lead bullets wouldn't do anything against the black dogs, but to the people watching, the gun would look like a reasonable safety precaution. A human form of protection. Domin was Henry's best friend—his only real friend—but there were still some things Domin didn't understand about the human world. Some things even Henry didn't understand.

Of course, Fitzhugh was bending the truth when he said Domin was using Henry for his own ends. Domin wasn't like the other Fay.

"I think we've chased the hounds away for now," Domin said.

"But why are they attacking? What do the Fay hope to gain by this?"

Domin squinted at the cloudy sky as if it might offer him an answer. For all Henry knew, maybe it could. "The Dark Lady must pay her tithes to Hell before another winter sets in."

Henry tightened his grip on the gun. "Fitzhugh is fighting *against* the dogs. So the Seelie Court must have summoned them, not the Dark Lady. He seems to think whatever he's doing is going to bring the Fay out of hiding."

"That is worrisome," Domin said.

Henry swept his hand through the energy and the unnatural fog swirling around him. "And this. The Seelie Queens don't have the power to enchant the whole village, do they? Or does the Dark Lady?"

"I don't know. Her power will be at a low ebb until she pays her tithes. The Seelie Queens... perhaps they could for a while. It will cost them, though." He paused. "I sense Seelie and Unseelie magic here."

"Whatever they're after, it must be worth a great deal to them."

"Yes. It would be safer for everyone to return to their homes where the Fay cannot enter. Now, while the hounds are absent."

"How do we convince them? No one's going to listen to either of us."

Domin shrugged. They walked back to the small knot of villagers crowded in the doorway of the inn while the rest of the guests continued their dance. The musicians played on in the background as though nothing unusual were happening. Fitzhugh's glamour blanketed the assembly. It was unlike him to care about keeping people calm, so Henry assumed he had some other motivation for spending the energy to enchant so many people.

Amy stood next to the Weaver sisters and their nurse. Cassandra still wore the white rose buds Henry had sent her. She was the only young lady who hadn't torn off her roses, except for Amy, who loved to flaunt the flower as a reminder that she was allied with the Seelie Court. Jairus might get to look like the hero, but at least Henry had helped Cassandra protect herself from Fitzhugh. Now, he just had to worry about everyone else.

"Did you stop them, then?" Amy's gaze flicked to the gun in Henry's hand, and Cassandra stared at it with wide eyes.

"For now. We'll patrol the streets tonight to make sure everyone gets home safely." Henry paused. "Where's Robert Ashby?"

Amy gestured behind her. "Still inside, dancing."

"Can you fetch him? He might have the clout to break up the party."

"I don't know if I can"—Amy glanced at Cassandra, who was watching the conversation with a quizzical expression—"uh, get his attention. He's so *entranced* with the ball."

Domin stepped forward. "Everyone's safety is at stake, and you are not without your own charms. Unless you have some other motivation for not wanting to help?"

"Of course not!"

Amy huffed and forced her way back into the inn. She was being more reasonable than Henry had expected. If she wasn't an elf, he would almost think of her as a friend. But she could have something to do with the Seelie Court's plans.

That reminded him of Cassandra, who stared at Domin with her eyebrows raised. His friend's interaction with Amy would seem strange. Cassandra caught Henry's stare. Her eyes reflected her wariness of him, yet she had worn the roses. Maybe it was possible for Henry to have a friend in the human world. He stepped closer.

"Are you all right, Miss Weaver?"

"Yes. Or, no." Cassandra lowered her gaze. "I'm frightened. Do *all* those dogs have rabies?"

"I'm not sure, but we're going to find out. In the meantime, I'll make sure you and your sister get home safely. Did you walk?"

"No. We came with the Ashbys."

"What happened to Mr. Fitzhugh?" Sophie asked wistfully. "Did you see how brave he was?"

Cassandra watched her sister with concern. Their nurse had a grip on Sophie's arm like the girl was caught in a flood and might wash out of her reach.

Amy and Robert parted the crowd and directed the exodus from the ball, sending people home in groups. Lingering strands of Fitzhugh's enchantment clung to everyone, but without the Unseelie elf there to manipulate them, they complacently followed Robert's leadership.

Cassandra and her sister would be safe from the dogs in the Ashby's carriage, but Fitzhugh had gained too much sway over the Ashbys, especially given his interest in the Weaver sisters.

"It may be some time before the Ashbys leave," Henry said. "I'll escort you home."

A moment of stubborn defiance flashed in Cassandra's eyes, but then she glanced at her sister, who was still scanning the crowds dreamily. "That's probably for the best. Thank you."

Henry informed Robert he was seeing Cassandra home and returned to offer her his arm. She took it hesitantly then tightened her grasp. After Fitzhugh's taunts, her trusting touch warmed Henry. He adjusted his hold on the gun and led the Weavers up the lane. The old nurse dragged a pouting Sophie along. Domin followed silently behind.

Cassandra's nervousness seeped into Henry as they passed the outskirts of the village. He drew energy from the currents of the night air and fed it into the breeze, clearing the fog around them, but he still imagined shadows creeping closer. If he could touch the Faerie power crackling around them, he could clear the whole village of fog and shadows. But even if it were possible for him to control the Fay's magic, it would take him a step away from what little was left of his humanity.

"Oh, fairy lights!" Sophie said dreamily.

Henry pinned Cassandra's arm against him and spun to see Sophie reaching for the pale orbs floating in the fog.

The old nurse held Sophie back. "No, my lamb. Leave them be!"

"But Nancy, in your stories they lead to treasure." Sophie tried to twist free of the nurse's grip.

"Or to monsters," Cassandra said, but Sophie paid no attention.

"Ignore the lights," Henry said. "You see them all the time around here, but if you follow them, you'll end up lost in the woods." The lights wouldn't hurt them—the will o' the wisps were some of the weakest Fay, a barely sentient flash of energy—

but they might be under the control of a more dangerous Faerie creature.

Cassandra frowned and tightened her grip on Henry's arm.

"If you like, we can follow the local custom for scaring them away," Henry said, looking back at Domin. His friend nodded and slipped into the soft folds of the mist. The orbs danced away from him.

"Local custom?" Cassandra asked.

"Turn your cloak inside out."

A weak smile crept onto Cassandra's lips, and she followed Henry's example as he flipped his coat around. Nancy forced Sophie to do the same.

"What's this supposed to accomplish?" Cassandra asked.

"Will o' the wisps aren't very smart. It confuses them." Henry paused. "Um, that's what people say, anyway."

"I suppose you hear quite a few folk stories out here," Cassandra said as they walked on.

"Yes," Henry said. The lights flickered from time to time out of the fog, but there was no sign of Domin. "Will o' the wisps are said to help lost travelers who flatter them, but I wouldn't trust a Faerie creature. At best, they're only interested in their own amusement, and too often they use people for their own ends, not caring if they're destroying the person in the process." He cleared his throat. "In the stories."

"What do you think the lights are, really?" Cassandra asked.

"Hmm." He could tell her the truth, but if she didn't believe him, he'd look like a fool, and if she did, it would draw her into the dangers of his world. He would always have to keep any humans in his life at arm's length. He forced a light tone. "I've heard people blame them on spontaneous combustion of elements in the air. What do you think?"

"That's a frightening thought, that fire could just spring up around us. I wish I could believe they were little fairies. The world could use more beautiful things."

Henry choked on his response and turned it into a cough. He relaxed when he saw the soft glow of the white roses climbing the Weavers' front porch. Their scent mingled with the damp smell of the fog. Cassandra released his arm and walked up the steps to rap on the door.

"Thank you again, Mr. Stewart," Cassandra said when the maid unlocked the door. She paused. "I hate the thought of you being alone out there with those mad dogs."

He stared at her for a moment. She was worried for him? A glimmer of warmth bloomed in his chest. "Thank you, Miss Weaver, but Domin's close by." He hoped that was true. "And I have a gun," he added.

Looking reassured, she waved goodnight and retreated inside with her sister and Nancy.

Henry bowed, watching the door even after the bolt slid shut. A will-o-the-wisp drifted near, and he snapped out of his reverie. Cassandra was safe now, but where was Domin?

Chapter Twelve

The Faerie lights danced and bobbed around Henry, teasing him to follow. He chased them through the inky night into the woods beyond the Weaver's orchard. If Domin had followed the lights too, they might lead Henry where his friend had gone. Branches snagged at his coat like bony fingers, but he snapped through to a clearing around a pond.

He stumbled to a halt as the lights swirled around the water. An old woman in gray robes hunched over her wash. Banshee. Dark stains seeped into the pond. Henry swallowed. If he could see whose clothes the banshee was washing, he would know who was doomed to die, but he couldn't force himself close enough to recognize the blood-soaked garments.

The Fay hag snapped her pale face around and wailed. The sound burrowed into Henry's heart. He covered his ears. Her wail broke into a rasping caw. The woman shrank into the form of a crow, black wings stirring the fog as she flew off. Her gruesome laundry dissolved into the mist lingering over the pond.

Henry tightened his hands into fists to stop them from shaking. If a banshee was in Drixton, the Morrigan—queen of battle spirits—might be drawing near. She was almost as bad as the Dark Lady, trailing bloodshed behind her.

The will-o'-the-wisps scattered, and a black mare crashed through the trees—the pooka. A snarling gray wolf dodged her hooves. The wolf yelped as a blow connected with his head. He rolled away and came up on his feet, shimmering into the form of a panther. The black cat bunched his thick muscles and sprang onto the mare's back, dragging her to the ground.

She shrieked. Her shape writhed into that of a woman with black hair and a face too long and angular to be human. The panther dissolved into Domin's form.

Domin wrapped his hand around a few of the pooka's hairs and yanked, but they didn't break. She grabbed Domin's dark hair and drew his face close, as if to kiss him. His eyes widened, and he strained to pull away. As the pooka's breath brushed his face, his skin turned sunken and dry. Black veins spiderwebbed up his arms where he touched her.

Henry grabbed his iron knife and caught a handful of the pooka's hair. She cried out when he severed a few long strands.

"Stop!" Henry shouted as she twisted from Domin's grasp.

She froze in place.

Domin rolled onto his feet and blurred through several shapes. The wasted flesh and black veining had healed when he resumed his human form.

"What now, changeling?" the pooka asked, golden eyes fixed on Henry. "You turned down Fitzhugh's offer to use me so you could control me yourself?"

He twisted the long, thick hairs between his fingers. He could put a geas on her—order her to drive all the Fay from Drixton and create a refuge for the people who lived there.

Wasn't their safety worth more than her freedom? Of course, if she encountered one of the Faerie Queens or the Morrigan, she'd have to fight them, and they would likely kill her. Or, perhaps she would kill one of them. Either way, it meant one less Fay in the world.

Henry looked into the pooka's inhuman eyes, and his stomach tightened. He'd raged against the injustice when the Fay forced him to use his control of the elements for their own ends. His life—his freedom—meant nothing to them. This wasn't the same, was it? She was one of the monsters. Yet that justification rang hollow.

"I'll make you a bargain, pooka."

"Henry, do not ensnare yourself," Domin said.

"You can warn me if I misstep." He straightened his shoulders. "Pooka, I will release you if you promise never to cause any harm to a human again, directly or indirectly."

The pooka's golden eyes narrowed. "I will not agree to such a bargain. That promise is eternal, while my slavery at your hands would end with your death."

Henry frowned. "Pooka, I will release you if you agree not to harm any human, directly or indirectly, for seventy times seven years."

"I will agree to seven times seven years, and nothing more."

Henry looked at Domin, who shrugged.

"Very well. I release you, on the condition that you do not harm any human, directly or indirectly, for seven times seven years."

She nodded. "I agree."

Henry felt a tug of regret as he ignited the hairs in his hand.

Domin stepped forward to face the pooka. Henry caught his breath. He had said she could not harm *humans*. Stupid. He had not thought his bargain through well enough. But the pooka didn't attack, only watched Domin warily.

"You are not part of the Unseelie Court, pooka," the shape-shifter said. "Will you tell us what the Dark Lady seeks in Drixton?"

"That is a Faerie matter. It does not concern outcasts." She resumed her equine form, baring her teeth and snorting before fleeing into the woods.

"Was that a mistake? Should I have used her?" Henry asked.

"You already know the answer to that."

Henry ran his hand through his hair. "I saw a banshee."

"What?"

"She was washing clothes in a pond. I didn't see whose they were."

Domin frowned. "Even if they were yours, the final design of destiny can be altered by changing the smaller patterns. Take it as a warning, though. More than ever, you cannot afford to be reckless. There is always Telesm's—"

"No. I won't abandon all of them."

In the distance, beyond the woods, the dim lights from the villagers' windows pierced the fog. Each one that winked out pricked Henry's heart with lonely dread. He hoped everyone had the sense to stay inside.

Familiar energy moved through the air, and he tilted his head back. A storm brooded over the village, growing powerful and hungry as the clouds fed on the magic in the night sky. It was so swollen with energy that Henry had only to give it a light push to puncture it. He smiled as the first drops of rain spattered his face.

"That will help keep people in their houses."

Domin nodded, but Henry's satisfaction eroded as the mist

and rain drifted around them. Even with his friend's help, there was nothing he could do about the powerful magic blanketing the village. He was trapped between two warring forces, and he didn't even know what they were fighting over.

Chapter Thirteen

Somewhere distant, as through fog, a bell sounded, and Cassandra blinked and rubbed her eyes.

She was sitting at her dressing table holding the bell cord. The roses she'd worn at the ball littered the table, dripping wilted petals over her fan and dance card. She recalled taking the flowers off as she got ready for bed, but her memories since then were vague, churning shadows. Patches of morning light filtered through the lace curtains onto her gray-striped gown. When had she woken and dressed?

Beth didn't respond to another pull on the cord, so Cassandra ventured downstairs. An unnatural stillness hung over the house.

Sophie lounged in the drawing room, watching the hands on the clock with a slack expression. Strands of blond hair had fallen loose from her braid, and she had dribbled tea on the blue cotton wrapper she wore over her nightgown.

"Sophie?"

Her sister blinked but didn't look away from the clock. Cassandra hurried to her side.

"Are you ill?" She touched Sophie's forehead, but it was cool.

"I'm fine." Sophie smiled, but it didn't change the vague look in her eyes. "I'm sure we'll have callers along any moment. Mr. Fitzhugh said he would see me again soon."

Cassandra drew back. "Sophie, it's much too early for callers." Not to mention that Sophie would never meet Mr. Fitzhugh in her nightgown and wrapper. "I think you're unwell."

"I'm fine," Sophie repeated.

"You're not fine!"

Sophie just smiled vaguely. Cassandra backed away. Where was everyone else? She limped down the corridor to the dining room. Beth sat at the table, dragging her fingers through a clinking pile of silver utensils.

"Beth?" Cassandra whispered.

"Yes, miss?" The maid's voice was hollow, and she didn't turn her empty stare from the silverware.

Cassandra shook her head and hurried upstairs to her parents' room. She burst through the door without knocking. Her mother lay on her side, her expression blank and her reddish-brown curls in tangles.

"Mother?"

No response. Cassandra smoothed back her mother's hair.

"Cassandra." Her mother's voice was barely more than a whisper.

Cassandra sagged against the edge of the bed. "Yes, Mother. I'm here. But I think Sophie and Beth are ill."

"Sophie?" her mother muttered. "It may be better if Cassandra doesn't go to the ball."

Cassandra flinched, but her mother closed her eyes again. Cassandra felt her forehead. It was cool, but something was wrong with her, just like Sophie and Beth. Her father chose the worst times to be gone on business. No, he was always gone, so when the worst times came, the women were alone. Like when the fever had struck.

The fever. It had left Cassandra crippled and Georgina deaf. What damage would this illness do to an unborn child? Cassandra put a hand on her mother's belly and held her breath. The baby moved under her fingers. Cassandra sighed in relief. She wished she could grasp the baby's tiny hand, keep it safe.

"I'll watch over you," she whispered.

The baby stirred again, as if responding to her voice.

Cassandra hurried down the corridor to the nursery. Her younger sisters sat entranced at Nancy's feet as the white-haired nurse read them a story in a droning tone. Only Georgina stood, paintbrush slashing the wall with dark colors to create a mural of swirling shapes that reminded Cassandra of her nightmares.

"Nancy?" Cassandra asked. She put a hand on her sister's shoulder. "Georgie?"

Georgina didn't turn, and Nancy continued her story without pause. Cassandra leaned against the wall and rubbed her forehead.

A thin, white trail of fine powder sparkled along the windowsill. Cassandra rubbed the gritty stuff between her fingers and sniffed it. It looked like salt. Why was there a line of salt in front of the window? There was no one left to ask.

Cassandra finger's shook. She dug them into the folds of her skirt. Her family had moved to the country to be safe from the city's plagues, and now she—the invalid, the cripple—was the only one still well. She had to find help before she succumbed to this mysterious sickness too.

She limped downstairs to the front door, but before she could slide the bolt, someone outside gave a sharp rap. Cassandra hesitated a moment, then opened the door. Amy St. Clair stood on the porch, purple visiting dress and blond curls neat and dry despite the drizzle of rain behind her.

"Lady St. Clair!"

"Miss Weaver. Are you well?"

"Yes. Well, no. That is, my family's ill. I was just going to go ..." Cassandra's mind didn't provide her with a destination.

"To the apothecary's?" Amy supplied. "Church services seem to have been canceled, so I would guess he's at his shop."

Cassandra swallowed. "Services? Isn't it Saturday?"

Amy shook her head, and Cassandra tightened her grip on the door. How could she have missed an entire day?

"Would you like me to accompany you?" Amy asked. "You don't seem quite the thing this morning."

Amy had behaved rather oddly at the ball, and Cassandra didn't trust her. But Amy was a guest of the Ashby's and a friend of Henry's, and Cassandra didn't trust herself at the moment, either. What if she ended up ill, wandering the streets aimlessly? "Yes, I think that would be best."

"Shall I wait while you get ready?"

Cassandra straightened her dress and grabbed a bonnet— even in an emergency, she must remember The Rules. She considered her cane for a moment, but she could do without it. "I'm ready now. It's rather urgent."

Amy shrugged. She opened a silk umbrella that matched her dress down to its purple fringe, then stood close enough to shelter them both from the cold drizzle. Clouds blanketed

Drixton like smoke, wisps drifting down to mingle with the fog. The thick, dank air tickled Cassandra's throat.

As they walked past the woods, Cassandra's scalp prickled as though someone was watching them. She scanned the trees, but no one was there.

She and Amy picked their way along the winding, muddy road to the village. There, only the occasional creak of a shop sign broke the rain's rhythmic patter. Ghostly figures moved behind spattered panes. The few people who shuffled past them on the lane wore the same vacant expression as Cassandra's family.

Cassandra glanced at Amy, but her companion appeared unconcerned about the villagers' strange behavior. Amy didn't have the same lost look as the others, but her disinterest wasn't normal either.

By the time they reached the apothecary shop, Cassandra had worried herself into a headache. She pushed open the heavy door, wrinkling her nose at the overpowering scent of medicine and herbs. The shop was empty.

"Hello?" Her voice sounded too loud in the quiet. She fought down her hysteria, aware of Amy, silent, behind her.

"Miss Weaver?" Henry appeared in the doorway of the upstairs living quarters, Domin behind him.

Henry looked alert. Confused, but alert. Normal. At last! Cassandra took a breath. "Mr. Stewart."

"Are you well?" He hurried down the stairs. "What are you doing out in this weather?"

"Please. Can you tell me what's wrong with everyone?"

Henry ran his fingers through his hair, not meeting her eyes. "What do you mean?"

She glanced at Amy. The blonde woman quickly turned her attention to her closed umbrella dripping rainwater onto the wood floor. There *was* something going on, and both of them knew it. And to think Cassandra had started to believe that Henry wasn't a self-absorbed scoundrel after all. For all she knew, he had something to do with whatever had happened to the village. Hadn't Beth said that Domin was some sort of magician? Cassandra gestured toward the village outside the window.

"What have you done to them?"

Henry's eyes darkened. "*I* haven't done anything but try to protect them. There are dangerous forces at work here, and you would be safer waiting at home." He gave Amy an annoyed glance, and she looked contrite.

"Dangerous forces? What's that supposed to mean?" Cassandra remembered Jairus's guns and his talk of dangerous times.

Before Henry could reply, the front door creaked open, and a slight figure stepped inside. Mary Leland looked more pale than usual. She paused and blinked at the group gathered there, her gray eyes swollen and red-rimmed.

"Miss Leland, what's happened?" Cassandra said.

"It's my father, miss...I think he's ill."

"Everyone's ill," Henry said curtly. "It should pass soon."

Mary risked a quick glance up. "There's something different wrong with him."

Henry rolled his eyes.

Cassandra glared at Henry and took Mary's arm. "I don't know why everyone's acting strangely, but I'll come with you and do what I can to help."

"As will I," Amy whispered.

"There's nothing either of you can do," Henry said.

Cassandra whirled on him. "Well, at least I'm willing to try. I may not understand what's going on, but I'm not going to hide in here like a coward. Come, Miss Leland. We'll find someone else to help us."

Henry narrowed his eyes and hurried forward to block her path. "What kind of help do you think you'll find out there?"

Cassandra raised her chin. "I'll fetch Mr. Hale."

Henry scowled. "How do you know you can trust him?"

"Well, he saved my life." And he seemed to know how to deal with strange occurrences.

"I believe he's trustworthy, Henry," Domin said quietly.

"Very well," Henry said. "We're coming, too. I'm probably going to regret this."

"I don't believe I asked for your company," Cassandra said. Henry opened his mouth to protest, so she added, "But Miss Leland wanted your help for her father, so you may join us."

Henry scowled and grabbed a leather satchel and his bowler from the counter.

Cassandra looped her arm through Mary's, her grip tight as they passed through the drizzle falling over the silent village. Amy trailed behind them, purple umbrella dripping with rain, while Henry and Domin followed at the back, arguing in whispers. Mary stopped in front of a shop window crammed full of clocks and toys. She led the way inside to a room overflowing with mechanical devices on shelves and worktables, the air rich with the warm scents of pine shavings and oil.

Cassandra maneuvered her skirts between benches displaying music boxes and toy carousels. "Your father makes these things?"

"Yes, miss." Mary stared at the floor.

"These are extraordinary," Cassandra said, "but I'm surprised there's enough business in Drixton to support him."

"People come from all over the world to buy his clocks and automata. He could move to London and make his fortune, but"—Mary's voice caught—"he thinks it's healthier for me here."

"Probably correct," Domin said, examining some windup soldiers with a frown. "Do you assist in making these?"

"Yes," Mary said, fidgeting. "Please, my father is this way."

She gestured to a dim corridor leading from the workshop. Amy hung back in the shop to admire an intricate clock with wolves carved on the case. Cassandra followed Mary into the corridor connecting two cramped bedrooms and a small kitchen. Mary pointed to one of the bedrooms, and Cassandra stepped aside so Henry and Domin could squeeze in.

The thin, graying man who had escorted Mary from the church now thrashed and muttered on a narrow bed that took up most of the room. Henry held the man still long enough to feel his forehead and examine his eyes.

"I don't think he's ill," Henry said.

Domin nodded. "He's fighting it."

"Fighting what?" Cassandra asked, unable to keep the frustration from her voice.

Henry nodded at Mary. "Ask her. For all we know, she has something to do with it."

"I don't know anything," Mary said in a trembling voice. "I never mean to—"

Mary caught herself, but Cassandra prodded.

"Mean to do what, Miss Leland? What could you do to make people sick?"

"Nothing. I didn't do anything, I promise, miss. But sometimes things happen. I don't want them to, but I know it's my fault."

"This is ridiculous." Cassandra glared at Henry. "It almost sounds like you think she's a witch, and you've got her believing it herself."

At the word "witch," Mary moaned and sagged against the door frame. The clocks in the shop chimed in a cacophonous racket. Cassandra remembered the organ at church, and goose bumps ran up her arms. She shook her head. Drixton was strange, but the frail girl standing in front of her couldn't be responsible for all the odd things happening there. She grasped Mary's arm.

"You're not a witch. I know we're out in the country, but this is the nineteenth century. You can't possibly believe in such silly things." Cassandra turned to Henry. "You people are impossible. I'm going to find Mr. Hale now. At least Americans aren't so superstitious."

Henry laughed. "Americans who carry guns loaded with silver bullets?"

Cassandra paused.

"You're not surprised." Henry raised an eyebrow. "So you knew? Maybe you shouldn't be so quick to rule out superstition."

"Regardless of Mr. Hale's bullets, I refuse to believe this girl is a witch."

"Of course she's not," Domin said, "and she's not to blame for what's happening here, Henry. You may wish to find out what Amy knows, though."

"Is someone going to invite me back, then?" called Amy.

"Absolutely not." Henry moved into the corridor so he could see Amy in the shop. Cassandra wondered why she needed an invitation. That sounded like something out of one of Nancy's fairy stories.

"Do you know who's doing this?" Henry asked.

"No," Amy said. She glanced at the window, and her eyes widened. "But I suspect Fitzhugh does."

They all turned their attention to the street, where Fitzhugh sauntered toward the shop.

Henry bolted for the entrance, narrowly avoiding several of the tables. Domin followed on his heels. Cassandra limped forward cautiously with Mary shadowing her.

Henry stopped in the doorway, blocking it. Fitzhugh grinned and leaned against the frame.

"Fitzhugh," Henry said. "What are you playing at?"

"If I told you, it would stop being fun."

"This isn't a game," Henry said.

The wind lashed rain at Fitzhugh, sending drops spinning off his black hat. His grin widened. "You're young. You have so much to learn. Ask Domin. It's always a game. It's the only thing that makes all this time bearable. Want to make a wager on who wins this round? No? What about you, Domin? Or Amy, my dear? You must be bored or you wouldn't be here. Where's our American friend? I bet he'd be willing to play."

"What are you doing here?" Henry asked.

"Oh, I'm here to make sure Miss Weaver stays safe."

The mocking way Fitzhugh looked at her made Cassandra feel anything but safe.

"Miss Weaver?" Henry glanced at her. "You're here for her?"

"I am. Oh, and for the angry mob."

"Angry mob?"

"You're doing it wrong, Henry." Fitzhugh gave an exaggerated sigh. "You're supposed to say, 'What angry mob?' and then I say"—he stepped aside—"this angry mob."

Through the doorway, Cassandra saw a crowd of blank-eyed villagers huddled together in the square. The driving wind tugged at their coats and ripped away their hats.

"Fitzhugh, what are you thinking?" Amy cried. "Those are innocent people!"

"Are they? But I can't make them do anything they don't want to. That's the interesting thing. I thought Domin would be a convenient target. All in good sport, of course. They do hate anyone who's different." Fitzhugh smiled. "But your conversation gave me an idea. Do they think the little changeling is a witch? We haven't seen a good old-fashioned witch hunt for ages. It would be refreshing to be on the other side of one for a change. I'm not sure Henry would even try to stop me. I don't know whom to choose." He looked at Cassandra. "What do you say, Miss Weaver? Miss Leland or Domin?"

"What's the matter with you?" Cassandra pulled Mary behind her. "Leave her alone."

"Very well, my pet. You've made your choice. Domin it is."

Cassandra flushed. "I didn't mean—"

Fitzhugh raised a hand. "A deal is a deal. Don't worry. Domin's gotten out of tighter spots than this one. I'd recommend standing back, though."

Chapter Fourteen

Cassandra clutched Mary's arm and stared at Domin. He curled his lips back in a snarl.

Fitzhugh lifted his cane and drew the sword hidden in its sheath.

Then he froze. The smile melted off his face. He let the cane and sword clatter to the ground and raised his arms.

"That's right, Mr. Fitzhugh. That's a gun full of iron shot pointed right at your heart." Jairus's voice drawled over the wind. The American was dressed as Cassandra had first seen him: long coat, wide-brimmed hat, and an ammunition bag and leather baldric slung across his chest, with a shotgun sheath at his hip. "Now, release whatever hold you've got on those folks out there, and we'll discuss the terms of your surrender."

Henry motioned Cassandra and Mary back as he drew a revolver from under his coat. Cassandra pulled Mary behind a table of toy trains.

Fitzhugh smirked. "Even if I wanted to, Priest, I couldn't. I can manipulate them, but I'm not the one who has the hold over them."

"I don't believe you."

"He's telling the truth," Henry said. "He can't lie."

Cassandra looked between Henry and Fitzhugh. Not being able to lie was another common theme in fairy tales.

"If you shoot me, Mr. Hale, you may also hit Henry and Domin, perhaps even Amy," Fitzhugh said.

"What makes you think that would bother me in the slightest? They're all tainted, just like you. You're just the one who reeks of it the most."

The crowd of villagers lurched toward the shop with an awkward, single-minded motion.

"Watch behind you, Mr. Hale!" Henry shouted.

Jairus glanced over his shoulder at the mob, keeping his gun leveled at Fitzhugh. Fitzhugh smacked the gun aside, and the American pulled the trigger. The blast pelted the eaves of the shop. Fitzhugh jerked back, his shoulder bleeding from the stray shot.

Jairus shoved Fitzhugh away from the door and rushed inside, bolting it behind him. He looked around at the clocks and toys.

"This looks like a terrible place for a fight. Is there a way out the back?"

Amy stared at him. "You just said you wanted to shoot us."

"Nope." He grinned. "I just asked him why he thought I wouldn't."

Amy frowned, but Domin motioned to the back. "There is another door through there. Miss Leland, please invite Amy to come with you."

"Of course she can." Mary's voice trembled. "But please, my father, his shop ..."

"Your father's not in any immediate danger," Henry said. "Domin and I will go out the front, and they'll leave this place alone."

Cassandra looked out the front window where Fitzhugh clutched his injured shoulder and gestured orders at the approaching mob. For now, better to escape. They could worry about what was happening once they were safe. She tugged Mary along, and Amy followed. Jairus raced down the corridor with the women, shotgun in hand. They passed through the little kitchen into the alley behind the shop.

Thunder crashed overhead, and wind roared through the warren of tiny gardens and alleys, ripping Amy's umbrella away. Cassandra's boots slipped in the rain-soaked muck deposited from butchers and grocers, and she tried not to think about what sort of filth was staining the bottom of her skirts. Amy covered her nose, gagging at the stench. Mary stumbled, and it was all Cassandra could do to keep herself and the frail girl upright. Amy grabbed Mary's arm and hoisted her from the other side. Following Jairus's lead, they emerged on the main road, the mud slurping at their boots.

They stumbled along, past the last of the village shops, to the open countryside, rain pelting their faces. Jairus stopped where the road split. He nodded and gestured as if he were having an animated conversation with himself. Finally, he turned to the women and motioned toward the hedgerow.

"Go through there. Stay low." The trees and bushes had grown together over the years to form a dense wall separating the road from the fields, but there was a gap where a tree had fallen.

Cassandra hesitated, but the hedgerow was probably safer than being out in the open, and Jairus seemed competent, if a bit eccentric. She pushed her way in, the branches tearing at her clothes and face. Mary and Amy scrambled through behind her. When they reached the other side, the three women huddled together, crouching against the trees and shivering as water dripped onto their faces and down the necks of their dresses.

Through a gap in the branches, Cassandra watched Jairus pace, obscuring their footprints. The pounding of hoof beats broke through the moan of the wind. The American stepped to the middle of the lane and raised his shotgun.

"Go back, or I'll shoot." His voice carried over the storm.

"You can't cover for her forever, Priest." Fitzhugh reigned in his stallion. "You're meddling in things that are none of your affair."

"I'll decide what's my affair," Jairus said.

"You don't know the game. You're going to get people killed. Where is Miss Weaver?"

Cassandra froze, not even daring to breathe. Jairus shot a quick glance, not at their hiding place, but up the winding road leading away from the village. Fitzhugh shouted in triumph and spurred his horse forward. The bay stallion bared teeth that looked surprisingly canine, and Jairus leapt out of the way as Fitzhugh sped past.

A gray wolf tore by in the horse's wake. Henry followed, shouting for Jairus to stop Fitzhugh.

"Don't worry!" the American chuckled. "He's been misled." He gestured for the women, and Cassandra helped Mary to her feet, glad to move her cold hands.

Henry gave a start when they emerged from the hedgerow. "That was a risky gamble."

Jairus held up his revolver. "Not as risky as trying to hold him off with an empty gun."

Henry stared at him. "I'm beginning to wonder if you're insane."

"Just now?" Jairus chuckled. "I'm glad to see you haven't lost my other gun, though."

Before Henry could reply, Domin appeared, walking down the road Fitzhugh had taken moments before.

Cassandra glanced up the lane. How had Domin gotten ahead of them? Only Fitzhugh and the wolf had run that way. The wolf. She shivered at a chill that ran deeper than the cold from the rain.

"Well?" Henry asked.

"Fitzhugh is keeping watch down the road," Domin said. "I think he believes the women have gone back to Miss Weaver's home."

Cassandra brushed the dirt and wet leaves from her dress and helped Mary do the same. At least the storm had subsided again to a gentle drizzle. Amy smoothed out her dress and hair. Her appearance gave no hint that she had been scrambling among the bushes, except for a smudge of mud across her nose that was obnoxiously charming.

Cassandra pulled a broken twig out of her hair. What a fright she must look. Sophie and her mother would be horrified.

"Oh, no!" She covered her mouth.

"What's the matter?" Amy took Cassandra's arm.

"I have to get home. Sophie's expecting Mr. Fitzhugh, and she's not thinking clearly. I shouldn't have left her alone. And my mother and sisters, they're not well."

Cassandra turned to follow Fitzhugh up the road, but Jairus held out a hand.

"Miss Weaver, I agree we should make sure your family's

safe, but going off half-cocked will only put you in danger too. You need to know what you're up against."

He motioned her under the shelter of a tree overhanging the lane. The others shuffled to join them.

"Do *you* know what's going on, Mr. Hale?" Cassandra asked.

"Not exactly. I'm still trying to put the pieces together myself."

Cassandra and Jairus turned to Henry expectantly.

He sighed. "The people in the village are under an enchantment."

Cassandra found the idea far-fetched, but not unbelievable. "Mr. Fitzhugh must be some kind of hypnotist." She cast a wary glance at Domin. "Or a magician."

"A bokor," Jairus suggested. "This reminds me of voodoo."

"No, he's an elf," Henry said. "One of the Fay."

Cassandra stared. "Aren't they supposed to be very small?"

Amy laughed. Mary looked between the others, her face pinched with worry. Cassandra couldn't blame her. They sounded like a pack of lunatics.

Henry shook his head. "He's an elf, not a pixie. There are a number of races among the Fay. They're all residents of Faerie —the Otherworld that exists woven around the human realm— but some, like elves, can seem almost human."

Cassandra pursed her lips. In Nancy's tales, elves and their kin were always abducting children, punishing trespassers, and robbing travelers. Those were just stories. But she had no other explanation for what she had seen. "If Mr. Fitzhugh is using magic, why doesn't it work on us?"

"Some of us are protected by our own magic," Amy said, "and Mr. Hale is a priest."

Jairus cocked his head. "Why do y'all keep calling me that?"

"Isn't that what you are?" Amy asked.

He looked thoughtful. "Not the sort who does much preaching, but God and I do have a sort of working arrangement. He points me to the monsters, and I deal with them."

Henry raised his eyebrows. "God talks to you?"

"Yep."

"As in, you hear voices?"

"Something like that."

"And you do as they say?"

"It seems foolish not to."

"Oh, good. You *are* insane." Henry snatched his hat off and ran his fingers through his hair. Cassandra thought Henry might be right. She put up her petitions to God, but she'd never really expected to hear an answer.

"Could be," Jairus said, "but it hasn't steered me wrong yet." He glanced at Amy. "How can you tell about that, though?"

"Your devotion to your faith makes you slippery. It's hard for our magic to touch you." Amy shrugged. "And, Miss Weaver, you managed to avoid Fitzhugh's influence and my own little test at the ball—"

"Test?" said Henry. "What did you do to her?"

"I just asked her some questions, nothing that would hurt her."

"It felt so confusing ..." Cassandra's eyes widened. "You're saying you're an elf too?"

"I am." Amy gave Henry a defiant look. "I only wanted to see why Fitzhugh couldn't affect her"—She turned back to Cassandra—"and based on how well you evaded my influence, I suspect you're Sabbath born."

"What's that?" Cassandra asked, giving in to the madness of

the conversation.

"Faerie magic is affected by belief and symbolism," Henry said, "so people born on holy days are harder to charm."

"Being born on a Sunday gives a person some resistance against magic," Domin said, "perhaps like Miss Leland's father" —Mary backed away when he motioned to her—"but you must have been born on an especially potent day, such as Easter or All Hallows' Eve."

"Yes," Cassandra said, her throat tight. "Hallowe'en. I always thought it was an unlucky day." Unlucky left-handed. Unlucky birthday. It had hung over her all her life.

"Not for you." Amy's smile dimpled her cheeks.

"But I missed an entire day yesterday. I can't remember anything between getting home from the ball and pulling the bell cord this morning."

"No human is completely immune to Faerie magic," Amy said, "but you're able to break through it. The bell probably helped, especially against Unseelie magic."

Henry mumbled something about roses, but Cassandra didn't catch it.

"What's Unseelie?" Jairus asked. "This Faerie business is new to me."

"Well..." Amy wrinkled her forehead. "It's...not Seelie."

"Unblessed. Unholy. Dark," Domin said. "Not that the Seelie Fay are particularly benevolent."

"The Seelie draw their power from the cycles of the natural world," Henry said. "The Unseelie thrive on human suffering."

A howl sounded in the distance, answered by others that encircled them in a ring of hollow cries. Mary clutched Cassandra's arm. Black dogs with glowing red eyes were in Nancy's stories too: harbingers of death. Icy tingles slipped down her spine. The existence of Fay might explain all the strange things she'd seen in the village.

"Sounds like a fight's headed our way." Jairus grinned and flipped his shotgun around to load it.

"We cannot stay here in the open," Domin said. "There's a place nearby where we can take refuge while we devise a plan." He gave Henry a questioning look, and Henry returned an exasperated shrug.

"I can't leave my family in danger," Cassandra insisted.

Domin fixed his green eyes on her. She resisted the urge to look away, but her heartbeat echoed in her ears as she thought of the wolf.

"Your family is safer than you are," Domin said. "The Fay cannot enter a dwelling without an invitation from a member of the family who lives there. The invitation has to be given willingly and not as the result of an enchantment."

Cassandra didn't like the idea of trusting her family's safety to superstition, but another howl, closer than the others, made up her mind.

"I'll go, for now." She glanced at Mary and Amy. "You're coming, too, aren't you?"

Mary hesitated, looking back to the village.

"Of course," Amy said. "It wouldn't be at all the thing for these gentlemen to leave us to deal with the hell hounds and Fitzhugh on our own."

"But whose side are you on this time, Amy?" Domin asked.

"I can hardly answer that honestly when I'm not yet certain what the sides are." Amy lifted her chin to meet Domin's gaze. "But I have no desire to harm anyone, and I would like to counter whatever trouble Fitzhugh is causing. That's why I followed him to Drixton."

"Very well." Domin turned away and set off at a jog toward the woods, not glancing back.

Henry followed, motioning for the others. Howls sounded behind them, and Jairus dropped to the rear, shotgun held ready as they stumbled through the tangled old trees. Twinges of pain raced up Cassandra's right leg, but she bit the inside of her cheek and tried to ignore them.

The path turned to follow the dark waters of a stream. Its burble mocked Cassandra.

Come to me. Come to me. Come to me.

She shivered. Was this the same water that ran along her property? The same stream where she'd met Henry and Domin? She might be following them to something worse than what waited in Drixton.

They reached the dark opening of a cavern. The stream flowed swift and cold from the blackness, the path just a narrow strip of damp earth beside it.

"Wait!" Jairus called. He jogged forward and peered into the cavern. "Where are you taking us?"

Domin turned back, his face lost in shadow. "You are standing on the edge of Elfland—the Faerie realm. This is one of the places where the edges of the worlds touch, and humans and Fay can cross through. There's a refuge through here—a place where none of the Faerie Queens can reach us."

Cassandra glanced at Henry. He looked unhappy, but not afraid. Amy motioned them forward and walked ahead into the darkness. Mary clung to Cassandra's arm.

Jairus looked heavenward. "I hope you know what you're doing."

He gestured for Cassandra and Mary to go first. Cassandra looked at the uneven ground then back at the village. If there was any truth to the stories of Faerie and magic, she was going to find out. She scooted forward, her leg muscles tight and uncooperative as she tried to find sure footing. For a few moments that seemed to stretch forever in the darkness, there was nothing but the musty taste of cavern air and the sound of rushing water.

She flailed forward, and a strong hand caught hers in the darkness. She could make out Henry's form in front of her, a darker shadow against the deep, endless gray. She wished she didn't *have* to have his help—that she could choose to take his hand instead of being forced to by her own body's weakness—but she was glad for his sure-footed guidance.

Her eyes adjusted enough to see the dim light ahead, growing brighter as she pressed forward. The path angled upwards, and she stumbled as she fought the aching weariness in her leg. Mary hung tightly to her, nearly pulling her off balance and into the dark waters racing beside them in a foamy, white waterfall, but Henry kept her on her feet.

At the end of the cavern, the rock gave way to rough tree bark. Cassandra stepped blinking into the light to find herself under an arch of intertwined hawthorn trees, their branches bright with white blossoms as if it were spring and not autumn. A wide, shallow river flowed in front of the cavern entrance. A branch of it broke away to crash under the hawthorn arch, forming the stream. Domin and Amy waited on the other side.

Henry led the way down, and Cassandra waded after him into the river. It tugged at her skirts and petticoats, and her weak foot dragged through the silt, but the riverbed was relatively smooth and firm, and Mary had let go of her once they reached the sunlight. Cassandra waded up the other side of the riverbank. Into the Otherworld. Elfland.

Jairus half-ran, half-jumped his way across the water, then Domin led them away from the river. The trees thinned to a clearing with a little stone cottage. A chimney rose from the home's thatched roof, and thick rose bushes clambered up the walls, wrapping it in an embrace of white and red blooms. It was exactly the sort of fairytale cottage Cassandra had half expected to find in the woods behind her house. Shafts of sunshine broke through the canopy and insects flew in lazy circles in the light. The peace of it wrapped around Cassandra like a shawl and warmed her chilled skin.

"It looks like a storybook," Mary whispered, "like it's not real."

Cassandra caught herself. Mary was right. Most beautiful places weren't so perfect when you got to see them up close— dirty, or musty, or falling to ruin—but this clearing looked like someone had captured a perfect image and fastened it in place. Only four lion statues, twice her height and set in pairs to guard the approach to the cottage, marred the serenity of the scene. She imagined their stony gazes following her as she passed beneath the pedestals where they lounged.

"It is safe," Domin said, "but try not to disturb anything."

"What is this place?" Jairus asked as they reached the cottage door.

"A refuge under the protection of an elf named Telesm. He's not here, but he would not mind us taking shelter. You are all welcome, for now."

Domin stepped into the cottage. Henry hesitated before crossing the threshold, and Cassandra limped in after him.

The cottage looked impossibly large on the inside. A staircase ran around the outside of the room to a loft full of books above, and windows brought a flood of sunlight into the open main floor. The huge room overflowed with a jumbled collection of swords, pieces of armor, mirrors, boots, jewelry, and other odds and ends, as though some explorer had abandoned his findings on the table and chairs. A life-size statue of a beautiful girl dressed in armor stood alone by the door, her expression a haunting mixture of determination and despair.

Jairus came in last, squinting in the dimmer light. When he saw the statue he made a strangled noise and backed away. "Good heavens! She's alive. What sort of wicked place have you brought us to?"

Chapter Fifteen

Henry's scalp prickled at the gray tears frozen on the girl's stone face. A living statue? That was a magic he didn't know.

Cassandra backed into him, staring at the statue. He reached out to steady her, but she tensed at his touch. He lowered his hand. She distrusted him now; she would hate him when she knew what he was. What he'd done.

Amy reached out to the statue, her expression a mix of wonder and pity, but Domin caught her arm.

"Don't touch anything." He turned to Jairus. "And be careful how you judge what you see, Mr. Hale. This cottage is a sanctuary guarded by powerful magic. The Faerie Queens' power cannot enter it, nor can any violence be done here."

Amy studied a thin, double-edged dagger unsheathed on the table. "Can the elf who created this place—Telesm, you said?—help us against the Fay, then?"

Domin looked uneasy. "He does not like to be drawn into the affairs of the Fay, and his temper is... unpredictable. We are only safe here if we remain neutral."

"But what about my family and everyone else?" Cassandra asked. "What's to keep them safe from those monsters?"

"Uh, Miss Weaver." Jairus cleared his throat. "I'd be careful about how you use the word 'monster,' seeing how we're keeping company with folks who aren't exactly human."

"Oh." Cassandra glanced at Domin and Amy. Then she met Henry's gaze and raised her eyebrows.

He took a deep breath. He couldn't put it off forever.

"I was human once." He looked down. "I'm a changeling."

"A changeling?" Cassandra asked, her expression more confused than surprised. "Isn't that a Faerie baby left in place of a human one?"

"That's a Faerie changeling," Henry said. "Human changelings are the children they steal. The Fay keep us as slaves, altering us with their magic. And some counterfeit takes our place in the human world."

His gaze went to Mary, almost against his will. Her eyes widened.

Henry looked away quickly. She hadn't known. Was ignorance bliss? It was dangerous, at least; he was sure of that.

"You don't mean that you and Miss Leland were... switched?" Cassandra whispered.

"No," Domin said. "Henry is not the Leland's child."

Henry paced, restraining the impulse to kick aside the rusted helmet and gauntlets in his path. "But she's here because some human child was ripped from her family."

"You're saying I'm—" Mary's voice cracked. "That I'm not —" She choked. "Is that what's wrong with me? I've never meant to hurt anyone."

She gasped out a sob, and a mechanical songbird on a perch trilled out a matching tone. Everyone glanced between Mary and the bird.

Domin silenced it with a touch and frowned at Henry. "The elf child is just as much a victim as the human one. Most Faerie changelings don't survive the switch. Her human parents must have realized what she was and loved her enough to keep her safe from iron and other Faerie poisons."

Henry looked away, his gaze catching on a framed mirror protected by a gossamer cloth. The hazy reflection turned his face into something sharp and pale. Cruel. Inhuman. He quickly turned his eyes elsewhere. He resented Mary—everything she stood for—but the situation wasn't her fault any more than it was his. She had been lucky to find a caring home. The Fay knew nothing of love.

Mary wiped her eyes, and Cassandra put a tentative arm around the girl's shoulders.

"Why do they do such things?" Cassandra asked. "And what do they want with Drixton?"

"The Courts are always hungry for power," Domin said, "trying to tilt the balance of the natural elements in their favor. I don't know why they have chosen your village for their latest battleground."

"What will they do to everyone?" Cassandra glanced at the door as if ready to bolt back to her family.

Henry hurried to reassure her. "If everyone stays inside, they should be safe. Fitzhugh said they were hunting for something, and once they find it, they'll leave."

"Hunting for some*thing*?" Amy asked. "More likely some*one*. The Dark Lady's sacrifice."

"The Dark Lady?" Jairus cocked an eyebrow. "Let me guess. She's not friendly?"

Henry gritted his teeth at the American's casual tone. "This is nothing to joke about, Mr. Hale. Every seven years, the Dark

Lady sacrifices a human to pay her tithes to Hell. And she doesn't just kill him—"

"Or her," Amy added quietly.

"She corrupts him—or her—first," Henry went on. "Her tithes are due on Michaelmas—in three days."

Jairus's jaw tightened. "I ain't taking this lightly. If she's hunting us, I say we bring the fight to her." He rested a hand on his revolver.

Henry rolled his eyes. "Just because you held off a couple of hell hounds doesn't mean you know how to defeat the Unseelie Queen."

"Henry! Don't draw her attention." Amy glanced out the window.

Henry went cold at his mistake. He was out of practice with the Faerie world. "At least I didn't say her full name."

"In that old story," Cassandra said quietly, "about the changeling Tam Lin, the Faerie Queen was going to sacrifice him. Is the Dark Lady after Mr. Stewart?"

Henry grimaced at being compared to that debauched Unseelie changeling. Apparently, the Weaver's nurse had been unusually thorough in her bedtime stories.

Domin's brow furrowed. "It is possible."

"I don't plan to let her corrupt me," Henry interjected, "and I'm hardly as depraved as Tam Lin."

"Of course not." Cassandra's face turned bright red.

"Besides," Henry said more quietly, "Fitzhugh has shown little interest in me, and he's part of the Unseelie Court."

"But he has shown an interest in the Weavers," Amy said.

Cassandra paled. "My sisters."

"He said he's protecting you, Miss Weaver," Henry said. He didn't add that the Unseelie elf could be protecting her now in order to sacrifice her later.

"Hmm." Jairus scratched his chin. "From those devil dogs, most likely. They only showed up when the Weaver sisters were around."

Cassandra looked like she was going to be sick. Henry wished he could say something to reassure her.

"But this is all so simple," Amy said with a smile of triumph. "If the Dark Lady is after Miss Weaver, or any of us, we just have to wait here until after Michaelmas and we'll be safe."

"And if she's not after one of us?" Henry asked. "Then we're trapped here while she can hurt whomever she wants out there."

Jairus flourished his pistol. "I ain't no fence sitter. Y'all said we were just coming here to regroup. God sent me to fight monsters, not to sip tea and sniff roses in a magic cottage."

Domin's eyes grew distant for a moment, then he focused again on the room. "The Faerie Queens are hunting for us. There are hell hounds nearby. If we choose to leave, there will be no other refuge. We might be throwing ourselves into their hands."

"If we're in here," Cassandra said, "then who is out there, protecting my sisters?"

The cottage grew silent. Henry opened himself to the energy permeating the clearing. A bitter sting shuddered through him like the icy touch of a winter wind. Domin was right; powerful magic was near. Hungry, hunting.

"No one," Henry said. "If not us, there is no one else, and we leave the villagers defenseless."

"I won't let that happen," Jairus said. "I can't."

Mary shivered, her gray eyes rimmed with red. Amy opened her mouth and shut it again, indecision furrowing her forehead.

"I have to go back," Cassandra said. "I can't leave my sisters alone if they might be in danger."

Henry nodded. "I'm fighting, too. I've been hiding long enough."

Domin gave him a warning look, which he ignored. He was probably being rash, but what of it? He had a multitude of past sins to atone for.

Amy raised her chin. "We have to stay together. If that means we fight, then we fight."

Chapter Sixteen

Henry took a deep breath, inhaling the rotten tang of the dangerous magic awaiting them: hell hounds, and something more.

"Very well." Domin rummaged through the piles heaped in the corners, setting some objects aside and placing others on the table. "I will need everything back when we're safe, but we need to borrow a few things."

"You told us not to touch anything," Jairus said.

"Yes, but now it might help us to get Telesm's attention. He'll forgive me, eventually. Here, Mr. Hale. I believe you will be able to use this." Domin slipped an iron sword from its sheath, its dull, leaf-shaped blade pitted with age but sharp and bright along the edges.

The American raised an eyebrow. "Well, I've used a saber, but I'm more comfortable with my gun. If there are hounds nearby, it won't be too hard to pick them off from here."

"You cannot commit violence within this sanctuary, and

even if you shoot from beyond the bounds, you'll run out of iron—or luck—eventually. Few Faerie creatures can stand against this sword, though."

Domin offered the blade, and Jairus wrapped his hand around the smooth, wooden hilt. His eyes widened. He hefted the sword and turned it over to admire it.

Cassandra backed up when Domin passed her a round metal shield. "I would be in the way in a fight. Can't you see, I'm..." Her face reddened. "I mean, can't we just hurry back through the cavern?"

"They'll be watching it." Domin stepped closer, offering the shield again. "But any creature that charges this shield will be fettered by fear and confusion. All you have to do is stand next to Mr. Hale. Keep the hell hounds back."

She hesitated before taking the shield. Henry felt the stir of magic when she ran her fingers over the geometric designs etched into the metal. The sword in Jairus's hand also pulsed with quickening power, like a heartbeat growing stronger. What kind of magic awakened to the touch of normal humans?

After frowning at the things scattered around him, Domin gave Amy a small harp and handed Mary a tiny vial filled with silvery liquid, like moonlight captured in glass.

"What am I to do with this?" Amy touched the harp's tarnished silver strings and the cracked, strained wood of its soundboard.

"Play it if they threaten to overwhelm us. Try something soothing. You know how to manipulate emotions well enough."

Henry raised his eyebrows at the bite in Domin's words, but Amy looked more thoughtful than offended.

"Why don't I just play it now, and we can all walk out?" She ran her finger over the strings. The bright notes raced up Henry's spine, jolting him to attention, and the others jerked like puppets connected to a single string.

"It's an enchanted harp, Amy," Domin said in exasperation. "It amplifies your inborn abilities enough to affect all of us, Fay or not. These things are here because they're dangerous. We're only using them to reach the entrance to the human world. They cannot go beyond the trees at the edge of the clearing without awakening their guardians."

Amy nodded and lowered the instrument. Henry looked away. Domin trusted her with a dangerous object, but not him? Henry knew he was rash sometimes, but was he that irresponsible?

"Miss Leland," Domin continued, "if anyone is seriously injured, put just one drop of that liquid on the wound. Do not waste it. Henry, you provide cover."

Henry nodded. Jairus offered him the reloaded shotgun, but Henry waved it away; the touch of iron on his skin would interfere with his magic.

"How're you going to provide cover without a weapon?" Jairus asked.

"Just worry about your part of the fight. I'll take care of mine." Henry wasn't armed with guns or magical swords, but at least this time he was in Elfland: familiar territory. Of course, that meant Miss Weaver would see how much he belonged to this world. How much he did not belong to hers. He rolled his shoulders, trying to shrug off the sting of the thought. It didn't matter. He couldn't pretend forever, anyway.

Jairus peered out the window. "I see a pack of hell hounds at the edge of the clearing near the river. I could get a couple of good shots in and clear the way."

"As long as you are beyond the lion statues when you pull the trigger," Domin said.

Jairus shoved the door open and sprinted past the stone lions, sword in one hand and shotgun in the other. Cassandra hefted the shield and gathered her skirts to limp quickly after him. Henry plunged through the doorway, past the lions' fierce gazes. He stopped beside Cassandra and Jairus.

Black fur and bright teeth hurled at them from the edges of the clearing. Jairus fired off two shots. The pack of hounds splintered, fanning out across the crescent-shaped clearing between the statues and the woods, blocking the way out. Henry tensed when one of the animals bounded toward them, but it balked at Cassandra's shield and circled back, head low.

Jairus holstered his empty gun and lifted the sword.

A snarl from behind pricked the hairs on Henry's neck. Domin dashed past in panther form to tear through the hounds' line. They yelped and slammed into each other, scattering. One broke for the trees, but the huge cat wrestled it to the ground.

They just had to clear a path. Henry drew on the natural energy in the air, separating it from the Faerie magic like a tailor pulling apart the strands of a thread. That was the trick in Elfland: he couldn't use their own magic against them, but he could use the elements, and here they were purer, stronger.

Something dark and leathery flashed at the edge of his vision. Wyverns. His breath caught. The small, dragonesque creatures folded their bat-like wings and plummeted into the clearing.

He lashed out with the energy coiled in his hands. A gust of wind slammed the wyverns through the trees at the edge of the clearing.

Cassandra stared at him in confusion. He didn't meet her gaze.

Jairus and Domin fought off the hell hounds, but the wyverns circled back. Henry gritted his teeth and pulled at the air currents. Clouds exploded into the sky like smoke from a cannon. The leaves on the ground tumbled into rustling circles that rose toward the gray churning overhead. Too much. He was out of practice, and he was letting his emotions take control.

"What the—" Jairus jerked his gaze from the wyverns to the funneling clouds.

Cassandra snapped the shield up against the flapping creatures. Too late. One of wyverns caught Jairus's arm with yellow talons, tearing a bleeding gash. Jairus swore and flailed, dropping the sword.

"This would be a nice time to do something useful, Mr. Stewart!" the American yelled, throwing himself behind the shield.

Henry grimaced and urged the wind on. It whirled through the clearing, scattering the wyverns. Sweat rolled down his temples. The elements here were wild, fighting him, hungry to tear through enemy and ally alike.

"Miss Leland! Mr. Hale is injured!" Henry called over his shoulder.

Mary hovered at the edge of his vision, trembling and clinging to the lion statue with one hand while clutching the shimmering vial with the other. Amy urged her on, but the girl shrank back, tears in her eyes. Henry shook his head in disgust. Amy raised the harp uncertainly, her gaze shifting to Domin.

The remaining hounds backed the shape-shifter against the edge of the clearing. The wyverns dived, burying the panther in a tide of beating, leathery wings.

Henry grasped the wild energy and drew it tighter until a thin funnel of wind and forest debris danced in front of him like a charmed cobra. Cassandra gaped at him, her hair whipping across her pale face. He pushed the whirlwind forward, snatching the wyverns from the air and battering their bodies against the ground.

The black dogs scattered. One of the beasts dashed toward Jairus. He snatched his sword and slammed it into the hound. The blade stuck deep in its ribs. Jairus wrestled with the hilt, trying to jerk the weapon free. The two remaining hounds dodged Cassandra to charge him. Domin caught the one closest to him, tumbling to the ground in a tangle of teeth and claws.

The last hound leapt for Jairus. The American abandoned the sword still stuck in the dead beast and lifted his injured arm to shield his face. The creature slammed him to the earth, jaws locking on his forearm. Jairus's scream carried over the noise of the wind.

Cassandra, too far away to protect Jairus, threw the shield at the creature, smacking it in the side. The hound yelped and circled away, and the shield rolled out of Jairus's reach.

Jairus clutched his arm to his chest and dragged himself toward the shield. The beast rose, drool dripping from its bared teeth. It crouched to spring.

Henry pushed the whirlwind after the hound, but he wouldn't reach the creature in time.

The sweet bell tones of a harp lullaby rang over the noise. The hound sagged to the ground. Jairus collapsed, rivulets of blood drenching his sleeve. Henry's head swam. The energy slipped from his hands, freeing the fierce wind to tear through the clearing and strip leaves and ropes of bark from the trees. The siren call of the enchanted harp invited him into the darkness swirling at the edge of his vision. Henry watched helplessly as Cassandra sank to the ground. Domin, still in panther form, shook his head and moved as if wading through deep water.

"It's enough, Amy," Henry whispered. "Stop."

But the music continued, and the blackness rose to devour him. Perhaps Amy had betrayed them after all.

Chapter Seventeen

Henry blinked and lifted his pounding head. A breeze stirred the mossy smell of the woods, and scalloped oak leaves danced overhead to the fading echoes of the harp. Purple silk rustled at the edge of Henry's vision. He rolled over. Amy stood next to him, a dagger clutched in her hand.

"Amy!" Henry scrambled to his feet, dark spots swimming before his eyes.

One of the hounds growled and staggered to its feet, ears flat. Amy raised the dagger. Before she could strike, Domin slashed his hooked claws into the hound. Henry yanked Amy back as Domin dragged the creature to the ground and silenced its desperate yelps.

Cassandra bolted upright, jerking the shield with her. Jairus dragged himself close enough to reach the hilt of his sword, yanking it from the withered hell hound corpse in a spray of black dust. The last hound lifted its head groggily. The American twisted and thrust the blade into the creature's chest, then collapsed with a groan.

Silence fell over the clearing.

Domin stretched into his human form, dark fur melting into a black suit in less than a heartbeat. Cassandra stared, eyes wide. Mary whimpered and covered her face, huddling against one of the lion's pedestals.

"What were you thinking, Amy?" Domin's gaze locked on the dagger. "You took that from the cottage!"

She glared back. "With everyone asleep, I could easily have killed the hounds. It was a good plan. If I hadn't awakened Henry—"

"Then one of the hounds might have woken first and killed you." Domin held out his hand, and Amy hesitated, staring at the slender, double-edged blade.

"Give it to me, Amy," Domin said with quiet urgency. "The longer you hold it, the more hungry it will become and the harder it will be to resist using it."

Amy slowly turned her gaze from the blade and set it in Domin's palm, then shuddered and wiped her hand on her skirt. Domin placed it at the feet of one of the lions.

"Why would anyone create such a thing?" Amy whispered, glancing at the dagger.

"Partly because he was foolish," Domin said, "but what it turned into was not what he intended. Telesm is a Faerie changeling; his magic is unpredictable."

"Mr. Stewart?" Cassandra's voice cut through Henry's curiosity.

As he turned, she tightened her grip on the shield. He took a deep breath. She seemed to be taking the Faerie world in stride, standing against the hounds with a magic shield, but fighting monsters was not the same as befriending one, as he had feared.

"Mr. Hale needs help," she said, not meeting his gaze.

Jairus lay on his back, staring at the sword still clutched in his good hand. Henry approached him cautiously.

White bone poked through the American's shattered forearm, and blood welled from the wound, staining his shirt. Henry remembered the banshee's bloody laundry, and his hands turned cold. Had the clothes been Jairus's?

"I think it's broken." A smile curved the corners of Jairus's pale lips.

"Setting this may be beyond my skills." Henry yanked off his cravat to tie it above the injury, stilling the exhausted tremble in his fingers long enough to pull the knot tight.

"Beyond anyone's. I know." Jairus clenched his jaw and looked away. "Do what you have to."

Henry nodding his understanding. Jairus knew he might lose the arm. Battlefield surgery was far outside Henry's experience, but he would have to try.

Domin frowned. "Where is Miss Leland?"

Mary inched forward, clutching the tiny vial with its shimmering liquid. She offered it to Domin, but he shook his head and pointed at Jairus. Henry scooted out of her way. The American eyed the liquid as she twisted the cork and let a drop fall into the wound. Silvery mist pooled around it.

The mist clung to his forearm and beaded into the wound like drops of quicksilver. Jairus inhaled sharply through clenched teeth and screamed. The liquid dissolved into a faint silver glow on his skin.

As the glow faded, Jairus drew long, shaky breaths.

"Well, now it's numb." He lifted the arm and frowned at the new, pink skin showing through his ragged sleeve. "Is that normal?"

"I believe the sensation will return soon," Domin said. "I've never seen it used successfully before."

"What!" Jairus lifted his head and paled. He fell back and closed his eyes. "What was that stuff?"

Domin studied him. "It's distilled from the horn of a unicorn."

"You killed a unicorn?" Amy's face crimsoned.

"The unicorn gave Telesm a shaving from its horn. I had little to do with it. The elixir can cure almost anything, short of death. Though it cannot turn stone to flesh." A hint of sadness slipped into Domin's voice as he stared toward the cottage with its living statue.

"Who was she?" Amy's question broke the silence.

"Someone we should have protected better."

Henry raised an eyebrow. We? He could press for the story later, but Domin wasn't likely to share it.

"You're a daemon!" Jairus exclaimed, pushing himself up to stare at Domin. "I was guessing djinn for a while, but daemon fits better."

"How can you call him a demon after he helped you?" said Henry.

Domin shook his head. "Not demon, Henry. Daemon, with an 'ae'. The meanings are significantly different." He looked back at Jairus. "You're surprisingly astute, Mr. Hale, though I'm only half daemon."

Henry stared at his friend. Daemon? That was either a Faerie creature he'd never heard of or one of the spirit beings outside the Faerie realm. Henry had always assumed Domin to be one of the ancient solitary Fay who sometimes took a benevolent interest in humans. Why would he hide what he was?

Jairus rose to his feet unsteadily. "It took me a while to put it together, but I've read about guardian spirits bound to serve certain bloodlines. You didn't seem like the type to have one, Mr. Stewart, but I can see I may have underestimated you."

"Bound to serve?" Henry stared at Domin. The shape-shifter refused to meet his eyes. "As in, you're under some kind of obligation—forced to act by a geas? Because of my bloodline?" Henry lowered his voice as the reality sunk in. "Fitzhugh was telling the truth. You've been deceiving me this whole time."

Cold swirled around Henry and seeped into his chest. His one friend wasn't a friend at all. Did Domin secretly search for a way out of his enforced companionship, as Henry had sought to be free of the Fay? Henry should have known better than to trust any supernatural creature. The cold tightened into a sharp, icy pain. He should have known better than to trust anyone.

"Whom do you really serve?" Henry asked, remembering the rest of Fitzhugh's warning.

Domin remained silent and still.

Jairus cleared his throat. Embarrassment warmed Henry's face. At least he might have found out in private instead of laying his humiliation out for everyone to see.

"Um." Amy's voice broke through the tension. "Where did the statues go?"

The four pedestals in front of the cottage were empty.

"Miss Weaver," Domin said urgently, "return the shield to the clearing."

Cassandra had backed away from the argument, taking the enchanted shield just a step beyond the rough gray trees marking the boundaries of Telesm's clearing—the boundaries the objects were never supposed to pass. She limped forward and set the shield down, her face bright red.

Wind rippled through the clearing, and Henry's hair stood on end. The air crackled with energy. Trees swayed in the breeze, but the whisper of leaves was drowned out by the roar of the stream behind them as it poured faster and deeper along its course, spilling up the banks. Jairus scrambled away, collecting his discarded gun and hat.

"Henry?" Amy asked.

"That's not me." The energy was unfamiliar, but it hummed with angry purpose.

"We have triggered Telesm's defenses." Domin raised his voice over the wind and water. "If there are any other Fay in the area, this will certainly attract their attention. Put down everything from the cottage so the guardians do not pursue us if we are able to escape."

Mary placed the vial next to the shield and scurried away from it. Jairus wiped the sword clean on a patch of grass before setting it with the other things. The crackling in the air dissipated, but the rushing of the river grew more fierce, like a floodgate had been opened. The water was forming itself into the shape of a huge, shimmering lion.

"Is there another way out?" Jairus asked, pulling Cassandra and Mary back with him.

Domin shook his head. "Not without crossing through a vast stretch of Elfland, past whichever Fay are headed this way. I think that would be more dangerous than fighting one lion, elemental or not. Henry?"

"Well, what do you expect me to do?"

"Anything would be good at this point." Amy pointed behind them, where the ground rose in the shape of a lion's head. The beast slowly pulled up from the earth that formed it.

Henry held his hands out and stepped toward the water. Currents of energy flowed through it, woven with magic. The watery lion snarled and leapt, engulfing him in a liquid embrace. He flailed back, struggling for air. The lion dragged him into the raging water, battering him against the rocky riverbed and knocking his breath away. Water poured down his throat. He didn't know which way was up in the churning dimness, and his lungs burned.

An iron grip locked onto his arm and jerked him upwards. The lion tugged him back into the suffocating cold, but the strong hands yanked him from the river's grasp and onto the bank. Someone slammed his back. He coughed up muddy water, choking and gasping for air.

Domin released his arm and studied him, black hair plastered against his head and green eyes bright with concern. Henry swept his own dripping hair from his face and nodded grudgingly. They scrambled farther from the watery beast pacing the river and roaring its frustration.

Jairus's revolver trailed the shimmering lion, but he spared a glance over his shoulder for the earth lion, which had almost fully emerged from the ground.

"Right!" Henry said. "I can't use the water. I'll need something else." He extended his hands to feed his pain, anger, and embarrassment into the wild energy in the air. His arms and chest ached with the cold, and his breath turned to mist.

Frost gathered at the edges of the river. The lion shook its head and lunged to escape the ice creeping up its limbs. Icicles formed in its tail and mane. Its movements slowed, and its features froze in an expression of frustration and rage.

The earth lion, only its rear legs still trapped in the soil, turned its head in their direction. It roared, and the ground trembled.

"Well, let's get out while we can," Henry gasped, teeth chattering.

Jairus raced across the frozen water and reached a hand out for the women, who slipped and scurried after him, holding their skirts. Mary's lips were blue, and Cassandra hunched her shoulders, not glancing at Henry as she hurried past.

"Go," Domin said to Henry. The shape-shifter paused to look up at the frozen lion. "Tell Telesm I'm sorry for the mess."

Henry edged across the ice and followed the others down the cavern trail, emerging into the old woods. The stream flowed along its course, its surface dappled by the light rain curtaining Drixton.

"Keep moving." Jairus motioned them onward, and the shivering ladies followed.

Henry reached for the strength to warm the air, but the energy in the human world felt like lead. With each step, the same loneliness he had known in Elfland yawned before him, a void separating him from the human world as well as the Faerie one.

Domin matched his dragging pace, but Henry refused to look at the shape-shifter.

"I suppose I'm not able to release you from your geas," Henry said in a low voice.

"You are not. I made a vow long ago to... to someone important to me that I would watch over her bloodline. Your bloodline."

His bloodline again. It was all the Fay—any of them—seemed to care about. As if he were nothing more than a vessel for a past and a heritage he felt entirely disconnected from. A tool and not a person. "And what Fitzhugh said about using me?"

"He was distorting the truth as always. To embrace my daemon nature—to overcome my Fay shortcomings—I must keep my oath to serve your lineage. Protecting you allows me to do that." He hesitated. "I could not keep the Fay from taking you when you were a child—the... arrangement binding you to them is beyond my powers to break—but once you escaped, I was able to fulfill my promise again."

Henry felt like he might be sick. "I never asked for this. Any of it."

"I know." Domin glanced at Amy's back and whispered. "Over the generations, I have learned the dangers of trusting too readily, but I am sorry I did not tell you more, and sooner. I'm not used to guarding those who know me for what I am."

Domin's face registered regret and something else. Something almost like hope. Or fear. As isolated as Henry was being a slave in the Faerie realm and an outsider in the human one, how must it be for Domin to serve generation after generation of humans who didn't even know who or what he was, to be forever hiding? Not just a moment of loneliness, like being left out of a joke, but the kind of cold emptiness that stretched on as far as the night sky, a deep, never-ending blackness that reached farther than the faintest pinprick of starlight and left one feeling very small and very lost.

"I suppose I can understand that," Henry said warily.

Domin nodded and strode forward to lead the others.

Trying to understand was the best Henry could do for now. Trust... he didn't know if it would come again. If it was worth the effort or the pain.

Chapter Eighteen

Cassandra's hands trembled, even after the walk through the woods forced warmth into her tingling fingers and toes. She'd almost cost Henry his life by forgetting Domin's warning about the shield. It was all too much, this new world of magic and monsters.

Her weak foot dragged through the slippery leaves as she limped behind Mary, and spasms of pain shortened her steps. She regretted leaving her cane at home. She resented her crippled leg. Could the elixir that cured Jairus have healed her as well? Or Georgina, if she'd been able to bring some back? She glanced over her shoulder toward the entrance to Elfland.

Only Henry walked more slowly than she, weariness hanging over his shoulders like a damp cloak.

She stumbled on a root, and Henry grabbed her arm. His other hand braced her waist, warm through the damp layers of her dress. Her heart stuttered, and she tensed.

He slid his arm from her waist. His expression reminded her of the white stag, wounded and wary. She wanted to flee the impossible things she'd seen Henry do. No wonder he was arrogant, holding the power of air and water in his hands. Yet he'd been quick to help her, treating her like a whole person instead of a cast-off cripple. Certainly, he knew the pain and loneliness of feeling out of place. She managed a hesitant smile for him before trudging after the others. His eyes lit with a hope so honest and vulnerable it made her heart ache in sympathy.

"So, do we have a plan?" Jairus asked.

Domin's glance swept over the group. "We are going to confront Fitzhugh again, if we can get him away from the villagers so they're not endangered. We may be able to force or trick some useful information from him about the Dark Lady's plans."

Jairus frowned. "I don't understand. He's your enemy, but you saved him from the hounds last night. Or at least I assume the wolf was you."

"It was. My main concern was stopping the hounds, but daemons do not shed blood needlessly. If anything, Fitzhugh deserves our pity for the miserable servitude he has chosen."

"Hmm." Jairus folded his arms. "I ain't fond of killing either, but I'll do it if I have to."

Domin shrugged and forged ahead, finally reaching the orchard. Cassandra sighed at the sight of her house nestled among the roses and elderberries, safe and undisturbed.

The splash of hoof beats over the muddy ground brought everyone to a stop. Even through the apple trees and misty rain, she recognized Fitzhugh's graceful figure atop his bay stallion. Jairus stepped to the front, the click of his shotgun's hammers a counterpoint to the smooth rhythm of the horse's canter.

The elf smirked as he reigned in. His coat and shirt were ragged where Jairus had shot him earlier, but the skin that showed through bore no traces of injury. "Very clever, my friends. Had a bit of an adventure, have you? You're all trailing glimmers of Elfland behind you. It's safer here, you know, especially for Miss Weaver." He grinned at her. "The Seelie Court has your scent. They can track you anywhere in your world or ours, and they won't stop until they find you."

Cassandra's breathing tightened as if someone had over-laced her corset.

"Why?" Amy asked.

Fitzhugh shook his head and dismounted. "I'm not playing that game with you, Amy. We know each other too well. I'm here to make an offer to Miss Weaver. A proposal, if you will." He winked at Cassandra.

She lifted her chin. "What are you talking about?"

"I'm offering you a better refuge. Come with me to the Unseelie Court, at least until Michaelmas is past, and I'll keep you safe." His deep voice soothed her like warm water, inviting her to forget her fears. "You don't belong in this backwards village. You deserve better than this place has to offer."

She met his sympathetic gaze. He was right, wasn't he? She deserved to be appreciated instead of treated like a worn-out piece of furniture shoved in the attic. Her mother pinned all her hopes on Sophie's sweet smile and pretty manners, but this time, it could be Cassandra's turn to be recognized and admired.

Sophie. Her sisters. Cassandra blinked. Putting her safety in the hands of a rake like Fitzhugh? What was she thinking?

"You think I'd leave my family? And my friends?" she asked.

"You may bring your sisters and your mother. The rest are none of my concern."

"I can't do that." Cassandra shook her head. "Why would you even make such an offer?"

"I want to show you I'm your friend, little pet, and I can do more for you than these pathetic outcasts. I'll even prove it. You may ask me ten questions, and I'll answer each one. Yes or no questions only." He shook his finger at Amy. "And no prompting from the rest of you. Do you agree, Miss Weaver?"

He flashed his handsome smile, and Cassandra's mouth went dry.

"Phrase every question carefully, Miss Weaver," Domin said.

"That doesn't count as prompting," Amy interjected.

Fitzhugh shrugged.

"Very well." Cassandra took a deep breath, trying to calm her racing heart. She would never believe Fitzhugh was her friend, but if it might help her family, she'd play his game. "Did the Dark Lady send you to protect me from those hounds?" She pressed a finger into her palm, counting down questions.

"Yes." He flipped the reins in his hand, his expression bored.

"Are you protecting my sisters as well?"

"Yes."

Cassandra shivered. How could her family be of interest to creatures she didn't even believe existed until today? She bit her lip. Maybe it wasn't just about them.

"Are the hounds targeting anyone outside my family?"

"No."

He smiled again and stepped closer, radiating charm. Her heart fluttered, and she scooted back. He was trying to distract her. Three fingernails bit into her palm. What did she most need to know? "Is one of my family meant for the sacrifice on Michaelmas, then?"

"No."

She let out her breath. Wasn't her family's safety all that mattered? It wasn't her concern what the Fay were doing.

Jairus cleared his throat. Cassandra's focus snapped back to

Fitzhugh and his cocky grin. His game was about more than the questions she asked; he was pushing her emotions around like the wind toying with a lost bonnet. She found her anger and clung to it. She wouldn't let him win so easily.

"Do these attacks have anything to do with the tithes to Hell?" she asked.

The smile melted from Fitzhugh's face, and he paused. "Yes."

"Even though none of us is the victim?" Cassandra blurted out, then slapped a hand over her mouth. "No, wait! I meant—"

Fitzhugh grinned like a snake. "Yes."

Cassandra winced and looked at the others. Amy gave her an encouraging nod. Henry shuffled in place, his mouth pinched shut. Cassandra chewed her bottom lip, trying to reason through what little she knew about the Faerie world.

"You're protecting us from another of the Faerie Queens." She met Fitzhugh's gaze. "So the Dark Lady needs us for something, and one of the queens is trying to interfere with her plans?"

"Yes," Fitzhugh said, eyes narrow.

"Do you know which queen is sending the hounds?"

The elf's expression relaxed. "No."

"Is there a way we can stop the hounds from attacking"— Cassandra paused as a wicked grin spread across Fitzhugh's face —"without harming anyone?"

His grin faded and he remained silent. Hadn't he heard? Cassandra caught the question before it escaped. She couldn't afford to waste another one.

"He doesn't know the answer," Amy said, "so according to his own rules, he can't say anything. You get another question." She looked at Fitzhugh. "That's still not prompting."

"Hmm," Cassandra said, "but the Dark Lady will lift the enchantment on the village after Michaelmas, correct?"

"Yes."

She nodded. That confirmed that the Dark Lady caused the enchantment.

"What about—" Henry began.

Domin lashed his hand out. "Quiet, Henry! If you prompt her, the game is over and she misses out on the last question."

Cassandra drew a slow breath. If she asked another question Fitzhugh couldn't answer, she might learn something and gain more time to think. Of course, she couldn't afford any mistakes. Fitzhugh watched her with a grin, but was he really so sure of himself?

"I wonder how much your Dark Lady trusts you, Mr. Fitzhugh. Did she send anyone else to help protect us?"

He opened his mouth then clamped it shut with a frown. Cassandra smiled. He wasn't sure. If he was busy protecting her family, would he also know about the sacrifice?

She wet her lips. "Is the intended victim for Michaelmas someone in Drixton?"

"Yes," Fitzhugh said.

She grimaced. A better question and she might have discovered more.

The smile crawled back onto the elf's face. "Not bad for your first game, my pet, but you can see that you're in over your head. I can help you and your sisters if you bring them to the Unseelie Court. I'll even promise immunity to any of your friends who wishes to join us."

She recoiled. "But you're the ones who dragged us into this. If you want to help, stop playing games and tell me what's going on."

"I'm not going to lay my cards on the table without getting

something in return. Agree to go back with me, and I'll tell you more."

Cassandra shook her head. Fitzhugh stepped closer, but Jairus swung his shotgun into the elf's chest. "The lady said no."

The elf sneered and pushed the gun aside.

"I don't think you're going to harm me now, Priest, when any misstep might place you on my Lady's altar. That's what you need to understand about this game: we can't lose. My Lady's plans are rolling forward, and she will have her sacrifice. There are so many victims to choose from." He leered. "Maybe one of you, if you refuse the hospitality I'm offering."

Jairus snorted, and Fitzhugh sneered down at him.

"You would make a nice sacrifice, Priest, and you wouldn't be so hard to corrupt. You look skeptical. Would you care to *bet* on it?"

Jairus paled, and Fitzhugh went on.

"Oh, yes, you want that risk, that challenge. You need it like some humans need alcohol or opium. What did you lose to your addiction? Love? Money? Respect? No matter what it took from you, you'll never stop wanting it. It will stalk you for the rest of your life, even if you never pick up another card. I could get you to bet your very soul, if I made the game interesting enough."

"I don't gamble," Jairus said through clenched teeth.

Fitzhugh turned on Cassandra.

"Or you, my pet. You're feeling smug now, but you're so ordinary. And damaged. Just a burden on your family. If you came with me, you wouldn't have to be. Our magic could heal you. Heal your deaf sister."

His voice slid through Cassandra's mind like silk, and her heart whimpered at his words. Facing the hounds, she had felt brave, like she could do anything, but in truth she was broken, helpless, useless.

"Fitzhugh, stop." Domin stepped up to him.

The elf pushed past the shape-shifter to Mary.

"Poor elf child. You've never fit anywhere, but you would finally belong in Elfland. It is your home, after all." He sneered. "But, of course, we have no use for you. That's why we left you here in the first place."

Mary flinched, and her gray eyes filled with anger.

"My dear Amy," Fitzhugh said, lifting the blonde elf's chin and standing so close it made Cassandra blush. Amy's eyes widened as he lowered his face to hers. "You're so beautiful, so accomplished, so close to perfection." He traced a path along her pale cheek and whispered, "But no matter what you do, it's not quite good enough, is it? You'll never be good enough. Not for your mother. Not for Henry or Domin. They don't want you. But we do. You know there's always a place for you in the Unseelie Court."

Amy trembled, and Domin stepped toward her. Fitzhugh dropped her chin, and she sagged like a broken marionette.

"Oh, Henry," Fitzhugh said, "I haven't forgotten you. You're the easiest of all. You just want your freedom."

Henry shook his head. "Freedom isn't a gift you can give me."

"But we can." Fitzhugh reached a hand toward Henry and then snapped it into a fist. Henry gasped and clutched his chest, eyes wide. Domin snarled, but Fitzhugh raised an eyebrow. "Down, mutt. I just wanted to prove my point." He opened his hand, and Henry sucked in a deep breath.

"You see, Henry, you can hide from the Fay, but not from what you are. Our magic is part of you now, and you'll never escape it. We turned you into a monster. A freak." Fitzhugh spat the word, and Henry winced. "But with the Unseelie Court, you'd be free from all these constraints you've put on yourself, all this control and fear. You could embrace your power and finally get the revenge that's rightfully yours. You would be free to make the Seelie courts tremble, make them pay for what they did to you and your family."

Henry's expression darkened. Cold wind howled past the trees, and Cassandra flinched from the branches thrashing and creaking above her.

Domin stepped forward, hand extended. "Douglas Fitzhugh, stop!"

His words reverberated through the orchard. Cassandra's mind awakened from the mesmerizing spell of Fitzhugh's voice. She wrapped her arms around herself, feeling that her heart had been stripped naked in front of everyone.

Fitzhugh's head rocked back like he'd been punched, but he laughed.

"Domin, that was rather elvish of you. Are you going to step down from your daemon pedestal and start playing by our rules, now? Because it would be delightful to see your blood spilled on my Lady's altar."

Domin smiled coldly. "If I ever did cross that line, what do you think would stop me from taking over the Unseelie Court myself? You should pray that day never comes, if you still remember how. Leave this place now. We are finished here."

"You have no authority to send me away. You should be glad of my help, for Miss Weaver's sake, if nothing else. While you've been playing in Elfland, I've fended off threats here: things much more unpleasant than hell hounds."

Cassandra remembered the monsters from Henry's book and felt ill. But Fitzhugh was no different from the everyday bullies who came into her father's shops, harassing her sisters or the shop assistants because they thought no one would stand up to them. She took a limping step forward. "I don't want your help, Mr. Fitzhugh. I want you to leave my family alone."

Fitzhugh's eyes narrowed, and he smirked. "Perhaps I will. We'll see how many of your friends die protecting you before your pride breaks and you crawl back to me."

Fitzhugh swung onto his horse and spurred it toward the lane.

"What did I just do?" Cassandra asked.

"The right thing," Henry said quietly. "You don't want Fitzhugh as an ally. But we should get inside."

She nodded and led them to the house, though its walls seemed a thin protection against Fitzhugh's warnings.

Chapter Nineteen

Silence greeted Cassandra as she swung the back door open. Her skin tingled at the strange stillness.

"Miss Weaver?" Amy stood back from the threshold, her face pale. "Will you invite me in?"

"Oh." Cassandra paused. She hardly felt in a position to refuse entry to a titled lady—even if that lady was also Fay—but she was responsible for her family's safety. Would inviting Amy in endanger them?

"I have no intention of harming anyone in this household." Amy glanced at Domin. "I made a mistake once and betrayed a trust, but I'm trying to make amends."

Rain dripped from Amy's blond locks and splattered on her purple dress. Her head hung down, and Cassandra's sympathy stirred, but she couldn't make her decision based on kindness alone.

"Why did you come here this morning?" she asked.

Amy sighed and met her gaze. "I'd been watching your

house. I suspected you'd break from the enchantment eventually, and I wanted to help."

"Help whom?" Domin asked. "Be direct."

Amy straightened her shoulders. "I wanted to help Miss Weaver because I saw that she was in danger from Fitzhugh and the Unseelie Court. I also wanted to help myself, to prove ..." She drew a long breath. "To prove that I am more than my mistakes."

The Fay couldn't lie, but they could bend the truth. Amy sounded sincere, but Cassandra felt too muddled to be certain. Cassandra looked to Henry and Domin.

Domin studied Amy, then gave a slight nod.

"Very well," Cassandra said quietly. "Lady St. Clair, you're welcome here. As are you, Miss Leland," she added, uncertain if a Faerie changeling needed an invitation. Mary blinked rapidly and smiled at her.

They all followed Cassandra into the house. Cassandra limped to the drawing-room as quickly as her throbbing leg allowed. Sophie still sat in her chair, eyes glazed by the enchantment and a forced smile on her lips. At least she seemed unharmed.

"Sophie!"

Her sister's gaze flicked in her direction. "Hello, Cassie. Did you sleep well?"

Cassandra knelt by her side. "We're going to fix this."

"Of course. Everything is lovely."

The others lingered in the entrance to the room. At least Cassandra wasn't alone. She stood to face them.

"What now?" Cassandra asked. "Is it true that my sisters are safe from the Dark Lady's sacrifice?"

Henry ran his hand through his hair and paced. "Fitzhugh

said the Dark Lady has other plans for your family. We need to know what they are."

Cassandra looked helplessly around the drawing-room decorated with her mother's bric-a-bracs as though some answer could be found among the hand-painted flower vases and lacquered pencil boxes.

"Let's start with the tithes." Jairus stepped into the room and rested his elbow on a stand holding a globe. "Can the Dark Lady sacrifice anyone?"

"More or less," Domin said. "But she'll want the sacrifice to be someone talented or idealistic. The farther the person falls, the more strength she gains from the ritual. Also, the person she intends to sacrifice will not be enchanted. She can deceive or entice them, but they must betray the things they value of their own free will."

"Someone corruptible, then," Jairus said.

"Isn't everyone corruptible?" Amy asked quietly.

Cassandra's stomach turned. The Fay, or at least Fitzhugh, certainly knew how to entice. How often had she thought she would give anything to feel accepted and appreciated?

"Could she be using the Weavers as bait?" Jairus asked.

"If that's the case, the sacrifice may very well be one of us," Domin said.

Everyone looked at each other uncomfortably.

Henry tapped a staccato pattern on the side table. His fingers left a trace of ice on the polished wood. "Fitzhugh said he wasn't hunting me."

"He wasn't, but the Dark Lady could be," Domin said.

"Well, she has to corrupt us, and we won't let that happen." Henry paced the length of the room to the piano at the far end and turned back. "Who else is a likely candidate?"

"Miss Leland's father is very talented," Amy said.

Domin glanced at Mary, who shrank against a curio displaying ceramic animals.

"Perhaps," Domin said, "but he *was* enchanted, and some of the wonder of his creations are because Miss Leland helps make them, leaving traces of her magic."

Mary shook her head, looking close to tears.

"What about the pastor?" Cassandra asked quickly to divert attention from the poor girl. The pastor seemed idealistic, speaking of gratitude at the Harvest Festival.

Amy looked away from one of Georgina's paintings on the wall. "Or your apothecary."

Henry frowned. "Mr. Tanner has been missing all day."

Cassandra imagined the apothecary with his thin hair and stooped shoulders. It was hard to imagine him hurting anyone.

"Do either of them have a connection to the Weavers?" Jairus plopped down in a chair, resting his elbow on an embroidered sampler pillow that read, *Seek to be good but aim not to be great, Cassandra Weaver, Age 10, 1861.*

"We've met the vicar and the apothecary," Cassandra said. "I don't know if that qualifies as a connection. The Ashbys befriended us as well."

Lady Ashby would probably be happy to sacrifice someone to stop her husband from associating with such low acquaintances as the Weavers. And Elizabeth had seemed to be their friend, but she had shown a nasty side at the ball.

"Sir Walter is a possibility." Henry ran his hands through his hair. "Amy, you're his guest. How well do you know him?"

"We move in the same circles, but I don't know him well. I had to use some, uh, persuasion on Lady Ashby to receive an invitation when I found out Fitzhugh was coming here."

"How is Fitzhugh acquainted with him?" Henry asked.

"Through shared social circles," Amy said. " Fitzhugh

might just be using him as a convenient way to find acceptable lodging in Drixton."

Cassandra's gaze flashed to the elf. Amy and Fitzhugh had both used the Ashbys. For all everyone said that the two Faerie Courts were different, Cassandra had trouble seeing much distinction.

Domin frowned. "Fitzhugh might have used his influence to get Sir Walter's help with disabling the church bell as well. He would have needed an ally outside of the Unseelie Court to do that."

"What about Mr. Rushford?" Jairus asked.

Cassandra shuddered at the memory of the man prodding at her skull.

Henry cocked an eyebrow. "Sir Walter's friend? He wouldn't have far to fall."

"Maybe," Jairus said, "but listen. I've dealt with some nasty things: ghosts, vampires, and plenty of other monsters I won't talk about even in the daylight. I know trouble when I spot it, and Rushford and those Grigori are neck-deep in it. That's why I followed them here."

"Did you say Grigori?" Domin turned on Jairus. "What are you talking about?"

"The Order of the Grigori. Mr. Rushford's friends. It's a gentleman's club for people with occult interests. They claim their interest is just academic, but I don't believe it."

Domin grimaced. "The name Grigori refers to fallen angels who deal with humans. I doubt they chose it by accident."

Cassandra sank into a wing chair, more than half certain she would wake up to find everything a strange dream. "I don't understand what any of this could have to do with my family."

Henry sat across from her. "This may be uncomfortable, but we're going to have to ask you some questions."

"If you don't want to talk in front of everyone, I can leave the room," Jairus said.

She wondered what The Rules would say, but she was drifting beyond their help. "I don't think we have any great secrets, and maybe with more people thinking about it, it'll be easier to find an answer. What do you need to know?"

Cassandra braced herself as they sifted through her family's everyday life, looking for something that might connect them to the Fay. Had anyone in her family had extraordinary good fortune? Did strangers ever show an unusual interest in them? Did she suspect either of her parents had been unfaithful?

No. No. No.

Cassandra did her best not to squirm at the questions. While her family might not have secrets, they had many moments formed around the grit of life like pearls, almost too precious to pour out in front of others: Sophie caring for her and Georgina as they recovered from the fever; finally getting Sophie to smile again after her suitor jilted her for a girl with a larger fortune; Georgina giving up her painting lessons so their younger sisters could afford to study drawing.

Dusk stole into the corners of the room. Mary fell asleep huddled in one corner of the sofa, and Jairus muffled his yawns in his torn sleeve.

"We're getting nowhere." Henry stood and stretched. The cuffs of his shirt inched up enough to reveal thick scars on each wrist. He quickly covered them again, and Cassandra looked away, rubbing her own wrists.

"Is it unusual for your father to be absent for so long?" Henry asked.

"Not really," Cassandra said. "He's always attending to some business or another."

"Leaving a household full of women." Henry tilted his head. "Is it only women here?"

"At the moment. Is that significant?"

"Perhaps. Only because it's a little unusual. Can we meet your other sisters?"

"Yes. It would be best to get Sophie upstairs anyway."

Sophie smiled complacently as Cassandra guided her up to their room. The others followed, except for Mary, who snoozed on the sofa. When Cassandra led the others to the nursery, Nancy and her sisters took no notice of the strangers. Cassandra sighed. She'd hoped to find something different.

Georgina had covered an entire wall with dark, swirling colors. Cassandra imagined a vague figure in the center of the painting, but even when she squinted, she couldn't bring it into focus. Domin studied Georgina like a scientist watching a rare bird, but finally, he shook his head.

"She's painting what she senses happening around her. It shows some intuition and talent, but not enough to attract this much attention from the Fay."

"You do have quite a few sisters," Henry said. "Six girls total?"

Cassandra flushed. "My father has always been able to provide for all of us."

"What? No, that's not what I meant. Anne—my mother— had more children than that." Sadness settled back over his expression. "I was just thinking out loud."

Cassandra nodded and led them from the cozy room. As they tiptoed past her mother's door, her thoughts drifted to her unborn sibling. She jolted to a stop, nearly tripping up Jairus. "My mother's in confinement. If the baby's a girl, we'd be seven sisters. That's significant, isn't it?"

"It's interesting," Amy said, "but it would only be

significant if your mother was also the youngest of seven sisters."

There was a hint of joking in Amy's voice, but Cassandra's skin went cold.

"Is she the youngest of seven sisters?" Amy asked.

Cassandra nodded.

"She has no brothers, and neither have you?" Henry prodded. "Living or dead?"

"None. She's always said it was lucky. I mean, she hasn't had a son, but she hasn't lost a child."

"Domin?" Henry asked.

Domin closed his eyes and tipped his head back. "The child is a girl."

Chapter Twenty

Cassandra didn't ask how Domin could know her mother was expecting a seventh daughter. She wasn't sure she could handle the answer. For now, she only had to understand what it meant for her family. For her unborn sister.

"So, I've heard of the seventh son of a seventh son," Jairus said.

Domin nodded. "It is the same. The seventh daughter of a seventh daughter will always have some exceptional talent or ability, provided there are no males who interrupt the line, and," he looked at Cassandra, "provided all six of the child's sisters are alive at the time of her birth."

A long silence settled over the corridor.

"Ah," Jairus said.

The walls seemed to close in around Cassandra. "So the Dark Lady wants the baby, and some other Faerie Queen is trying to kill one of us so she'll be—"

"Normal. Just another baby girl. Of no interest to the Dark Lady," Domin said.

Cassandra limped toward the bright comfort of the drawing-room downstairs. "There's another way, isn't there? One of my sisters or I don't have to die to keep the Dark Lady from taking the baby?"

"No," Jairus and Domin said in unison. They looked at each other, then Domin said, "Once the child is christened, the Dark Lady won't be able to take her, at least not until she's old enough to choose for herself."

"So, we just have to protect all of you until the baby is born and we can find a priest," Henry said.

"We already have one." Domin fixed his green eyes on Jairus.

The American cleared his throat. "I ain't Anglican, you know."

Amy laughed. "It doesn't matter. The Fay have been around much longer than the Church of England."

"The exact ceremony is not as important as the act of claiming the child," Domin said, "giving her a place in this world so the Fay can't take her to theirs. As a priest, you have that authority."

"Is that right?" Jairus glanced up at the ceiling. He shrugged and looked back at Domin. "God agrees, so I'm game."

Cassandra wondered again if everyone in the room was insane, but she reminded herself of what she'd seen at Telesm's cottage. She was out of her depth, and she needed help, for her sisters' sakes if not her own.

Henry sat on the sofa in front of the window. Mary started awake and shrank as far from him as she could without actually changing seats. He didn't seem to notice.

"Then we just have to find out who the victim is and protect him as well," Henry said. "We'll drive the Fay out of

Drixton, and maybe even punish them in the process—show them they can't keep toying with human lives."

"Perhaps," Domin said, "but beware of your motivations, Henry. Fitzhugh is trying to entice you into using your abilities for the Unseelie Court. Everyone needs to be cautious and watch each other for the Dark Lady's influence. It would not do to save the victim only to allow one of us to become the sacrifice."

"And if we think someone is falling under her sway?" Jairus asked.

"Incapacitate them if they will not respond to reason."

Everyone exchanged uneasy glances. Cassandra forced down a hysterical giggle at the thought of trying to incapacitate any of the others.

"What are you drawing?" Henry asked Jairus.

The American had found a dusty side table and was tracing a broken figure eight. "The Grigori use this symbol. I'm still wondering how they fit into all this. Could they be working with either of the Faerie Courts?"

"It's unusual for the Fay to seek human allies," Domin said, "but not impossible."

"I've seen that symbol, too," Cassandra said. "On the wall of the church near the belltower."

"Then the Grigori are probably allied with the Dark Lady," Domin said.

Cassandra stared out the window. Were there Fay out there, watching and hoping they would make some critical mistake? It made taking tea with her mother's sharp-eyed society friends seem relatively relaxing.

She moved to close the heavy curtains and froze, crushing the thick fabric in her grip. Tiny lights floated around the house, illuminating dark shapes that paced the shadows. A whimper escaped her throat, and the others rushed to the window.

"Can they get inside?" she asked, hating the way her voice cracked.

"No," Domin said, but his brows drew together as he stared into the darkness. "Without Fitzhugh here, other Faerie creatures are flocking to the house. The roses around the porch will keep the darkest ones away, and none will be able to cross the threshold without an invitation."

"But if Fitzhugh was the one holding the Seelie Fay back, what's stopping them from doing whatever they want now?" Jairus asked. "If they want to kill someone, they just have to burn down the house."

"Mr. Hale!" Amy stared at him. "Isn't that rather blunt?"

"No," Cassandra said. "He's right, isn't he?" Bile soured her throat at the thought of her sisters trapped in a burning house because she had lost her temper and sent Fitzhugh away. If she had just stayed at Telesm's cottage, he would be guarding the house and her family would still be safe.

"I can control the fire if they try to burn down the house," Henry said.

"All right, but what if they try something else?" Jairus pressed. "We're trapped here."

Domin nodded. "The Seelie Court will still be wary of the Dark Lady's powers at night when she is strongest, but in daylight, they may attack. We will need a plan for dealing with both courts."

"Plan?" Jairus pulled out his revolver. "We make our stand."

"Against what? Will o' the wisps?" Henry asked. "Until our real enemy makes an appearance, we have nothing to fight."

Cassandra stepped between them and turned to Henry.

"Was I wrong to turn down Fitzhugh's offer? Could we still go to Elfland, my sisters and I?"

"It's your choice," Henry said, "but you would be at the mercy of the very worst of the Fay. Some things—" He shook his head.

"Some things are worse than being dead," Jairus finished quietly.

Cassandra considered that. She had wanted to be useful to her family—protect her sisters and the new baby—but now that she had that role, she realized how inadequate she was. She took a deep breath. "Then what are we to do?"

"Sleep," Domin said. "I'll keep watch, but you should take advantage of the brief peace the darkness has brought us. In the morning, you'll need your strength."

"I wish this enchantment affected me too, then," Amy said. "I can't imagine sleeping with the Seelie and Unseelie courts sparring outside the house."

Henry shook off his gloom and picked up the apothecary's satchel he had dropped by the sofa. "I can make a tea that will help with that. It won't force you asleep, but it will make it easier to drift off. Miss Weaver, if you'll show me to your kitchen?"

As they walked down the corridor, Cassandra stole glances at him. His forehead creased with worry and a frown dulled his eyes. What must it cost him to confront the Fay? Even talking about them at Telesm's cottage had pained him. At the ball, Amy said he had done something brave, that he was hiding from someone. Cassandra guessed that had to do with the Fay, and now she'd dragged him back into that world.

"I'm sorry," she blurted out as they headed below stairs to the kitchen.

He blinked. "For what?"

"For...well, to start, for calling you a coward this morning."

"Oh." He rubbed the back of his neck. "I might have deserved it. I had some idea, at least, of what was going on. I should have done more."

Cassandra found a clean pot and filled it with cool water from the pump. "No, it was unfair of me. I didn't know—"

He took the pot, and she jumped at the touch of his hand.

His expression crumpled. "You *are* afraid of me."

"I-I suppose I am, a little. Or, at least of what I saw you do. This is all a bit much to take in at once." She remembered Fitzhugh's taunts and touched Henry's arm. "But I don't think you're a monster."

He stared at her hand as if a songbird had lighted on his sleeve. One corner of his mouth turned up. "What about a freak?"

He set the pot down on the stove and hovered his hand over it. In a matter of moments, steam rose off the clear water.

Cassandra swallowed her unease. "That's very useful. If you decide not to be a surgeon, you could open a tea room."

Henry laughed and went about his work as if he were an ordinary young man making tea in her kitchen. An ordinary young man who could summon the wind and order water to boil. But also someone who was risking his well-being to protect her and her sisters.

He finished the tea and poured it into the cups Cassandra had gathered, filling the kitchen with an earthy lemon scent. Picking up the tray, he gestured for her to lead the way back to the drawing-room.

Amy and Mary thanked Henry as they took their cups. Cassandra offered one to Jairus, but he shook his head.

"No, thanks. I like to keep my head clear, and I've learned to sleep on the battlefield." He stretched out on the sofa in front of the window, pulled his battered hat over his eyes, and said, "Goodnight, y'all."

Everyone stared at him, then at the other sofa.

"We don't all have to sleep in here, do we?" Cassandra asked. She might as well throw The Rules out the window at the Fay.

"No," Domin said. "You should be safe anywhere in the house. I will keep guard."

"Lady St. Clair, Miss Leland, I can make space for you in my room," Cassandra said.

"Thank you," Amy said as Henry settled on the empty sofa. Domin stood at the window, as still as a cathedral gargoyle.

"Goodnight," Cassandra mumbled as she retreated from the room, grateful now that everyone else in the house was enchanted. What would they say if they found three men encamped in the drawing-room? Amy and Mary followed her upstairs, where Sophie snored in her bed.

"I'll share with Sophie if you two don't mind taking the other," Cassandra said.

Amy shrugged. Mary washed her hands and face in the chilly water on the dresser. Cassandra left them and checked on her mother, who was asleep in her room.

Cassandra placed a gentle hand on her mother's belly and felt the baby—her youngest sister—stirring. Strong kicks for someone so tiny. But the Dark Lady was out there, waiting to steal the child if Cassandra and her sisters survived until the birth. Cassandra was weak, but the baby was even more helpless, and her mother and sisters were in no state to defend themselves. There was only her. How could she ever be enough?

She limped back to her room. Mary had curled up on the bed in her dress. Cassandra picked at her mud-crusted sleeves. It made sense to sleep dressed, but her stiff bodice chaffed her neck and arms. She pulled out a soft, blue-green dress and shucked off her gray one, loosening her corset enough to sleep comfortably.

"I'm sorry I don't have anything small enough to fit you," she said to Amy.

"Well, at least this way I'll only have one dress ruined if we're to fight tomorrow."

Cassandra's hands froze over her filigree buttons. "Do we have any chance of winning?"

"I don't know. It's an odd thing to be glad the Dark Lady is on our side, but she'll try to protect you as long as she needs you alive. After that ..." Amy set down the pins she had pulled from her golden hair. "Well, our friends downstairs aren't insignificant either. Especially Domin."

"Domin?" Cassandra asked. Shape-shifting didn't seem as formidable as Henry's control of the weather or Jairus's shotgun.

"It was before my time, but I've heard he almost killed the Dark Lady once. He chose to become a protector, but were he to step out of that role and embrace the full extent of his elvish abilities: controlling others' emotions, creating illusions, exceptional strength and speed...Well, I don't know what he'd be capable of. But since the Faerie Queens don't either, they're cautious of him."

Cassandra nodded. It was Domin who had disposed of most of the hounds at Telesm's cottage. Her sisters were going to be safe. They all were. She repeated the thought like a desperate prayer as she shucked off her brace and rubbed her sore leg.

As she brushed through the snarled mess of her hair, a piece of jewelry on the dresser caught her eye. She picked up

Georgina's little rose brooch and slipped the iron pin through the fabric of her bodice. Protection against dark creatures.

She tried to roll Sophie over, but her sister was a dead weight. Amy set down the hairbrush to help her. Sophie's eyes snapped open to stare at them before sagging back into sleep.

"Is she going to be all right?" Cassandra asked.

"She should be. I've, uh—"

Cassandra looked at the elf, then down at Sophie. "You've enchanted people before?"

"Well, yes." Amy met her eyes. "Nothing like this, though. You have to be extremely powerful to do something like this. I can just be quite...persuasive. And it never seems to harm anyone."

"Hmm. Is everyone going to starve? Or will they do something dangerous and hurt themselves?"

"No. People who are enchanted usually go about their normal activities—so they'll eat and drink if they need to—and even a Faerie Queen can't make someone act against their nature."

"But will everyone remember what happened?"

"They'll find a way for it to make sense to them. Humans are amazingly good at fitting things to what they want to believe. They'll probably say it was a fever." Her gaze slid to the floor. "I'm not proud of the things I've done, you know. I understand why you hesitated to invite me in. In your place, I might have slammed the door."

Cassandra stifled a yawn, Henry's tea blurring her thoughts. "I've made mistakes too, and I wouldn't want anyone to hold them over me."

Amy sat on the edge of the feather bed where Mary had already sunk into sleep. "It doesn't sound like you've ever done anything to be ashamed of, though. I thought I was going to help people and stand up against an injustice, but I got people—my friends—killed. If it wasn't for Domin, it would have been much worse. I try, but I always seem to make the wrong choice." She plucked at the top of the soft mattress. "I guess I'm too silly to think things through."

"If you thought you were doing right—"

"I helped my friends attack the king and Parliament when they threatened another round of witch hunts. The Fay always suffer the most at such times. My mother was furious, not that I tried to kill the king, but that I failed."

"The king? Witch hunts?" Cassandra asked. Queen Victoria's consort was dead, and witch hunts were something out of darker times.

"James Stuart. King James the First."

"King James? Are you talking about—" Cassandra covered her mouth. "Are you talking about the Gunpowder Plot—Guy Fawkes Day? You tried to blow up Parliament?" She didn't ask how old Amy must be. The fifth of November had been notorious for well over two hundred years.

"Not personally, but I helped the conspirators cover their tracks. If Domin hadn't detected my deception, we might have succeeded. I'm glad we didn't, of course. I'm still paying for my mistakes as it is." The elf sighed. "At the time, it seemed like a brave thing to do."

Cassandra considered that. "I suppose I've never done much to be ashamed of, but I don't think I've ever done anything brave either."

"No?" Amy asked. "You were brave today."

"That was just the shield," Cassandra said. Fitzhugh's words still stung.

"No, I felt the way Telesm's magic works. He's a Faerie changeling, like Miss Leland, so his magic can encourage or seduce, but not coerce." Amy leaned forward. "Domin didn't give you the shield to make you brave. He gave it to you because he saw that you were brave and its strength would awaken in your hands."

Cassandra sat back and fidgeted with Georgina's brooch. Fitzhugh only saw the ordinary in her. Domin, though, saw bravery, enough that he had entrusted her with everyone's lives. Fitzhugh's voice was easier to listen to—it demanded less—but something in her heart stirred at the thought that she might be stronger than she knew.

"Thank you, Lady St. Clair."

The elf wrung her hands. "Would you call me Amy? That title is an unpleasant souvenir from my past. I use it because it's convenient, but I don't like being reminded of the... situation that bestowed it on me."

The "situation" had to be marriage, but guessing how old Amy must be, it was no longer surprising that she had been wed at some point. Still, for someone of Cassandra's station to call a titled lady by her first name was so informal, Sophie would call it vulgar. "I don't know. What would people say? I hardly feel I should be so familiar..."

Amy studied her with a curious expression, half amusement and half concern. "You give so much weight to human titles, then? I wonder... You may someday find that attitude at odds with your happiness. But I overstep." She sighed. "We elves don't share our true surnames—names have too much power—so we usually go by our given names among ourselves, and since you know about us now ..."

Cassandra considered that. "What about Mr. Fitzhugh? None of you use his first name."

Amy glanced down. "He renounced it when he joined the Unseelie Court. Names are very important to us, Miss Weaver."

It was a different set of rules, and it seemed fair to respect them. "Then please call me Cassandra, Amy."

Amy smiled and settled into bed, and Cassandra stretched out by Sophie. She turned the events of the day over in her mind, like a rock tumbling in a stream, until some of the sharpest edges wore away. Finally, the soporific effects of the tea dragged her into a sleep filled with prowling shadows.

Chapter Twenty-One

Shouting shattered the early morning stillness.

Mary started awake with a gasp. Something touched her arm, and she flailed before remembering where she was. Amy gave her a worried look, golden hair framing her heart-shaped face, then released her arm and hurried out the door after Cassandra.

Mary pulled the covers up to her chest. She should just stay here and go back to sleep. Ignore the events of the last few days, the claim that she was something less than human.

But she couldn't ignore the mad sense behind what they said. She'd always been sickly and strange things happened around her. She *felt* like she didn't fit, but she'd had no evidence, no reason to think she was anything besides a misfit. Until now.

She crept down the stairs behind the other women and joined them in the tiled front entrance, where Jairus sat surrounded by guns and knives. He was sharpening the point of a black metal pole with a blacksmith's file.

"What's going on out there?" Amy asked.

"A boar." The steady sound of rasping faltered. "A really big boar with, um, poisonous bristles."

"The roses will keep it away, won't they?" Cassandra asked.

"Domin says it's Seelie, so the roses won't stop it, and it's big enough to batter the walls down. He's keeping it at bay for the moment, but—" Jairus quickened his work. "Well, the bright side is, it scared away all the other Faerie creatures. Miss Weaver, does your father have any guns? We're going to want more than what I've got with me."

"Yes, in his study. I'll get them."

Cassandra ran to one of the rooms lining the corridor and returned a few moments later, arms laden with a pair of birding guns and several bows and quivers.

Mary pressed against the wall. Her hands itched at the thought of iron touching her skin. It was an odd sensitivity that caused her father to use only brass in his shop.

"Was that my mother's plant stand?" Cassandra asked as she set the weapons down by the sharpened metal poles.

Jairus shrugged. "We needed iron."

"What am I going to tell her when she notices it's missing?"

"Tell her it was ugly," Jairus said.

Cassandra rolled her eyes, and Amy choked back a snicker.

Henry edged his way to the open front door, his eyes fixed on the tumult outside. The women scooted closer to see as well. Henry glanced at Cassandra, his eyes taking in her face like he was hungry for it. She looked down shyly and smoothed back her hair. Mary scowled. Why would someone as kind and brave as Cassandra act silly over bad-tempered Henry?

Mary looked past the curtain of rain dripping from the eaves of the porch, and her eyes widened. A boar the size of a plow horse snorted and charged across the lawn. It slashed with yellow tusks at a panther, who bounded and dodged to keep ahead of its attacks.

Mary retreated into the entryway. Jairus bolted past her onto the porch and fired at the boar twice in quick succession. She flinched and covered her ears.

"Anything you can do about the rain, Mr. Stewart?" Jairus asked as he retreated to reload. He wiped droplets from his chin with his sleeve. "It's not working in our favor."

"I can try to redirect it."

Henry furrowed his brow and reached his hand toward the clouds. It looked absurd, but Mary felt something shift in the air. The rain battered the roof with renewed intensity, and the wind whipped cool moisture around her in the entryway.

"Not what I had in mind!" Jairus said, shielding his gun with his tattered coat.

"Would you like to try, then?" Henry snapped. He narrowed his eyes and raised his hand again. The rain slackened to a slow drip plinking half-heartedly off the roof. On the lawn, Domin kept the boar pivoting after him, churning the muddy ground.

"That's more like it! Grab a gun. They're loaded with iron." Jairus motioned to the double-barreled birding guns.

Henry took one and handed the other to Cassandra.

"I've never shot a gun," she said.

"It's already loaded," Jairus said, "but you have to pull the hammer back all the way before it'll fire." He lifted his shotgun to demonstrate. "Then just aim and pull the trigger. There'll be a kick. You need to brace yourself for that. And there are two triggers, one for each barrel. Don't pull both at once."

Their footsteps rattled the front porch then stopped suddenly.

"What the—" Jairus exclaimed.

Mary peeked around the edge of the door.

A flock of crows circled the front lawn. They pulled into a tight spiral until Mary couldn't tell one bird from another. Their dark forms melted into a tall female figure armored from head to foot like a storybook knight, wielding a huge, two-handed sword.

"Heaven help us! The Morrigan!" Amy grasped Cassandra's arm.

"The what?" Jairus asked, aiming at the armored fighter.

"No!" Amy pulled his arm down. "She's a spirit of battle and death. Don't draw her attention."

The Morrigan danced lightly around the boar, swinging the enormous blade as easily as a birch switch as it whipped gashes into the creature's tough hide. For all its size and brawn, the boar moved like a creaky wind-up toy compared to the Fay warrior.

Domin shifted into a wolf and leapt to catch the boar's ear in his teeth. He hit the ground and scurried back, tugging the creature off balance and exposing its neck. It bashed Domin's side with its tusk, leaving a gash in his fur, but Domin didn't release his grip. The Morrigan plunged her sword into the boar's neck and twisted. Mary gasped and covered her face.

The scene grew quiet, and Mary looked up. The boar lay still. Domin backed away from the Morrigan, teeth bared and hair standing on end. She pulled off her helmet, revealing an angular face and long, golden-red hair plaited into a braid. Mary crept forward. She had never imagined women wearing armor and fighting, but it seemed to be something that belonged to this world of magic and monsters.

"Come, Domin, we can't talk like this." The woman's voice rang as clear and strong as a battle trumpet.

Domin shifted into human form. He retreated into the

roses arching from the porch as the Morrigan approached him, a predatory smile marring her fair features.

"This is no way to greet an ally, Domin."

"Are you an ally?" he asked.

"Long ago I saw your battle fury, and I want to fight by your side again. Can't you smell the blood in the air?" Her eyes shone.

"I do not wish for bloodshed."

Her laugh rang under the eaves of the porch. "You want me to believe you are made of ice, but I have seen the fire burning in your veins, as it does in mine." Desire flashed in her eyes. "Side by side, we felled entire companies of men. Do you not recall? And now the battle has started anew. All you can do is choose sides."

"I will not join either."

She stepped closer but hesitated at the white roses nodding around Domin. "You're caught between the Faerie courts. Even you cannot survive them both without my help."

His eyes narrowed. "What price do you demand, Morrigan?"

"I am in need of a consort." She smiled and ran her fingers down his chest.

He shoved her hand away. "Do not touch me."

"Are you still pining after that human girl? By now she is dead and rotted to dust."

Domin straightened. Something changed in the profile of his face: a terrible sharpness beneath the surface that Mary hadn't noticed before. She shrank from it, but the Morrigan chuckled.

"There's the Domin I remember. I knew you weren't lost to me."

Domin grabbed one of the long rose canes arching next to

him and whipped it across the Morrigan's face. She stumbled back, her face torn by thorns, white petals clinging to her hair. She gasped and tore the petals away.

"Very well then." The Morrigan's smile turned cold as the gashes on her face sealed themselves and disappeared. "I can get almost as much enjoyment fighting against you as fighting by your side."

Her sword dissipated into dark mist. She dissolved into crows that circled the corpse of the boar and melted into the bleeding body. Under the Morrigan's control, the mangled creature shuddered and struggled to its feet, cloudy eyes staring without blinking.

Domin looked up at the others. "We need iron and fire. Destroy the body. Do not touch the skin. The bristles are poisonous."

He shifted into panther form and charged the boar, slashing at its face and throat with his claws and bounding away to keep it circling after him.

"So, fire?" Jairus asked Henry, gesturing toward the boar.

"Don't you think if I could just set things on fire, I would have done so already? To do that, I'd have to sear everything between myself and her. I doubt even you're crazy enough to think that's a good idea. Now, if there was a fire already burning, I could work with that."

"Oh!" Cassandra said and dashed back into her father's study.

Jairus blinked after her, then shrugged. "All right, the old-fashioned way, then. Grab the guns and bows." He offered Henry a sharpened iron stake. "Here's the best I could do as far as swords."

Cassandra returned, a bottle clutched in her hand.

"Mr. Hale, Mr. Stewart, would this burn?"

Jairus's eyebrows crept up as he studied the label. "Brandy? I should think so."

He ripped a strip of fabric from the tattered end of his sleeve and shoved the scrap into the bottle.

Amy strung both bows with experienced ease and pressed one of them into Mary's hands.

"Draw it like this." Amy demonstrated.

Mary tried to imitate the elf's confident stance, but her arms trembled as she pulled the string to her cheek. Beautiful, bold Amy was everything Mary could never be.

Amy handed her a quiver of arrows. "Be careful of the tips. They're iron."

Mary nodded. She stood aside with Amy as Jairus motioned Henry and Cassandra behind him. Henry lit the brandy-soaked rag with a match from Jairus's ammunition bag, and the American hurled the bottle at the reanimated monster chasing Domin.

The bottle shattered when it hit the creature's bristly hide. Flame splattered onto the ground at its feet. Henry lashed his hand toward it and the fire roared up like a living thing. The boar squealed and writhed. Flames slithered around it, grasping with hungry fingers.

Jairus stepped out the front door, a manic grin stretched across his face. He fired his gun, and the boar shook its head madly at the iron shot. It dropped into the mud, rolling to quench the flames. Domin darted after its exposed belly. The boar heaved itself onto him, engulfing them both in the fire.

Henry shouted and drew his hands back, and the flames sputtered and died in the mud. Domin pulled himself free, his skin blistered and pink through his singed fur. He blurred through a shape change, restoring his smooth black coat.

The boar charged the house. Henry snatched up the gun,

and Cassandra followed him out the door. The guns roared against the boar. It shrieked and barreled closer. Domin buried his claws in its neck, and it swung its tusks after him.

Mary gaped at the scene. She didn't belong here. She belonged in her shop, where everything was orderly. Predictable. Safe.

Amy prodded her to the edge of the porch. Amy's bowstring twanged as she loosed an arrow into the boar's nose. Mary felt like her head was wrapped in wool. Everything was a muffled rush of noise. She drew the bowstring back as far as she could. It snapped her wrist when she released it, and her arrow jumped to the side.

Henry and Cassandra fired again. The boar squealed, and Domin hissed as some stray shot pelted him.

Mary waited for the white smoke to clear. She forced another arrow onto the string with shaking hands. Afraid of snapping herself again, she released it too soon, and the arrow fell into the rose bushes. She tried to retrieve it, but the thorns snagged her arm. One of Amy's arrows sang by her ear, and she jerked back, ripping her sleeve.

Amy reached into her empty quiver and frowned. Mary handed Amy the rest of her arrows and huddled against the house, wiping away the tears that blurred the bloody scene in front of her. She waited for someone to berate her for her uselessness, but they were too focused on the fight.

The boar's face bristled with arrows, and its body oozed from raw wounds, but it still slashed at Domin. The panther hobbled away, favoring his bleeding leg. Mary wrung her hands. Why didn't he change shape?

Jairus and Henry clattered down the porch steps with their guns and iron swords. Cassandra held the third sharpened pole at the top of the stairs. The boar swept its tusks at Domin again, gashing his side and sending him rolling across the grass, where he lay motionless.

Henry yelled and ran forward to fire his gun twice into the boar's flank. It turned from Domin. Henry tossed the empty gun behind him and yanked the iron skewer from his belt, holding it like a dueling sword. The boar lowered its head.

Jairus fired his gun at the monster. The boar shrieked and whirled on him.

The American raised the shotgun to fire the second barrel. Nothing happened when he pulled the trigger. He looked at the gun as he might a treacherous friend then tossed it aside, grabbing his makeshift sword.

Mary's mind itched as she looked at the discarded gun.

A shout snapped her attention back to the fight. Henry stabbed his skewer into the boar's ribs. It spun, yanking the pole out of his hands and sending him tumbling across the grass. He slammed into the fence and collapsed. The boar charged him.

Domin rose and stumbled between Henry and the boar. The creature flung Domin aside. Henry pulled himself to his feet. Jairus jabbed his iron pole into the boar's side. It roared and swung its tusks.

Cassandra started forward, but Amy grabbed her arm.

"You're the one they're trying to protect."

"Which is why I can't just sit here and watch them get hurt."

Mary crumpled back. How did it feel to be brave? The men stumbled to keep ahead of the raging boar. This time there was no magic elixir to heal their wounds, even if she could find the courage to bring it to them.

Jairus's gun lay ignored near the porch, one shot still trapped in the barrel. Its broken mechanism cried out to Mary like a music box stuck on a single note.

Amy held Cassandra back. "It's Domin that the Morrigan is after. You can't afford any more enemies among the Fay."

The Fay. The ones who had supposedly tossed Mary aside as worthless. She admired their boldness, but she didn't see much else to mourn in their loss. Her human mother and father had wanted her, though, and her father had taught her well.

Mary scurried down the stairs, unnoticed. She grabbed the broken gun and then jerked away, hands blistered by the iron in the steel. She grasped the wooden handle to pull the gun to the shelter of the porch steps. Reaching through the small slit in her skirts, she fished a few simple tools from her pocket. When she held them, all the shouting and scuffling faded away, leaving her alone with the broken mechanism.

She'd watched Jairus load the gun, so she knew how to remove the explosive percussion cap before she took the firing mechanism apart. The problem was simple. Just a bit of oil and dirt jamming the parts. It only took a moment to clean the clog. As she fit everything back into place, the mechanism hummed under her fingers, almost alive at her touch.

The fight jumped back into focus. Cassandra guarded Mary with the iron pole. The boar shoved Henry aside and twisted its head after Jairus. Gore dripped from the monster's wounds, leaving splotches of dead grass and bubbling mud in its wake.

Jairus slipped in the muck and fell, scrambling back as the beast bore down on him.

Mary jumped to her feet, clutching the gun. The dangerous power of the iron shot in its barrel soured her stomach. She tried to cock the hammer back with her thumb as Jairus had done, but it took her whole hand to click it into place. She pulled the trigger, anticipating the momentary delay before the gun boomed. It slammed into her shoulder, and she tumbled against the porch. She dropped the weapon to suck her blistered fingers.

The boar snorted and turned from Jairus to Mary. She scurried up the porch stairs. The American jumped up and jammed his iron pole deep into its leg.

"Miss Weaver!" He stretched out his hand, and she tossed him her pole. He slammed it into the boar's other knee. The creature crumpled.

Mary hid her face. The boar's angry squeals grated her ears.

"Watch out!" Amy cried.

Mary forced herself to look. Birds rose from the broken body, swirling together. Amy waited until the Morrigan was nearly solid then let an arrow fly through the figure. Bird-shaped wisps of smoke dissipated, and the rest of the crows scattered. Jairus wrenched one of the poles free from the boar to slash at them, leaving a trail of black mist in his wake. The rest of the Morrigan's birds scattered. As the flock fled, a woman's laugh drifted on the breeze.

Henry rushed to Domin. The shape-shifter, still in his panther form, bled from numerous gashes, some of which already festered with yellow ooze.

Cassandra limped onto the lawn, hand over her mouth, to where Henry bent over Domin. It seemed impossible that the shape-shifter was still breathing, but Mary saw the shallow rise and fall of his side. Henry used a small knife to pluck several pieces of iron from Domin's shoulder. As soon as he removed the last one, the shape-shifter's body shuddered and reformed into his human guise.

Henry tossed the shot aside and smiled weakly. "That wasn't so bad, was it?"

Domin gave Henry a humorless look and stalked back toward the house. Blood stained the shoulder of his coat, though Mary couldn't see an injury or even a tear in the fabric. As she watched, the stain shrank and disappeared. She shivered.

Domin paused next to the corpse of the boar, almost as tall as him. "Burn it."

Jairus struck a match from his bag and tossed it into the body. Henry gestured, bringing the flames up like a puppet master. Jairus shucked off his gore-stained duster and tossed it into the fire.

Mary gagged at the stink of burning hair and scooted back from the stinging heat. They watched the crackling bonfire in silence until only ash and fragments of charred bones littered the grass. Henry sank back, face pale. The rain began again, sizzling in the blackened mud.

Jairus wiped his forehead on his sleeve and jabbed his homemade sword into the ground. He picked up his gun and cocked an eyebrow at Mary.

"It won't jam anymore," she said, looking down.

"Thanks," Jairus said. "I didn't know you were familiar with guns."

"I'm not," she whispered, glancing up, "but they're like clocks. Just pieces that have to fit together right."

"I suppose." He smiled. "That was nice shooting."

Her heart bounded into her throat, and her cheeks burned. Even homely young men ignored her; a handsome one had certainly never smiled and complimented her before. He didn't even mention her failures; none of them had. Was this what it was like to have friends? She ducked her head and hurried after Cassandra into the sanctuary of the house.

Chapter Twenty-Two

Henry leaned heavily on the railing of the porch stairs as a wave of dizziness washed over him. He inhaled the sweet fragrance of the roses, hoping to chase away the stench of the boar and clear his pounding head.

"Mr. Stewart, your back is bleeding," Jairus said.

Henry found the ragged tear in his coat. He winced at the sting, and his fingers came away sticky and red.

Domin strode over. "Did this happen when the boar threw you, or did the bristles cut you?"

"I ..." A few images from the fight hung frozen in Henry's mind, but the rest blurred together. He swallowed. "I'm not sure."

The ladies had already retreated inside, so Henry pulled up his shirt. Stony silence filled the space behind him.

Henry's throat tightened. "If you can tell me what kind of poison was on the bristles, maybe I can—"

"All those scars," Jairus whispered. "The Fay did this?"

"Yes," Domin said.

Jairus rattled off a string of curses. Henry tried to look at his back.

"The wound is not poisoned," Domin said, taking a handkerchief from Henry to dab it clean. "It's only a scratch."

Henry eased his shirt down and wiped his fingers on the stained handkerchief.

"Who sent that monster after us?" Jairus asked.

"One of the Seelie Queens," Domin said. "Whichever is trying to kill the Weaver sisters before the Dark Lady can claim the child."

The American scratched his stubbled chin. "Do the queens ever work together?"

"Sometimes," Henry said. "The Seelie factions are generally at peace with each other, but they have different characteristics and goals, just like human nations."

"Which one does the Morrigan belong to?"

"She is one of the solitary Fay, independent of the queens," Domin said. "Her allegiances shift, but she is drawn to places where there is likely to be strife and bloodshed."

Jairus stared at the distant village with a haunted look. "I've seen enough bloodshed for a dozen lifetimes. We have to end this." He shifted his grip on his shotgun and then grinned. "Well, we drove off that Morrigan creature. We'll send the rest of them back into the fairy tales where they belong." He trotted up the porch stairs, whistling a battle anthem.

Henry shook his head, but he caught the thrill of the American's excitement. They *had* defeated the Morrigan, if just barely. Perhaps, together, they had a chance against the Faerie Queens as well. He could help save the Weaver child from the hell he had endured. The weight of his weariness lifted at the thought, and he followed Jairus inside.

In the drawing-room, Amy and Cassandra stood by a tea

tray laden with bread and cold meats, laughing over something Jairus said. Mary hovered close to them, a flush lending life to her pallid features.

Henry's heart jumped when Cassandra smiled at him. He washed up in the basin beside the food and joined the others.

"May I play your pianoforte, Miss Weaver?" Amy asked. "I think we need some music."

"Of course," Cassandra said.

Amy struck up a waltz. Jairus whooped and grabbed Mary, spinning her across the drawing-room. She tripped along, face crimson as he guided her through the steps.

The intriguing scent of soap, flowers, and gunpowder drifted to Henry. Cassandra stood nearby, smiling at the music. If Fitzhugh was right, and he could never be free from the Fay, it would be a mistake to let himself become too fond of her. But the Fay were held at bay for the moment, and she was here, close enough to touch.

He held out his hand. She glanced at him and hesitated.

He felt a stab of embarrassment and pulled his hand back, but Cassandra caught it and smiled. He took a deep breath and wrapped his arm around her waist, pulling her close and swinging her into the dance.

Her skin was soft and warm under his fingers, and her weak right hand curled tightly against his. He was suddenly quite glad his hands were occupied with the dance, or he might have given in to the temptation to caress her freckled cheeks, and he doubted she would welcome such a familiar gesture. Still, she grinned at him as they turned between the grand room's chairs and tables, and he found his gaze drifting to the soft, pink curve of her lips.

"I'm not sure there's much to celebrate, since you have yet to defeat your real opponents." Domin's gloomy pronouncement carried over the music, breaking Henry out of his reverie.

Amy played more loudly. Henry scowled at Domin, and Cassandra stumbled in his arms. He caught her back into the rhythm.

"He's right, isn't he?" she asked.

"We still have the Faerie Queens to deal with, but I don't see why we can't enjoy this moment," he said.

But Domin *was* right. Fitzhugh had been holding the Seelie Court's attacks off before, but now they were on their own. Their luck wouldn't hold forever. Between fighting the Seelie Fay and the Dark Lady, some of them would likely die, as Fitzhugh predicted.

Henry tightened his grip on Cassandra's waist, and she gave him a curious glance. They needed a truce with the Fay, but for that, they had to know which Seelie Queen was leading the attacks and how to make her listen. His injured back stung when he guided Cassandra through a turn, but the flare of pain gave him an idea.

The song ended, and Amy started another upbeat piece. Jairus and Mary stopped near the pianoforte, leaving Henry and Cassandra alone on the other side of the room.

He slid his hand to her elbow, keeping her close enough to whisper. "Don't act alarmed."

"Is there a reason I would be?" she asked, her smile tightening.

"I need you to distract Domin for me, just for a few minutes."

"Distract him? Why?"

"I'm going to do something he won't like. It's nothing bad —just a little risky—but it won't work if he's with me." Cassandra hesitated, and he squeezed her arm. "Trust me."

She fidgeted with the brooch on her dress and glanced at Domin. "How do I distract him? I mean, he always seems to know what's going on."

Henry grinned. Cassandra trusted him. He wouldn't let her down—or any of them. "He likes us to think that, but he's not omniscient. Just talk to him."

She turned away, mumbling, "Just talk to him? Goodness, about what?"

Cassandra poured a cup of tea from the lukewarm kettle, her thoughts swirling like the amber liquid in the delicate bone-white china. Cradling the smooth cup in her hands, she stared down the corridor where Henry had slipped away. Perhaps Domin should know he was planning something. But Henry had trusted her. She couldn't betray him.

Drawing a deep breath, she approached Domin, who stood keeping watch by the front window. He gave her a questioning look.

She offered the cup, forcing a bright smile. He took it with a nod and went back to staring outside.

"Don't you ever rest?" she blurted out.

He raised his eyebrows. "Of course."

"I mean, I know you're, um, not human, but you still eat, and I would guess you need to sleep too."

"I do. I am alive, after all." His lips twitched, and Cassandra wondered if he was laughing at her.

Jairus's foot paused from tapping to the beat of Amy's music. "You're not mortal, though, are you? It doesn't seem like you can be killed."

Domin set down the tea and folded his arms. "Were you planning on trying?"

Jairus laughed. "I ain't that crazy." He leaned forward in his chair, resting his elbows on his knees, and his expression grew serious. "It's just...I don't generally work with other people—I don't like the risk."

His words were heavy with sorrow. Cassandra sensed a story behind them, but even if The Rules didn't forbid her from asking, she wouldn't pry into his pain.

Domin's expression softened, and he nodded.

Jairus met his eyes. "If I'm going to work with allies, I'd like to know their strengths and weaknesses."

"My life is bound to Henry's," Domin said. "As long as he is alive, I will not die easily."

"Does that mean if Mr. Stewart dies, you do too?" Cassandra asked. Did Henry know Domin's life might hang in the balance while he went about his risky scheme? Domin studied her, and she felt as clear as glass.

"Henry is the last of his line. If he were to die without an heir or betray his heritage, I would have to find another branch of his family to serve, or I would become...vulnerable."

"That iron shot hurt you, though," Jairus said.

"Yes. Magic is a kind of energy, and iron interrupts its flow."

Jairus cocked an eyebrow. "But not silver?"

"Silver can reflect magical energy and throw off its balance. It works best against humans using a magic that's unnatural to them. If you're looking for new weapons, rowan wood absorbs magical energy. It's slower but effective."

"Good to know." Jairus rubbed his lightly stubbled chin. "So, can you change into anything you want?"

"Within reason," Domin said.

Jairus chuckled. "I'm not sure what that means when it comes to shape-shifting."

"I cannot significantly alter my size or take a form very different from my true nature. I have never tried to change myself into something inanimate because I'm uncertain if I would be able to shift back."

"You can look like anyone, though? I fought a skinwalker in Sante Fe—"

"I am not a skinwalker." Domin curled his lips back in disgust.

"I ain't saying you are," Jairus said quickly. "I'm just trying to understand how what I've seen fits into this larger world that you're a part of."

"You have encountered humans attempting to tap into deeper powers unnaturally, using blood that's not their own or invoking the help of malevolent spirits. But not all spirits are evil, and what you call magic—the ability to manipulate energies of the natural world—comes naturally to some beings and some bloodlines." He shrugged. "I can imitate anyone if I'm familiar with their appearance."

"But if you can look like anyone you want, why do you choose to look like—" Cassandra stopped as heat prickled over her face.

"Myself?" Domin finished for her.

"I—I'm sorry." She tripped over her apology in her rush to cover her thoughtless words. "I only meant... wouldn't it be easier not to be different?"

He waved her words away. "I can blend in if I have to, but this is who I am." After a moment he added, "And if you pretend to be something long enough, it's hard not to lose yourself in the pretense."

Amy faltered at the piano then resumed playing with more energy. Domin's gaze lingered on her.

"Are there many...beings who can change shape naturally?" Jairus asked.

Domin dragged his attention from Amy. "Many of the Fay can use glamours to disguise themselves, but only a handful can truly change form."

Cassandra's grip tightened on the hard wooden arm of the chair. "If there are Fay who can look like anyone, how do we know whom we can trust? I mean, that people are who they appear to be?"

"Most Fay are limited in the forms they can assume, such as the Morrigan, who can only turn into crows or possess a body killed in battle."

"Charming." Jairus grimaced.

"Indeed." Domin smiled a little. "Also, it's difficult to imitate someone's mannerisms, especially to those who know them well. I'm not even sure I could keep up appearances as Henry for very long." He glanced between them. "Another thing you should know is that shape-shifters cannot change their eyes. Watch."

He melted into Henry's form. The resemblance was almost perfect, though he didn't have Henry's mischievous grin, and his eyes were bright green instead of blue like Henry's. Cassandra leaned away.

"You have not known Henry all that long, but it would be fairly easy for you to tell that I am not he." Domin's serious tone sounded wrong in Henry's voice.

"That's eerie," Jairus said. "So, can you do his"—he waved his hands in imitation of Henry manipulating the weather—"too?"

"No, his abilities are tied to his blood, not his form. That's why the Fay have allowed him to live this long; he's the heir of a potentially powerful bloodline—too valuable for them to waste."

Cassandra frowned. Her weakness—something she couldn't help—made many people think less of her. But would it be any better to be valued for something outside of your control? Either way, as Domin suggested, they might lose who they really were—who they wanted to be—beneath the image others painted over them.

Music and conversation followed Henry out the back door and into the garden as he left the sanctuary of the house. He turned to stare up at the rain-freckled windows. What was it like, to know that some tiny corner of the world was a refuge where you could always seek shelter—a place that belonged to you and where you belonged? The private world of human homes was as strange to him as the Faerie realms would be to someone like Cassandra.

Cassandra. Warmth rolled through him as he thought of the feel of her in his arms as they danced. But he couldn't let that distract him now.

The spicy scent of damp herbs led him through the garden and orchard to the edge of the woods. Closing his eyes, he reached out to the land around him. He sensed the nearness of the stream and the direction and strength of the storm, as well as the slow change of the seasons from summer to autumn: energy moving through the land in a complicated web.

If he abandoned his restraint as Fitzhugh suggested and truly drew on the energies around him, he wondered just how much he could do: summon floods or fires, change the seasons, call down mountains to crush the Fay? He was not yet skilled enough to control it, though. The land and all of its people would suffer if he unleashed his temper. He would become even more of a monster than Queen Titania had tried to make him.

Searching deeper, Henry found the thin thread of magic that tied him to Elfland like a leash. He called out a name, sending it vibrating along the cords of magic.

"Queen Mab, Lady of the Mountains, I summon thee."

The wind caught the words and carried them off toward the distant mountains. He didn't know the queen's full name—few did—so she could ignore the summons if she wished. He paced, running his hand through his hair. Maybe it was a mistake to call her. She was one of the harshest of the Seelie queens. But that meant she was also the most likely to lead the attack against humans.

He glanced back at the house. He needed to do something to protect the people he had come to care about—to atone for past mistakes—but this might be rash, drawing Mab's attention to them and risking her wrath. Before he could decide if he should return, a figure emerged from the shadows of the trees.

She wasn't as tall as Henry remembered, but he had been much younger the last time he saw the Lady of the Mountains. Her hair cascaded down her back and over her shoulders in a waterfall of dark ringlets. Swirls of tiny blue and white glass beads adorned the hem of her white dress, catching the light like flecks of snow. Though the sky continued to drizzle, the rain did not touch her.

She stood as regal and unfeeling as the mountains she called home, making her look older than most Faerie ladies, though no lines marred her perfect, pale skin. Her eyes betrayed her weariness, however, and Henry repressed a grin. That kind of exhaustion only came to the Faerie Queens by expending a great deal of energy, such as summoning creatures to attack the human world.

"Henry Stewart." Queen Mab's lips turned up in a smile that was, perhaps, even a little sincere. "Does my sister know of your absence?" Her voice was deep and musical, like the wind sighing through high mountain caverns.

He took a deep breath. Queen Titania, Lady of the Woods, was his nominal master. He risked offending both queens by going to Mab for help, but Titania wouldn't bargain with him.

"Yes, Lady. She banished me."

"I did hear that she was wroth with you. You refused marriage to her daughter if rumor speaks true. The daughter is a comely little elf, but I think you acted well. You would be better matched with someone more powerful. Think of what you could become, in the right hands."

Henry gritted his teeth. He couldn't afford to lose his temper with Mab, especially now. "I wished to live among my own kind."

"I cannot imagine why. You belong more to our world than theirs." The elf queen frowned at the house across the orchard. "Why have you summoned me to this place?"

He drew a long breath. "I wish to make a bargain."

"Oh?" She arched her perfectly-shaped eyebrows. "Are you free to do so?"

"As far as I know."

"What manner of bargain do you seek? There are few things I can offer you that my sister cannot."

"I know. I wish for you to call off the attack on the Weavers."

"Weavers?" She tilted her head. "Why would I care about weavers?"

"Um, I meant the family whom you are threatening in

order to prevent the youngest daughter from being taken by the Dark Lady."

Her eyes narrowed. "They should be grateful that I would keep the child from her. You must understand that."

"They don't want to die."

"They have such short, meaningless lives. What can a few extra years matter?"

"If their lives are so short, all the more reason not to take those years from them," Henry hated the impersonal words that widened the chasm between himself and the human world.

"I will not risk letting the Dark Lady capture the child. One human life is a small price to pay to prevent her from gaining a vessel capable of great power." She sighed. "But I am merciful. I will allow the humans to choose which of them should die. Two of the girls are marred by illness. They might find it noble to sacrifice themselves for such a purpose. Or they could kill the child and be done with it."

Cold air stirred around Henry. Marred? Cassandra had her limp, but she was kind and brave—worth more than any of the Seelie Court. He clenched his fists until his knuckles ached, and the energy in the storm called to him.

He took a deep breath and forced his hands to relax. Attacking Mab wouldn't help Cassandra or her sisters, and argument wasn't likely to change the Faerie Queen's opinions. He spoke in slow, measured words. "I will stop the Dark Lady from getting the child if you leave the rest of the family in peace."

"Are you willing to kill the child before you let the Dark Lady take her?"

"No. I'll keep all of them alive and safe."

"Why should you care about them? What are they to you?"

"Nothing," Henry said, pushing aside thoughts of

Cassandra's gentle hand on his arm, or the life of manipulation and torture awaiting her baby sister if he couldn't protect her. He tried to reason like an elf. "But why destroy the child's potential if there's another way? She could prove useful in the future."

"I doubt it is worth the risk. With such a powerful tool at her command, the Dark Lady's strength would grow immeasurably, perhaps enough to start another war among the humans. We are still recovering from the French Revolution." Mab lifted her chin. "If you wish to be the child's protector, you will have to owe me something should you fail."

A heavy lump formed in his chest. A magical war could destroy the human world, and he knew what Mab would demand of him if it came. "What do you ask, Lady?"

Her smile chilled Henry. "Your servitude, to begin with. Your talents at my disposal, for seven years times ten, the length of a human life. After that, my sister may have you back, but I will need all the power you can muster to battle the Dark Lady if she has the seventh daughter of a seventh daughter in her thrall."

Henry's stomach twisted, though it was what he had expected. Everyone in the human world would suffer if the Dark Lady dragged the Fay into the war Mab feared. He couldn't allow that if he had any chance of stopping it. This truce between him and Queen Mab would halt the fighting and keep his friends alive long enough to stop the Dark Lady. It meant he couldn't afford to fail, for his own sake as well as the child's.

He cleared his throat. "You said, 'To begin with'?"

"You cannot think that you are worth as much as a seventh daughter. You are an oddity—a useful tool—but she could be molded into such a weapon as the Fay have rarely seen." She tilted her head. "I have heard rumor that you managed to fight your way free from Telesm's refuge. There are items there that interest me."

Henry blinked. Maybe he should have brought Domin along. But Domin wouldn't have let him bargain with a Faerie Queen. "We only escaped because we left everything behind. I can act as an agent to try to negotiate with Telesm."

"No. He is not reasonable. If not that, you will agree to marry whom I choose for you, and allow me to raise your children as my servants. Your bloodline may yet produce more powerful magic."

Henry's lips curled back. "No."

She frowned. "Would Domin come with you, if you joined my court?"

"I don't know. I don't command him."

"I fail to see the advantage this bargain has for me. It seems wisest to destroy the child's potential and any who stand in my way." She lifted her hand.

"At what cost?" Henry asked before she had time to act against him. "How many of your resources will you have to sacrifice, especially to kill Domin? You've already lost hell hounds, wyverns, a boar, and a pooka."

Mab's eyes widened. "What have you done to my pooka?"

"We forced her into a bargain. If you keep fighting, you might stop the Dark Lady from getting the child, but your forces will be so depleted that she will still have the advantage. Declare a truce with us and save your strength to fight her, adding our forces to yours and preserving the child's potential."

"A truce." She pursed her lips.

"Yes." Henry met her eyes.

"I will still demand your life as a surety. And if you fail, I will not treat you like some favored pet as my sister did."

His back twitched at remembered pain. "Very well."

"Strike the bargain, then." She folded her arms. "Let us see how well you have been taught."

He took a deep breath, choosing each word with care.

"The Lady of the Mountains, all of those under her dominion, and all of her allies in the Faerie courts will do no harm to any member of the Weaver household, nor will they enter the Weaver's property, or interact with any member of the Weaver household directly or indirectly from the time that this bargain is struck until after the Weaver's seventh daughter is christened. In return, I, Henry Stewart, guarantee the safety of the Weaver's seventh daughter from the Dark Lady and her allies until the child's christening, or—" he choked on the words, then spit them out in a rush, "I forfeit myself to serve in the court of the Lady of the Mountains for seventy years."

"Done." The elf smiled, and Henry gasped as the chain of Faerie power tightened around his heart, searing the bargain into his being.

As Queen Mab slipped back into the shadows, a shrill scream echoed from the house. Henry's skin turned cold. Perhaps he had not chosen his words carefully enough.

A discordant clang jerked Cassandra's attention to Amy. The elf hunched over the pianoforte, her head clutched in her hands. A visceral shriek tore from her throat and she tumbled to the floor. Her shuddering gasps filled the stunned silence.

Mary gaped and backed away. Cassandra and Jairus moved toward Amy, but Domin bounded to her in a burst of inhuman speed, not bothering to drop Henry's appearance. He knelt by the elf. She opened her mouth to scream again, but only a rasp escaped.

"I don't know what happened." Mary trembled. "Did I do something wrong again?"

"You could not have caused this," Domin said without taking his eyes from Amy's terrified gaze.

The elf reached out for Domin, tears spilling down her cheeks. Cassandra covered her mouth. She couldn't guess what was wrong with Amy, much less how to help her.

Domin hesitated then grabbed Amy's outstretched fingers, placing his other hand on her forehead. His face contorted, and he hissed in pain. A wave of agony slammed into Cassandra, knocking her breath away. Jairus stumbled back, grabbing his head, and Mary cried out.

"What's happening?" Jairus shouted.

Domin jerked away from the elf's touch, but his voice was gentle when he caught his breath again. "I'm sorry, Amy. It is too much pain for me to deflect, and I cannot counter it."

She mouthed the word "please." Her body shuddered and blood trickled from her nose.

Domin straightened his shoulders. "Sleep," he commanded, and Cassandra felt the push behind the word.

Amy's eyes rolled back and closed.

"What's going on?" Jairus asked.

"She's dying," Domin said, his voice tight. "Someone is tearing the magic from her body. It makes no sense. I don't know what to do."

Amy jerked and went rigid. Her breathing stopped. Cassandra choked back a sob.

Footsteps pounded down the corridor. Henry stopped short in the doorway. "Get her outside!"

"I cannot touch her," Domin said.

Jairus rolled Amy's stiff body into his arms. Cassandra opened the door so he could race onto the porch.

"Off of the property," Henry shouted. "Go to the lane."

Jairus jogged through the drizzling rain, holding the elf to his chest and ducking his head to shelter her. Cassandra hurried after him, but her boots slipped in the mud. Henry and Domin passed her, reaching Jairus as he lowered Amy onto the damp grass beside the road.

The elf's breathing returned to a deep, steady cadence. Pink seeped back into her waxy face as raindrops splashed against her skin, shimmering like splinters of broken glass.

Henry's hands moved restlessly, checking her pulse and lifting her eyelids to see the whites of her eyes. "Oh, Amy! I didn't think—I'm so sorry. Is she going to be all right?"

"I don't know," Domin said. "What did you do?"

Henry sat back on his heels and closed his eyes. "Please forgive me, Amy." He looked at Domin. "I banished her from the Weaver's property."

"What!"

"Not on purpose. I made a bargain."

"Henry..." Domin's eyes narrowed.

Henry stood and looked Domin in the eyes. "Can you please drop that guise?"

Domin blinked, then shifted back into his own form.

"Thank you." Henry pushed back his wet hair. "It was the only way to make them stop, and I was the only one she would bargain with."

"With whom did you bargain? We don't even know—"

"I realized it doesn't matter. When it comes to the Dark Lady, all of the other Fay are allies."

Domin's jaw tightened. "You did not—"

"No, I didn't go back to the Lady of the Woods," Henry

said, "I have no bargaining power with her. I summoned the Lady of the Mountains. I thought she was most likely to be behind these attacks, and I was right."

"What deal did you make?" Domin asked through clenched teeth.

"She called off the attacks on the Weavers, and in exchange, I promised that the Dark Lady would not get the child."

Domin wiped the rain from his face and rubbed his eyes. "What words did you use?"

Henry closed his eyes and recited his bargain so quickly that Cassandra didn't catch every word until he got to the end.

"... or I forfeit myself to serve in the court of the Lady of the Mountains for seventy years."

Cassandra muffled her gasp. Henry had put his life on the bargaining table to buy them a few days of peace. Perhaps to save her and her sisters. She wanted to throw her arms around him in gratitude, and at the same time shake him for taking such a risk.

The shape-shifter's green eyes turned hard, but before he could speak, Henry looked at Amy.

"I forgot that Amy might qualify as an ally of the Lady of the Mountains."

"You are extremely fortunate that neither you nor I apparently qualify," Domin said, "or then where would we have been? You should not have spoken to her alone."

"I knew you'd try to stop me." Henry looked at Cassandra. "Miss Weaver, please keep your distance from Amy. If she tries to speak to you—or even send you a message—at any point before the baby is christened, it will harm her."

Cassandra nodded and backed away. Poor Amy. She'd only been there because she wanted to help.

Jairus folded his arms. "We can't leave her lying in the road."

"She can stay at my house until she's better," Mary whispered. "I'll tell her what happened. And... I want to check on my father."

"That's not a bad idea," Jairus said. "And if the immediate threat to the Weavers is passed, I want to see what Rushford and the Grigori are doing *and* try to stop the Dark Lady's sacrifice."

His words tightened the discomfort around them like a noose. Cassandra had been so worried about her sisters that she'd forgotten Michaelmas was just two days away.

"We should look for Mr. Tanner and the vicar and check on the Ashbys," Henry said.

Domin nodded. "I can see what their situation is, but we still have to worry about the Dark Lady attacking here to gain control of the child."

"Then you should stay," Jairus said. "I'll scout out the village."

"You are needed here. Once the child is born, you have to christen her," Domin said.

Cassandra glanced between the men. She dreaded being left alone, but they had to stop the Dark Lady from kidnapping or killing anyone.

"I'll go," Henry said.

Domin shook his head. "You have made yourself more a target to the Fay than ever."

Henry scowled and opened his mouth to protest, but Jairus cut him off.

"For now y'all can protect the Weavers better than I can. I didn't stand much of a chance against the Morrigan on my own. I'll just check on the village and come back. I can't stand being cooped up, and I ain't going to let someone be sacrificed if I can stop it."

"The Dark Lady could use the infant's power to drag the

human world into chaos, but she will tear the village apart to get her sacrifice," Domin said, his expression turning thoughtful. "Very well. See what you can find out and return as quickly as possible."

Jairus nodded. "I understand. Miss Leland, if you'll show me the way, I can carry Lady St. Clair back to your home." He glanced at Henry and Domin. "I assume it's safe to move her?"

Henry nodded.

"Just let me get my things." Jairus ran back to the house and returned with his ammunition bag slung across his torso and his guns back in their holsters. Henry offered him the revolver he'd been carrying, but Jairus shook his head.

"You may need it. Magic can't solve every problem."

"Neither can bullets," Henry countered, but he slipped the gun back under his coat.

Jairus lifted Amy. Her head lolled back, spilling damp blonde curls over his arm. Cassandra restrained an impulse to try to make Amy more comfortable. She had to stay away from the elf. With a nod to the others, Jairus followed Mary down the road toward the village. Cassandra wondered how long it would be before she saw them again.

Chapter Twenty-Three

Fat drops of rain soaked Cassandra's dress. She limped for the shelter of the porch before looking down the lane after Jairus, Amy, and Mary. Clouds hung low over the village, reaching cold, misty tendrils to hide the houses below.

Cassandra shivered and ducked inside, retreating to the drawing-room, and Domin and Henry followed. Domin took up his station by the window, and Henry paced. Sharp tension radiated from their silence.

"I'm going to check on my mother and sisters," Cassandra mumbled.

As soon as she was out of the room, she heard Domin say to Henry, "How am I supposed to protect you when you sneak off to do something foolish?"

"I didn't ask to be protected." Henry's voice followed Cassandra down the corridor. "And I probably saved all of our lives!"

Cassandra hurried up the staircase and found her younger

sisters and Nancy just as before. In her mother's room, the wooden cradle with its white blanket waited for its tiny occupant. Would her sister ever have a chance to use it, or would the Fay snatch her away before she ever knew the comfort of being rocked and loved?

Mrs. Weaver cried out in her sleep, and Cassandra rushed to soothe her back into a fitful rest.

Cassandra returned to her room, where Sophie sat at the dressing table brushing her hair. Her sister's gaze was still dull, but at least she was doing something normal. Cassandra sat on the bed and wrapped her arms around a pillow, running her fingers over the soft ridges of its embroidered flowers.

"Oh, Sophie, I wish you were yourself. I would love someone to talk to." Her sister nodded, and she went on. "I'm afraid for Mother and the baby. Amy got hurt, and Mr. Stewart made a dangerous bargain. What if I let them down? Let all of you down?"

The sibilant whisper of the brush never paused, making it easy to imagine Sophie was slighting her. She rubbed her elbow where her sister's nails had cut her at the ball.

"Everyone tells me the Fay can't make you do things you don't want to. So those things you said about me at the ball... that I'm hopeless and awkward..." She hugged the pillow closer. "I guess you really must get tired of watching after me sometimes. But it's not like I asked you to do it. I can take care of myself, you know. Or, at least, I thought I could."

Cassandra glanced up to meet Sophie's eyes in the mirror. Something whisked past the doorway in the reflection.

Cassandra jerked around to stare at the empty corridor.

"Mr. Stewart!" She knocked the pile of pillows off the bed as she scrambled to her feet. Sophie gave her a blank stare and then went back to brushing her hair. Cassandra grabbed the little stork-shaped scissors on the dressing table and edged toward the door. "Mr. Stewart!"

Henry burst into the room, jolting to a stop when he took in the bed chamber. He reddened and stepped back, then his gaze fell on the ineffective weapon clutched in her hand. "What's wrong?"

"Has anyone else come upstairs?" The dryness in her mouth kept her voice to a whisper.

"No, of course not. Why?"

"I saw something in the mirror. Out in the corridor. Trying to sneak past. If everyone is enchanted, they wouldn't be sneaking, right?"

He nodded and put a hand on her arm. She leaned into his warm, steady touch as he called back down the stairs. "Domin! Can you come up here, please?"

There was no sound of footsteps, but Domin appeared in a few heartbeats. "What happened?"

"We may have an uninvited guest," Henry whispered.

"Who?"

"I don't know, but there was someone," Cassandra said. "They went down the corridor, toward the other bedrooms."

Henry nodded at her and pulled out Jairus's revolver, then he and Domin slipped down the corridor. Cassandra peered out behind them. The two men tiptoed from room to room. Soon, they had checked everywhere but the nursery.

Domin leaned his ear against the closed door then gestured Henry forward. Henry pointed the revolver up and swung the door open. Cassandra held her breath. Her sisters sat on the rug around Nancy, oblivious to Henry. He looked around and lowered the gun. After checking in the wardrobe and under the beds, he holstered the gun and turned back to Cassandra.

"There's no one here but the children and the nurse."

"I know I saw something," she said.

She checked the rooms just as the men had. Her mother slept, but Cassandra noticed horseshoe nails pushed into the foot of her bed. She touched the iron and frowned.

"Mr. Stewart?" she called and showed him the nails. "I don't think these were here before."

He rubbed the iron with his thumb. "A good deterrent against lesser Fay, though not enough to stop a more powerful one. Is your mother superstitious?"

"Not really."

"All right, this is strange. Let's keep searching."

Cassandra walked past the cradle again, and a chill ran up her spine. A pair of scissors lay open on the white blanket. "Mr. Stewart?"

He lifted the scissors. "Another remedy for protecting babies from being taken. They weren't here before?"

She shook her head, her stomach churning. Someone had been in her mother's room, and they had done it in the short time that Cassandra had been with Sophie. The shadows around the cradle seemed to deepen, hiding unseen enemies. Cassandra stayed close to Henry as he inspected the rest of the chamber.

They found nothing else odd in her mother's room, so they returned to the nursery. Nancy knitted mindlessly while the children looked halfheartedly at picture books, except Georgina, who daubed gray onto the ceiling, matching the sky outside. Cassandra squinted at the picture, and this time the figure in the mural stood out. It was the Dark Lady from Henry's book.

Cassandra clutched Henry's arm. His eyes widened as he recognized the image. He pulled her closer.

"What does it mean?" Cassandra whispered.

Henry shook his head and looked to Domin, who frowned. "Has she seen Henry's herbal?"

"Yes," Cassandra said, "before the ball."

"She is somehow connecting the enchantment with the Dark Lady. Was she born on a Sunday?"

"I don't know."

Domin nodded. "She is likely Sabbath born, and she is gifted. If such talent is common in your family, your youngest sister will have exceptional abilities. Perhaps she will be a seer."

Cassandra's sisters paid no attention to their conversation. For the moment, they seemed safe. Cassandra breathed out a sigh and loosened her grip on Henry's arm.

Then she noticed Nancy—how the nurse's hands trembled.

Domin followed Cassandra's gaze and stepped toward the nurse. Nancy dropped her knitting and bolted for the door. Henry grabbed her, twisting her bony arm behind her back. Nancy cried out but didn't struggle.

"Be careful!" Cassandra cried.

"She was pretending to be enchanted," Henry countered. "Do you realize what that means?"

"But she's been with our family since Sophie was born."

"The Dark Lady could have sent her to watch your mother, knowing her potential as a seventh daughter."

"I don't know any Dark Lady," Nancy protested.

Domin leaned closer, trying to look at her eyes. She shrank away, but he said, "I think she may be telling the truth, Henry." He bent to see her face. "Miss ..."

"Mrs. Page," Nancy whispered after a long pause.

"Mrs. Page, what do you know about Fay?"

The nurse kept her eyes fastened on the floor. "Nothing. Just stories I tell the children."

"Mrs. Page, this is important," Domin said. "We are not

going to hurt you or the children, but we cannot protect this household if you don't tell us what you know."

Nancy looked at Cassandra with wide eyes. Cassandra's heart ached. Nancy had taught her and her sisters to read their first words, cleaned and kissed their scraped knees, and soothed their tempers when they fought. She stepped forward to touch the old woman's arm, and Henry loosened his grip.

"Nancy, you're part of our family," she said, "I don't believe you'd hurt us, but you have to tell us what you're hiding."

The nurse's wrinkled face sagged, and she looked down at the floor, her eyes troubled. "Very well, Miss Cassandra." Nancy took a deep breath. "I've seen the Fay before. After my husband and son died, I became a midwife and got a pretty good reputation. One night this woman came to my door. Oh, she was beautiful. Too beautiful and cold to be human. She wanted me to deliver a baby. She gave me something to put in my eyes and everything looked different. Sharper. Brighter. I delivered the baby, and then she said ..." A tear spilled down her cheek. "She said if I ever told anyone she would put out my eyes."

"That will not happen. She'll never know you told us," Domin said gently.

"But you look like them, all bright and lovely. Aren't you one of them?"

Cassandra stared at Domin. He was handsome, in a stern sort of way, but clearly, Nancy saw things Cassandra couldn't.

"Not exactly," Domin said. He met Cassandra's curious gaze. "One of the elves used a Faerie ointment on her eyes. It allows her to see things most people cannot: glimmers of magic. It also allows her to see through enchantments and glamours and avoid being snared by them. Elves must do this for human midwives when they need their services, but the elves resent it because it makes the midwife resistant to their powers."

"But, Nancy, why did you pretend?" Cassandra asked.

"I'm sorry, Miss Cassandra. I was scared. Ever since we came to this place, things have been wrong. I thought I could protect the children and the mistress better if no one knew I was awake. I've been doing what I can to keep the elves away from them."

"And that was you sneaking past my room?"

Nancy nodded.

"You put those nails and the scissors in Mother's room and the salt in front of the window. You were spying on me?"

"I knew you were awake too," Nancy whispered, "but I didn't know why. Then there were elves in the house, and it was you who invited them. And all that fighting." Her eyes were dry now, but her shoulders still slumped.

"She's telling the truth, Henry. You can let her go," Domin said.

Henry released her.

She rubbed her arm, and her voice trembled. "I've seen the Fay one other time. When the children were sick with the fever, an elf lady came to me. She told me how to help them. I'm not sure they would have survived if it wasn't for that, especially Miss Cassandra and Miss Georgina."

Cassandra furrowed her brow. "You're saying the Fay were watching us? They helped us?"

The nurse nodded. Cassandra remembered Nancy's hands, with their parchment-thin skin, reaching through feverish nightmares to cool her forehead and feed her herbal broths and elderberry syrup. Cassandra grimaced, her recollections warped by the thought of foul magical concoctions disguised beneath the vinegar smell of Nancy's medicines.

"What does this mean?" Cassandra asked.

Domin frowned. "It means the Dark Lady, and possibly

other of the Faerie Queens, knew about your sister's potential and guided your family's destinies."

"Guided our destinies?" Cassandra shivered.

"They have played a role in your lives," Domin said, "manipulating events to transpire in the way they wished."

Cassandra narrowed her eyes. "What kinds of events?"

Domin shrugged. "They may have guided your father's business fortunes, even nudged him toward moving you to Drixton."

"But not more personal things such as... as Sophie being jilted?"

"It's possible," Domin said quietly. "They do not leave things to chance."

Cassandra gaped at him. Was everything she understood about her life just an illusion, an act scripted by some malevolent Faerie playwright? She clenched her fists. "That's not fair! Why do they think they can play with people's lives?"

Henry's eyes were full of sympathy, but he didn't offer an answer. She wrapped her arms around herself and glared at the floor.

"It's good that you're not enchanted, Mrs. Page," Henry said when the silence became too heavy. "You can help deliver the baby."

Nancy nodded. "I've been checking the mistress, and her time is getting close."

Cassandra took a shaky breath. It would all be over soon. "I guess I should ..." She swallowed. "I should put the house back in order, then." There would be no getting back to normal, though. Normal didn't exist anymore... if it ever had.

"We'll help," Henry said, "if Mrs. Page will keep an eye on your mother."

Nancy nodded, and Henry and Domin accompanied Cassandra downstairs. She stood in the doorway of the drawing-room and stared blankly at the mess: rugs pushed aside, dirt tracked over the floors, used dishes scattered on the tables, and an overturned chair near the window. Domin stacked the teacups into a leaning tower and carried them down to the kitchen. Cassandra glanced at the shadows stretching across the grass and yanked the draperies shut.

Henry shoved a fallen cushion back into place. "Miss Weaver? I'm sorry about...well, what your nurse said."

"I wish the Fay would just leave us alone." She clattered used plates into a stack, resisting the urge to throw them and watch the shattered pieces fly across the floor. Setting the plates aside, she sank onto the sofa and lowered her head into her hands. The rain played a staccato rhythm against the house. Henry touched her arm, and she gave a start.

He jerked his hand away and settled on the sofa an arm's length from her. "I suppose I should know what to say, but I don't."

Cassandra sighed. "Georgie and I may be alive because of them. I should probably be grateful, but I hate them."

"I know." Henry's voice dropped. "All my siblings died young. I'd be dead too if the Fay hadn't taken me. But they ripped me from one life and didn't really give me another. Domin tells me if I hate them, I'll never find myself. I'll never have peace. He says the best revenge is to make the most of the life I have. I guess it makes sense, but it's not as easy as it sounds."

"No, it's not." Cassandra fidgeted with the brooch on her dress. "We're only human, after all."

Henry smiled wryly. "That's nice to hear you say. I'm not

always sure how much of me is still human. But I do feel happier in this world than in theirs."

"And you risked going back there to help us. I mean...thank you."

He shrugged. "I'm glad I was able to do something."

"It's not the only thing you've done. At least you know how to face them. I feel completely lost." She bit her lip. "Why did you give me that book?"

"Book? Do you mean the herbal? I thought if I tried to tell you what was going on, you'd think I was insane. But if you figured it out for yourself, or even just went along with the superstitions, you could keep yourself and your family safe. I didn't want to get you involved, but I had to do something about Fitzhugh." He hesitated. "And I thought you might be homesick and need something to distract you."

"Oh." She sighed. "You were right. I mean, I don't think I would have believed you if you had just told me. And I have been homesick, so it was kind of you to think of me. Not to say that you were thinking of me—" She shook her head. "I'm sorry. I'm rambling."

"Don't be sorry." He smiled and leaned closer. "It's refreshing after listening to the Fay talk circles around the truth. You're handling all of this better than I would have expected from anyone. You haven't fainted once."

He flashed her a teasing grin, and she laughed.

"I'm surprised myself," she said. "Maybe I'll faint later when it's all over." She paused a moment and traced designs onto the crisp velvet of the sofa. "Parts of it have even been rather exciting. I shouldn't admit that, though. I'll get a reputation for being bold."

"An elf would take that as a compliment, but you say it like it's a bad thing."

"Well, it's not very ladylike, and since my family's social position is not well established, it might reflect badly on us...to say nothing of shooting my father's gun on the front lawn or any of the dozen or so other things I've done wrong over the past couple of days." She buried her face in her hands.

"I still don't understand how human society works sometimes," Henry said. "Domin's tried to teach me, but you may have noticed that social grace isn't one of his strong points." She smiled at the understatement, and Henry continued, "It seems to me, though, that you've done exactly what you needed to under the circumstances." His voice dropped. "And you may have to do it again, now that you've gotten involved in their world."

Cassandra huddled against the sofa, but the back was stiff and upright, offering her no comfort. She edged closer to Henry instead. "Are there many Fay around?"

"Not the powerful ones, but minor Faerie creatures sometimes turn up in out-of-the-way corners like Drixton. I think all the steel and railroads are making them desperate for some unpoisoned place. That's part of the reason I chose to live here. The Faerie Queens don't notice my magic with the traces of minor Fay coming and going through the old woods."

She thought that over, along with what Domin had said about the Fay guiding her family to Drixton. "Mr. Stewart, may I ask you...I don't know if all of this is too uncomfortable to talk about." She was certain it was against The Rules, anyway.

He shrugged. "I think you have the right to answers. I'll provide them if I can. What do you want to know?"

"Mr. Fitzhugh hurt you with magic. Can the Fay do that to anyone?"

"No. That, at least, you're spared from, as long as you don't put yourself in their power. Lesser Faerie creatures can use elf-shot to attack a person directly with their magic, but it drains them or even kills them if they use too much. Fitzhugh was using my magic against me. Only the most powerful elves have enough command of magic to weave it together with a human's natural energies and talents. It gives the person their own sort of magic, but it lets the elves control them too."

"You must hate having magic if it ties you to them," she said quietly. He pulled back, but she grabbed his arm. "I'm sorry. I didn't mean to offend you. I was just trying to understand."

Henry stared at her hand. Cassandra blushed but didn't release her grip. His gaze found hers, his blue eyes warm and intense, drawing her in.

"I don't hate my magic. Maybe I should, and I hate the way it keeps me away from everyone else and forces me to lie. But it's amazing to feel all the life and energy around me. It's as if ..." He glanced down. "I've never tried to explain this to anyone before. Um, do you like music?"

She nodded, and he leaned his head back. "Magic—my magic, anyway—makes everything seem like a symphony. There's all this energy around us, and it all comes together to form something bigger than the individual parts." He looked at his hands. "And I can touch it. It's like being able to catch the melody from a violin and direct it higher or faster."

"That's...beautiful," she said.

"Yes. I guess for everything the elves took away, I should be grateful I got something in return." He touched her hand. "I'm glad they didn't let you die, when you were sick."

Cassandra's skin tingled as his fingers brushed hers. She cleared her throat. "So am I. But I still hate the feeling that I owe them something. Why *do* they bother with us?"

He sighed. "To some extent, they need us. Not just as slaves to entertain them and do their work. The Seelie Faerie gain most of their power from the natural energy in the world, and humans are part of the cycles of life and death that feed them. The Dark Lady learned long ago how to become even more powerful by drawing solely on negative emotions." His fingers pressed hers. "But I think they're jealous of us, too. They're always comfortable and entertained, but they're so busy manipulating each other that they know little of human traits like love and kindness."

Cassandra frowned. "Humans aren't always kind."

"I know. But they...*we* have a capacity for feeling that I think most Fay have lost. I suppose, living so long, they become numb to it. One of the reasons they love human singers and artists is that the Fay—the pure-blooded Fay like the Queens—can only imitate, not create. They can't even have children unless they take a human consort, and even then the child is often sickly."

Cassandra's face warmed at his frank talk of consorts. Henry reddened in return and chuckled. "I shouldn't say such things to a lady, should I? I'm sorry to make you uncomfortable."

"Well, their rules are much different than ours—uh, mine. Not that you're not... I mean..." She shook her head at her own discomfort. "I mean, I'm glad you're willing to tell me."

"I'm glad you're willing to listen."

He smiled, and his gaze traced her face, resting for a moment on her lips. The warmth in her cheeks spread down her neck, and her pulse quickened.

A creak in the corridor made them jump apart. Cassandra darted to her feet as Domin came in, his hands still damp with dishwater. He picked up the plates Cassandra had stacked, then glanced out the window and frowned.

"What's the matter?" Henry asked.

"Mr. Hale should be back by now, and dark creatures are gathering outside."

The flush Cassandra had felt at Henry's closeness quickly turned cold, and she backed away from the windows, grateful that she couldn't see the monsters prowling in the darkness.

Chapter Twenty-Four

Jairus paused in the steady drizzle. He had scouted the back roads of the village, but all was unnaturally still. The streets of Drixton were deserted, but the stone shops hedged him in. Something was watching, stalking him. He could feel it like a prickle between his shoulder blades the whole time he was walking.

He strolled back to the Leland's shop, glanced over his shoulder, then darted inside. The ticking of clocks sounded like hundreds of guns being cocked. He shut his eyes and saw the battlefield, smelled the gunsmoke and blood, heard the screams of dying comrades.

He grasped his revolver in its holster and opened his eyes, searching for an anchor to keep him from drifting into memories. He took in the two doors plus the windows—four exits if they were attacked. Plenty of cover behind the work benches. Then he spotted a row of pocket watches on a table, worth enough to get him through quite a few poker games.

A strong gust battered rain against the windows, and he flinched.

"Mr. Hale?" Mary's voice reached him like a lifeline. His hands relaxed. The clocks ticked gently now behind the patter of the rain. The present had enough monsters; no need for those from the past.

"Yeah, it's me," he said, wiping the sweat-salted rain from his face. He wove his way to the back. Mary sat by Amy, who still lay unconscious on the narrow bed where he'd left her.

"Did you find anything?"

"Nothing." The Queen's Head inn had been quiet. No sign of Mr. Rushford and his Grigori. No sign of the apothecary, Mr. Tanner, anywhere in the village. Jairus had found the vicar babbling a half-formed sermon to the empty church. The man had called Jairus a demon and chased him down the aisle, swinging the Bible like a hammer, but Jairus counted that as normal for a person only half under a Faerie enchantment. He turned his attention back to Mary.

"How's your father?"

"Resting," Mary said. She looked back at Amy. "Is she going to be all right?"

"Mr. Stewart said she would be, and I guess he knows what he's talking about."

Mary didn't answer, and Jairus remembered that Henry wasn't exactly friendly to her. Well, Henry had his own crosses to bear. They all did.

Jairus cleared his throat. "It's kind of you to take care of Lady St. Clair."

She shrugged. "I'm glad to help a... a friend. I wish I could do something for those poor babies."

"Babies?" Jairus asked.

"Miss Weaver's sister and the one they want to trade her

with. That's what they do, isn't it? Leave behind the one they don't want."

"Oh, I suppose it is." Jairus had almost forgotten there were two children at stake in the Dark Lady's plan. A Fay child would be abandoned, possibly to die in the human world, apparently forgotten by everyone. Like Mary. "You have been a help, you know. You fixed my gun. You weren't a bad shot with it either."

"I like fixing things. It just...feels right to me."

"That's an impressive talent."

"It's not very brave," Mary said with a wistful glance at Amy.

"Fighting isn't the only way to be brave. In the war, I knew women who smuggled documents and medicine under their skirts since none of the soldiers dared search them. They never touched a weapon, and they saved lives." Amy stirred, and Jairus said, "We'd better let her rest."

"No, wait," Amy said, eyes springing open. She struggled to sit up.

He grabbed her arm to steady her. "Careful there."

"Where am I? What happened?"

"You're at Miss Leland's house. Mr. Stewart made a bargain with someone called the Lady of the Mountains to keep all her allies away from the Weaver home."

Amy's eyes widened. "Including me."

"He seemed real sorry about what happened to you."

"Hmph," Amy said. "But what could he offer her in exchange for a truce?"

"Himself, if we fail."

Amy fell back against the lumpy mattress. "Oh, Henry, you fool, what have you done?" She glanced at Jairus. "And what are we doing now?"

"Well, *you're* resting. I did a quick reconnaissance around the village, and as far as I can tell, everyone still here is enchanted. Rushford and the apothecary, Mr. Tanner, are unaccounted for, though, so they might have something to do with the Dark Lady. And I still need to go to Ashby Hall and see if the Ashbys are affected."

"I'm coming too," Amy said.

"You've had a rough day."

"And the best way to put it behind me is by doing something. Come, Miss Leland."

Mary looked at Jairus in panic.

"Now, wait," he said to Amy, "I was just going to take a look around the place. The more people there are, the harder it'll be to go unnoticed, and I work better alone." He paused. "It may be dangerous, and I don't want to be distracted by worrying about y'all."

"You forget that I am Fay," Amy said. "I can make certain no one sees us. And Domin said we should keep an eye on each other."

"Look, this is no picnic. God talks to *me*, so it's my job, and I'm doing it alone."

"You think you're expected to do everything on your own? Or is it that you still don't trust me?" Amy's eyes flashed with anger.

"No one else is going to die because of me!"

Jairus's voice reverberated in the tiny room. Mary flinched away from him, and Amy's eyes filled with tears.

"I'm sorry." Jairus rubbed the scruff on his chin. "I didn't mean to shout at you."

"It's not that," Amy said quietly. "I'm not as attuned as Domin, but when I'm this close to raw emotion, it hurts.

Please, I want to help. Wouldn't we be safer if we stayed together?"

Jairus hesitated. There might be something to what she said, but this was the first time he'd fought alongside the sort of creatures he usually hunted.

It was more than that, though. In America, everything he hunted had been a mindless monster to begin with or a person so depraved by the darkness they'd lost their humanity. The Fay were different. Domin claimed their abilities were natural and not inherently evil. Some were cruel and calculating, but others were compassionate and brave. Most seemed to be a mix of both. Pretty much like humans. Now the easy battlelines and easy targets were gone.

"Maybe," Jairus said, "but why not let Miss Leland stay here with her father?"

"We need to stay together, watch out for one another. Besides, I couldn't possibly travel alone with a man I'm not related to. It would be entirely improper."

Jairus stared, not sure if she was joking. A familiar voice in the back of his thoughts whispered reassurance, and he blew out his breath. "Try not to slow me down."

"Hmph," Amy said as she eased to her feet. She wobbled for a moment, holding her hands out to steady herself, then straightened. "I'm ready. Are you, Miss Leland?"

Mary looked like Amy had just offered to yank out her teeth, but she nodded and ran into the shop, scrambling to throw some tools into a satchel. Jairus shook his head. He'd long ago given up on trying to figure out the way women thought.

He led them outside, and they trekked up the muddy lane out of the village. Before they got within sight of Ashby Hall, he paused to peer into the woods. He wanted to approach the estate under cover, but whatever lurked in the trees might be worse than what waited at the house.

"If we're to cross through the woods, let me take the lead," Amy said.

"You?"

"Yes. I don't sense anything particularly dangerous nearby, and most Faerie creatures respect elves. They won't trifle with me, for my mother's sake, if not my own."

"Your mother?"

"The Lady of the Woods. She's unhappy with me, but I'm still protected as part of her court, at least from other Seelie Faerie."

"The Lady..." Jairus blinked. "Your mother is one of the Seelie Queens?"

"Yes, though my father had human blood. Mother says that's why my magic is too weak and my emotions are too strong. I'm a disappointment you, see." She glanced down. "I know this doesn't give you any more reason to trust me, but I'm trying to help. To not be a disappointment anymore."

Amy set off without waiting for a response, never hesitating as she wound her way through the deer paths and coppices. Jairus and Mary followed. He caught glimpses of things trailing them, dodging through deep shade and undergrowth, but Amy paid no heed, so he didn't either. Mary clung so closely to him, though, he was afraid she'd trip him up.

Finally, the woods gave way to a manicured lawn sweeping up to the Ashby's manor house. Jairus motioned for the women to duck into the shadows of the trees. The house's many windows winked in the shifting light of the late afternoon sun piercing the clouds. A line of carriages and wagons stood outside the front doors, and men—too well-dressed to be servants—moved back and forth, loading them with crates and boxes.

"What do you make of that?" Jairus whispered.

"I'd say something is afoot," Amy said.

"We need to move closer. We can hide behind that sort of ridge over there."

"Haha," Amy said.

"What?" Jairus stared at her.

"It's called a haha wall."

"Well, I call it cover." Jairus watched for a break in the revolving movement of people from the house. "Let's go!"

They darted for the grassy ridge and huddled behind the low wall.

Amy plucked stray bits of wet grass from her purple dress. "Now, if I'm still a welcome guest here and all this sneaking turns out to be for nothing, won't you feel silly?"

"Shh. I'm pretty sure Mr. Fitzhugh made sure we wouldn't be welcome."

"Someone's coming," Mary whispered.

Heavy footsteps approached their hiding place. Jairus pressed his back against the wall and caressed the smooth hammer of his revolver with his thumb.

Amy frowned and shook her head at Jairus. The footsteps paused. Jairus tensed. After a moment, the man grunted and meandered back toward the house. Mary exhaled, and Amy smiled.

"Did you do something?" Jairus whispered.

Amy nodded. "I cast a glamour to make him think that we were sheep."

"Sheep?"

"Yes. He finds them peaceful. Bucolic. I don't care for sheep, myself. Humans are so odd."

Jairus looked around to make sure no one else was approaching and leaned closer. He could never resist getting a peek at his opponent's hand. "Is that what Mr. Fitzhugh did when he stirred up that mob in the village?"

Amy nodded. "Darker emotions are easier to manipulate: fear, confusion, anger. Almost everyone feels some of those on a regular basis, so it's fairly easy to give them a focus, especially against someone like Domin whom people are a little afraid of anyway."

Jairus's mind drifted to cramped slave quarters, battlefields littered with broken bodies, and burned-out farms. "I can believe it. I've seen plenty of people do that without magic. But you can't do that to me? Or to Miss Leland?"

Amy shook her head and smiled at Mary. "Miss Leland is an elf too, so she has her own magic, even if her ties to the Fay have been cut off. That magic is... distracting. Hard for even the most powerful elves to work around." She looked back at Jairus. "Sometimes I can get a sense of your emotions, but they feel vague. Your devotion to your cause makes your mind hard to reach." She paused. "But you carry a heavy pain. You lost someone?"

He glanced up quickly. For someone who couldn't read minds, she was awfully close to the truth. He stared into the distance. "My nephew. He thought I was some kind of hero and wanted to help me hunt monsters. I was too wrapped up in a card game to pay attention when he told me there was trouble. He died alone facing down a wendigo. All I could do was bury him and tell my sister what happened to her boy."

He looked at the ground, feeling the stares of the women in the awkward silence. He would never, ever have to bury an innocent child again, not if there was anything he could do to stop it. And he wasn't going to let the Faerie take them, either.

If he could save the Weaver child, maybe it would make up, a little, for failing his nephew. "Can you tell us anything about what's going on in the house?"

"It's far away, but I can try," Amy said quietly. She closed her eyes, but they flicked back and forth behind their lids. She clutched her head. "There's so much darkness. With the enchantment hanging over everything, it's hard to get a clear picture, but it feels...inky. Thick. Black. It leaves a bad taste in my mouth, like metal. I don't know what that means, except that the Dark Lady's influence is here too. At least some of the people are enchanted, which should work in our favor."

"Is Fitzhugh nearby?"

"With all the magic floating around, I can't tell."

Jairus sat back with a sigh. He wanted to just walk in and deal with whatever happened. In some ways, it made sense. They didn't know that Fitzhugh was there. He might be waiting for their downfall elsewhere. They didn't even know if Sir Walter Ashby was still in the house, or if he was free, or enchanted, or being held as a prisoner. Jairus wrapped his fingers around the hilt of his gun. No, he couldn't afford to be reckless.

"Whatever you decide, Mr. Hale, we're with you," Amy said, and Mary nodded.

"All right." Jairus let their courage guide his decision. "Let's go."

Chapter Twenty-Five

Jairus watched the activity in front of Ashby Hall.

"It looks like they're focused on loading the wagons," he said. "We're going to take advantage to sneak in. Our main goal is to find out if the Ashbys are unharmed and whether or not they're under Fitzhugh's sway." He hesitated, listening to the worrisome warning prickling in the back of his mind. "We also need to find out what those men are doing with all those boxes. I have a feeling it's connected to the Dark Lady's plans."

Amy and Mary followed him, creeping behind the ridge, away from the front windows. Clinging to the scattered stands of trees and shrubbery punctuating the rolling green lawn, they reached the wall surrounding the kitchen garden. Jairus paused to scout out the landscape then pointed to the stables.

"If anything goes wrong, we meet back there. It'll make for an easy escape."

The women nodded, and they slipped into the gardens. Their boots crunched on the gravel-lined path, and Jairus winced. He tiptoed to the kitchen door. It creaked open into the cavernous kitchen, its massive black stoves and well-worn tables at rest for the evening.

Amy stepped up behind him and whispered. "The Ashbys' invitation to me as their guest still stands—the magic isn't preventing me from entering."

"Is it possible to rescind an invitation to a Fay?"

"Yes, but they either aren't thinking of it or don't see me as a threat."

Jairus nodded. That seemed to bode well for the Ashbys.

A maid came out of a pantry and walked across the kitchen without a glance at them. Jairus had been counting on the household being enchanted, but it still gave him goose bumps. At the far end of the kitchen, he peeked into the hallway to make sure it was clear then led them up a short staircase and through several doors into the main part of the house. Voices and laughter spilled from the study, and he motioned for the women to move quickly.

They hurried around a corner and crashed into Elizabeth Ashby. Mary scurried back around the bend, leaving Amy and Jairus to face Elizabeth. The girl took in Amy's disheveled dress and Jairus's coatless attire, with shirtsleeves rolled up to hide the tattered ends, and she wrinkled her nose.

"Well, I guess now we know why you've been so difficult to find, Lady St. Clair. You could at least pretend to be ladylike, though, as long as you're our guest."

Jairus almost laughed, but Amy's cheeks turned crimson, and he caught himself. A spoiled reputation was nearly a death sentence for a woman of her social standing.

Elizabeth turned and flounced away.

"Miss Ashby!" Amy hissed.

Elizabeth paused. "Yes?"

Amy's gaze darted around, as though searching for help.

She lifted her chin. "How is my cousin? You've been seeing quite a bit of him, haven't you?"

Elizabeth flipped her dark curls over her shoulder. "Mr. Fitzhugh can hardly bear to be apart from me."

Amy smiled thinly. "You know, some men take it amiss when people spread uncomplimentary tales about their relations. Just something to consider the next time my name comes up."

Elizabeth nodded, and her eyes took on the vague look Jairus had come to recognize in people influenced by the Fay. He was careful not to look at Amy, not wanting his discomfort to show.

Robert Ashby appeared at the end of the hallway.

"Elizabeth, Mother was—" The fair-haired young man noticed Amy and Jairus and gave a start. "Oh, uh, Lady St. Clair. We thought you'd left."

Amy tilted her head. "Where would I have gone, Mr. Ashby? I'm your guest."

"I...uh." Robert swallowed and adjusted his sleeves. "Sorry. What? Never mind. Elizabeth, Mother is looking for you." He grabbed his dazed sister and dragged her away.

"I'm sorry." Amy sighed. "That should have gone better. He was so surprised to see us, I pushed it into confusion and disbelief, but I couldn't make it hold very well. I'm afraid we don't have long until our names reach unfriendly ears."

"They're not under the Dark Lady's enchantment," Jairus said, "so either of them could be the sacrifice?"

"Possibly. Fitzhugh is toying with Elizabeth Ashby's mind. He has been since the ball, and probably before. She's not normally so nasty—or at least, she doesn't let it show. I don't know if that means the Dark Lady isn't interested in her, but Robert Ashby could be in danger."

Jairus pressed his lips together. "We'll make the most of the time you earned us, then."

He guided them to a lesser-used wing of the house. They tried several doors and found dusty, unaired rooms with covered furniture. In one, Mary bumped into a vase and sent it crashing to the floor. They hurried away. Finally, they came to a locked door. Jairus listened at the thick wood but heard nothing.

"What do you suppose is worth hiding in here?" He rattled the lock, wondering if he could break the door without attracting too much attention.

Mary put a light hand on his arm and pulled him back. She knelt in front of the door, skirts heaped awkwardly around her, and pulled something out of her satchel. She fiddled with the knob until it clicked. The door whispered open.

Jairus gave Mary an appreciative nod and then slipped inside, revolver in hand. He let his eyes adjust to the dim room then motioned the women in and locked the door behind them.

The grand room had been stripped of furniture, and heavy curtains blocked the window. Crates with the broken figure-eight symbol lined the walls. Jairus wrinkled his nose at the peculiar chemical smell and slowly moved closer to a hulking mass, draped with white sheets, brooding in the center of the room. The odd, lumpy shape stood as tall as a person and just as wide.

Jairus lifted one of the sheets. Metal glinted in the dim light, and he relaxed. He'd half expected the thing to be alive. The women met his gaze with wide eyes.

"What is it?" Amy whispered, as though afraid she would wake it.

"Hate," Mary said. "It was made to hurt."

"You can tell that?" Jairus asked.

Mary nodded.

"I can too," Amy said. "I thought it was my imagination, but it's like they left traces of their feelings when they made it."

"They always do," Mary said, "just not so strongly."

Jairus stepped back. "So, is it magic?"

"I don't think so," Amy said. "But perhaps an elf or someone else with strong magic helped build it."

Jairus shook his head. "All right," he said. "Then what does it do? Is it a weapon?"

He pulled off the rest of the sheets and stood back. It was a wooden chair with leather restraints. Jairus grimaced. He circled around, examining the needles, wires, and metal plates attached to the chair. Some of them were hinged so they could move. He stopped when he saw something he recognized. Amy was just reaching to touch one of the metal plates.

"Wait!" he shouted, forgetting to be quiet.

"What?" Amy jerked her hand back.

"I've seen these before, in telegraph stations." Jairus pointed at a dozen copper cylinders, each containing a clay pot and a mix of chemicals. "They produce electricity."

"What?" Amy repeated.

"Electricity. Energy. They use them to power the telegraphs. I don't see anywhere for the electricity to go except into those wires and plates."

"What does it do, then?" Amy stepped back.

Jairus's stomach turned. "The only thing I can figure is that it's meant to pump electricity into the person in the chair."

"I would guess from those straps that the person would not be a willing participant."

"Not that I would imagine."

"Would it kill them?" Amy asked.

"I don't know if the shock would be that strong, but it would hurt." It could be a form of torture—entertainment for a sick mind, perhaps—but Jairus suspected the chair was intended to do more than that.

They fanned out to examine the crates. Jairus found several filled with glass jars and vials.

"Mr. Hale, I think you should look at this," Amy whispered, her voice tight.

She handed Jairus a leather-bound book. He blinked a few times to make sure he was seeing correctly. The neat ink drawings showed a hell hound in various stages of dissection.

"This is why Rushford wanted the hound alive," Jairus said. "The Grigori are studying magic. Maybe learning how it works."

He almost admired their ingenuity, until he remembered the chair. It was built for a human. Or, perhaps, for an elf. He flipped through the book's stiff pages, stopping when he came to a page showing the same design etched on the crates: the serpent in a figure eight. He studied the cramped writing.

"Does this symbol mean anything to you?" he asked. "It's like an ouroboros—the snake eating its tail."

Amy chewed her lip. "Maybe wisdom or rebirth?"

Jairus frowned and gestured at the room. "Is this something the Dark Lady would be involved in?"

"It causes suffering, so perhaps," Amy said.

He lifted the lid of another crate and froze, unable to look away. Amy peeked in then turned away gagging.

"Is that real?" he asked.

"I think so. It's...it was a pixie."

The tiny, desiccated, human-like figure lay tacked to a board by its wings like a butterfly in a scientist's collection. Jairus slammed the lid shut and turned away from the other crates.

"We're getting out of here." His eyes focused on Mary examining the machine, touching it gingerly and moving parts around. "Miss Leland! What are you doing?"

She jumped. "Just...seeing how it works." She ducked her head. "I think I can fix it so it shocks the person who turns it on, instead of the one in the chair."

Jairus grinned. "I like the way you think. Do it fast, though."

She nodded and flexed her hands. Her fingers moved deftly around the wires.

Thumps in the hallway froze the three of them in a frightened tableau. A key turned in the door. Jairus motioned the women behind the machine and took cover with them, his revolver poised in his hand.

The door opened and a footstep creaked on the floorboards. Jairus berated himself for not covering the machine and disguising their presence.

Amy closed her eyes, lips moving as if in silent prayer. Jairus itched with uneasiness, sensing that she was using magic again, but he had chosen to trust Amy because it felt right, and he knew better than to switch horses midstream.

The man in the doorway muttered and walked back into the hallway, pulling the door shut behind him. Jairus sighed and looked over at Amy. She opened her eyes and gave him a weak grin.

"That was tricky. He was anxious, so I helped him think he was forgetting something. It may not last long."

"Who was he?"

"I couldn't tell. Human, though."

"We're leaving," Jairus said. He checked the windows, but they were nailed shut. Gun in hand, he led Amy and Mary out into the hallway.

He didn't slow his pace until they neared the study again. The door was ajar, and Fitzhugh's voice filtered out. Jairus tightened his grip on his gun, but he'd already pushed his luck far enough for one day. Then the sound of shuffling cards reached his ears, calling to him like the trickle of water to a parched man. Warnings of danger whispered in his mind, but he ignored them; Fitzhugh was speaking again.

"Everything appears to be going well. I'm impressed."

"Of course it is. You just keep up your end of the bargain," Rushford said.

"You know I can't lie."

"You say that, but I'll wait to see proof before I believe you."

Fitzhugh laughed. "Suit yourself."

The sweet whisper of cards being dealt caught Jairus's heart like a barbed hook, and he leaned closer. What would it be like to play against an opponent who could read your emotions?

"Hmm," Fitzhugh said.

"What is it?"

There was a long pause. Jairus clenched his teeth. What had Amy said about strong emotions? He backed away from the door and motioned for the women to go.

"I thought I sensed something—or rather someone—but it's gone now," Fitzhugh said. "I wonder if we're going to have company this evening?"

"I'm still waiting for you to tell me what we're doing about the child," Rushford said.

Jairus froze.

"I'll tell you when the time comes," Fitzhugh replied. "Don't trouble yourself over it. Our plans are moving forward. You needn't fear that we have forgotten you, either. One way or another, we'll make sure you have a chance to conduct your experiments. I'm rather interested in your results myself."

"Well, if you're willing—"

"Not interested enough to volunteer," Fitzhugh said, a smile in his tone. "I've seen your methods, remember."

Jairus swallowed. Rushford and Fitzhugh were allies, for now. The only remaining question was whether the Ashbys were co-conspirators or dupes.

"I say!" A newcomer's voice hit Jairus like a bullet to the back. "What's this? Eavesdropping?"

Jairus swung around and knocked the bespectacled man to the ground.

Amy and Mary fled for the kitchen. Jairus had to make sure they escaped.

Fitzhugh jerked the door open. Jairus had only the time it took to raise his gun to make a decision. He fired a lead bullet into Fitzhugh's chest, and the elf staggered back.

Jairus ran in the opposite direction from the women. Footsteps pounded close behind him. He veered into a room and shut the door. When someone turned the doorknob to follow him, Jairus yanked the door open. Rushford stumbled forward, right into Jairus's waiting fists. Rushford fell back into the pursuers gathering in the hallway, and Jairus slammed the door shut again, bolting it. Shouting and cursing accompanied the thumps on the door. Jairus ran for the window and slid it open to jump onto the lawn below.

Chapter Twenty-Six

Amy pulled Mary into the stable and swung the door closed. The welcoming smells of leather, hay, and horses wafted around them. A dozen equine heads turned in their direction, and Amy's Faerie pony, Isabel, whickered a greeting. The strength of Jairus's desire for them to escape still pushed Amy, like a wave surging over a storm wall. She hurried to her pony and threw her arms around its gray-dappled neck, relaxing into the creature's simple, peaceful emotions.

"Lady St. Clair? What do we do now?" Mary asked.

"We have to tell—" Pain surged up Amy's throat like bile, choking her. Tears stung her eyes, but she squeezed them back. "Drat! Henry was too careful when he made his bargain. I can't even talk about—" She gasped as the sensation returned.

"We need to tell Miss Weaver what we heard?" Mary asked.

Unable even to nod, Amy kicked the stall door, blinking away a fresh set of tears. "I've been an utter failure in this escapade!"

Mary stared at her. "But I saw you shoot the Morrigan. You hit exactly where you meant to. And you used magic to keep those men from seeing us."

The words fluttered against Amy's heart, but she dismissed them. She couldn't afford to be pleased with herself, not until she atoned for all of her past mistakes. "And look where that's gotten us. We need a plan, and whatever I choose is certain to go wrong." She straightened. "No, Mr. Hale needs help. And Henry and...our friends need Mr. Hale for the christening. We have to get this right. I can fix this."

She fastened on Isabel's rope bridle and sidesaddle. Then she looked at the row of horses. Picking the fastest-looking one, she led it out and saddled it.

"What are you doing?" Mary asked.

"Getting a horse ready for Mr. Hale if...*when* he gets here."

The stable door burst open, and Jairus rushed inside.

"What are you lollygagging here for?" he asked.

Amy sagged with relief.

Jairus glanced over his shoulder. "Those men'll be right behind me!"

"We're ready to ride," Amy said.

"Then ride!"

She shoved the second horse's bridle into his hands and led Isabel to the mounting block, swinging up and motioning to Mary.

The changeling backed away. "I've never been on a horse before."

Amy held out a hand. "Isabel won't let any harm come to you."

Mary paled and scrambled up to sit astride behind Amy, taking a tight grip on Amy's waist. The pony shifted under the extra weight but didn't protest. Jairus pulled himself onto his mount and looked out through the open door.

"We're going to make for the woods. Are you a good rider?"

"I'll be able to keep up. Don't worry," Amy said.

Jairus did look worried as he glanced at Mary clinging behind her, but he led them out of the stable, pushing his horse into a gallop. Shouts followed them over the grassy lawn, and Jairus didn't slow when they reached the trees.

The wind whipped at Amy's hair. She smiled, even with Mary's grip on her waist throwing off her rhythm and squeezing out her breath. They were away and rapidly putting distance between themselves and any Grigori or Fay who might try to follow.

Jairus's horse snorted and tossed his head.

Jairus reigned in. "Watch out. Something's up."

Amy focused on the energy in the air, and her skin crawled. "There's Unseelie magic here."

Something moved at the edge of her vision. She snapped her head around but saw only rough brown and gray trunks. She squeezed the reins and turned her gaze up.

A giant brown spider hung above her.

She screamed.

The beast's body was as big as a person's torso, and each knobby leg taller than a grown man.

Jairus whipped his revolver up and fired. Thick, black sludge oozed from the spider's abdomen. Amy's stomach churned. The creature leapt for Jairus. Another blast from his gun knocked it aside, and it skittered back into the trees.

"It's an attercrop!" Amy choked out.

"How does that help me?" Jairus asked, pulling on the reigns as his mount danced in a circle. "Can it be killed?"

"With iron."

The hairy creature scuttled into the branches above them, its swollen body swaying like a buoy on a rough sea.

Jairus grabbed his shotgun from its holster and fired. The blast exploded through the leaves like startled birds. The attercrop jumped to a higher perch. "Are there more of them?"

The edges of Amy's vision were hazy. The only thing she could see was the huge spider darting among the branches. She blinked. "Um, probably not. They're usually solitary. They're very poisonous, though, and fast."

"Perfect." Jairus grinned humorlessly. He took aim as the creature scurried above him. "Keep riding. I'll cover you."

Amy nearly suffocated beneath Mary's grip as she spurred her pony to a canter. Jairus's gunshot cracked the air behind them. All around, other dark creatures stirred, waiting for night to fall. She needed to get somewhere safe while there was still light, and she wouldn't be able to enter the Weaver's property. She could head for Elfland—Faerie ponies were adept at navigating its strange ways—but there was no guarantee they would be any safer there than in Drixton. Of course, she didn't want to lure Unseelie monsters back to a village full of innocent victims. Either decision could be a mistake, but she had to choose something.

She gave Isabel free reign. The pony understood, veering toward the nearest entrance to Elfland. Mary bounced behind Amy like a bag of rocks.

Jairus raced to keep up with them, shouting something that was lost in the wind. Of course, he had no idea where Amy was going, but she couldn't explain at that distance and speed. Her pony plunged into a small pond ringed with hawthorn trees. They pushed through a heavy curtain of magic, an almost-physical pressure that eased once they were on the other side.

Past the magical barrier, the little pond widened into a shimmering, shallow lake that reflected the bright sun overhead. Trees with gold and silver trunks circled the lake, dripping white and pink-petaled flowers onto its surface. Mary gasped and loosened her grip, and Amy took a deep breath of sweet-smelling air laced with magic: the air of her mother's realm.

She looked back to see Jairus's mount splash into the water. As soon as the horse reached the border of Elfland, it balked, throwing Jairus forward in the saddle. Jairus urged his mount onward. It bucked, and Jairus tumbled into the water. He came up splashing and yelling at the horse.

Amy's breath caught. Dark figures moved in the woods behind Jairus.

"Watch out, Mr. Hale!" she yelled.

Jairus didn't seem to hear. Amy frowned and turned Isabel back. The pony snorted and went straight-legged. Amy shouted for Jairus again and jumped into the waist-deep water, leaving Mary clinging to the frightened mare.

Amy sloshed forward, her sodden skirts dragging behind. She slammed into the veil between the worlds, now as solid as a wall, and fell back into the water. Why had it been sealed off? Sputtering at the pond water dripping down her face, she struggled to her feet, using the invisible barrier to brace herself.

"Lady St. Clair?" Mary urged Isabel forward, but the pony tossed her mane and backed away with the changeling clutching the saddle.

A group of mounted men emerged from the woods on the other side, led by Mr. Rushford. Jairus wiped his face and lifted his revolver.

Amy pressed her palms against the barrier. Solid magic pushed back against her.

"What are you doing here, child?"

Titania's voice sliced into her heart like a scalpel. Amy turned slowly. Elves dressed in all the shades of the forest lined the shore of Elfland, mingled with an assortment of other Faerie courtiers drawn from the highest ranks of the Fay: dryads, centaurs, and even a glaistig with her goat legs hidden beneath a flowing green dress. Amy's mother stood in the center, arms crossed and bright green gown trailing through the leaves.

Amy pushed her dripping curls from her face and glanced at Jairus. He pulled the trigger, but the waterlogged gun didn't respond. Amy gasped.

"Mother! Help him! He's a priest. He can keep the Dark Lady from taking the seventh daughter."

"The Unseelie Queen's forces are on the other side," Titania said. "That's why I closed the way. I can't risk rushing into battle unprepared just for one human, priest or no."

The American charged the mounted men, swinging his shotgun like a club.

"But, Mother—"

"As always, you're not thinking things through, child. When we've gathered with Mab's forces, we'll be prepared to defeat the Unseelie Queen, and we can capture or kill the child as needed. She's only one part of the picture."

Jairus's assault unhorsed several of the men, but they circled him, punching and jabbing him from every side, like hyenas tormenting a wounded lion.

"Did you truly expect to best a Faerie Queen with such paltry allies?"

Her mother's sneer sent heat pulsing through Amy's veins. She clawed at the invisible barrier, as smooth as glass beneath her fingers.

"Please, help him!" Amy yelled, not sure if she meant the words for her mother or someone else.

"Foolish child." Titania chuckled. "You were the one who led them here. You have no one but yourself to blame for the priest's predicament."

Amy winced and pushed against the barrier with all the force of her pain and anger, but her mother's magic was too strong. Tears blurred her vision as Jairus staggered under the barrage of fists and rifle butts. She slumped against the barrier, wiping her damp cheeks.

Jairus sank to the ground. The black-coated men kicked him.

"No!" Amy threw herself at the transparent wall, slamming her fists against it until the bones in her hands ached.

"Stop her," her mother said coolly.

Two elves grabbed Amy by the arms and dragged her toward the shore. Mary watched with wide, tear-filled eyes.

"Mr. Hale!" Amy twisted back.

Rushford's men lifted Jairus's limp body, his arms hanging at odd angles. Amy sagged, and the elves dumped her at her mother's feet.

The Lady of the Woods frowned at her. "Now, tell me why you have left London."

Amy stared down silently, salty tears rolling past her lips. Her mother wouldn't have the satisfaction of laughing at her failed plans.

"I don't understand how you came to be so inept," Titania said.

Amy pressed her lips together. The familiar pain of her mother's reproach was almost comfortable compared with her aching fear over Jairus and the rest of her friends.

Titania shook her head. "I gave you leave to amuse yourself so long as you put yourself in the way of influential men. Your magic is weak, but with your fair appearance, it should not be so difficult to find one willing to marry you. Instead, I discover you traipsing about the countryside with a group of neophyte aristocrats and, if I understand correctly, Henry Stewart and Domin. Is it true that they are here? Speak!"

Amy opened her mouth at the command, but her tongue stuck in place. She smiled sadly. Her careless promise at the ball not to reveal Henry's location had saved her from betraying him.

"Worthless girl," her mother hissed.

Amy flinched and dug her fingers into the soft ground.

"I am at a loss about what to do with you, especially with war brewing." Titania frowned. "Perhaps, since you cannot secure a husband of your own choosing, I will arrange one for you."

"No," Amy whispered, cold gripping her stomach.

"Your weak mind must be guided by a firm hand, and I don't have the time to correct you."

Amy shuddered at the memory of her first husband's firm hand, and his possessive, demeaning touch. "I won't do that again."

"You have no choice."

Amy looked up at her mother's cold, beautiful face. Titania had spoken those same words to Henry, trying to force him to take Amy. After a lifetime of gathering misery and discontent, he had finally flung it all back at Titania, on Amy's behalf as well as his own. Amy pushed herself up to her knees.

"I do have a choice," she said hoarsely.

"If you refuse me, I will turn you out into the world, exiled from my court. Your silly schemes will get you nowhere. What could you do, besides marry some poor human besotted with your looks, or follow a debauched life charming men into caring for you?"

Amy staggered to her feet. "You don't understand the human world as well as you think. You chose my last husband for his title and his seat in the House of Lords. A helm for turning human affairs, you said, especially if we produced heirs. But you forgot that the vile monster you pushed on me also had wealth, and I made certain that it stayed in my hands when he died. Thanks to your matchmaking skills, I don't have to rely on you."

Titania stared down at her daughter, eyes dark. "You will obey me. We are at war. Everyone must make sacrifices."

"Including you? No. You lost the right to my obedience when you stopped caring about anyone's well-being but your own." Amy squared her shoulders. "I will never again let you force me into degradation. I have bought my freedom and I will die before I relinquish it. Rip your magic from me and let me crumble to dust, if you will, but I am not yours anymore."

The clearing grew still except for the gentle lap of the lake against the shore. The Lady of the Woods raised her hand. Amy closed her eyes, wanting the savory taste of freedom and the sweet smell of flowers to be the last thing she experienced.

Her mother's slap jolted her eyes open. A hot sting pulsed through her cheek.

"I will deal with you after this battle is over, insolent child." Titania's eyes narrowed. "Don't think your insults will be forgotten."

Amy breathed deeply, grateful for each lungful of air. Even the throb in her jaw was a welcome sensation of life. The breeze brushed by her face, scattering delicate petals to kiss her skin and hair.

She wished she could believe Titania's mercy came from love, but she was the sole carrier of her mother's bloodline. Like

Henry, she owed her life to the fact that the Lady of the Woods didn't destroy tools that might be useful someday.

"I hope you have at least learned enough not to interfere. You botch every task you touch." Titania sneered at her. "The Dark Lady's human allies have your priest now, and her servants are moving to take the child. While she's distracted, we'll surround her forces and destroy them."

"No! You have to stop them now!" She stepped toward Titania, and her mother gestured. Magic slammed into her, knocking her to the ground.

"You do not command me. Remember your place before you speak to me again."

Amy couldn't lift her head. A gentle hand touched her arm, and she opened her eyes to find Mary huddled over her protectively. The Faerie host streamed past them into the woods without a glance for a disgraced elf. If Amy hadn't humiliated herself, she might have convinced some of them to help her, but it was too late now.

Fitzhugh's offer surfaced in her mind. Would joining the Unseelie Court make her more powerful? Perhaps it was possible to learn to use Unseelie magic without letting it corrupt her. Fitzhugh had certainly become crueler since joining them, but there had always been a streak of unkindness in his humor: one that she'd overlooked until it was too late.

She sighed and pushed the thought away. Everyone else might have given up on her, but she wasn't yet ready to give up on herself. Sometimes she wasn't sure why she kept trying to make things right, but the last spark of rebellion in her heart refused to be extinguished. She would find a way to help Domin and the others. Make up for her past failures. Stop Fitzhugh and the Dark Lady. Prove her mother wrong.

Amy looked back across the barrier. Rushford and his men

were gone, along with Jairus, whether he was alive or dead. The sun's last rays colored the clouds gold, violet, and pink before slipping away to let the night begin its reign. Shadows crept through the trees. The Dark Lady's forces were converging on Drixton, while Amy and Mary sat sheltered and helpless in Elfland, trapped behind the border Titania had sealed.

Chapter Twenty-Seven

Hail rattled off the roof of the Weaver's house. Cassandra clutched Henry's book of plant and Faerie lore and huddled under the warm light of the lamp, grateful for Henry and Domin's presence, despite their ongoing argument.

"It's getting worse out there," Henry said. "We need to go after Mr. Hale."

"And leave this house and the child unprotected? Do you think that's what Mr. Hale would want? He's resourceful, and he knows he's needed here."

Henry stared at the curtained windows with a skeptical expression. The house groaned under the thrashing storm. Cassandra flipped through pages of the herbal, searching for anything that might help against the Dark Lady. She flipped quickly past the images of redcaps and banshees, wondering if any of them were lurking outside in the dark. Then, she stumbled over a passage in French illustrated by a sword piercing a snake-like beast.

"Mr. Stewart?" she asked, her voice nearly lost in the howl of the wind. "Can you help me with reading this? My French…"

"Is atrocious?" he asked, his teasing grin momentarily erasing the worry lines on his forehead.

"It really is," Cassandra admitted with a weak smile. Her confession to him at the ball seemed years ago.

Henry sat next to her, bringing the pleasant scent of cinnamon and cloves. Cassandra leaned in as Henry shifted the book to scan it. He traced the text on the rough paper, and his hand brushed hers, sending a thrill over her skin. His cheeks reddened slightly, and he cleared his throat.

"Uh, it's talking about the legends of Charlemagne—his defeat of a dragon. I don't see anything helpful in it."

He stood quickly, and Cassandra glanced down at the book to hide her confusion. Had she done something wrong?

"There's another hand guiding this storm." Henry returned to his pacing. "I can sense it. I didn't think the Dark Lady could do this."

"She has many allies," Domin said, "and I do not know all of their abilities. Perhaps she has another changeling like you in her thrall."

Henry paused. "Is that possible?"

Domin shrugged.

The room dimmed, despite the lamps. Angry voices whispered in the wind. The words tumbled together in a threatening hiss, but a few stood out to Cassandra.

Weak. Broken. Pathetic.

Cruel laughter wove through the words. She cringed, reminded of how often she humiliated herself, like tripping at the ball. The memories rode on the wind like a wave, with Sophie's angry words riding the crest.

Hopeless. Awkward. Embarrassment.

Cassandra's eyes stung. She glanced at Henry and Domin for reassurance, but the wavering light cast strange, hard shadows over their faces.

Something outside scratched at the windows. Cassandra stumbled to her feet, grateful the draperies were closed. Henry put a reassuring hand on her shoulder, his presence muffling her fear. Still, the unease seeped under her skin. Who was she to stand up to the Fay, to fight against such powerful magic?

Sophie screamed upstairs.

Cassandra broke away from Henry's touch and hobbled quickly for her room. Sophie huddled on the bed, lashing out at nothing and shrieking. Tears streamed down her face.

"Make it stop!" Sophie cried, rocking back and forth.

Her eyes rolled back and her limbs jerked. Blood drooled from her mouth. Cassandra rushed to her sister. Henry knelt by her side, and she jumped, unaware that he had followed her.

"What's happening? Is she dying?" Cassandra put a hand on Henry's arm. "Can you help her?"

He leaned forward to examine Sophie without shaking off Cassandra's hand. The lines of his face softened. "She had a fit and bit her tongue. It will heal."

He rolled Sophie onto her side and pulled pillows around her. Cassandra grabbed a cloth to dab up the blood. Sophie groaned, her gaze unfocused.

Henry checked her eyes and pulse then shook his head. "There's nothing else we can do. The Dark Lady's magic is touching her mind."

"I thought we were safe inside the house."

"She can't enter physically, but her influence can, just like with the enchantment."

Cassandra covered her mouth. Down the corridor, the wails of her younger sisters rose in a chorus of agony. Hot tears coursed over her hand. Henry hurried to the nursery, and Cassandra limped after him.

You don't have to be cast off.

The voice came more clearly than the others, a whisper in her ear. She turned to look over her shoulder, but no one was there.

You have hurt for so long. Body and mind. It doesn't have to be that way.

Numbness washed over her like she had fallen into a dream. And as in her dreams, there was no pain or fatigue in her limbs. She glanced down at her right hand. The tight fingers uncurled, free from their infirmity as though a band around them had been cut. She turned them over and flexed them. A simple motion, but it meant everything. Before the fever, she hadn't understood the miracle of fingers that straightened and bent at will. Now, she shook with silent sobs of joy to see her hand made whole again.

I understand suffering. I take broken things and make them mine. Better than they could ever be on their own.

The numbness faded, and Cassandra's fingers curled again into a helpless palsy. The burning prickles washed down her right leg again, and she gasped.

But those who defy me know the true meaning of pain.

Her sisters screamed again. Cassandra bolted to the nursery, dragging her aching leg. Nancy scrambled from one girl to another as they writhed on the floor. Henry dropped down to help the nurse soothe each girl. Georgina clawed at her skin and shrieked in agony, and Lottie sobbed for their mother. Cassandra leaned on the doorframe, tasting bile.

Come to me and all of your pain—your sisters' pains —will end.

Cassandra could stop all of this suffering. What did it

matter what happened to a broken thing like her, especially if she could help her sisters? She choked on her tears and fled the room. This was how she could finally be of some value to her family. She rushed down the stairs, catching herself on the banister when her useless, worthless right foot twisted and she stumbled. The ghostly laughter echoed all around her.

Henry caught hold of her at the bottom of the steps.

"Let me go!" She tried to twist away. "I'll make her stop. Even if she takes me—"

"Miss Weaver!" His fingers dug into her arm. "Listen! Please listen. This isn't the Seelie Court. This is the Dark Lady. What price will you pay her? Your baby sister's life? Your soul?"

He forced her to face him. With his free hand, he gently brushed the tears from her cheeks. "Please, don't listen to her. Listen to me." She sagged against his hold on her arm, but he held her gaze. "If I let go, will you promise not to go to the door?"

Cassandra nodded dully, the horrible voices still pressing against her skull.

"Look." He rolled up his shirtsleeves. Thick scars formed a band around each wrist.

"What happened?" she whispered.

"When I was just developing my abilities, T— um, the Lady of the Woods wanted me to practice by flooding the field of a farmer who had offended her. He had children—even younger than me—who'd be left hungry without that crop. When I told her I wouldn't do it, she dragged me back to Elfland and tied me up, leaving me locked alone in the dark for days, without food, or water, or any idea of what time it was. Her servants woke me from time to time to torment me, and they let my injuries fester."

"That's terrible." The word felt small and dry in

Cassandra's mouth.

He put a finger under her chin, making her meet the pain and anger in his eyes. "That's not the worst part. They took me back, after, and I flooded the field. I was sorry for it, but I did that and every horrible thing they asked of me, for many years."

He moved his hand away, but the intensity of his gaze kept her eyes locked on his. "And these were the Seelie Faerie. Think of what the Unseelie Queen would do to your baby sister. The Dark Lady is making the other girls suffer, trying to lure you into giving up, but she can't kill them, and she wouldn't, since then your seventh sister would lose her abilities. Their suffering won't last. Can you say the same for the child, if she falls into hands like those?"

Useless. Silly. Craven.

Cassandra squeezed her eyes against the tears burning them. When her sisters shrieked again, she whimpered and sank into Henry. He leaned back for half a breath then wrapped her in a tight embrace. She melted into the safety of his arms and muffled her cries in his shoulder.

When her gasping sobs slowed, he guided her back to the drawing-room. She sat on the sofa, and he stood by her side. Cold rolled around him, chilling her. He began pacing again.

"There must be something we can do to end this," he said.

Domin shook his head. "We cannot attack the Dark Lady unless she shows herself. We just have to endure."

Henry brought his hands to his head. "Can't we at least stop this noise? I can't take another minute of these voices."

Cassandra started. Did Henry hear the same words she did or did the Dark Lady whisper different secrets to each of them?

"Music would help." Domin glanced at the piano and then at her.

"I can't play anymore, since the fever." Cassandra let the

weak, useless fingers of her right hand curl in her lap.

Henry drew Jairus's revolver from under his coat and studied it in the dim light.

"That will do us no good," Domin said. "Put it away."

"Apparently, it's enough for Mr. Hale, though."

"His situation is different."

Henry turned on Domin. Cassandra wrapped her arms around herself as the temperature plummeted. Henry's breath hung in the air as he spoke. "He's not a monster, you mean."

"It would be best for you to stop using that term," Domin said.

The two young men glared at each other, their faces dark in the faint light. Cassandra stood slowly. This wasn't right. This wasn't them. It was the Dark Lady. What was Cassandra supposed to do? Subdue them, if they wouldn't listen to reason, Domin had said. She held back a hysterical giggle at the notion.

"Would you like to tell me where I fit into all this, then, since you're so wise?" Henry asked.

"You're a reckless fool chasing impossibilities."

"Stop it!" Cassandra said, coming between them. She faced Domin. His dark features were etched sharp with anger and frustration, but she met his green eyes. "You're Henry's friend. You don't want to hurt him."

Domin's face softened.

She turned toward Henry but stopped short. A faint blue glow rose from his skin, and a vacant look took hold of him, much like the enchanted villagers. She glanced back at Domin, whose eyes widened in alarm.

"If I embrace the Dark Lady's gift, I don't have to worry anymore about where I belong." Henry's words echoed themselves as if two people shared his voice.

"Henry, this isn't you," Domin said. "It's the Dark Lady.

You have to fight her."

"I'm tired of fighting." Henry dropped the gun. He held his hands out, and sparks of blue electricity danced in his palms. "With her power, I can protect everyone. Better than I ever could on my own." His echoing voice carried a pleading undertone.

Domin stared at Henry uncertainly. Cassandra looked between them. Had Domin never learned to aid or comfort a friend? No, perhaps he hadn't. Social grace wasn't one of his strong points, after all.

Cassandra stepped closer to Henry. "But, Mr. Stewart, we need *you*. You don't belong with her. You belong here, with us. Please, come back."

He didn't look at her, but something of himself flickered back into his eyes. His forehead wrinkled in consternation, and his jaw set. He clutched his head and shouted, his strange, echoing voice unraveling into two. His own sounded tortured, while the alien one roared in pain and frustration until it faded back into the storm.

The energy crackling along Henry's hands died. He gasped and swayed as if he might collapse, but caught himself on the arm of the chair. Finally, he looked up at Domin and Cassandra.

"I'm sorry. I let her in—inside my head."

"But then you resisted," Domin said, "and it hurt her."

Henry looked down and shook his head. "Part of me didn't want to resist. The power she offered felt so enticing."

"Yet you did not give in," Domin said quietly, "and listen to the storm now."

Only a soft patter of rain dripped off the roof, and the angry voices faded into a calm whisper. The warm light of the lamp had sprung up to chase away the gloom.

"The wild energy is gone," Henry said.

"Yes." Domin cocked his head. "You weakened her enough to buy us some peace, perhaps even until tomorrow night." He hesitated. "If you want me to search for Mr. Hale, this would be the best time to do it, but I do not like the idea of leaving this house vulnerable."

Henry ran his hands through his hair. "Without him to christen the child when she's born, we'll have to endure attacks like this—or worse—every night until we find a way to drive off the Dark Lady, or we break. And Mr. Hale will need help fighting his way back if her servants are abroad. What do you think, Miss Weaver?"

Cassandra jumped. "You want my opinion?"

"Of course," Henry said. "This affects you too."

"Once the baby is christened, will the Dark Lady stop?"

Domin looked thoughtful. "She'll be angry, but this assault is costing her a great deal of energy. She won't keep attacking if she has nothing to gain. The Fay are not forgiving, but they're too far-seeing and patient to waste resources out of rage."

Cassandra sat back, biting her lip. Mr. Hale would have returned by now if he could, and if he was in trouble, Domin could help. She thought of the blood trickling from Sophie's mouth and her little sisters screaming. "We need Mr. Hale back so he can christen the baby and this nightmare can end."

Henry nodded. "I'll stay here in case there's trouble, but the Fay can't get inside, and the Dark Lady doesn't want to kill any of the sisters. I think Miss Weaver and I can handle it."

His words propped up her sagging courage, especially when Domin examined them both and nodded before heading to the front door.

Henry sighed. "You should get some sleep, Miss Weaver. I'll be keeping watch tonight."

Chapter Twenty-Eight

Cassandra woke slowly, squinting at the predawn light. She bolted upright. Had Domin and Jairus returned? She limped into the corridor. Her nightgown fluttered around her legs, and she reddened and hurried back to her room. Had she forgotten The Rules completely? She couldn't appear in front of Henry —or the others—in such a state.

Her favorite green-striped gown caught her eye, and she pulled it on over her corset and crinoline, adjusting the overskirt atop her white petticoat as well as she could without help. She left her brace off to give the blisters on her leg a chance to heal, but she stuck the little iron pin of Georgina's rose brooch through the fabric of her bodice on her way downstairs.

She peeked into the drawing-room, and her heart sank. Domin and Jairus were still missing. Henry slept in an overstuffed chair facing the window as if he had just meant to close his eyes for a moment while he watched. Only the ticking of the clock and his slow, steady breathing broke the early morning quiet. Cassandra crept forward, not wanting to be alone.

Henry's brown coat lay tossed onto the sofa, and he'd taken the time to wash his face before settling down for the night. Seeing his peaceful expression, she decided to let him rest, though she had to fight the desire to brush the tousled brown hair off his forehead. To sink into the reassurance of his arms again. Perhaps to feel his lips on her mouth, his touch on her skin.

She drew back, cheeks burning.

Holding her skirts to hush their rustling whisper, she fled the room, but she couldn't escape the images she had conjured up. Ridiculous fantasies, especially when her sisters were still in danger. Whatever closeness she imagined with Henry could easily vanish along with the monsters when the baby was christened and they escaped the Fay. Was it likely that Henry would come calling on her after it was all over? She glanced at her cane, almost forgotten in the entryway. Why would anyone confident and capable want her when she would only be in their way, a burden?

And yet, Henry never treated her like a burden.

She jumped at the sound of footsteps. Beth marched down the corridor. A carving knife glinted in the maid's hand.

"Beth?" Cassandra asked. "What are you doing?"

Beth shoved Cassandra aside and continued into the drawing-room.

"Mr. Stewart!" Cassandra yelled and grabbed the back of the maid's dress, yanking her to a stop.

Beth spun and slashed. Cassandra stumbled to the ground. The knife flashed a hand's breadth from her face. She covered her head and kicked out, just missing Beth's knee.

Henry raced into the corridor, stopping short when he saw the girls. "What—"

"She's gone mad." Cassandra scrambled to her feet. "She has a knife!"

He lunged for Beth's arm. She lashed out, slicing his hand. Drawing a sharp breath, he smacked her hand. The weapon clattered to the floor, but she clawed his face. Two red lines welled up on his cheek. He pushed her away.

Cassandra threw herself at Beth, knocking her to the ground. The maid rolled and reached for the knife. Kicking the weapon away, Henry grabbed Beth and twisted her arms behind her back to pin her face-down against the carpet.

"What's happening?" Cassandra asked.

Beth snarled and thrashed, throwing Henry off balance. He leaned his knee into her back. "In my satchel, find the laudanum. Brown bottle. It's labeled."

She nodded and slipped past. The maid uttered guttural, inhuman sounds and tried to sink her teeth into Henry's arm. Cassandra found his bag in the drawing-room and dumped it out, sorting through the clinking bottles until she found the right one.

"Here it is," she said, but when Henry reached to take it, Beth got an arm free and flailed at him. He flipped Beth over, pinning one of her arms under her body and holding the other down with his knee. Avoiding her gnashing teeth, he held her shoulders against the floor.

"You're going to have to administer it while I hold her. Twenty...no, twenty-five drops."

Cassandra uncorked the bottle, wrinkling her nose at the bitter smell, and fished out the glass dropper. Henry pinched Beth's mouth open while Cassandra counted each drop aloud.

Huddled so close, Beth's sweaty, animal reek made Cassandra gag.

When she counted the last drop, Henry forced Beth's mouth shut until she swallowed. The maid swore at them and writhed, her eyes rolling back. After a few long minutes, her movements lost their vigor, and her growls turned to muffled grunts.

"What happened?" Cassandra asked. "Is she possessed?"

"Not exactly," he said. "I'm sorry I didn't think about your servants. The Dark Lady must have found some dark desire in the girl's mind that she could twist into action. The maid didn't go after you, though, did she?"

"No." Cassandra wrinkled her forehead. "No, she pushed right past me ..." Her eyes widened.

"To attack me." Henry sighed. "The Dark Lady knows we're alone here. She can't harm any of you without destroying the child's potential, but if she killed me, there'd be no one left to protect you or the baby."

The maid's eyes fluttered shut.

Cassandra leaned back. Poor Beth. She had looked so envious when they'd left for the ball, and Sophie was always ordering her around. Was that why she'd come to hate them so much? "Is she going to be all right?"

"Eventually, I imagine. You'll have to think of some reason to get your mother to let her go, though."

"Yes, I can't imagine keeping her on after this, though we've only just hired her."

"Really? Who recommended her?"

"Lady Ashby. You don't suppose she knew Beth would turn on us?"

"It's possible. If Lady Ashby is working with the Dark Lady, she may have sent someone whom they could use against you."

Cassandra groaned. "I'm always going to be watching over my shoulder, aren't I?"

"Why don't you take a moment to recover?" Henry said gently. "I'll lock the maid in the servant's quarters so she can't do any more harm, and I'll check on the other servants too, just in case."

"There's just the cook at the moment." Cassandra got to her feet as Henry lifted the maid.

Bottles and bandages from Henry's satchel lay strewn across the drawing-room rug. As Cassandra stowed them back in the leather bag, something tangled around her fingers: a tarnished chain holding a worn silver locket of the sort sweethearts exchanged.

Her heart caught. She had hoped there might be more than friendship in Henry's words and touches, but he did seem to be holding something back. The roses he sent for the ball were a neutral white, promising nothing, only meant to ward off Fitzhugh—an act of kindness. Why hadn't it occurred to her that his affections might already be engaged?

She put the locket back and shoved a few more items into the bag without really seeing them. Whose image was in the locket? A human lady, or a Fay one? No doubt someone Cassandra could never compete with. Someone more worthy.

Cassandra ground her teeth. She glanced at the empty corridor and yanked the locket out again, hating her curiosity.

The locket clicked open. She blinked at the faces there: Queen Anne and her consort, Prince George. Frowning, Cassandra studied the ornate trinket, worn by years of use. Why would Henry carry lovingly preserved portraits of long-dead monarchs? The queen was only significant for being the last of the Stuart line.

A chill spread across Cassandra's shoulders. Henry's mother

was named Anne, and all of his siblings had died young. And he was a Stewart, last of a family line important enough to have its own daemon.

She shook her head at the preposterous idea. If Henry was Queen Anne's son, he'd be over a hundred and fifty years old. She paused. Of course, more than two hundred and fifty years ago, Amy—who looked little older than Henry—had tried to kill James Stuart in the Gunpowder Plot, only to be stopped by Domin. If Domin had been protecting King James, it proved he guarded the Stuart line. She covered her mouth, thoughts whirling.

"Miss Weaver?" Henry asked from the doorway.

She closed her hand around the locket.

"What's wrong? You look like you've seen a ghost." A smile quirked his lips. "You haven't, have you?"

"I'm sorry." Her cheeks burned.

"What's happened?" No suspicion clouded the concern in his blue eyes. They looked very much like Anne's in the picture. He held out his uninjured hand. "Please, tell me what's wrong."

"Your locket fell out." She shoved the trinket into his hand. "I shouldn't have opened it."

Understanding swept the confusion from his face. "Oh, Miss Weaver. Please, don't...I can explain. You shouldn't be so distressed."

She swallowed and pointed at the locket. "Are you related to them?"

"Yes," Henry said, kneeling to meet her eyes. "They're my parents."

Chapter Twenty-Nine

Cassandra gaped at Henry, a buzz of disbelief ringing in her ears. "So you *are* a Stuart, and that means—"

He settled across from her. "What does it mean?"

She couldn't meet his gaze. "You're nobility. I mean, do you have a claim to the throne? And I'm just the daughter of a shopkeeper. I shouldn't even be in the same room with you. I shouldn't—" She wanted to sink through the floor when she thought of her growing feelings for him, now so impossible to mention, but by his long pause, she wondered if he guessed them. When he shifted closer, she fought her urge to back away.

"I don't think you can say I'm nobility. I'm apprenticed to an apothecary. I spend my time hunting for rare plants and grinding up medicines... But that's not all that's bothering you."

"You're...how old *are* you?"

He chuckled dryly. "I'm not sure what the honest answer is. I was born about a hundred and eighty years ago, but the Faerie

Queens manipulate the passage of time in Elfland, so I was lifted out of its normal flow. I suppose I'm as old as I look."

Still avoiding his eyes, Cassandra studied the floral patterned rug. Did it matter when he was born? At least he seemed about her age. He didn't carry the weight of all those years on his shoulders, as Domin did.

"I'm still the same person, aren't I?" He touched her sleeve. "Why should it matter who my parents were?"

Cassandra shook her head. How would he understand how completely unworthy she was? How small and stupid she felt?

She pulled away. "I don't know what to make of all this. It isn't fair. It's not just that you're a changeling. You're—" She tried to catch the hurt and anger slipping from her tongue, but the escaped words hung in the air, sharp and dangerous.

"I'm what? A liar? Monster? Freak? What am I, Miss Weaver?" A pleading note underlay his harsh words.

She buried her face in her hands. After a long pause, his footsteps crossed the room. She peeked up. He stood at the window, studying the locket with a pained expression before placing it on the sill above the sofa. He wrapped his injury with linen from his bag and struggled to tie off the bandage one-handed. Blood soaked into the pale linen.

Cassandra bit the inside of her cheek. Henry's blood. The thing about him the Fay fixated on. And now she was reducing him to nothing more than a bloodline as well. Just as most people reduced her to a crippled leg. She rose and tiptoed across the plush carpet to touch Henry's arm, reaching for the loose end of the bandage.

She felt his gaze on her face as she fastened the soft linen. She lifted her eyes to meet his, not releasing his hand even as heat blossomed on her cheeks.

"I'm sorry," she said. "You've been a friend to me. I shouldn't have snapped at you."

Warmth flickered back into his eyes. "Well, you may be right. Even I'm not certain what I am." He glanced away. "I'd hoped you might help me to...to work it out."

"I want to, but I can't begin to understand what you've been through." She looked at the locket on the sill. "How did the Fay manage to take you? I would think you'd be well-guarded, being nobility. And with Domin protecting your family ..."

"My mother wasn't queen at the time, and even Domin can't interfere with a Faerie bargain. They're bound by strong, old magic."

Cassandra's stomach flipped. Queen Anne had come to the throne by a roundabout, improbable route. "You're not saying your parents bartered your life for their own advancement, are you?"

He stared past her. "No, it was my grandfather, King James II. He was so desperate for a male heir to secure his throne. When his son died at birth, he turned to the Fay, begging for a replacement, and offered his daughter's next male child—me—in exchange."

"That's not fair!" Cassandra said, tightening her grip on his hand.

He shrugged. "Not much in life is." His voice dropped. "He destroyed his family and allowed the Fay to put a changeling on the throne, just to keep his power. And it was all for nothing since Parliament was suspicious of the child. They denied the Faerie changeling the crown and called him James the Pretender." He shook his head. "More apt than they realized. And my mother ended up as queen after all."

Cassandra didn't pull her hand away, even as the cold

hovering around him chilled her fingers. "You must have lost so much. I mean, your family, and ..." she took a deep breath, "that whole life. I'm so sorry."

He put his fingers over hers, tracing her hand with a light touch that made her forget the cold. "You think I'm sorry that I wasn't king? I wouldn't trust myself with that kind of power. I have enough to repent of from my time with the Fay."

"They made you do those things, though."

"Did they? They can't force anyone to do anything, even their slaves."

"They would have killed you."

"Perhaps," he whispered. "Perhaps I should have let them before I used my abilities to harm people. Do you understand why I can do these things?"

"Because the Fay did something to you?"

"They enhanced my inborn talents. The bloodline of the kings of Britain has always been tied to the land, like the story of the Fisher King being healed to save the kingdom, or in Macbeth when a false king throws the elements into chaos."

Cassandra nodded.

He went on, "That connection is meant to protect the land and its people, and look what I did with it. As long as I was obedient, the Fay treated me like a prince. They educated me and let me mingle with them. But it rotted away my humanity, especially using my abilities against my people—the people I should have been helping."

"You had enough humanity left to know it was wrong," she said. "And you found a way to escape."

He grinned crookedly. "Actually, I found a way to offend them. The Lady of the Woods finally pushed me too far, and when I stood up to her, she threw me out. She meant it as a punishment, but it was glorious. I was free." His smile faded.

"At least until I got hungry and realized my family was long dead and I had no way to survive. Thankfully, Domin found me. He couldn't interfere with my grandfather's bargain, but he helped me find work that interested me, that I could pursue with no real assets or connections. I wanted—I want—to be normal."

"But you can still do magic," Cassandra said quietly.

"Yes, well, I suppose I've been hiding from myself, as well as the Fay." He squeezed her hand. "But I have to try. I don't want to watch the world pass by without ever experiencing any of it. Being hungry sometimes, and...well, lonely, and the hard work ..." His grin crept back. "Even getting cuffed on the ear by Mr. Tanner when I don't work fast enough—it's all worth it if I can be free."

His long fingers tightened around her hand, like a drowning person afraid of slipping under water.

She grasped his hand in return. "You remind me of the Lady of Shalott."

"Who?"

"You don't know it? I would think the Fay enjoyed Tennyson's poems." He shrugged, and she went on. "The Lady of Shalott is a Faerie lady in a tower who can only view the world through an enchanted mirror. She decides she needs to see things for herself and leaves her tower, even knowing she could die. To me, she's very brave."

Henry dropped her hand and looked away.

Cassandra cleared her throat. "I'm sorry. I didn't mean to give offense. Sophie's always telling me I need to talk less. I guess I do ramble..."

He caught her arms and drew her close. So close, she was only aware of him, his scent of cloves, the rise and fall of his chest.

He leaned his forehead down to hers. "You don't talk too much, Miss Weaver. Or, if you do, I like it. I like quite a few things about you." His gaze traveled over her face and to her lips.

"Oh," Cassandra murmured, finding it strangely difficult to breathe.

He met her eyes again, his expression pained. "But I'm not as free as I would like."

"Oh?" she repeated.

"It's been four years since I left the Fay, but I haven't aged a day—not even enough to need my hair trimmed. The Lady of the Woods wants to punish me, not let me go. I'm still tethered to Elfland, pinned in place by the magic they wove through me, and even if I could find a way to break the connection..."

Cassandra remembered Nancy's fairy stories. "When humans leave the Faerie realm, the years they missed catch up with them. They..." She took a deep breath. "They turn to dust."

He nodded and relaxed his grip, but she flung her arms around him. His chest rose in a long sigh, and he returned the embrace. His fingers trailed softly up and down her back. She melted into the warmth of his body against hers. She was defying The Rules, but it felt right. As if, with his arms wrapped protectively around her, with her head buried in his shoulder, she finally fit somewhere. She was no longer hiding or blending in: she belonged.

But it couldn't last. Not with the Fay hunting them. Dread seeped into her chest, cold and heavy—a fear that if she let go, Henry would crumble to dust in front of her. Or that she would feel time carrying her forward while he stayed behind, trapped and un-aging.

"I hate the Fay," she said, breathing in the scent of his shirt.

"I know." His voice echoed in his chest. "Fitzhugh was right. They turned me into a freak. A monster."

"No." Cassandra pulled back to look up at him. "They've trapped you, but you would only be a monster if—" She stopped, thinking about his temper and its dangerous possibilities.

"If?" He watched her carefully.

"If you let yourself be one," she said. "It doesn't sound like your magic is bad. It's just a part of who you are. Maybe it's even good that you're not normal. I mean, you can help people." She blushed at the intensity of his gaze. "I'm glad you decided to help me, anyway."

He smiled and brushed back a loose strand of her hair. The touch of his fingers on her forehead sent a pleasant shiver over her skin.

"I'm glad you bullied me into it," he said.

"I bullied you?"

"Certainly. You called me a coward and held up Mr. Hale as the hero. It was more than my masculine pride could take." He grinned. "But I am glad. I'm glad I could help, and ..." His smile faded. "I hope we're still friends, at least? I know the reality I live in is difficult to accept, and perhaps it would be easier not to have anything to do with it."

Cassandra looked away, searching for an honest response. Friends. It was hard to see a way around it as long as the Fay held him captive. But there had to be some hope for him. For them. It was an insane idea, but Henry wasn't like anyone else she knew. He didn't treat her like something broken, and she longed to stay near him—a sensation at once exhilarating and frightening.

"I think this has become my reality, too," she said. "I mean, now that I know about it, I can't see how I could just forget or ignore it. And I wouldn't be much of a friend if I turned my back on you just because you're in difficult circumstances."

He smiled. "I'm glad, and perhaps someday—"

Pounding rattled the front door.

"That must be Domin," Henry said.

Cassandra tried to hide her disappointment at the interruption. They needed Domin back, after all, and Mr. Hale too. She turned toward the door, but Henry caught her arm. "Wait here, just in case."

He ventured into the entryway, leaving the drawing-room door open. She peered out after him.

"Domin?" Henry asked through the bolted door.

The door frame burst apart with a splintering crack. Shouts and heavy footsteps poured into the house. Cassandra whisked behind the wall separating the drawing-room from the entrance, wincing at the grunts and thuds on the other side.

Her cane clattered to the floor and rolled closer, ignored in the chaos. She grabbed the end and pulled it over, clutching it in front of her. A short, bald man in a tailored suit stepped into view, his back to her. She hesitated, rolling the smooth wood in her left hand.

Henry raised Jairus's gun at one of the men. The man froze, but Henry hesitated. His opponent knocked the gun aside and punched Henry in the face.

The man in front of Cassandra chuckled. She gritted her teeth and swung. The cane connected with his head, and he dropped to the ground. She gaped at him and backed away.

Two more men raced to the doorway of the drawing-room. Blood pounding in her ears, Cassandra broke for the window. One of the men caught her in a few steps and wrenched the cane away. She punched his gut, but he grabbed her arms and dragged her into the entryway.

Henry lay on the floor, hands manacled behind him. Seeing Cassandra, he kicked the man closest to him and rolled onto his knees. The man swore and knocked him back.

Cassandra's assailant tossed her to the ground. She slid on the tiled floor, bringing her face to face with Henry. A gash on his forehead oozed blood. The man holding him down had a bloody nose, and another man curled up against the wall. Mr. Rushford looked down his nose at the chaos, his wormy little mustache twitching.

Henry struggled as a man with a trim beard locked his feet in manacles. "Leave her alone! She has nothing to do with this!"

The man kicked Henry in the ribs. "Quiet, freak."

Rushford gave the man a stern look but said, "Bind her, too."

The bearded man hesitated, wrinkling his forehead. "I thought we were only here for the freak. Mr. Fitzhugh said—"

"Since when do we do everything Fitzhugh says?" Rushford snapped. "The girl is a complication."

Henry shouted and thrashed closer to Rushford. Cassandra twisted, but they locked her wrists behind her. The cold metal bit into her skin, and she grew still. Struggling would only exhaust her now. Her cane lay on the floor a few feet away, and she longed to pick it up and swing it at Mr. Rushford.

"What about the infant?" the bearded man asked.

Cassandra caught her breath, and Henry tensed.

"We're to wait until it's safely born. We'll leave someone to guard the house and return for the child at our leisure."

The men dragged Cassandra and Henry outside. A pair of town coaches waited for them on the road. Henry jabbed and kicked his captors as they shoved him into the second coach. Rough hands pushed Cassandra after him, forcing her onto the upholstered seat across from Henry. One of the men pressed a cloth over her mouth. Another did the same to Henry. She shrank back but had to take a breath, and she tasted something sweet. Relaxation spread through her body like slipping into a warm bath.

"Now, Mr. Stewart," Rushford said from the carriage door. "I'm not taking any chances on the iron manacles being enough to stop you, so we're placing this ether diffuser in the carriage to keep you quiet." He hung a glass globe from a hook on the ceiling and clicked the door shut. The heavy drapes blocked the morning light.

"What's he talking about?" Cassandra asked.

"It's a threat. The ether will keep us unconscious, and it's also flammable. Even a small spark could ignite it. Not that it matters. With this iron on my wrists, I don't think I can do anything anyway."

Cassandra remembered how iron had affected Domin. "Does it hurt you? The iron?"

He shook his head. "No. I'm not an elf, remember. It's actually kind of...peaceful, though that could be the ether." He paused. "I can still feel the magic there. I just can't do anything with it."

"Oh." Cassandra's thoughts were fuzzy. "We're going to be the sacrifice, aren't we?" The idea was frightening, but only in an abstract way. A pleasant sleepiness stole over her.

After a long pause, Henry said, "I'd like to think neither of us could be corrupted by tomorrow, but I don't know what they're planning. I'm sorry you've been dragged into all of this." Henry's voice slurred. "You should lie down so you don't fall over."

Cassandra slumped down, too warm and comfortable to respond. Fuzzy darkness wrapped around her as the carriage rattled down the road.

Chapter Thirty

Domin's paws ached, but he continued his steady lope as he circled back to Sir Walter's estate, nose close to the ground. The wind ruffled his gray fur, carrying lingering hints of Jairus's scent, but that trail had gone cold as he tracked it into the dawn. Now, the sun stood high in the sky.

At the sealed entrance to Elfland, he lost the last trace of Amy and Mary, heavily spiced by anguish and terror. The smell of blood in the churned, muddy ground conjured images of Jairus's battered body. He snarled, and a stiff ridge of fur rose along his back.

He shook out his coat and focused on Henry and Cassandra. At least he could still protect them. He raced through the woods, the ground flying under his feet. The borders of Elfland wove and danced across his consciousness. As he neared the Weaver's property, the feel of Faerie magic grew stronger.

He charged forward, head low and teeth bared. A dappled

gray elf pony wound through the trees ahead of him, its coat blending with the lacy shadows. Domin bounded to a stop when he recognized Amy and Mary on its back.

The pony snorted and tossed its head, and Amy jerked around. She cried out when she spotted Domin and stumbled from her pony, leaving Mary clinging to the saddle. He barely had time to change shape before Amy threw herself into his arms.

Her emotions flooded him. Happiness. Relief. Safe harbor in his embrace. Closing his eyes, he let the sensations flow through him. The strands of hurt, doubt, and guilt she always carried rose to overpower her initial feelings. There had been a time when her touch had been soothing, but now he ached at her pains as if they were his own.

He recognized Titania's mark in the deep scars and raw wounds crossing Amy's heart. Only traces of the carefree friend he had once known lingered, like a spider web: fragile and nearly invisible. The Lady of the Woods had destroyed so much over the years. He tensed and pulled back before his anger overwhelmed him. Daemons did not seek revenge, but the buried part of him that was Fay longed to make Titania choke on the centuries of suffering she had caused.

Amy stepped away. Just before she let go, he sensed something new in her, but she broke the physical connection before he could define it.

"I'm sorry." Her shoulders slumped. "I was just so relieved …"

"I'm glad you're unharmed. What happened?"

"Fitzhugh saw us at Ashby Hall, and we ran. I thought we would be safe in Elfland, but my mother closed the passage, with Mr. Hale stuck on the other side. Mr. Rushford's Grigori caught him...Domin, I don't even know if he's alive. We rode all night, and Telesm's clearing was the only passage open. I can't get much closer to...our friends, but I thought Miss Leland could warn—" Amy clutched her head in pain and frustration at the strength of the geas locking her tongue. She whispered, "It's worse than we thought. Mr. Rushford and his Grigori are doing experiments on Faerie creatures. They'll track us down. It will be like the witch hunts again."

Domin tensed. He'd been so focused on the Fay that he'd forgotten the threat humans presented. "Rushford has Mr. Hale? He could enter the Weavers' home, too."

Eyes wide, Amy nodded.

His muscles tightened, caught on the edge of transformation. "Go to Miss Leland's home and barricade yourself in."

He dropped onto padded gray feet and tore through the woods. How much of a head start did Rushford have? Too much. Before he reached the front porch, he knew Henry and Cassandra were gone. Their fear and anger lingered, almost tangible in the air, and he could smell Henry's blood. The other human scents were familiar from the scene of Jairus's abduction.

He growled and pushed himself into human form to rap on the battered door, tearing off a thick splinter hanging from the shattered frame and tossing it aside.

Scraping sounded from behind the door before Nancy wedged it open. Fear and worry deepened the lines in her face, and her eyes were swollen and red.

"Tell me what happened," Domin demanded, remembering too late not to frighten the old woman.

"Some men took poor Miss Cassandra and Mr. Stewart this

morning. I hid upstairs with the mistress and the children. They left someone behind, but when he fell asleep, I bashed him on the head and tied him up." Her voice shook as she spoke, but her hands were steady where they gripped the doorframe.

"Is he conscious?"

"No, and he won't be for some time. I gave him something to keep him out, and I know how to mix my medicines."

The man might have been useful, but Domin had no time to wait for him now. "You did well. Is Mrs. Weaver's time close?"

"Drawing near, but not here yet."

"Good. Block the door and do not open it again. Stay inside. Keep the children safe."

She nodded and shut the door. It rattled as something heavy thumped against it. Domin shoved it to check its security then slipped into his wolf form, circling the lawn.

At the lane, he encountered a chemical smell he could not place. The scents and emotions faded from there, and carriage tracks led away. He dashed after them, eyes on the muddy ground and ears flicking back and forth. The trail joined a main road past the village, crossing with older ruts until Domin lost all trace of them. He loped back to Drixton, head and tail drooping.

One of the black-and-white hogs the villagers fed on their garbage trotted across his path. It squealed and skittered away, and he braced his legs against the instinct to give chase. Instinct. Emotion. Nothing but distractions from his purpose.

He shook his head and stretched out of the wolf form, thick pelt giving way to smooth, black cotton. The village smells of food, animals, and waste dissipated, and his thoughts sharpened, along with his sense of the enchantment permeating Drixton.

He jogged to the Leland's shop and banged on the door. Amy swung it open and stepped back to let him in.

"Domin, what's happened?"

He rubbed his temples. "Henry and Miss Weaver are gone."

"Gone?"

"Yes. Rushford and his Grigori have them. I didn't even consider the possibility of humans..." He pushed his guilt aside. It helped nothing. "I cannot track them. I need to know where they might have gone."

After a long pause, Amy whispered, "Do you think they're still alive?"

"I know Henry is, at least."

"You're certain?"

"I... share in a measure of the pain when one of my charges dies."

Amy's eyes filled with sympathy. "You never told me that. How can you bear it?"

He shrugged. "I have to, though it's certainly one of the least pleasant aspects of my role. If I were a full-blooded daemon, at least I would be able to sense Henry's location."

She reached out a hand but stopped short of touching him. "Well, how *do* we find them?"

Domin closed his eyes. "I will search Ashby Hall again and see what I can learn about Mr. Rushford and the Grigori's activities there. Perhaps they left some clues."

"Yes, that's where we should start," Amy said.

"We?" he echoed.

"Of course. I'm not useless. I'm coming with you, and so is Miss Leland."

"Me?" Mary squeaked from the corner where she had been watching the exchange.

Domin studied Amy, trying to decipher the change stirring in her. He could not afford to trust her as he once had, but he would not turn his back on someone whom he had once laughed with and confided in.

He grasped her hand. Her eyes widened, but she hesitantly curled her soft, white fingers around his dark ones. Her emotions coursed over him until he identified the strengthening pulse of confidence and hope struggling against a tide of self-doubt.

"What did you do?" he asked.

"What do you mean?"

"Something happened since Henry banished you from the house. What was it?"

"Oh." Pink tinted Amy's cheeks. "I...I stood up to my mother. Is that what you mean?"

"Yes. I think it probably is." Domin studied her. "You may come if you wish, though I will not force Miss Leland to follow us into danger."

"But if they're hunting Fay, they could come for Mary as well. She's not safe either way."

Domin shrugged. It was not his decision.

Mary looked around the shop, her eyes full of longing, then stood. "I...I want to go. Just let me check on my father, please."

Domin nodded. "We need to hurry. Michaelmas is tomorrow, and the child will be born soon."

Mary scurried into the back rooms.

"You don't think one of our friends is the sacrifice, do you?" Amy asked.

"Possibly. I'm certain this is related."

"What if it's a ruse to draw us away from the real victim?"

Domin hesitated only a moment. "You may do what you like, but my duty is to protect Henry."

"It is, isn't it? Then we're coming too."

"Why are you doing this?" he asked.

"I want to help my friends." Amy frowned. "You still don't trust me, do you? It was over two centuries ago!"

He shrugged.

"Well, I'm trying to make amends." Her eyes flashed with anger, then her expression softened. "How long will it be until I've paid for my mistakes?"

"I'm not the one asking you to pay," Domin said softly. "I forgave you long ago."

"But you don't trust me!"

"Forgiveness and trust are not the same. I bear you no ill will, but I remain uncertain of your loyalties." Domin shook his head. "If this is about Fitzhugh...Amy, you cannot hold yourself responsible for his decisions."

"I'm the one who talked him into getting involved in the Gunpowder Plot. Before that, he didn't care about trying to change things, and he never would have turned to the Unseelie Court." Her shoulders sagged. "I think he still believes he's going to win freedom for the Fay, so we don't have to hide in shadows and behind glamours anymore."

"Perhaps," Domin said, "but he made his own choices. You cannot say 'what if', because there are an infinite number of other things that could have happened, especially over two centuries. Perhaps it's time you forgave yourself."

"I can't!" she wailed, her agony tearing through Domin like a sword thrust. Amy lowered her voice. "I don't deserve it. Not yet. But, Domin, I'm...I'm afraid. I'm afraid my mother's right. No matter what I do, I'll never be good enough. I'll never be worth anything."

Domin took a slow breath to diffuse the physical pain of her misery. "Amy, everyone has worth. You certainly do."

She shook her head, eyes brimming with tears.

Mary came out of the back rooms with her satchel slung over her shoulder. She gave Domin a dark look. He turned away. She might blame him for Amy's pain, but it was not his place to explain.

"We had best get moving," he said.

Chapter Thirty-One

Amy hesitated at the grand steps of Ashby Hall. The windows stared across the landscape like empty eyes. No human emotion reached her from inside, but traces of dark desires lurked in the uneasy stillness.

"Is it empty?" she whispered.

"Some of the servants are here," Domin said, "but they are enchanted. This is our best chance of tracking the others. If we find no trace of our friends, Fitzhugh, or the Grigori, we at least might discover where they've gone."

Amy nodded and clutched Mary's arm to follow Domin inside. Once again, no magic held Amy back—the Ashbys still had not uninvited her. Amy and Mary tiptoed behind Domin as he strode from room to room, emptying drawers, tapping for hidden compartments, and even slitting open the mattress in Fitzhugh's room. Mary picked the locks he couldn't force open, but they found nothing hinting at the elf's or Rushford's plans.

The room that had housed the machine now stood empty, but hatred still radiated from its dark corners. Mary refused to budge from the corridor. Domin grimaced when he stepped inside, but he took his time searching under the rug and sifting through the ashes in the cold fireplace. Amy stooped to help him, catching her skirts on the ornate iron fireplace grate and ripping off a long strip of fringe. Domin tugged the purple trim loose and handed it to her. She mumbled her thanks and backed away to let him work alone. Always a disgrace.

Back in the corridor, Domin sighed and ran his hands through his hair. Amy blinked at seeing him copy Henry's familiar gesture. She'd never known him to mimic the mannerisms of his charges before. Of course, he didn't often get to guard a friend. It must make it harder, more personal.

"We should try questioning the servants," he said.

"While they're under the Dark Lady's enchantment?" Amy's eyebrows arched. "Or are you going to break it?"

He shook his head. "Even at my best, I'm not sure I would have been able to, and I certainly cannot now, but you might be able to twist the enchantment to work in our favor."

Amy took a step back. "You want me to use Unseelie magic?"

"Of course not. I just want you to nudge their thinking in the right direction. It's not particularly difficult."

"So you say, but you're not the one doing it," she snapped.

Domin frowned at her, and she sighed.

"Very well. Can you disguise yourself as Robert Ashby? They'll be more inclined to talk if they think you're one of the family."

He shrugged and shifted into Robert's appearance. Amy smothered a laugh. The features were Robert Ashby's, but there was no mistaking Domin behind the expression.

"You might have to smile," she said. "Robert isn't so dour."

"Let's get to work," he said with a scowl.

Mary hung back, keeping Amy between herself and Domin. A handful of staff wandered the corridors, but they only mumbled or shrugged when Domin and Amy pressed them for Sir Walter's whereabouts. The enchantment muted so much of their emotions that Amy had nothing to work with. Domin's frown deepened as they walked. Had she disappointed him again? How would she ever redeem herself if she couldn't do anything right?

They ended in the kitchen, where the scullery maid ignored them. Amy and Domin glanced at each other in silent concern.

"What's that noise?" Mary asked.

Faint clinking sounded from the pantry. Amy opened the door on a portly, gray-haired woman counting silverware.

"The housekeeper!" She grinned. "They always have their fingers in the family gossip."

The woman paid no heed to Amy and Mary but curtseyed to Domin when he stepped into view. Amy gestured for him to do something with this sign of recognition, and he smiled, though it looked more like a grimace.

"I'm looking for my father," he said. "Can you tell me where he is?"

"Yes, sir," the housekeeper said.

"She's not really listening," Amy whispered.

"That's your job. Push her to pay attention."

Amy nodded and closed her eyes, shutting out everything except the housekeeper's feelings. "She's like the others. There's not much of her own will here."

"See if you can find anything that would make her want to speak."

Domin's voice sounded like Robert's, and on hearing it, Amy felt a prickling of emotion from the housekeeper. "Oh! She has a soft spot for you."

"What?" Domin stepped back from the woman.

"Well, for Robert. You have to be sweet to her."

"You want me to flirt with the Ashbys' housekeeper?"

Amy snickered at the thought of Domin trying to flirt. "It's not like that. Just be gentle with her. She's lonely, and she cares about Robert. She probably watched him grow up. Yes. She feels motherly toward him." Her grin faded. "It doesn't seem right to use those feelings against her."

"We're not hurting her," Domin said softly, "and if Robert Ashby is involved with the Dark Lady in any way, he's in terrible danger. She would want to help him."

"Yes, I suppose that's true. Very well. Just talk to her, and I'll nudge her emotions along." Amy sighed and turned back to the housekeeper.

Domin sat on a barrel next to the housekeeper and smiled. There was some sincerity in his expression, and Amy felt a stab of regret. There had been a time when Domin smiled more. Her feelings mingled in sympathy with the housekeeper's, who missed Robert's boyish smiles, and she pushed on that, encouraging the woman to look up at Domin.

"I need to find my father," he said. "Can you help me?"

The woman's desire to help was there, so Amy grabbed the thread and pulled, trying to tug it out of the haze of Unseelie magic clouding the housekeeper's mind.

"He left with everyone else, Master Robert."

"But where did they go?"

"The ladies went back to London, though it's an odd time of year for it. The men was right mysterious about where they was going, though."

"Surely you know something?"

After a long pause, the woman said, "They might've gone to the old estate. I heard 'em complaining that the roads was bad."

"That sounds promising," Domin said to Amy and Mary. "It's probably clandestine." He turned back to the housekeeper. "Where is the old estate? How do we get there?"

"I don't remember the name of the village nearby, but I think it's north, almost a day's ride."

"North. Yes, that's the direction I tracked Mr. Hale. Can you tell me anything else about it?"

Another long silence stretched around them, and the woman's glassy gaze made Amy think she hadn't heard. Finally, she said, "Pines grow there. You brought me the cones when you was a child."

"Thank you," Domin said, and the woman smiled serenely.

"Is that enough information to go on?" Amy asked, releasing her hold on the woman.

"I think so," Domin said. "I saw some records in Ashby's desk dealing with his properties. We'll check them and find the one that matches her description. The Grigori have quite a head start, though."

Amy's heart sank. Once again, her friends' lives were at stake, and she was too far away to help them. But her steps regained their bounce as she guided Mary down the corridor. Maybe this time she could finally make things right.

Chapter Thirty-Two

Cassandra forced her eyes open. Her nose and throat burned, and the dim light in the carriage pierced her pounding head. She tried to sit up, but the manacles dug into her chafed wrists. The drugs had left her stomach churning.

The coach rolled to a stop.

Henry slumped in the seat across from her, his eyes still drooping. He met her gaze and shifted straighter.

"Miss Weaver?" His raspy voice made her throat ache in sympathy. "Are you awake enough to listen? We may not get another chance to talk."

"Yes," she whispered, grimacing at the sickly sweet taste in her mouth.

"I hesitated with Mr. Hale's gun, and that was a mistake. The first chance I get, I'm going to make Rushford and his Grigori regret ever touching either of us. Cooperate with them if it keeps you safe, and run if you see the opportunity. Even if I can't get free, Domin will find us eventually, and he'll help you."

Voices approached the carriage. Henry watched the door with eyes narrow and lips drawn tight. Cassandra remembered what Domin had said about watching each other. Henry's temper looked close to the snapping point, and it might be just what the Dark Lady wanted.

"Mr. Stewart?" she whispered. His gaze softened when it shifted back to her. She took a deep breath. "Regardless of what happens, I wouldn't want anyone hurt for my sake. I mean, I understand you may have to do certain things for us to escape, but not for revenge."

Henry's forehead wrinkled, but he nodded. Cassandra tensed for the chance to get away. Not that she was likely to get far with her bad leg and not even her brace to support it. But if she could create a distraction, it might help Henry. The carriage door opened. She flinched from the bright light.

"He's really one of them, then?" a man asked in the crisp accent of London's West Side.

"We'll make certain once we get them inside," Rushford answered.

"Who's the girl?" another man asked.

"An anomaly. She's immune to magic, but she doesn't seem to have any. I believe she has the potential to be useful to me... or us."

Cassandra's stomach rolled, and she pressed against the cushioned seat.

One of the Grigori grabbed Henry's arm. Henry rocked back and kicked out with his manacled feet. A man in a wrinkled brown waistcoat caught Henry's legs and yanked him off the seat, slamming his head against the carriage floor. The man reached in to haul him up. Henry pitched forward and slammed his forehead into the man's nose. The first man punched Henry in the face and dragged him outside.

"Don't damage him," Rushford said with a sigh.

Cassandra scooted away from the men's reaching hands. The heel of her boot tangled in the hem of her skirt, but she tore her foot free and lunged for the far door of the carriage. Someone caught her manacles and yanked. She whimpered at the pain tearing through her shoulders and let them pull her into the late afternoon light. The rough movement roiled her stomach, and she fought the urge to gag.

Dirt and gravel crushed by numerous wheel ruts swung across her vision as the men forced her to the steps of a hulking old manor house. She looked for something to orient herself before they pushed her inside, but the building sat in a low, wooded park, and the drive curved out of sight.

She expected a dim interior full of spiders or mice, but bright paraffin lamps illuminated the polished wood floors in the entrance. Servants moved about, taking hats and coats from the well-dressed Grigori and paying no attention to their unwilling guests. They didn't look enchanted, just uncaring. As if they'd witnessed this kind of scene before. The Rules said they should obey their master, so they did.

"Bring them back here. We'll get to work directly," Rushford ordered.

One of the men tugged Cassandra's arm, forcing her past ornate furniture and paintings of long-dead lords and ladies. After limping down a corridor and up some stairs, she finally stumbled to a stop in what might once have been a hall for dancing or fencing. Tables scattered around the room held microscopes and brass instruments for taking measurements, and lamp light spilled through rows of glass containers with colored liquids, casting strange rainbows on the walls. The chemical smell wafting from the place burned Cassandra's nose and prodded her uneasy stomach.

"Test him first," Rushford said.

Two of the Grigori lifted Henry off his feet. He twisted, but a broad-chested man cuffed him in the face. Cassandra winced in sympathy. They refastened Henry's shackles in front of his body and strapped him to a flat, narrow bed. The broad-chested man cut away his sleeve, while another pushed over a small, wheeled table with glass orbs and metal tubes.

Rushford slid a brass needle into Henry's arm. Henry flinched, but the men held him fast as blood flowed through the needle into a vial. When it was full, Rushford pulled out the needle and held the vial to the light, swirling the blood around the glass. Henry's arm oozed.

"Staunch that wound," Rushford said, his eyes fixed on the vial. He placed a drop or two of blood in each of the containers on the wheeled table. The other men gathered around, whispering and craning their necks. The liquid in a few of the orbs changed colors, and one developed a faint glow.

"Interesting," Rushford said as he made some notes. "Very interesting. I believe your time with us will be enlightening, Mr. Stewart." He leered at Cassandra. "Bring the girl now."

"Leave her alone!" Henry shouted, rattling his chains, but the men didn't even glance in his direction.

Cassandra didn't struggle when they shackled her hands in front. But when they shoved her onto a hard, narrow bed, she tried to roll off the other side with the desperate desire to crawl under and hide. One of the men jerked her back and fastened leather straps across her shoulders and waist. She turned her face from their curious stares and pulled her stockinged legs up under her skirts.

The broad-chested man cut through her green and white sleeve. Just that morning, she had put that dress on hoping to look nice for Henry. Before Beth had attacked them. Before she knew Henry was stranded outside of time. Before she'd been kidnapped from her own home. A lifetime ago. Hysteria fluttered beneath her ribs, and she clamped her mouth shut, not certain if she wanted to laugh or cry, but knowing she wouldn't be able to stop doing either once she started.

Rushford traced a cold finger down her arm and then plunged the needle into the inside of her elbow. Sharp, warm pain raced up her arm. She didn't dare move for fear of tearing the needle out, though she couldn't stop herself from trembling.

She realized she was holding her breath, but before she could exhale, Rushford drew out the needle and placed a rag over the wound. The men turned their attention to the table as he dribbled her blood into fresh orbs. She twisted her head to watch.

After a few minutes of hushed muttering, Rushford said, "Nothing at all."

"She's perfectly ordinary," another man said.

Cassandra met Rushford's calculating gaze. *Pretend to be normal.* She'd made up that rule herself. She could have laughed if the man's icy look wasn't freezing her in place.

"Maybe she's made a pact with some magical creature for her safety," Rushford said. "What do you say, Miss Cassandra? Don't you want to be helpful and tell us what you know? Why doesn't Faerie magic touch you?"

Henry had told her to cooperate, but she couldn't bear the thought of helping the Grigori. She avoided looking at Henry and said, "I don't understand what you mean."

"I doubt that's true." Rushford smiled without any trace of humor and leaned closer to whisper in her ear, "Cooperate, and we will find a way to cure you. I will make you my Galatea."

Cassandra shuddered and turned her face away.

"Maybe she'll talk if she sees our other methods of getting information." The broad-chested man licked his lips and grinned. She glared back, but her stomach flip-flopped like a trout on a line.

One of the men cleared his throat. "I didn't sign up to torture girls, Rushford."

"No, we shouldn't have to resort to that," Rushford said. "The freak here probably knows the answer, and we have her blood to study. If she won't cooperate, we'll put her to another use."

"What use could that be?" asked a man with a polished London accent.

"With her and the other one for the ritual, we'll be able to keep Mr. Stewart around longer. Take her downstairs. We have more work to do here."

Cassandra shouted and kicked as rough hands lifted her from the bed, dragging her along well-lit corridors and down steep stairs that led underground. The darkness thickened as they descended, drawing around her like a winding sheet. She might never see daylight again, or her sisters, or even Henry. She stopped struggling and turned to watch the light vanish behind her, trying to remember the way back.

They arrived at a cavernous stone room. The fireplace on the far end was so large a man could easily walk into it and be lost in the shadows. Dungeon cells lined the wall. Cassandra's nausea swelled at the stench of decay emanating from the space. She balked, but her captors pushed her forward.

"Mark her and put her in one of the empty cells," one of the men said before leaving the room. The broad-chested man unlocked her shackles. Cassandra whirled to break his grasp, but he pulled her back and slapped her so hard spots swam across her vision.

"Touch her again, and I'll put a lead ball where your heart should've been." The familiar voice echoed off the stone walls. Jairus!

Cassandra twisted to see him, but the broad-chested man tightened his grip on her arm and pulled a hot iron out of the coals in the fireplace. She shouted and squirmed, but he shoved her down and knelt beside her, pinning open her crippled right hand.

The hot iron pressed into her palm for several seconds. Searing pain and the smell of scorched skin brought tears to her eyes. Only after the man pulled it away did she realize she'd been screaming the whole time. She turned and vomited. Her captor made a disgusted noise and hauled her up, wrenching her arm.

He yanked open one of the cells and thrust her inside. She stumbled onto the cold floor and curled into a tight ball. The creak of the iron lock and the slam of the room's wooden door echoed as if from a great distance. Trembling racked her aching muscles, and tears rolled down her cheeks as she cradled her hand. The lingering smell made her heave again, but nothing came up.

"Miss Weaver?"

She blinked through the haze of darkness swarming her head like wasps and concentrated on catching Jairus's words, following them back to awareness.

"I need you to listen to me," he said. "You've been through something terrible, and your mind is likely in shock. I'm going to keep talking to you, and I want you to focus on what I'm saying."

The fireplace cast a red glow over the room, just enough to see the large, empty space beyond the cell. Keeping her injured hand close to her chest, she crawled to the bars.

"Mr. Hale? What are you doing here?"

"Being held captive, same as you." His voice sounded close —perhaps in the neighboring cell—but she couldn't find an angle that let her see him.

"Now pay attention," he said. "I'm going to tell you what to do for your hand. Do you have any clean cloth? Maybe part of your dress?"

Cassandra took a shaky breath and studied the remnants of her striped skirts, dirty from the stone floor. The petticoat beneath was fairly clean. "Yes."

"Good. Tear off a long strip of the cleanest fabric you've got and wrap it very gently around the burn. Make sure the whole thing is covered. You don't want it too tight, but it shouldn't be so loose that it'll slip around."

Fingers still shaking, Cassandra managed to rip a ruffle from her petticoat and wrap it around her injured hand, tucking in the loose ends. "I did it."

"Good. Hmm. I don't want to embarrass you, Miss Weaver, so I'll just say you should make yourself as comfortable as possible. Make certain you can breathe well."

"I understand." She wriggled her good hand up the back of her bodice and pulled the ties on her corset, loosening it as much as she could without undressing.

"You need to keep talking. Can you tell me how you ended up here?" Jairus asked.

She sought out her scattered memories, pulling them together a little at a time, like a braid catching loose strands of hair. "They attacked my house and drugged Mr. Stewart and me. Where are we?"

"A house out in the country. I'm afraid there's no one close by."

"Oh." She leaned against the bars, and the cold soaked through her cotton dress. "How did they catch you?"

"When I got back to Sir Walter's estate, I ran into some of Mr. Rushford's men. I was too badly outnumbered…"

She gingerly touched the soft bandage swaddling her hand. The blistered, red mark on her palm was the same one Jairus had traced in the dust in her sitting room, the same one carved into the church: a snake coiled into a figure eight. "Why did they do this to me? Burn my hand?"

He was quiet for a long time, then she heard him sigh. "I guess it's better for you to know than not. The brand means you're to be sacrificed. And me—I've got one as well."

"So we *are* going to be the Dark Lady's sacrifice?" Her stomach twisted again. Had her disregard of The Rules sullied her past saving?

"I don't plan on letting them sacrifice us to anyone, Miss Weaver, but the being they mentioned is called the Leannan, not the Dark Lady. What happened to Mr. Stewart?"

"They have him upstairs. They took our blood and did some tests. His…reacted."

"Did it now? They tested mine too, when they brought me here, and tossed me in this cell when nothing happened. I'm not sure how it's possible to test for magic, but it looks like they've found a way. That might be good news for Mr. Stewart or it might not, I suppose. At least he's not stuck down here."

"I think he was going to be. They said that since I was here, they could keep him around longer." She hesitated. "What will they do to him?"

Jairus paused again, and she got the sense he was holding something back. "These Grigori study the supernatural. I reckon they want to find out what sort of magic Mr. Stewart can do, and maybe if there's a way for them to do the same."

She shuddered. "Do you think they *can* learn to use magic?"

"I don't know, but it's not something that comes naturally to us humans."

The door to the room crashed open, and she shuffled back from the bars. Rushford burst into the dungeon as if he had been shoved. Fitzhugh strode in behind him, giving the man another push. The elf stopped outside Cassandra's cell and crouched to look at her face, concern in his blue eyes.

"What have they done, little pet? Are you injured?"

His baritone voice soothed away some of her shock and confusion. Letting go of whatever dignity she had left, she nodded, tears welling in her eyes.

Fitzhugh snarled and jumped to his feet. Cassandra scrambled farther back as he slammed Mr. Rushford into the cell bars, holding him by the coat.

"How dare you touch her! I allowed you to take Henry Stewart—a sacrifice on our part—but you were not to harm the Weaver girls. They are under my protection." Fitzhugh hammered Rushford against the bars again and leaned in to sneer at him. "Don't forget, if I withdraw my recommendation, my Lady may choose to claim *your* soul tomorrow night."

"I haven't forgotten," Rushford choked out. "We won't kill the girl, at least not until after the baby is born."

Fitzhugh threw Rushford to the floor and grabbed the iron bar of Cassandra's cell. He hissed and jerked his hand away, staring at the burn crossing his palm. The anger coloring his face faded as his hand healed, and he chuckled. "I apologize for the accommodations, my pet, but if you had come to Elfland with me, you would be much more comfortable right now. Maybe this is fitting, after how troublesome you've been. As long as I keep your human overseers in line, you're safer in here than off doing something foolish."

Fitzhugh spared a smirk for Jairus before following Rushford out of the room.

Cassandra sank back, shaking.

"Fitzhugh just bought you some time," Jairus said. "That's something to be grateful for. You ought to rest if you can. We have some excitement ahead of us."

"Y-yes," Cassandra managed to say.

She doubted she could sleep, but she curled up on the dirty stone floor and took long, slow breaths, trying to imagine being anywhere else. Her hand throbbed in time with the beating of her heart, and her head and throat ached. Still, the lingering effects of the ether and her injury overcame her, and she slipped into a shallow sleep with mercifully few dreams.

Chapter Thirty-Three

The cell bars dug into Jairus's shoulder as he slammed against them, but they didn't give under the onslaught. He grunted and picked up his discarded belt buckle to resume chipping at the mortar. At least when the Grigori took his weapons, they'd overlooked the damage a little bit of metal could do if one had a few hours to work on the problem.

The damp chill of the dungeon stiffened his fingers, even as sweat tickled the back of his neck. He paused to rub his hands. At this point, he would play poker with the devil if the stakes included a warm bath and clean clothes, so he was grateful Fitzhugh hadn't made any offers.

A muffled whimper escaped from the neighboring cell, which had been quiet for some time.

His jaw tightened, and he scraped harder, rubbing blisters into his fingers. "Miss Weaver? Are you all right...given the circumstances?"

"Yes," she said. "I just can't stand being... useless. Is there anything I can do to help?"

He stopped, resting his head against the cold bars. "Did they leave you with anything metal, or sharp?"

"I didn't have anything like that to begin with. Just a little brooch. If only I had put on my brace this morning."

"They probably would have taken it, anyway. Try to rest for now."

"I'm not tired anymore. Is it day or night?"

"I don't know, but I'd guess it's close to Michaelmas." The stone walls loomed over him, heavy and jagged in the dying glow from the fireplace outside their cells. "I was trying to keep track, but I slept a bit too."

He tossed the buckle aside and paced, running his hand along the rough stones in hope of finding one loose. Covering his nose, he stopped by the old latrine hole in the back of the cell. Too narrow to climb down, even if he could brave the stench.

The door to the room creaked open. He rushed back to the bars. A Grigori with black mutton-chop whiskers frizzing from his jowls trudged in and shoved a shallow bowl of cold, lumpy porridge under each of their doors. Jairus tensed to grab the man's hair and yank him against the door, but the Grigori stayed just out of range. As soon as he left, Jairus took his bowl and shoveled the mush into his mouth.

A spoon. If the devil offered him that poker game, he'd ask for a spoon too. It would be easier to dig with and might work as a weapon.

"Are you eating, Miss Weaver? It'll keep your strength up."

"Are you certain it's safe?"

"I tried a little bit last time they brought something and I'm no worse off. I don't think they're going to poison us."

Her bowl scraped the stone floor.

Jairus forced down most of the porridge. His stomach

ached for more food, but he gagged at the cold, gray blobs quivering in the bowl and closed his eyes.

Hot, roasted meat dripping with gravy. Thick-crusted bread still steaming from the oven. Pie stuffed with spicy, sweet-tart apples. His mouth watered at the vision. If the Dark Lady herself showed up now and made the offer...

He frowned. Why *wasn't* she trying to corrupt them? They would be easy targets now. Jairus took inventory and didn't think he'd done anything to make himself the sacrifice, but with so many gaps in his armor, he couldn't be sure he had them all covered. And the voice in his mind stayed strangely quiet.

The door swung open. He jumped, but it was just the whiskery guard. "Dinner's over. Give me your bowls."

Cassandra's rattled under her door, but Jairus wrapped his fingers around the smooth wood.

"Come on, hand it over," the man said.

"Come get it." Jairus held the bowl just inside the bars.

The man rolled his eyes. "Keep the bowl, then. That was your last meal anyway. Stupid Yankee."

Jairus bared his teeth and flung the bowl sideways through the bars. The Grigori stepped back, but the bowl smacked his face and splattered him with the remnants of the porridge. The man cursed and fled the room, wiping his whiskers with his sleeve.

"Never call me a Yankee!" Jairus drew several deep breaths as his stampeding temper ran itself out. Not the best time to lose control. He sighed. "Sorry for the outburst, Miss Weaver. I hope I didn't offend you."

She replied with a muffled noise. Jairus frowned. Crying seemed like a bit of an overreaction. But, no, she was laughing.

"I only wish I'd thought of that." She took a shaky breath.

"I'm sorry to laugh. What were you planning to use the bowl for?"

"Absolutely nothing," Jairus said. Then he dissolved too, letting the tears of nonsensical laughter wash some of the grime from his face. When his mirth drained away, he felt cleaned out, like a gully after a storm.

"Well, I did hope you had a plan, but the look on his face when you hit him ..." She snickered again, then her voice grew serious. "If I can ask, why did it make you so angry that he called you...that?"

"I saw the things the Yankee soldiers did." He leaned against the rough wall. "The Rebels, too. I never agreed with the Rebel cause, but war can turn anyone into a monster. My sister, Kate..." He buried his bruised face in his hands, trying to stop the memories that swarmed him.

The silence waited, heavy, and he kept talking just to fill it. "My parents moved us to the Utah Territory before the trouble started. They were from the South, but they didn't want anything to do with the war or with slavery, just to follow their religion and their consciences in peace. Kate felt the same way, but she married a man who kept her in Mississippi. He died a year into the war, and she was defenseless when the soldiers came and burned her out of her home." Jairus paused. As much as Cassandra had suffered, she didn't need to know about the hellish reality for women and children homeless, crying for hunger, bare feet cut and bleeding as they fled over the frozen ground to escape the soldiers, Rebel and Yank both.

"The war wasn't over," Jairus went on. "So I went back to help her and her children. Protect them." He paused. "Sometimes we have to grow up too fast, to help the people we love."

"Yes," she said softly.

He paced again, kicking aside some of the debris scattered on the floor and trying not to think much about where the tufts of black fur and torn fabric came from. He picked through the rags with the toe of his boot. Something solid caught on his foot, and he shuffled the mess apart to find a dull white bone about as long as his forearm. He couldn't tell if it was human.

"Can you tell me about America?" Cassandra asked. "I mean, not the war part."

He hesitated, staring at the bone. "Well, I'll tell you about the West. The war hardly reached out there. It's kind of its own world." He closed his eyes and let his mind roam out of the cell as he described the tall mountains that held their snow into July, the towering red rocks sculpted by burning winds, and the sweet smell of sagebrush after a rain.

"It sounds beautiful. I can see why you miss it," she said when he fumbled to a stop.

He shrugged, trying to banish the homesickness his descriptions conjured up. The bone rattled against the floor when he nudged it. He picked it up and brushed his fingers along the rough, dry surface, pausing over the gnaw marks. Rats? No, something bigger. "I'm just telling you the nice parts. It's a harsh place too."

"Is that why you came to England?"

He paced back to the cell door and stuck the bone between two bars, pressing to lever them apart. The iron didn't budge, but he hadn't really expected it to.

"Well, some monsters have a long reach." He picked up the belt, wrapping it around two of the bars and then winding it around the bone. He turned the bone like a ship's wheel, tightening the belt. "After the war, I...got into some bad habits. Gambling. Looking for fights. I guess the war never ended for me. I just went from fighting Yanks and Johnny Rebs to fighting monsters. One time, some powerful Southerners planned to summon spirits to possess the Yankee leaders, thinking they'd be able to control them then." He smiled thinly. "They didn't take it well when I stole their grimoire—their book of spells—and burned it, along with most of their plantation house. They sent men to hunt me. After that, no one I cared about was safe as long as I was around, so I came here. I had enough money from gambling to continue tracking some of my former enemies who'd come overseas, and they led me to Rushford and his Grigori."

"You sought them out knowing how dangerous they were?"

"So I could discover their plans and stop them. It's what I do. My calling."

He twisted the bone again, and the bars creaked under the tightening belt. Ignoring the pain stabbing his burned hand, he grinned and levered the bone around. The leather belt snapped, and the bone flipped up to smack his chin. He slammed the bone against the bars, and it cracked.

"What was that?" Cassandra asked.

"A minor setback." Jairus rubbed his chin and studied the jagged end of the bone. He grabbed the longest remaining piece of the belt and used it to tie the door to the bars next to it. When someone got close enough to untie it, he'd have a shot at them with the sharp piece of bone. Then the other Grigori would close in, though. He looked at the pathetic weapon in his hand and sank to the ground. The voice that had guided him through battles and monsters and across an ocean now offered no guidance or comfort. Perhaps there was none to give.

Frustration mingled with the ghosts of his memories and, like a riptide, pulled him back onto the battlefield. The hellish stink of sulfur. The screams of dying men and horses. The ground rumbling underfoot with each cannon blast.

"Mr. Hale?"

He smacked his head back against the bars. He wasn't in Mississippi. The gunshots and explosions and screams weren't real. What *was* real was that he was locked up, about to be murdered, and the innocent girl in the cell next to him needed him to keep his thoughts clear so he could save them both.

A bang echoed off the stone walls. Not another ghostly cannon, but the door to the room slamming open. Jairus's gaze jerked to a trim man carrying two bowls. More food? If Rushford wanted to fatten them up, he'd have to send something more appetizing. The trim man slid a bowl under his door. Porridge again. Jairus grimaced and pushed it aside. The man studied Cassandra with bright green eyes as he passed her bowl over.

"Miss Weaver, Mr. Hale, are you unharmed?" the man asked.

"Domin?" Cassandra's voice cracked.

"Of course," Domin replied, not dropping his disguise.

Jairus sagged against the door and shut his eyes in a silent prayer of thanks.

"Mr. Stewart thought you would come," Cassandra said. "Have you seen him? Is he all right?"

Domin hesitated. "He's not too badly injured, for now, but we need to get all of you out of here. The house is closely guarded."

"We?" Jairus asked.

"Amy and Miss Leland came with me."

Jairus nodded. At this point, Faerie magic was a card he didn't mind having up his sleeve. "Can't you get us out now?"

"Picking iron locks is not a skill I have acquired. I'm still looking for the keys."

"Miss Leland can pick locks." Jairus gripped a bar with his

uninjured hand. "Do you know where they put my things? If we're getting out of here, I'd like my guns back."

"I would like you to have them, but I've not yet found them." Domin glanced between Jairus and Cassandra. "What did they do to your hands?"

Cassandra must have shown Domin her wound because the shape-shifter's green eyes narrowed and his lips curled back.

Cassandra spoke up. "Mr. Hale told me they were going to sacrifice us to, uh—"

"The Leannan," Jairus said.

Domin's face blanched. "They are insane."

"Fitzhugh is here too. Is this Leannan part of the Dark Lady's court?" Jairus asked.

"No. Leannan are solitary Fay like the Morrigan. They are creatures of spirit who feed humans forbidden knowledge and inspiration while draining the life from them."

"Does this mark mean we belong to the Leannan?" Cassandra asked.

"Your soul belongs to no one but you, and only you could give it up." Domin paused. "That is not to say a demon mark cannot be troublesome." He shook his head. "The Dark Lady must be involved in this, but I am not yet certain why."

Jairus groaned. "She's always one step ahead. It's going to be tough to stop her."

"Regrettably, it usually is, but do not give up hope. I will free you soon, and perhaps we can find a way to stop her sacrifice." Voices echoed in the hallway, and Domin said, "I'll return shortly."

He lowered his face and turned to leave, still disguised. Sir Walter and Mr. Rushford sauntered into the room, giving Domin only a passing glance. Sir Walter's eyes widened when they fell on Cassandra. She gasped, and Sir Walter looked away.

He walked to Jairus' cell and stared in as if the American were a circus animal on display. One step closer and Jairus could grab him, maybe hold his life for ransom.

"It's unfortunate, Rushford," Sir Walter said. "Unfortunate. He could have been a useful ally."

Rushford pulled Sir Walter out of Jairus's reach and cast a taunting smirk at the American. "He'll be a desirable offering for the Leannan if he's a priest as Fitzhugh claims. Preferable over the crippled girl—I may have overestimated her potential. But after all these tries, we may finally have found someone whose life energy will entice the Leannan." He lowered his voice. "With a powerful Fay on our side, we'll no longer need to deal with Fitzhugh's arrogance and slippery promises."

Jairus gripped the cell bars. He wasn't interested in being an enticement for anyone.

Sir Walter turned his back on Jairus. "Are you making any progress with the boy?"

Rushford's hard eyes glinted in the torchlight. "He is close-lipped, but our experiments will give us a baseline for studying others, something to compare our results to. In the future, perhaps we can find more willing participants."

Sir Walter shrugged. "You didn't tell me you wanted volunteers. But I expect results after everything I've invested in your work." He stopped and looked back at Cassandra. "Perhaps it's good we're not giving the girl to the Leannan yet. The boy may not help us for his own sake, but I think he'll cooperate to spare her, once he sees her suffer a bit."

Jairus wrapped the fingers of his bandaged hand around the bone, looking for a chance to attack with it. "Y'all are fools. I've seen this kind of thing before, and it won't end well for you. There's always a price."

Sir Walter's face tightened. "It's getting late, Rushford. Prepare the men."

Rushford nodded and walked back out into the hallway. Sir Walter stood looking at the cavernous fireplace on the far end of the room.

"Listen to me, Sir Walter," Jairus said. "When humans meddle with supernatural forces, they always come out the loser. Do you think you can make a deal with a powerful spirit and walk away without any entanglements? It'll own you."

Sir Walter ignored him.

Jairus kicked the bars of his cell and paced to burn off his frustration. He rattled his door. "Well, you've been a lousy host, Sir Walter. Murdering your guests is...how do you Brits say it? Not 'the thing.'"

Still no reaction. After a long, tense wait, Rushford reentered the room wearing a long black robe and carrying a book. He handed another robe to Sir Walter.

"Are you sure this is necessary?" Sir Walter held the robe out like a filthy rag.

"It is. Summoning rituals require the correct forms to be effective, and we want to make certain we keep the Leannan under our control."

"Oh, very well, very well."

Sir Walter donned the black garment, and other hooded Grigori filtered into the room, taking up positions around the floor. A few carried torches, and one drew arcane symbols with white chalk on the stained flagstones of the dungeon. Jairus scanned the room, but if Domin was there, he gave no indication. Jairus shook his head when he spied Robert Ashby by his father's side. How had he gotten mixed up in this?

The men gathered into a circle around the diagram on the floor. Rushford handed Sir Walter a book, and he opened it to read. Jairus strained to understand, but the words were a hodgepodge of languages, and he could only pick out an occasional phrase. The cloying darkness of the ritual made his skin crawl, and he backed up. Clutching his broken piece of bone, he prayed for rescue.

Chapter Thirty-Four

Mary leaned against the rough bark of a pine tree, wishing it would open to admit her like a carved bird in one of her father's clocks. The smell of pine and chimney smoke hung thick in the night air, wrapping her in memories of her father's shop, where soft, curled golden shavings cushioned her footsteps, and the tick of its mechanical denizens gave order to the hours. A refuge where no one taunted her, or threw garbage, or muttered to each other when things broke in her presence.

Home would never be the same, though. She had things to fear now that even the workshop couldn't shelter her from, and —if what Domin said was true—her father had known the truth and hidden it from her. He might have done it to protect her, but how was she safer not knowing what was wrong with her or why strange things happened around her? A lie falling between two people knocked everything out of place, and Mary didn't know how to make the pieces fit right again. Maybe the only way she could return home was to face the truth and bring back her own answers about who she was.

She couldn't stop thinking about the child that had been stolen from her parents. They had cared for Mary—shown no resentment toward her—but the guilt of what she was gnawed at her stomach, circling there like an angry, living beast. Was the child she had replaced alive in Elfland somewhere, a slave, while she had lived its life, sheltered by kind, grieving parents?

Light flashed from a side door to the house. Mary shivered and shrank back next to Amy in the darkness. A low whistle announced Domin's approach. Amy stepped out from behind the tree, but Mary kept her hand on the wide trunk.

"Well?" Amy asked Domin, who still wore the guise of a trim, tawny-haired man. Mary took a step back. It wasn't natural, him changing faces the way some people changed hats.

"The situation is not good," Domin said.

Amy stiffened. "Are they alive?"

"Yes."

"Injured?"

"Yes, and you were right about these men. They are dangerous, experimenting with magic. The Dark Lady must be desperate for allies. For now, though, we need to get our friends out. We have less than an hour until midnight, so the Dark Lady cannot be far away."

"If her sacrifice is even here," Amy said. "We don't know for certain."

Domin shrugged. "Can you go inside?"

"No. It *is* a home, however twisted. But Miss Leland can."

Domin cocked his head. "Miss Leland, you can pick locks. Does that include iron ones?"

Mary shrank from his scrutinizing gaze. "Yes."

"Good. Come with me."

He turned back to the house. Mary looked to Amy, who gestured for her to follow. Mary hurried after Domin, her boots slipping on the slick pine needles carpeting the ground. As they crept through the side door, they passed an unconscious guard, bound and gagged, with the same face Domin wore. Mary dug her fingernails into the leather strap of her satchel and glanced back at Amy, wishing they could trade places. But Cassandra and Jairus had been kind to Mary, and now she might be able to help them. She could do for Cassandra's sister what no one had done for her parents' natural child—her sister, in a strange way.

Her footsteps echoed in the lofty, wood-paneled corridor as they passed gold-framed pictures and windows hung with velvet draperies. She scurried along like a mouse lost in a palace.

Summoning her courage, she whispered, "Mr. Domin?"

He paused and made a noise somewhere between annoyance and amusement. "It's just Domin."

Mary flushed. She'd never addressed anyone older than her by their given name. "Um, Domin. If I'm Fay, why can I come inside and Lady St. Clair can't?"

He pressed forward, speaking just loudly enough for her to hear. "She exists in a different state than you do, so she must follow different rules."

Mary pulled the idea apart and examined it like a broken music box. "But iron still hurts me."

"Elves are creatures of magic, and iron hurts magic. The Fay have cut you off from their world and their power, but that doesn't change what you are. Think about water. It can be liquid and dwell on the earth, or it can be mist and dwell in the air. Either way, it is still water, but it follows different rules depending on its state."

"I'm liquid, and she's mist?"

"It's only an analogy, but that is the idea."

"But she's here in this world just like me."

"Faerie magic still ties her to Elfland, like in nature how water vapor can...hmm." He trailed off, annoyance in his voice. "Well, I didn't say it was a perfect analogy."

"Did *you* need an invitation to come inside?"

"No. I'm part daemon. I can go anywhere I must to protect my charge."

That seemed like quite a bit of trouble over Henry Stewart. Mary shrugged to herself and trudged on in silence.

Domin led her up a flight of stairs. At the landing, they came upon a beefy man in a black suit.

He dropped his newspaper and stood. "What are you doing, Greene? No one's supposed to be up here right now."

Domin lunged and slammed the guard's head against the wall, knocking him out, then lowered him to the floor. Mary's trembling hands stilled when the guard drew a breath.

She scooted around the unconscious man and followed Domin past an open room full of cluttered tables. Her entire home, including the workshop, would have fit inside.

Domin opened the next door down the corridor and, after glancing in, motioned for Mary. She paused in the doorway. The machine from Sir Walter's home loomed in front of her next to an assemblage of microscopes, gauges, and other scientific instruments. Beside those were tables covered with jars and tubes of various shapes and sizes. Sharp surgical tools hung on the wall.

Domin disappeared through an entrance on the far side, and Mary scurried after, turning her face from the machine.

Several large iron cages stood in the far room. Henry lay curled up in one of them, his hands and feet shackled, his torso bare, and his face pallid under his cuts and bruises. Only the uneven rise and fall of his breathing proved he still lived. Small,

round wounds marked his arms and torso. Beneath those were
old, crisscrossing scars, some thin and others as thick as Mary's
little finger. Was that the life her parents' child faced? She
swallowed the taste of bile.

"Can you open this?" Domin's voice broke through her
horrified stare.

She dug her fingers into the strap of the satchel and tiptoed
across the room to examine the lock. One of the slender tools
from her satchel slipped easily into the mechanism. Sensations
whispered through her hands, drawing a diagram in her mind
of the internal levers as she manipulated each one. After a few
moments, she stepped back and swung the door open, curling
her fingers—blistered from the iron—into her palms.

Domin darted inside. He examined Henry's wounds with
care, but Henry made a sound somewhere between a whimper
and a groan. Mary looked away.

"Miss Leland." Domin gestured her over.

She stepped into the cage. The air, heavy with the stink of
iron, pressed around her. Domin pointed to the shackles. She
lowered herself next to Henry, the cold sting of the flat grid of
bars on the floor penetrating her skirts and stockings. She flexed
her hands and bent over the locks. The buzzing in her head
disrupted her concentration, but finally, the last lever clicked
open. She scrambled to her feet and fled the cage.

"Henry?" Domin pulled the manacles away with a hiss of
pain.

Henry woke with a gasp. He scooted from Domin and
raised his hands defensively, then blinked a few times and
relaxed.

"Domin?" Henry asked, his voice hoarse. "I was starting to
be afraid you wouldn't find us. You are here, aren't you? They
drugged me. Everything's hazy." He ran his fingers through

his hair. "They wanted me to tell them about what I can do, what I know. I don't think I told them anything, but I don't know how long until I would have. One of the men had a cigar..."

Mary clutched her satchel to her chest and backed away, understanding the fresh marks on his body. Some of her anger toward Henry dissolved under a flood of pity.

"It's over now," Domin said gently. "We're leaving."

Henry shook his head. "Miss Weaver. They have her. I'm not sure where."

"I've seen her. Mr. Hale is here, too."

"We're going after them, then." Henry pushed himself up. Domin held him back, but Henry shook off his hand. "No, I can get up. It was mostly the chemicals, and they're wearing off now." He rubbed his eyes, frowning when his gaze reached Mary. "Ah, uh, Miss Leland."

She lowered her eyes to the scuffed wooden floor before she could decipher his expression. Disappointment, perhaps, or embarrassment?

"Miss Leland opened your cell," Domin said.

"Oh. Well. Thank you. I—" He winced and grabbed one of the iron bars for support.

Mary sensed an apology in his tone but wasn't sure she was ready to forgive him.

"We need to go." Henry straightened. "Where are the others?"

Domin hesitated. "Miss Weaver and Mr. Hale are downstairs. Amy is outside. It might be better if you waited with her. Fitzhugh is here, and the Dark Lady may be near."

"I'm not going to wait outside with Amy," Henry snapped. "Look." He held out his hands and a breeze whirled through the room. Mary shivered. The lamps flickered then surged up more brightly. Henry lowered his hands. "I'm not useless. I'm coming with you."

Mary started at his words: the same ones Amy had used back in Drixton. Of course, Amy was still standing out in the chilly darkness.

"Very well," Domin said. "Let's go."

Mary paused when they passed the machine. Hatred seeped from it like putrid sap from a blighted tree. "Would a distraction help?" she whispered.

The men stopped.

"What did you have in mind?" Domin asked.

She turned from them to stare at the lurking machine. She had disabled it, but that wasn't enough. "A fire. It could destroy all of this before they put it out."

A grin spread over Henry's face as he surveyed the room. "With all the chemicals in here, we could make it better than just a fire: an explosion. Like that ether. Even the vapors are combustible. How far are we from Miss Weaver and Mr. Hale?"

"We are at the top of the north wing. They are below the main building." Domin frowned. "We have to be careful not to make the explosion too large, and we need to give ourselves time to get away before it brings everyone here." He opened a satchel hanging over his shoulder. "I found Mr. Hale's possessions. I'm certain he has something...Yes." He pulled out a cartridge of gunpowder. "But how will you light it without being caught in the explosion?"

Mary pointed to the machine. "This has electricity."

"Yes." Henry nodded. "They tried to use it on me—to see if they could control my magic with it—but it shocked the man who pulled the switch. Knocked him out cold."

Mary suppressed her triumphant smile. "I could make it spark. We'd have to turn it on and run before the fire caught."

"It would ignite the ether, and if we put the gunpowder in a container, it will make a lot of noise when it catches." Henry took the powder and placed it inside a lidded metal jar then set it on the machine's wooden chair. "Miss Leland?"

Mary rearranged the wires she had taken apart at Ashby Hall, moving them so they were close but not touching. Henry handed her an open container of ether, and she set it on the machine. "It's ready."

"I'll pull the handle," Domin said.

"That switch over there." Mary pointed. "It won't shock you now."

Domin motioned for Henry and Mary to go as he grabbed the large handle and flipped it up. The electric current flowed, sparking as it jumped the gap between the two wires.

Henry ran with a halting limp, but Mary allowed him to take the lead, averting her gaze from his bare, scar-puckered back. The guard still lay unconscious on the landing. Domin, catching up with them, stopped to lift the man over his shoulder. Green light flashed in the landing and a whoosh thrummed against Mary's eardrums. A bitter smell stung her mouth and nose, and she covered them with her sleeve. The building rumbled. Several smaller explosions popped in quick succession.

Mary stumbled at the bottom step. The stairs seemed much shorter going down. Domin let the guard slump to the floor and rolled him over, removing the man's jacket. He handed it to Henry and led the three of them down a dim side corridor.

As Henry eased the jacket over his injuries, a group of men in archaic-looking robes ran down the main corridor toward the staircase, shouting at the sight of the fire.

"These back corridors let the servants move about without

disturbing the family," Domin whispered. "They will get us downstairs unseen."

"Then what?" Henry asked.

"You and I create a distraction so Miss Leland can open the locks."

Mary nodded, her throat as dry as sawdust. Clutching her satchel, she hurried with the men down the narrow corridor.

Chapter Thirty-Five

Cassandra huddled against the cold cell wall, out of reach of the flickering torchlight and the swaying shadows of the bars. She wrapped the torn remnants of her green-striped dress more tightly around herself and rubbed her fingers over Georgina's brooch.

The Grigori mingled in front of the cells, their murmurs humming through the cavernous room. Rushford scowled at his pocket watch and then at the door. The men he had sent to investigate the splintering boom from upstairs still hadn't returned.

"Does the exact number of men matter in the summoning?" Sir Walter asked.

"Father," Robert said in a low tone. "Perhaps we should wait..."

"Hush, boy, hush," Sir Walter said. "Rushford?"

"As long as we have at least thirteen."

"Good, good, then we continue."

The men spread into an uneven circle around the chalk

drawings on the floor and resumed their chant. Chills trickled down Cassandra's spine as their harsh droning echoed off the stone walls. In the torchlight, she caught glimpses of faces shielded by black hoods. None of them glanced in her direction, and she saw no sign of Domin. Sir Walter cradled his dark book like a hymnal in church. Rushford stood as still as a wax figure, except for his mouth, which snapped out each syllable of the chant. Robert's lips curved down and moved slowly, almost reluctantly, over the foreign words.

Wind whistled through the room, and the torches in the men's hands flickered. One flame bent too close to its bearer's robe, and smoke spiraled up from the fabric. A faint smell like burning paper mingled with the stench of the room. Jairus cleared his throat, and Cassandra edged closer to the bars.

"Fire!" Jairus shouted.

The circle of chanters scattered as the flames climbed the man's black garment. He flung the robe aside and dropped to roll on the filthy stone floor, smudging the chalk lines of their circle in an attempt to extinguish his smoldering clothes. The discarded robe blazed in the dark room. Hooded men crashed into each other, shouting for water. Rushford tore off his vestment and tossed it over the burning one, smothering and stomping out the flames.

The men stared at the smoking remnants of the robes.

"Do we have to start over now?" someone asked.

Cassandra bit back a hysterical giggle. Rushford's men were insane, but that fire hadn't been an accident. She grabbed the cell door, her pulse hammering.

Sir Walter straightened his robe and opened his mouth to speak, but the flames of the torches leapt up. Men shouted, and a few tossed their torches aside. A cold wind howled through the room, blowing out the flames and scattering red embers into the air. An animal snarl rumbled in the darkness. Men screamed and stampeded for the dim light of the corridor.

The lock on Cassandra's door rattled, and the hinges creaked.

"It's open," Mary's voice hissed beneath the shouting. Cassandra couldn't remember a sweeter sound.

Mary darted to Jairus's cell, a ghostly figure in the gloom. A lock clicked in the stillness, and Jairus slipped from his cell. Mary handed him his satchel. Cassandra limped toward the light of the doorway, but a whoosh made her ears pop. She winced at the sudden ache, and a feline snarl sent shivers swimming up her spine.

"That will be enough, Domin." A female voice rebounded through the room.

Cassandra froze, recognizing the alluring tones from the night the Dark Lady attacked her house.

Streams of sickly-pale blue light swam through the large room, illuminating a petite woman with white-blond hair, as pretty and uncanny as a living doll. The Dark Lady, Cassandra was certain. The Unseelie Queen stood in the mouth of the fireplace, which warped and sagged like the skin of a rotten melon. The raw edges opened into a place of cavernous black behind her. Veins the color of dried blood crept along the walls from the darkness.

Three desiccated creatures like dried human corpses with dark, unblinking eyes flanked the woman. Two clutched Sir Walter and Robert with bony hands, while another of the gray-skinned things stood in front of the Dark Lady. Cassandra backed away.

"Ghouls!" Jairus hissed to her. "Don't let them near you. Their bite draws out your strength and lets them mimic you."

He guided her slowly back toward the door. Cassandra

knew she should focus on sneaking away while the Dark Lady was distracted, but she couldn't break from the ghouls' empty stares.

The woman smiled over at Sir Walter. "Surprised to see me? You should thank me for interrupting your little performance." She gestured disdainfully at the chalk on the floor. "Your death at my hands will be quick, but the Leannan would have found pleasure in your screams."

Domin stretched into his human form and stepped forward. The unoccupied ghoul shuffled to match his stance.

The shape-shifter's lips curled back. "I will not let you have him, Lady. You will have to pay your tithes out of your own people this time."

"But Domin," the Unseelie Queen said, her smile still frozen on her face. "He is already mine. And you can't kill me to save him, *daemon,* since he's not the one you're meant to protect."

She glanced toward the corridor. Cassandra looked over her shoulder to see Henry silhouetted in the doorway, Jairus's shotgun clutched in his hands. He raised the weapon. "You can't defeat all of us."

"I don't have to, changeling."

The Dark Lady flung her hand out. Henry doubled over then snapped back to attention like a toy soldier, the gun still locked in his grip. A blue glow rose from Henry's skin. Cassandra wanted to run to him yet didn't dare move for fear of drawing the Dark Lady's attention. Jairus stared longingly at his shotgun, but he hesitated to take it from Henry's glowing hands.

"That should bind your arrogant tongue, princeling," the Dark Lady said to Henry. "Don't worry, Domin. It's not enough energy to kill him."

"This wasn't the agreement." Sir Walter struggled against the ghoul's knobby gray hands. "You promised me knowledge. I lured that shopkeeper's family to Drixton, and I helped Fitzhugh protect the sisters so you could have the child for your sacrifice."

A gasp caught in Cassandra's throat. She stepped forward, fists clenched. Jairus reached an arm out to stop her. Her hands trembled as she glared at Sir Walter. He had befriended her father, offered his advice, and looked after her sisters' needs, all the time with the intent of destroying her family.

Domin tensed, his eyes darting between Henry's still figure and the ghoul mirroring his movements.

"Don't do anything rash, Domin." The elf queen smirked. "You know the rules. Sir Walter challenged my word, so I must answer him. I wouldn't want anyone to say I didn't play fair."

She turned her pale blue eyes on Sir Walter. "You recall our bargain, but you never understood it. You *are* providing me with a sacrifice, and in return, I grant you this knowledge: the child is a valuable tool, like Henry Stewart. I wouldn't waste either of them on the sacrifice." She gestured at Cassandra, who flinched away from her attention. "And you were so distracted by the Leannan's promised secrets, you risked one of the sister's lives. Luckily for you, the child is safely born and under the guard of my servants, or I would make you suffer for that loss."

Cassandra's skin went cold. They were too late for her baby sister. Too late to save Henry from slavery to Queen Mab.

"Rushford!" Sir Walter licked his lips. "The Leannan was Rushford's idea from the beginning. Take him instead!"

"I will, eventually, but he still interests me." The Dark Lady shrugged. "The only thing you have to offer is your blood on my altar. I can take it from you, or from your son."

Sir Walter's eyes widened. He looked at Robert, who stared

at his father and shook his head. Cassandra covered her mouth, willing Sir Walter to be brave.

"Take him," Sir Walter said. "Take him and set me free."

Cassandra shook her head. Robert yelled and lunged at his father, fighting the ghoul's grip.

The Dark Lady laughed. "You see how thoroughly corrupted Sir Walter is, Domin. He once strove to make life better for everyone in his little village, yet now he is willing to destroy it and his own son in his lust for forbidden knowledge. He's been mine since he agreed to bring me the child, and now there's nothing left to save."

"There is always a chance for redemption," Domin said.

The Dark Lady grinned and pulled out a long, silver dagger. She shoved it into Sir Walter's side. "Not anymore."

Sir Walter shrieked and grasped at the dagger protruding from between his ribs. Blood dripped to the floor. Domin sprang at the Unseelie Queen, changing shape in midair, but the third ghoul leapt between him and the Dark Lady, latching sharp yellow teeth onto his neck. Domin yelped, and the wraithlike ghoul fleshed out, mimicking Domin's wolf form and dragging him to the ground.

The Dark Lady smiled and motioned for the ghoul to haul Sir Walter to the warped opening of the fireplace.

"No!" Cassandra shouted, but her voice was lost in the scuffle.

Dark power poured over Henry and swirled in eddies through the room. Unseelie magic pulsed through him, binding his muscles, threatening to burn him hollow. Behind it, he sensed the suffering of countless humans, victims of the Dark Lady's cruelty.

Robert rushed past Henry for the exit. The ghoul who had been guarding him turned on Jairus, while the second one wrestled Domin.

The Dark Lady followed the final ghoul, who dragged Sir Walter to the fireplace opening. Henry couldn't shout a warning or lift the shotgun clenched in his hand. He could scarcely draw breath. Magic crackled along his skin like blue static. Soon there would be nothing left of Henry—just dust and Faerie magic. He directed his silent scream of agony and frustration inward and shoved at the energy.

A breeze stirred in the room, hot and dry. Henry's hair stood on end. His muscles twitched as the pressure eased, and the shotgun clattered to the ground.

The Dark Lady paused her exit to frown at him. She raised her hand, and another wave of energy pounded him back. He gasped. Glimmering spots flashed across his vision. Only the magic held him on his feet. The energy pulsed like a heartbeat, flashing through every vein in his body, trying to consume him. Like the night he had let the Dark Lady into his mind.

The night he had fought back against her and banished her from his mind.

In the center of all that energy was the cord of power leashing him to the Fay. He pushed at the Faerie magic again, sending it coursing back along the tether.

The Unseelie Queen shrieked and clutched her head. The press of magic eased for the space of a heartbeat. Henry kicked the shotgun toward Jairus. The Dark Lady pushed more power through him, and he screamed before the pain punched the air from his lungs and locked his jaw.

"Douglas Fitzhugh!" the Dark Lady called.

Her words raced through the strands of Faerie magic, echoing in Henry's head. A summons.

Jairus reached for his gun, but the ghoul stumbled in his way. He paused and wove to the side. The ghoul copied him.

Henry strained against the cords of Faerie power binding his limbs, trying to get the gun, but Mary crept from the shadows and grabbed the weapon. The ghoul turned on her. Still kneeling, she pulled the first trigger. The creature crumpled to the ground in an ear-blistering explosion of white smoke.

"That's more like it!" Jairus whooped.

Fitzhugh bolted into the room, his face darkened by smoke and his clothes soot-stained from the fire raging upstairs. He snarled at Mary and elbowed her aside, snatching the shotgun from her hands. Henry wanted to scream, but his jaw remained locked. Helpless. Cassandra jumped after the gun, but Fitzhugh shoved her into one of the empty cells. Henry gritted his teeth and pushed at the Unseelie magic, but it was like trying to turn back a raging river.

Fitzhugh leveled the gun at Jairus. Mary shrieked. The sound reverberated with a hum that spilled into the magic in the air. The gun's percussion cap exploded—not to ignite the gunpowder, but to send a shower of sparks over Fitzhugh's hand. He cursed and shook his hand out.

Jairus lunged for the gun, wrestling it from Fitzhugh.

"Fitzhugh!" The Unseelie Queen stepped through the portal into Elfland on the heels of the ghoul and Sir Walter.

Fitzhugh dashed into the darkness, and the portal closed.

Lost.

Henry had lost everything.

Chapter Thirty-Six

The blue light dissolved, and the pressure on Henry slackened. The fireplace pulled itself back into solid masonry. The dark veins on the floor and walls crumbled to dust. The only light in the room came from the corridor and the energy coursing over Henry's skin. Cassandra crawled to Mary, checking her injuries.

Domin still grappled with the remaining ghoul, both changing form so rapidly it was impossible to tell who was who.

Jairus scrambled in his satchel for another percussion cap. "Domin! Iron!"

Domin resumed human form, fending off the ghoul's slathering bites. It mimicked his appearance and wrapped its hands around Domin's throat. Jairus pulled the trigger, peppering them both with iron shot. The ghoul shrieked and shriveled back into a corpse. Domin shoved it aside and glared at Jairus.

"Sorry, but it was the only solution I could think of," Jairus said. "That was the last of my iron shot, too." He shoved the empty gun in his satchel, then wrinkled his nose. "Where's all this smoke coming from?"

Mary moaned on the floor, her lip bleeding and her eyes unfocused. Cassandra cradled the girl's head in her lap.

Henry knelt beside Cassandra to check Mary, but he couldn't touch her. Faerie power crackled over his skin. He didn't want to inadvertently strike anyone with elf-shot like a careless Fay. The magic buzzing through him made his head spin and burned his chest. Behind it, his senses quickened, and he felt the capricious energy of the wind, the patient strength of the earth, the hunger of the fire, all just waiting for someone who could speak to them to summon their powers.

Domin limped over, bleeding from Jairus's shot. "We need to leave. The Grigori will likely send reinforcements."

"Also, I think the house is on fire," Jairus said. He gestured at the fireplace. "Can we follow them? Stop the sacrifice?"

Domin shook his head. "Only an Unseelie elf can open the portal."

"Then, it's over?" Cassandra asked quietly.

"The Dark Lady only said her servants were guarding the child," Domin said. "Since your nurse disabled the man they left behind, they'll be waiting for a human ally to go in and claim the infant. If we arrive first..."

Henry groaned. They were so far from Drixton, and some of the Dark Lady's human allies could already be on their way there. He ached with the energy pulsing over his nerves like electric shocks. And it was only a taste of what Queen Mab would do to him.

"Guns drawn!" Rushford's voice carried over the shouts and crashing of the men fighting the fire upstairs. Footsteps pounded down the corridor toward them.

The wild energy of the fire called to Henry's frustration. Fed by Unseelie magic, the flames would consume the Grigori in moments. The Fay wouldn't hesitate to do it. The Grigori probably wouldn't either, in Henry's place. He thought of the man with the cigar. The long days in the dark Faerie dungeons. Titania forcing him to burn a house, and he could only hope everyone had escaped alive. Now, he had to do it all again. All of his chances at being human were gone. Whatever he had allowed himself to feel for Cassandra would be gone. The Grigori would pay. If Henry was doomed to join the Fay, he would teach Rushford how the Fair Folk got revenge.

Henry stepped into the corridor and lashed out with his hands. A fierce, cold blast blew out all the lights, leaving the house in dusky dimness. Men yelled and stumbled away, and Henry's lips curled back.

"You wanted to know what I can do, so I'll show you," he said, his throat still raw from screaming under their torture.

"Henry..." Domin stepped closer, but Henry knelt to touch the floor, pushing Unseelie energy into the earth.

The ground rolled underfoot. One of Rushford's men fired his gun, but the floor bucked, and the shot went wild. The Grigori scattered like sheep before a lion. Caustic white smoke billowed down to fill the corridor.

A scent drifted to him through the choking stench: Roses. Cassandra. He glanced back to see her watching him, her hands clasped together. Afraid. For him, or of him?

He straightened slowly. Behind Cassandra was the empty fireplace where the Dark Lady and Fitzhugh had escaped. Through a portal that would only open to Unseelie magic. Henry glanced back at the corridor where the Grigori had fled.

If he let them go, they would be free to hurt people again.

Free to return to Drixton and steal Cassandra's sister. But if he called fire or earthquake to destroy them, he risked his friends' lives, too. What would that make him?

And if his friends cut through Elfland, they might have a chance of saving the child. It was too late for Henry to reclaim his humanity, but maybe—*maybe*—not for the infant girl.

He limped back to the fireplace and stood in its yawning black mouth. The thread of Unseelie magic vibrated through it.

"Henry?" Domin asked.

Henry didn't meet his gaze. "I think I can do this—open the portal with the Dark Lady's magic."

Domin shook his head. "Using Unseelie magic... I don't know what that will do to a human. To your mind."

"Lucky for us that I'm not completely human anymore, then."

Domin frowned and stepped back. Henry threaded the magic out, willing it through the gateway. It flowed away from him, a force building against the barrier until it yielded to his will. Someone behind him—Cassandra?—gasped. He pushed, and the gateway folded open, distorting the fireplace and pouring sickly blue light into the room.

Domin ran through the opening, and the others followed.

The energy crackling over Henry's skin faded. His vision dimmed. He tasted blood. His own, or the echoes of all the people the Unseelie Queen had hurt to get the power he was now using? If he stretched far enough, he could almost see them, yet they were countless. So much pain. Loved ones dead, gone too soon. Hearts crushed by unrequited love. Promises broken. Dreams shattered. Trust and innocence lost. Loneliness. So much loneliness. Was this all there was to the humanity Henry had sought for so long?

And now, there remained only darkness and smoke and the fire coming to claim him as the last of the energy left him and the world went black.

Chapter Thirty-Seven

If stepping into Telesm's clearing in Elfland had reminded Cassandra of a daydream, hurrying through the fireplace was entering a nightmare. She limped after Jairus into a cave sculpted of dark rock like black ice that had melted and dripped into grotesque, waxy forms. The only light was the blue glow from the entrance, and it was already dying, casting wan shadows.

Domin reached through the collapsing gateway and hauled Henry into Elfland.

Perfect, obsidian darkness fell.

Cassandra fumbled to the floor, afraid she would trip in the blackness. Her fingers roved over icy cold stone, smooth as glass and likely just as sharp. She drew a deep breath to call out to the others, but the total blindness choked her. She was all alone, so small, so helpless beneath a darkness heavy enough to grind her to dust. Dust that would blow away, forgotten, like she had never existed.

A whisper broke the black silence. The strike of a match. A

flicker of orange flared to life—tiny, but the darkness fled from the spark of light to its hidden places. Cassandra winced at the sudden brightness, but warmth spread over her chilled skin.

"I need something to burn," Jairus said.

Mary reached into her satchel and pulled out a partly carved piece of wood. Cassandra clutched her blistered hand and watched as Jairus held the wood to the flame. The fire flickered out, and the darkness rushed back, but then a red glow caught on the end of the wood, and Jairus held it aloft.

Domin knelt on the floor next to Henry's still form. The shape-shifter's face was ashen, his eyes pained.

Cassandra's eyes burned. "Is he... ?"

"He is alive. Beyond that, I don't know what the Unseelie magic did to him, body or mind." His voice was heavy. "Mr. Hale, scout the area. See if anyone has noticed our presence. Miss Leland, I need you to make me a weapon—something with a sharp iron point. And I need to borrow a knife."

Mary produced the knife and another piece of wood for Jairus to light, then they separated to their tasks.

Domin held the knife out to Cassandra. "Miss Weaver, I need your help as well."

"What can I do?"

"There's iron shot in my back."

Cassandra swallowed. "I've done some sewing. I guess—"

"You need not be a surgeon. As soon as the iron's out, I can heal myself."

Domin sat, and Cassandra knelt behind him. The light flickered over numerous wounds leaking blood down his back. She didn't even know where to start. "Um, do you need to take off your coat?"

"Just cut what you need to."

Cassandra took a deep breath and chose a wound near

Domin's shoulder. She dug the knife in to find the bit of iron, and his back muscles twitched.

"I'm sorry. Did that hurt?"

"Don't trouble yourself over it. Just remove the iron."

She tried to keep her fingers steady, but each time she found another injury, his back tensed under the knife. Of course, it hurt, even if he didn't show it. What a thoughtless question. Probably against The Rules. She almost gave into hysterical laughter as she imagined asking her etiquette teacher the most polite way to pick shot out of someone's back.

She tossed aside another piece of iron. "May I ask you something?"

The muscles across Domin's back tightened. "Yes, though I may choose not to answer."

"That's... that's fair. I just... Well, how do you always know what to do?"

He looked over his shoulder at her, his expression guarded. "What do you mean?"

"I've tried to do the right thing—to do what people need and expect of me, I mean—but now I don't know what that is anymore. The rules I thought I knew don't work."

"What did you hope they would do?"

"To keep myself and my family safe. To not embarrass them." To make herself enough. Enough to be useful. Enough to be loved.

"Those two are not the same. Social rules make people feel secure and comfortable. There's a place for that, but discomfort is sometimes necessary." His back twitched again as she cut out a piece of shot, and he lowered his voice. "I don't suggest being needlessly rude, but you're capable of making reasonable decisions. Using the wrong fork at dinner is a faux pas, a passing mistake dictated by fashion. Being kind to an awkward girl who doesn't belong, though, is right regardless of the fashions of the age, and you discovered that on your own." He glanced over to where Mary sat a short distance away, intent on her work.

Cassandra wiped her fingers on her ruined skirt and bent to examine another wound. "I suppose I'll always worry that I'm doing wrong."

Domin was silent for a long moment, and Cassandra wondered if she had said something offensive.

"Worry is a part of caring, and you should never stop caring," he said quietly, almost to himself. "Feeling, loving, living, they all have moments of pain."

"Yes, I suppose they do." She looked at her bandaged hand. It was lucky gloves were in fashion; she had enough other things to hide. "I want to do whatever it takes to protect my family. But I'm...broken."

"Not as much as you believe, Miss Weaver," Domin said with unexpected gentleness. "Life leaves everyone with scars. Yours are more visible than most, but those things that you consider imperfections might put you in the perfect position to do what you were meant to. You just have to trust yourself."

Cassandra swallowed hard. It was so close to what she longed to hear from Sophie or their mother. *We believe in you. We accept you. You are enough just as you are.*

She shook her head and pulled a piece of iron from below his ribs. As soon as she did, his back rippled faintly, like water disturbed by a falling leaf, and she found herself staring at smooth, black fabric. She glanced down at the blood on the knife and her fingers, the only evidence of his injuries.

"Wipe it off," Domin said, climbing to his feet.

She cleaned up as best as she could and sat by Henry, studying his pale, bruised face. What had caring cost him? His freedom, if they didn't save her sister. She brushed a stray lock of hair off his forehead. He stirred and blinked several times, his gaze coming to rest on her. She held her breath as confusion flickered over his face.

"Miss Weaver? Are we..." He squinted at the jagged black pillars surrounding them. "Ah, the Unseelie Kingdom."

He let his head sink back down. Cassandra resisted the urge to shout out the good news that he seemed to be himself. She glanced up and found Domin watching, his face still but his eyes concerned. Of course, Henry wasn't out of danger yet. None of them were.

Footsteps echoed off the ceiling, and Jairus reappeared from behind a black boulder that swooped upward like a hand reaching for help.

"Well?" Domin asked.

"There's no one around," Jairus said. "But I found Sir Walter. We were too late for him. There's an altar made all of silver, and, well..." He grimaced.

Henry groaned and rolled onto his side to push himself up. Mary stepped up to Domin, offering one of her chisels fashioned into a sharpened iron stake.

Domin nodded his thanks. "We might still be in time to save the child. If we find the Black Woods, they will take us to Telesm's clearing."

"I saw some black trees," Jairus said.

Domin helped Henry to his feet. Henry picked up the knife Cassandra had used and tucked it into his waistcoat. Together, the little group crept through the horrible magnificence of the black caves. The obsidian cavern opened into a rocky clearing bathed in cold light, though there was no hint of sun or even moonlight. The sky overhead was a continuous haze of pale, sickly red, like the smoke hanging over a thousand coal-burning factories, so thick that it cloyed

Cassandra's throat. On the other side of the clearing stood trees with black bark, their golden leaves shimmering in the eerie glow. Domin stepped out first, checking to see that their way was clear, then motioned for the others to follow into the open.

Goose bumps ran over Cassandra's skin, exposed by the cut in her sleeve, and she rubbed her arms.

"What's that? What did they do to you?" Henry gently grasped her hand to unwrap her makeshift bandage.

Cassandra blushed and stammered, "Uh, it's—"

"A brand," said Jairus from beside her. "A demon's mark they put on us before they tried to sacrifice us."

"Domin said it didn't mean anything—that it couldn't hurt us," Cassandra said.

"As long as it heals properly." Henry turned her hand carefully to examine the injury, sending tingles over her skin. "Burns are dangerous. It's too dark to tell. How much does it hurt?"

"It hurts like the devil," Jairus muttered, "but don't worry about me."

Cassandra's flush deepened. "It doesn't hurt as much as it did at first."

"I may never play fiddle again," Jairus said, a chuckle underlying his mournful tone.

Henry rewrapped Cassandra's hand and shot a wry look at Jairus. "When there's real light, I'll see to everyone's injuries."

"What about yours?" Cassandra asked.

He set his jaw. "I'll be fine."

She glanced doubtfully at the thin red marks splayed like tiny veins across the back of his hands.

They came to a stop under the canopy of the trees. Cassandra studied the leaves overhead. The false sunlight glinted off of them, and they hung stiff and heavy from the branches.

"Are those *real* gold?" she asked.

"Yes," Domin said, "but do not touch them. Don't eat, drink, or take anything from any of the elf queens. It comes at a heavy cost."

He pointed to the ground. Instead of the usual clutter of the forest floor, pieces of broken, yellowed pottery lay scattered over the rocky soil. No, not pottery. Fragments of bone. Cassandra covered her mouth and squeezed her eyes shut.

"How do we get out of here?" Jairus asked.

Domin guided them forward. Cassandra tried to watch where she stepped, but shards of bone crunched beneath her boots. No one spoke, and the absence of bird song and real light made the air dull and heavy. The trees grew so close together they were like the bars of a cage. Cassandra studied the black trunks to distract herself until she began to notice that in many places the bark was cracked and split like some cankerous disease afflicted the trees, and they oozed a sap as dark as old blood. Once, she thought she heard an echo of their footsteps elsewhere in the woods, but when she looked, nothing was there.

Several times, Domin had to pause, studying the sky and turning in every direction to decide how to lead them forward. Finally, he stopped and looked at Henry.

"The paths are changing as we walk them."

"Are we trapped?" Henry asked.

Domin surveyed the woods. "We'll find the way out eventually, but time is passing in the outside world."

Henry ran his hands through his hair. "Coming this way was a mistake. We could be here for years."

A snap sounded in the woods nearby.

"Quiet!" Cassandra said. The others stared at her, and she flushed. "I heard a noise."

Domin stepped forward, raising the sharpened chisel. Something white flashed in the trees and pushed its way past the black trunks and branches.

"The stag!" Cassandra limped forward. "I saw him in Drixton."

Domin lowered the chisel. "He's a spirit of the old woods, able to cross the boundary between worlds. He'll guide us back if we can keep up."

They all hurried after the stag. Henry offered Cassandra his arm, his gaze uncertain. She took his arm in a tight grip with her own, wondering if Henry was helping her, or if she was helping him as they limped side by side. Cassandra was afraid the stag would bound too far ahead of them, but it paused at times to look back, its massive antlers knocking golden leaves from the trees. The fallen leaves clanked to the ground and turned to ash.

Just as Cassandra was sure she couldn't lift her aching leg for one more step, she caught the scent of fresh air sharp with pine. Past the black trees, green shimmered under real sunshine. Focusing on keeping her foot from turning inward, she hobbled beside Henry for the light.

Chapter Thirty-Eight

Amy guided Isabel in another loop around Telesm's clearing. The silent cottage huddled behind its lion guardians. She felt their watchful readiness, an air of resentment in their stony gazes, but this was the only gateway between Elfland and the human world still open to her near Drixton. Domin and the others had never come out of the Grigori's manor house, even as it burned to a ruined shell. But Amy had sensed a shift in Faerie power around the house. If her friends had somehow escaped the fire and confusion through Elfland, this was where they would arrive. If they had not, Amy would do what she could to avenge them.

"Amy!"

Domin's voice. She had all but given up hope, but there he was, walking out of the trees as if he'd just been out for a stroll. As if everything was right again.

The others behind him looked considerably worse. Jairus's face was sooty and grim, Cassandra's leg dragged and her dress was torn to shreds, swollen bruises covered Mary's face, and Henry... Amy was surprised he was even on his feet.

Amy slid down from Isabel and ran to greet them, being careful not to come too close to Cassandra. The power of the geas forced her away, like the opposing ends of two magnets. She hadn't been able to get near the Weaver's house, either, though she'd seen the Unseelie creatures prowling the property, guarding it for their queen.

"You made it!" She wanted to hug them and cry and maybe give Domin a good shake for leaving her alone.

Domin nodded. "I'm glad you're safe as well. Have you been out there?"

"Yes. I couldn't get close, but the house is heavily guarded."

"Good." Jairus smiled. "That means the child is still there. We just have to fight our way through an army of powerful monsters and defeat an immortal queen who feeds on suffering and pain."

"Precisely," Domin said.

Jairus laughed. "Sounds like fun."

"If we can get you into the house, you can bless the baby and all this will be over," Henry said. "The Dark Lady won't be expecting us. Not this soon. We'll leave the ladies here and sneak in."

"There must be something we can do," Amy said.

"You cannot approach the house," Domin said, though his tone was soft. Almost sympathetic. "Miss Weaver and Miss Leland are injured and need to rest."

Cassandra looked like she wanted to object, but she nodded wearily.

"As do the rest of you," Amy said.

"There'll be time soon enough." Jairus motioned to the other men and marched forward.

Henry gave Cassandra a concerned look, then broke into a weary jog behind Domin and Jairus. The men crossed the river for the cavern that led back into the human world.

"I hate this—being useless," Cassandra said.

She didn't address Amy directly—Domin or Henry must have told her how the geas worked—but Amy ached for her. She looked at Mary.

"Come, Miss Leland, maybe we can provide a distraction to help our friends."

Mary looked confused, but she walked resolutely over to Amy and allowed the elf to help her onto Isabel.

"I think I'll walk," Amy said. "But Isabel can carry two."

She strolled away from the pony. Cassandra took the hint and climbed awkwardly onto Isabel. Did Cassandra know how to ride? Amy hadn't considered that, but Isabel was docile, and she would follow Amy.

Amy led the way out of Telesm's clearing, relieved to be away from the lion guardians. Isabel picked her way across the stream and through the cavern, and they emerged into the autumn woods.

The ache in Amy's head sharpened as they approached the Weaver's property. Moving forward was like pushing uphill through mud. She turned, using her pain as a guide to keep her on the edge of the property.

Deeper in the woods, shadows prowled: Unseelie creatures waiting for a chance to attack or Seelie ones who could not cross the threshold of the property until—*unless*—the Dark Lady claimed the child. Then the war would begin in earnest, and nothing would be left of Drixton but rumors and old stories.

The thump of hoofbeats approached. Mary whimpered and huddled behind Cassandra as Fitzhugh reined in from a canter. His kelpie stallion bared its sharp teeth at Isabel, who tossed her head and pranced back.

"Easy, boy." Fitzhugh grinned at Amy. His smile hadn't always had such a wicked edge to it. "I thought I sensed you near. What are you doing here?"

"I came to help."

Something like hunger flickered in his eyes. "You're here to help me?"

"Not in the way you think. Your queen claimed her sacrifice. Leave the child alone."

He shook his head. "The sacrifice was a necessary thing, but this child is the key. Don't you get tired of hiding all the time? My queen has plans, and this child's power will let her—all of us—move forward. The world is changing, Amy, and we have to change with it or risk extinction."

"I don't want freedom bought with an innocent life."

"We're not planning to kill her, just help unlock her potential. Can my queen possibly be crueler than yours? Join the Unseelie Court and you could help raise the child, see that she's treated fairly. Better than you were treated, certainly."

Amy stared at Fitzhugh, searching for the flaw in his logic. He wasn't capable of lying, and certainty lit his eyes. Perhaps the Unseelie Court wasn't as bad as she thought. Perhaps if she joined them, she could finally overcome her foolish shortcomings.

But what had it done to Fitzhugh? Turned his humor to cynicism and his charm to empty flattery. And what would happen to Henry if Amy helped the Dark Lady? What would Domin think of her? Amy couldn't hurt her friends. She was better off with the Seelie Court, despite her mother.

Amy glanced back at Mary clinging to Cassandra. No. Even the Seelie Fay tossed aside their infants for being weak. They enslaved children and tore families apart. Being a part of either court meant taking a role in their cruelty, no matter what her intentions were at the start. No wonder Domin hesitated to trust her. She was so confused that she hardly felt she could trust herself. But Domin said something in her had shifted, and that illuminated a path forward.

"I'm sorry, Fitzhugh. I don't want a part in either court anymore."

His eyes narrowed. "Suit yourself, my dear." He turned his attention to Cassandra. "My offer still stands, Miss Weaver. I will take you to Elfland. And as my Lady has shown you, our magic can cure you and your deaf sister. You and your family will be safe and provided for. Forever." His lip curled up. "You could even help us free dear Henry. After all, if the Seelie Queens are vanquished, their magic will break, and so will their hold on him."

Cassandra bit her lip and looked down, confusion in her eyes.

Fitzhugh shrugged. "Or, you can stand out here and watch as we kill your friends and take the child." He turned the kelpie stallion away.

"No, Fitzhugh." The whisper caught on Amy's lips. One thing she did see clearly was that the farther he traveled down this path, the more darkness he took on himself, and the less chance he had of ever being warmed by the light again. She found her voice and called, "Douglas!"

He looked back, eyebrow cocked.

She swallowed. "Be careful."

All joking disappeared from his expression, and something —doubt, sorrow, regret—flickered in his eyes. He gave her a nod and then cantered away.

"There must be some way to buy our friends time," Amy said.

She stared at the roofs of the village peeking out from the trees. A smile slowly spread over her face.

"What types of things can you fix, Miss Leland?"

"All kinds of things."

Amy's heart beat faster. "I have an idea. But we're going to need Isabel." She avoided looking at Cassandra. "I don't think anyone we know is in danger from the Seelie Court now that the baby is born. They just have to stay away from the Unseelie creatures."

Cassandra slipped down and stood aside, her eyes still downcast. Amy wished she could say something more to reassure her, but with the geas on her, Amy could only climb on Isabel with Mary and leave Cassandra alone.

Chapter Thirty-Nine

Jolts of pain flashed along Henry's nerves, and his skin itched like it had been stretched too tight, especially where the Grigori had burned him. Jairus had broken off rowan branches to use as weapons, but Henry leaned on his like a walking stick.

Part of him just wanted to curl up and sleep. Forget the pain and the hopelessness for a few short hours until Queen Mab summoned him for his punishment. Punishment he deserved. Not only was the Dark Lady on the verge of claiming the child, but Henry had used Unseelie magic. The coppery taste of it still coated his tongue. He'd proven he wasn't human and never would be again. And what was humanity but suffering? The Unseelie power had showed him the futility of it all.

Yet he couldn't watch the same torment happen to someone else—an innocent child—so he stumbled along behind Domin and Jairus. If they could reach the child before the Dark Lady did, Jairus could protect her, but the Dark Lady's forces were already at the house, only waiting for a human who could step inside and claim the child.

Magic hung heavily over Drixton along with steely black clouds. The church's belltower rose above the trees in the distance, but otherwise, they were cut off from the world. No songbirds took to the air and no natural creatures stirred. A crow flashed its wings overhead, and all three men pressed back into the shadows. A few heartbeats later, they continued.

Leaves rustled behind them. They swung around, rowan staffs at the ready. The pooka in horse form emerged from the trees. Her shape stretched into a tall, angular woman whose rippling black hair blended with her flowing gown.

"Daemon?" Jairus asked.

"No." Henry sighed. "Pooka." He glanced at Domin. "I'll speak to her."

Domin nodded.

The pooka shook back her hair and addressed Henry. "I bear a message from my mistress, Queen Mab. Because of your bargain, there is little she can do to aid you directly, but our ancient animosity with the Unseelie Court still allows us to fight them. I will make your way clear until you reach the boundary of the human family's domain. You failed to stop the sacrifice." She smiled, revealing long, flat teeth. "Don't forget what hangs in the balance if you fail to save the child."

"I haven't forgotten," Henry said dully.

She shifted back into a horse. Henry motioned the others forward. Before they'd gone far, a flock of crows circled above them.

"Get ready!" Domin said. "They've found us."

The crows swirled to the ground and melted together into the Morrigan's armored form. Her golden-red braid hung over her shoulder, and a long, double-edged sword materialized in her hand. She smirked. "Greetings, Domin."

Domin stepped in front of the others. "Let us pass, Morrigan."

"It seems you've forgotten how to negotiate. You're tired, your humans are injured, and the pooka's delightful powers of decay don't work on me. Not a strong position for making demands."

"We're not here to play games."

"Neither am I. I've spoken with the Unseelie Queen, and it seems we have common goals. Unless you're ready to offer me something I want, your journey ends here."

Domin stepped back and whispered to Henry. "I will keep her occupied. You and the pooka get Mr. Hale through."

Henry nodded, but his chest tightened as he stared across the woods filled with Unseelie creatures. What chance did they have?

"Well, Domin?" The Morrigan flicked her braid off her shoulder and swung her sword up.

Domin dropped into panther form.

Henry drew energy into his hands, gritting his teeth against the ache. It wasn't just natural energy that flowed through him, but Faerie magic as well. He couldn't separate them anymore. The lovely symphony of energies collapsed into a horrid screech in his mind like metal scraping on metal.

Before he could strike out with the tangled energy, a clanging sound tore through the air. The deep peal of a bell broke over the village like the dawn, tolling again and again.

The Morrigan shrieked and dropped her sword to cover her ears. She melted into dozens of crows and tore away. Henry flung the magic wildly at them, then shielded his face from the beating wings.

A flash of movement from the church belfry caught Henry's eye, and he laughed.

"What's happening?" Jairus asked.

Henry pointed. "Someone's fixed the church bells. They're driving the Unseelie creatures away."

Domin resumed his human form. "Hurry! The farther we are from the sound, the weaker its power becomes."

They raced along dirt paths, the deep toll of the bell fading behind them to a distant ding. Domin melted into wolf form to lope alongside the pooka. Wyverns circled overhead. Henry wasn't certain which court had sent them, but they didn't attack.

At the stream marking the edge of the Weaver's property, the pooka hung back. "I stop here until the child's fate is decided."

Henry nodded. The men crossed the rushing water. Henry drew a sharp breath at the sight of the Weavers' home through the orchard. A lindworm coiled in front of the house, its huge serpent head resting on its two scaly arms. Fitzhugh waited near it on his kelpie stallion, surrounded by redcaps. The short creatures with their blood-stained clothes spotted the three men. They sent up a cacophony of shrieks and hisses and rattled their pikes.

The wyverns plunged into the orchard. Definitely Unseelie. Henry reacted without thinking, drawing in a coil of energy and shoving it against the leathery creatures. He gasped at the pain burning through his hands, but the combination of wind and Faerie energy slammed most of them to the ground.

The few remaining wyverns dove for Jairus. He swung at them with his rowan branch, but the winged monsters dodged his blows. They clawed his back and shoulders through his tattered shirt before dropping lifeless to the ground. He nudged one of the dead creatures with his boot, his expression puzzled.

Jairus shook his head and motioned Henry and Domin to follow him. "We're almost there, form up!"

Henry managed a tired jog, keeping a wary eye on the jeering redcaps gathered around Fitzhugh. Behind them, the lindworm raised its head. A few goblins lurked in the shadows of the house away from the rose bushes, their horns devilishly sharp. Henry only had a small knife and a rowan stick to defeat them.

Fitzhugh smirked when they drew close. "You're wasting your energy and your lives. The child is ours, and your priest will die before he reaches her."

"We're not going to let you kill Mr. Hale," Henry said.

Fitzhugh laughed. "We already have. With that much elf-shot, he'll draw his last breath in a matter of minutes."

Henry turned to Jairus. Sweat beaded the American's forehead, and his skin was pale beneath his blossoming bruises —poisoned by the wyverns' elf-shot, the very last drops of their life energy.

The Lady of the Mountain's power tightened around Henry's chest, and he drew a struggling breath.

"That means we still have a few minutes," Jairus said. "Get me inside."

Fitzhugh shook his head. "If you turn back, the rest of you may survive. The bell drove away the weaker members of the Unseelie Court, but that just means I have the most fierce at my side. You're tired and injured. You don't have the strength to withstand my forces."

Domin smiled grimly. "I think you may have underestimated our resources."

Henry followed his gaze to the lane winding from the village. A rider charged up the road on a lathered gray pony.

Amy. The air behind her shimmered with heat. Domin dropped into panther form and raced to meet her.

Domin bounded to a stop before Amy's pony and changed shape, racing alongside her. He held his hands out for the harp clutched in her lap. "Give me the instrument before the lion guardian catches up with you!"

"I can play it," Amy said. "After I took Mary to the church, I realized I could put the Unseelie Fay to sleep if the bell didn't work. The harp didn't affect the lions, though."

"Of course not. Telesm would have thought of that."

Amy shook her head. "It seemed like a good plan."

He smiled. "It was better than you imagined. Give me the harp."

"But then its guardian will chase you."

"Exactly. And I can go where you cannot—near the house."

"Oh!" Amy exclaimed.

The lion guardian appeared around the bend. Flames swirled across its yellow and orange coat, and a fiery mane radiated from its face. Heat pricked Domin's skin, and each breath of dry air burned his throat. He changed into wolf form. Amy slipped the front pillar of the harp between his teeth, and he tore away.

A glance over his shoulder reassured him that the guardian had passed by Amy, focused only on the stolen item. Amy *had* brought him a weapon—not a harp, but a lion made of elemental fire.

Unless it caught him before he could use it against the Unseelie Fay.

In front of the Weaver's house, redcaps swarmed Jairus and

Henry, but the sight of the burning lion sent them scattering for cover like startled chickens. Domin sprang over the fence onto the Weaver's ruined lawn. The lion broke straight through, leaving behind cracked and smoldering planks.

Fitzhugh bore down on Domin with his sword drawn. "What are you thinking, you half-blood idiot? You'll burn down the house!"

Domin charged the lindworm. The monstrous serpent snapped at Domin, but he veered away, the lion close behind him. The lindworm rose on its coiled body like a cobra to face the lion. The enormous, fiery cat dodged the serpent's fangs and snapped down on the back of its neck. The lion gave a mighty shake and tossed the lindworm's body aside to smoke on the front lawn.

Then the lion turned back on Domin.

Domin raced forward, panting around the carved harp pillar rocking against his aching jaw. A few redcaps tried to stop him, but he bounded over their pikes, and the lion trampled them without pausing. Scorching heat touched the tips of Domin's ears, and he laid them flat. He just needed to buy a little more time.

Cassandra watched from the shadow of the woods as battle spread across her family's lawn and gardens. No Faerie creature had bothered her as she limped through the trees—as Amy had hinted, Cassandra didn't matter to the Fay anymore—but what could she do now? Fitzhugh tried to regroup the Unseelie forces against the fiery lion while Henry and Jairus fought their way through to the front of the house.

Another figure stood in the garden, watching from beneath

a silvery, hooded cloak. A wisp of impossibly white hair escaped in the breeze. The Unseelie Queen, enjoying the chaos while she waited for her chance to steal Cassandra's sister. The Dark Lady pulled her cloak tighter and backed into the shadows, away from the lion, while also keeping a wary distance from the elderberry.

Cassandra snuck through the orchard, limping from tree to tree, ignored in the chaos. Two red caps charged past her without even a glance. Why should they pay attention? A crippled young lady was no threat to them.

Fitzhugh rallied a group of horned monsters and advanced on Henry and Jairus. The Dark Lady clutched her fist as if crushing the two men. Cassandra slipped to the edge of the garden and hid behind the elderberry tree. The Unseelie Queen was near enough that Cassandra could have hit her with a pebble from the gravel walk.

Cassandra touched Georgina's brooch and thought of her sisters.

Sometimes we have to grow up too fast, to help the people we love.

She inched forward, walking gingerly so her boots didn't crunch on the gravel. Each step brought her closer to the woman who was the key to it all. Who held the cure for Cassandra's crippled body, for Georgina's deafness. Who could end the fight at that moment and spare all of Cassandra's friends. Cassandra took another careful step, her bad leg quivering with pain and exhaustion.

Move carefully and gracefully.
Do not draw attention to yourself.
Move carefully and gracefully.
Do not draw attention to yourself.

Cassandra was so close that she could see the jagged rise and fall of the Unseelie Queen's breathing. She sensed the power rolling off this woman who commanded torment and death and walked on the bones of her enemies. Cassandra's muscles locked in terror. Who was she to stand in the Dark Lady's presence?

She pictured her sister. Her new friends. People who needed her.

I am enough.

She had to be.

Cassandra pulled Georgina's pin from her dress and jammed the iron point deep into the Dark Lady's back.

The Unseelie Queen screamed. The shadows of the woods, the dark underbellies of the clouds, even the smoke rising from the burned orchard quavered and shrieked with her, a sound that went on and on and shook Cassandra to the ground. The pin broke off, leaving her clutching the painted image of the rose.

The Dark Lady fell, too, clawing at her back.

Cassandra scooted under the cover of the elderberry tree—protection from evil.

The sound of hoofbeats thrummed over the ground. Fitzhugh raced toward them on his stallion. He leaned down, grabbed the Dark Lady's extended hand, and swept her onto the saddle with him. With a deathly glance at Cassandra, he rode like a devil on wings for the sanctuary of the woods.

Henry covered his ears at the shriek resounding through the physical and magical world. He didn't understand it, but he recognized the power and pain behind it. Someone had hurt the Unseelie Queen.

Fitzhugh raced to her aid, and her forces fell back in

disarray. Jairus grabbed Henry's arm, leaning on him for support and nearly pulling Henry down, too. They stumbled for the safety of the porch with its curtain of white roses.

Cassandra appeared around the corner of the house, her weak foot dragging a furrow in the mud. Dirt smudged her face and her eyes were wide with panic as she checked over her shoulder. Henry didn't have time to wonder how she got there, but at least she was safe. He tried to force the front door open, but it was blocked from inside.

Cassandra limped up beside him and pounded on the door. "Nancy! It's us. Let us in."

Jairus leaned against the side of the house, eyes closed as he drew shallow breaths. "We don't have time for this."

He slammed the rowan stick through the window and knocked the shards of glass aside, then hauled himself in. He rolled across the sofa to land on the drawing-room rug, dragging pieces of glass with him. Henry knocked away more glass and pulled himself in after, then helped Cassandra climb through.

"That didn't work as well as I hoped." Jairus shivered as he tried to pick bits of broken glass from his hands. Fresh cuts welled on his arm to mingle with the injuries inflicted by the wyverns. "Bring the child so I can christen her before ..." His voice trailed off, and he gestured vaguely.

Henry looked up at Cassandra, who had tears in her eyes. "Please get the child, Miss Weaver. I'll see what I can do for Mr. Hale."

She nodded and limped from the room, keeping a hand on the wall for support.

Jairus sank back down, his breathing raspy. "Mr. Stewart, I have a sister. I've left everything I have to her. I want to tell you the details while I still can."

Henry shook his head. "No, Mr. Hale. You're going to get through this."

Jairus grinned weakly then curled forward, clutching his chest. "You practicing your bedside manners on me?"

Henry sensed the Faerie magic burrowing through Jairus. "I have an idea. I might know how to treat it, but it risks injuring you more."

"Then wait until after the child."

Nancy rushed into the room, cradling a sleeping infant. Cassandra hobbled behind her, her face full of pained hope.

Jairus motioned them over. "What's her name?"

"Mother never said." Cassandra and Nancy exchanged glances. Cassandra looked at Henry and asked, "What about Anne?"

Henry smiled and nodded.

"Good, bring her closer," Jairus said.

Cassandra took the baby and knelt in front of him, but a coughing fit doubled him over, and his face turned ashen.

"Mr. Hale?" Cassandra asked.

He closed his eyes and placed his hands on the baby's head.

The remaining creatures outside shrieked and roared, distracting Henry from the American's whispered prayer. Domin fought his way through a pack of goblins. There was no sign of the fiery lion. Henry snatched a rowan branch from the sofa and climbed through the window onto the porch. Domin changed form to reach up, and Henry handed him the weapon.

"Amen!" Jairus's voice echoed under the eaves of the porch.

The weight of the bargain with Queen Mab lifted from Henry's chest, and he drew a deep breath. He looked back to see Jairus take his hands from the child. Tears coursed down Cassandra's cheeks, and she pulled her baby sister close, all traces of pain and fear gone from her face.

In the renewed brightness of her eyes, Henry saw the cure for the Unseelie darkness still clinging to him: Determination. Hope. Love. Those were the things that let humans press on, despite all the pain and suffering in their world. They were the things none of the Faerie Queens could ever touch, or even understand. And as long as Henry held on to them, there would always be a part of him that was human.

Freed from Henry's bargain with Queen Mab, the pooka charged through the broken fence, followed by a swarm of pixies. The remaining Unseelie Fay scattered.

Domin bounded onto the porch. "It is done."

Jairus sagged back against the sofa.

"Mr. Hale!" Cassandra paled and handed the baby to Nancy. "Mr. Stewart?"

Henry clambered back in and dropped by Jairus's side. The American's eyes rolled back, and his breath rattled in his chest. Henry touched Jairus's chest, and the familiar sting lanced through his fingers.

"Henry?" Domin asked from the window.

"I think I can draw it out," Henry said.

The Faerie magic curled tight around the American's heart. Henry pulled, and the magic shifted under his hand. Jairus's eyes flew open, and he gasped.

Henry flinched at the power coursing into him. It hurt just as it had when the Dark Lady attacked him, but he opened himself to it, allowed it in. His skin glowed blue, and energy snapped and jumped over his hands. Faerie magic burned through his nerves until he thought his bones might crack from the pain and pressure, but he didn't let go until Jairus's breathing returned to normal. Cassandra cried and threw her arms around Jairus.

Henry staggered back against the sofa, his vision throbbing

with pain. The magic was poison, eating him alive. Outside, the body of the lindworm still smoldered. Henry fed all the energy into the blaze. The fire leapt like a thing alive, swirling a hundred feet upward into a tornado of flames staining the gray clouds orange. When the last of the elf-shot drained from his chest, he sank onto the velvet of the sofa by the window, his ears buzzing. The fire subsided to ash.

He could use Faerie magic. A bittersweet exchange for his hopes of returning to the human world.

"Is this a bad time?" asked an unfamiliar voice outside the window. "Because if someone cannot explain to me what was worth disturbing my sanctuary twice in one week, I might decide to turn my guardian loose again."

Chapter Forty

Henry bolted upright, a surge of alarm pushing away his exhaustion.

On the porch, a dark-skinned man in loose-fitting trousers and a knee-length, red silk robe stood face to face with Domin. The man's wavy black hair hung to his shoulders, and old wounds scarred his forehead and cheek, but the resemblance to Domin was unmistakable.

"Telesm," Domin said.

"Domin." Telesm slugged the shape-shifter in the shoulder, knocking him back two steps.

Domin snarled, but Telesm held up his hands. "A harp, brother? You at least could have stolen something worthwhile. I hope you are not trying to involve me in Faerie matters."

"Brother?" Jairus asked, joining Henry at the window. "Another shape-shifter?"

Telesm gestured to his scarred face with a hand missing its smallest finger. "If I was, do you think I would go about in this condition? No. *My* father was a Persian prince." He turned back to Domin and gestured to the lawn with a faint smile. "I suppose we have some cleaning up to do?"

Domin's nose flared. "Indeed."

Telesm grinned and drew the sword Jairus had wielded against the hell hounds.

Henry pushed himself up to join them, but a wave of dizziness knocked him back. All the energy had deserted him, and everything ached down to the soles of his feet.

Jairus smiled wryly at him. "I think we're sitting this one out, but I'd say those two can handle a few Fay."

The scattering of Unseelie creatures in the gardens fled before the half-brothers. Henry's hands twitched to fight the Fay as well, but perhaps this once he could leave it to someone else.

A pony carrying two figures trotted up the road from the village: Amy and Mary. Amy approached the Weaver's house without hesitation. Henry relaxed and leaned against the broken window frame. His deal with Mab was over, and he was still free from the Fay's grasp.

"Do you suppose Rushford survived the fire?" Jairus asked.

"I wouldn't be surprised," Henry said, "and whichever of the Grigori are left can't be pleased with us."

Henry turned back to see Cassandra marveling at her sister's tiny fingers. The Grigori would not be pleased with Cassandra either. A desire to protect her surged through him. She had proved more capable than any human had a right to be against the Fay, but he wouldn't leave her to do it alone.

Behind her, Nancy set up a tea tray laden with bread and sliced foods, as well as basins for washing. Henry's stomach grumbled, and he pushed himself off the sofa. As he did, he noticed something silver caught between the cushions, and he picked up his mother's locket, forgotten when Rushford's men had attacked. He grasped the thin connection to his humanity.

Jairus dipped his hands in one of the wash basins. "God tells me I'm not done fighting them."

Henry tucked the silver keepsake in his pocket and leaned over another of the porcelain bowls to scoop warm water onto his face. The cuts and bruises stung, but he scrubbed them clean, staining the water. "I doubt the Fay will leave me in peace, either."

Jairus nodded and wiped his face clean. "I've been thinking...monster hunting is a dangerous business. I've always preferred doing it alone, but I have to admit it sometimes goes better with company."

"Well, if you don't object to hunting monsters with a monster, I wouldn't mind joining you from time to time."

Jairus grinned. "I've met some real monsters, Mr. Stewart, and you're not one of them."

Henry smiled back. Maybe he could be not-quite-human without being definitely-a-monster. Maybe there was a place in-between for him.

Nancy *tsk*ed at the sight of Jairus's back. "Poor young man, let me clean that up for you." He hesitated, and she added, "Before you get blood on the floor."

He laughed. "Yes, ma'am. Just let me grab some food." He piled cold meat between two slices of bread and followed the old woman.

Cassandra stepped closer, still rocking her newborn sister, as Henry made a cucumber sandwich.

He swallowed a bite and closed his eyes. "This may be the best thing I've ever tasted, and I don't even like cucumbers." He grinned at Cassandra. She smiled sadly and looked away. He put the sandwich down. "Are you all right, Miss Weaver? Is your hand bothering you? I could take a look at it now."

"Yes. No. I'm just...jealous, I think. I'll be trapped inside decorating bonnets while you and Mr. Hale are off *doing* something to stop the Fay." She held the baby close. "On the other hand, I'm also terrified of encountering them again."

He ran his fingers down her arm, stopping at the warm skin where the Grigori had cut her sleeve. "I'll do what I can to keep them away." He cleared his throat. "You could help, if you'd like."

"Perhaps I will." Her eyes flashed with determination, then she glanced over at Jairus. "I think it's good that you'll be working with Mr. Hale, though."

Henry pulled his hand away and studied it, remembering how tempted he'd been to hurt people with the power he'd held. "He'll keep an eye on me, I suppose."

"Maybe, but that's not what I meant." Cassandra paused. "I have to admit it's hard to see how you could have a normal life, but that doesn't mean you can't have a good life, and a...a human one. Mr. Hale is not exactly ordinary, but he's definitely human, and he seems happy."

"He does seem to enjoy his insanity," Henry said.

Cassandra frowned.

"I'm sorry. I don't mean to disparage Mr. Hale." He hesitated. "You're fond of him?"

"Yes, I'm becoming very fond of him," Cassandra said.

The admission stung Henry, but he nodded. Jairus was, as she said, fully human. Like her.

Cassandra added, "If I had an older brother, I would want him to be like Mr. Hale."

"An older brother?"

"I think he's a good man, and very brave. I owe him a great

deal." She shifted the baby and put her free hand on Henry's arm. "I think the same of you."

He winced. But even sisterly affection was something he'd never had before. He would learn to be satisfied with it.

Cassandra tightened her grip on his arm. "I didn't mean...I meant that you're brave, and a good person. Not that I feel... that I don't feel ..." Her face flushed scarlet, and she looked down.

Warmth spread through Henry, making his limbs light. He smiled at Cassandra, but before he could reply, the Faerie magic tightened in his chest, jerking him to attention.

"Henry Stewart!" a female voice called from outside. "It is time for you to come home!"

Cassandra hugged her baby sister protectively and stared at Henry with wide eyes. Nancy took the infant and whisked it out of sight.

Domin strode back across the porch to stand in front of the broken window, placing himself between Henry and the Fay outside. "Leave this place, Titania. You are not welcome here."

The Lady of the Woods stepped forward, her loose blonde hair flowing around her shoulders. "I hardly care for that. I'm here to reclaim Henry Stewart, mine according to Faerie law and the decree of an ordained human king. You cannot interfere with such laws, Domin, as you well know. Come out, Henry, or I will force you out."

Henry's world, which seemed to have endless bright horizons just a moment before, collapsed back around him to the darkness of a cell in Elfland.

"Can she do that?" Cassandra asked.

"Yes," Henry said.

"Can't we make her leave?"

Henry shook his head. "I don't think any of us are strong enough."

Cassandra pressed her lips together and stepped forward.

Henry grabbed her arm. "Wait, Miss Weaver." Maybe he could never be truly free from the Fay, but he would live—or die—on his own terms. He pressed the silver locket into her hands. "I don't want her to get this. I'll be back for it." He hesitated. "Or, if I'm not, I'd rather someone had it who knew..." He shrugged. Who knew him. A friend who would remember him fondly and make sure some trace of him lingered in the human world, even if only in memory.

She clutched the locket. He walked to the lopsided front door and shoved aside the furniture blocking it. As he stepped onto the porch, Domin came to his side.

"Henry..."

"I've thought this through," Henry said. "I'm not being rash this time. Much." He forced a smile.

Domin nodded, and they walked down the steps together. Titania stood on the battered lawn, flanked by Seelie elves.

"Mother, no!" Amy raced across the charred grass. "Leave him alone!"

Titania sneered. "I have not forgotten you either, child. You are banished from my court. I do not wish to see you again until you prove yourself worthy."

Amy paled and staggered back, clutching her sides. Henry winced in sympathy. The geas enforcing banishment felt like someone pummeling the air from your lungs.

"I'm here, Lady," Henry said. "Leave everyone else in peace."

"You have not learned as much as I hoped if you think you are in a position to give orders, princeling. I thought to find you grateful for what I offer."

"Then you'll be disappointed."

Titania raised her hand, and Henry added, "I'll come back with you, but my mind and will are my own, as are my powers. I'll use them as I see fit."

"You will suffer for your disobedience."

"Perhaps." A smile crept onto Henry's face, though there was no humor behind it. "But I will repay that suffering. My abilities have grown in this world. I've learned to use Faerie magic. I'll send storms to destroy your gardens and I'll open the ground to swallow your meadows and woods."

Titania's face hardened. "If you are no longer useful to me, I will kill you."

Henry straightened his shoulders. "You can try, but I'll make certain it costs you."

The elf queen snarled and lashed out, and the cords of magic tore at his chest. He gasped and pulled back. It wasn't enough to stop the process, but it eased the pressure. Titania's skin flushed red, and fine lines appeared around her eyes and mouth.

Henry summoned the wind. It swirled around Titania and her Seelie companions, whipping them with ash and debris. Raw Faerie power built in Henry's chest, and he shoved it at Titania. She shrieked and yanked at his magic. Henry stumbled forward, losing control, and the wind rushed away in a wild flurry. Pain throbbed behind his eyes. Would he die all at once, or slowly age and crumble away?

The agony stopped, and he gasped for breath. Domin stood between him and the Lady of the Woods, Mary's sharpened chisel clutched in his hand.

"That's enough, Lady."

"You cannot interfere—"

"If you are claiming your rights, I can also claim mine. He

may be your changeling, but he is my charge, and I'm bound to protect his life. If you cause his death—here or later—I will destroy you and your kingdom."

Titania hesitated and glanced at the chisel poised near her heart. "A daemon does not kill in vengeance."

"No," Domin said. "A daemon does not. But I am only half daemon."

"You would give up your daemon powers for one human? Henry's not worth that much."

"He is my friend."

"Your friend?" Titania wrinkled her nose. "He is human."

"I do not expect you to understand. But I expect you to remember." Domin sliced his palm with the tip of the chisel and squeezed his fist until blood dripped at Titania's feet. "I make you an oath on my blood, daemon and Fay. If you kill Henry, I will kill you."

Henry gaped at Domin. How could he ever repay such a gesture? He felt as undeserving of it as Titania suggested. A different magic flowed between him, the shape-shifter, and the Lady of the Woods: Domin's oath binding them. Henry's skin itched, and he looked at his forearm to find a swirling blue mark wrapped around it, just above the scars on his wrist.

Titania scowled and turned to Henry. "This does not relieve you of your service to me, but the sight of you makes me ill. Leave my presence or I will make you suffer to the brink of death and bring you back again and again."

Henry's eyes narrowed, and he stepped forward. Titania needed to know he wasn't a dog to be summoned and dismissed.

Domin grabbed his arm and shook his head. "Another time."

Henry relented. Perhaps—occasionally—he could choose

not to be rash. The shape-shifter dragged him at a run through the orchard and toward the deer path leading away from the Weaver's house.

"What have you done?" Henry panted.

"Saved your life, and you're welcome."

"Of course, thank you." Henry looked at his friend. "Would you really kill her?"

"I will not have to. As long as I live, she will not kill you. She values her own life too much to gamble with it. I cannot protect you from her retribution if you seek a fight." Domin smiled a little. "But we frightened her. She will not request your services unless her need is great."

They slowed to a walk once the forest sheltered them in its shade.

"I have to leave, don't I?"

"It would be safer for the people in this village. She cannot kill you, but she will look for other ways to make you suffer."

Cassandra. Henry groaned. Was this the cost of whatever measure of liberty he'd managed to salvage from the Fay? To always be on the run? To leave behind the people he cared about? Well, as long as he was running, he wasn't dead, and there was hope for true freedom.

They emerged from the woods. The villagers would be shaking off the Dark Lady's enchantment and returning to wakefulness. They needed to leave before there were awkward questions. He didn't regret it much, except...

Henry stopped when they reached the apothecary shop. "If you'll gather our things, I'd like to wait."

"For what?"

Henry glanced back up the road. "I want to say goodbye."

"You think she will follow?"

Henry fought the red burning over his cheeks. "I hope she will."

Domin nodded with what might have been a gleam of sympathy in his eyes and went inside. Henry turned to stare through the window at the neat rows of medicines on their shelves. Medicines he would no longer be using to help anyone. He lifted his fingers and traced them down the warm glass.

Cassandra and Mary helped Amy into the house, where the elf struggled to catch her breath. In the front garden, Telesm spoke to Titania, gesturing angrily, though Cassandra wasn't certain if he was upset about Amy's banishment or something else. Jairus stood guard on the porch, one of Mr. Weaver's guns trained on the Faerie Queen's entourage.

Amy sank onto the sofa, and some color returned to her cheeks. Cassandra sighed and glanced back out the window.

"Domin and Henry?" Amy whispered.

"He's...they're gone." The words were heavy on Cassandra's tongue.

"Perhaps," Amy said, her voice a wheeze, "he hasn't gone far yet."

The elf managed a smile. Cassandra slowly grinned in return. Her leg was exhausted, but her cane waited by the front door. She grabbed it and slipped out the back. Henry and Domin had run toward the village. Would he wait, or would he simply vanish from her life?

Cassandra skirted the Fay and limped down the road, missing her brace each time she stumbled. At her agonizing pace, it took ages to reach the outskirts of the village. Hope was a painful thing clinging to her back, whispering in her ear, prodding her on even as it mocked her foolishness. What could she hope for from Henry, now or in the future? Nothing. But she had been enough to stand up to the Dark Lady. Maybe she was enough for Henry as well. She limped on.

She came around the bend in the road where she could see the apothecary shop, and she held her breath, prepared for disappointment. Yet Henry lingered there. Waiting for her?

A smile spread over her face, and Henry met her eyes. His worried expression came alive with happiness, and he stepped away from the window to meet her.

He reached out but hesitated just short of touching her. The elation in his eyes faded. "I can't stay."

"I know." Cassandra wanted to look away, to hide her dismay, but she kept her gaze on him, memorizing the lines of his face. "I'm sorry you have to go."

"I still hope I can be free someday. Then I can have my own life." He met her eyes. "And pursue my own interests."

"I'd like that," she whispered.

"I can't ask anything of you. I don't know what's going to happen. But we are friends, right?"

Cassandra's eyes stung, but she forced a smile. "Of course."

The sound of footsteps jerked their attention to the road behind them. Jairus ran up, panting, an unconscious man slung over his shoulder.

He stopped when he reached them and slid the man to the ground. Cassandra recognized the man as one of the Grigori who had attacked her house.

"What..." Cassandra stepped away from the unconscious Grigori.

"A little complication your nurse asked me to dispose of. When he wakes, he should have the good sense to run and not look back."

"And you?" Henry asked.

"I'm going with y'all, of course."

Henry shook his head, but he smiled until he looked back at Cassandra. "Goodbye, Miss Weaver."

Her voice caught. "Goodbye, Mr. Stewart."

"Ah, Mr, Stewart," Jairus grinned. "I have so much to teach you. In America, this is how we say goodbye to a pretty girl."

He stepped up and grabbed her hands, making her drop her cane, then spun her around to tip her back in his arms. She flushed and muttered a squeak of surprise. He winked before leaning in to kiss her cheek. She laughed.

Jairus spun her up and into Henry's embrace.

She met Henry's intense gaze, and the grin slipped from her face. He raised an eyebrow, his eyes uncertain, longing, as they found their way to her lips. She tilted her face to his. He slipped one arm around her waist, and his other hand traced a line of heat along her jaw. Her breath caught, and she closed her eyes. Henry's warm lips brushed hers, sending a thrill racing through her chest. Then he pulled her closer, his mouth lingering, questioning. She kissed him in return, running her fingers up his neck and into his tangled hair. Her pain and exhaustion fell away, and she wanted to stay in his arms forever.

He broke away with a sigh and brushed a stray hair from her forehead, his fingertips warm on her skin. "I'll come back when I can."

"I'll watch for you."

Jairus turned from where he had evidently been examining the church bell tower and slapped Henry on the back. "Now, make a graceful exit before you ruin the moment."

Henry chuckled and shook his head. His arm slipped away, leaving Cassandra to feel the chill in the autumn air. Domin stepped out of the shop, carrying several satchels, and the men hurried down the road. Henry looked back and grinned before they disappeared around a corner.

Cassandra leaned heavily against the side of the building, and the window caught her eye. Icy sketches of glittering white roses covered the glass. She touched one and smiled in the direction Henry had gone, though his creation had already begun to melt.

Epilogue

Cassandra sat in the garden with her writing slope, composing lies.

She could never tell her aunts the truth about the last few weeks. But she could honestly write that baby Anne was growing well and everyone else had recovered from their... illness. That was the story she and Amy decided on, and Amy had used her "influence" to convince Mr. Tanner and the rest of the town of it before leaving for London. Still, the villagers watched the old woods distrustfully and hung their doors and windows with horseshoes and rowan-wood crosses.

"Cassie!" Sophie called. "Papa wants to speak to us."

Cassandra wasn't sorry to set her writing slope aside and limp to the house, past where Georgina stood painting. Cassandra paused to look at her sister's work. Georgina was capturing the woods again—a peaceful scene except for the sharp oil-paint shadows of the trees reaching toward the house like black claws.

Georgina looked up, her eyes underlined by dark circles. "I

can't seem to get it right. I have horrible dreams, and they seep into everything I see."

"You'll feel better soon," Cassandra said. "The nightmares will leave you alone."

Cassandra would make sure of it. She had nightmares, too, but she was Sabbath born: able to stand between her world and the Fay. Georgina smiled wanly and turned back to her canvas.

Sophie grinned. "Papa said he has a surprise for us. I wonder if he's going to let us go to London."

Cassandra's interest prickled at that. London wouldn't be so bad. Maybe Cassandra could talk Mary into going with them. They could visit Amy. And Amy might know where Henry was hiding now. Was he in London, too?

Sophie laced her arm through Cassandra's as they walked into the house. "Is your hand hurting? It was good of you to take care of us while we were sick, but I hope you know better than to try to cook now. "

"It's healing well." Yet another lie. The demon mark under her glove had scabbed over well, but pain often lanced up her arm, curling her fingers, and the stench of burning flesh filled her nightmares.

Sophie studied her as if sensing that Cassandra was holding something back. "I'm sorry Mr. Stewart decided to leave, but it shows good sense that he wants to continue his studies elsewhere. Perhaps he'll be back."

"Maybe." Cassandra touched the silver locket hidden under her bodice. It felt warm next to her skin. "But I hardly knew him anyway."

Sophie squeezed her arm, and they stopped in front of their father in his study. He put his paper down.

"Sophie! Cassie! I have excellent news. I've arranged a French tutor for you. It's time you continued your lessons."

Cassandra tried to appear as delighted as Sophie. If they had to have a tutor, why couldn't it have been in something useful, or at least interesting? Of course, her father wasn't likely to hire someone to teach her Faerie lore or marksmanship.

"Thank you, Papa." Sophie's smile lit up her eyes. "We'll study hard."

"I know you will. You're good girls. Let me introduce you to your teacher."

He led them into the drawing-room, where a thin man with white hair stood staring at the papered-over broken window, a frown creasing his face.

"Monsieur Vibert, may I introduce your new pupils, Miss Weaver and Miss Cassandra Weaver."

Vibert nodded to each girl, and Mr. Weaver said, "Well, I'll let you get to work."

Once their father was out of the room, the man turned his frown on them.

"Yes, I believe we have our work cut out for us." His accent thickened his voice. "I have heard your French is atrocious."

Sophie's jaw dropped.

Cassandra met Vibert's bright green eyes and forced her grin away. "What a shocking thing to say!"

"Mademoiselle must learn not to take offense at the truth. Life is too short. Where are your books and papers?"

"I'll get them," Sophie said, hurrying out of the room.

"Domin!" Cassandra stepped forward. "I'm so glad to see you. What about—"

"Safe," he said without dropping his accent. "Best not to speak too much about it at the moment. I'm not convinced this is a good idea, but the Fay may not overlook the role you played in upsetting their plans. I have learned it was you who undid the Dark Lady."

Cassandra matched his serious gaze. "I found myself in the perfect position to do what I needed to do." She hesitated, then asked the question that haunted her the most at night. "Is she dead?"

"No, but severely weakened for now."

Cassandra's relief at not having blood on her hands was chased closely by fear. The Unseelie Queen lived.

Domin added with obvious reluctance, "And I will help you learn to protect yourself and your family."

Cassandra relaxed and smiled a little, not just at the prospect of learning from Domin, but also because he was reluctant. That could only mean Henry had talked him into it.

Sophie returned with their old French books, and they settled down to start their drills. Even as Cassandra stumbled over her verb conjugations, she caught herself grinning. It seemed her adventures weren't over after all, and if Rushford or the Dark Lady returned, she would be ready.

Notes on Lore and Left-handedness

I have tried to keep the lore in this book faithful to Celtic and sometimes broader European folklore, though I have mingled Irish, Scottish, Welsh, and even some ancient Nordic and Continental folk traditions. Beliefs in changelings, elf shot, and the dangers of the Fair Folk lingered well into the nineteenth century in the British Isles. Luckily, mortals had some protections in the forms of the Sabbath born who could see through enchantments, holy plants like rowans and roses, and the rules governing Faerie behavior—and, of course, iron. The Fay were thought to be fallen angels, the restless dead, or demoted gods and goddesses from pre-Christian times. The Tithes to Hell appear in early Faerie ballads such as Tam Lin, where they were due on Halloween; since debts were due on Michaelmas (September 29th) during the Victorian Era, I moved the Unseelie Queen's deadline accordingly.

Victorians considered left-handedness morally questionable at best, and often punished left-handed children and forced them to write with their right hands. Like Cassandra, I'm a leftie who was taught to write with my right hand (though my teachers thought left-handedness was inconvenient instead of evil). Also like Cassandra, I have an injury that left me with hemiplegia (partial paralysis on one side of the body), though my injury is on my left side instead of my right, so I'm grudgingly grateful that I already knew how to write with my right hand.

Cassandra's injury was caused by a spinal stroke (a stroke in the neck or back, cutting off blood supply and damaging nerves) resulting from scarlet fever, though medicine at the time would not have recognized those details. Strokes are often associated with the elderly, but they're not uncommon in younger people. My personal experience is with Brown-Sequard Syndrome from a spinal cord fracture, but the symptoms are almost identical to a spinal stroke. Despite being relatively common, spinal cord injuries aren't often portrayed in media (unless as a pitiable stock character), so I was excited to tell a story with a character who shows that spinal cord injuries take a lot from survivors, but they don't take everything.

Also by E.B. Wheeler

British Fiction:

Born to Treason

The Royalist's Daughter

The Haunting of Springett Hall

Wishwood (Westwood Gothic)

Moon Hollow (Westwood Gothic)

A Proper Dragon (Dragons of Mayfair 1)

An Elusive Dragon (Dragons of Mayfair 2)

A Subtle Dragon (Dragons of Mayfair 3)

Utah Fiction:

No Peace with the Dawn (with Jeffery Bateman)

Letters from the Homefront

Balm of the Heart (in *In the Valley*)

Bootleggers and Basil (in *The Pathways to the Heart*)

Blood in a Dry Town (Tenny Mateo Mystery)

The Bone Map

Nonfiction:

Utah Women: Pioneers, Poets & Politicians

Mysteries of the Old West

Acknowledgments

This story evolved over many years, and many people have helped to bring it into the world. My heartfelt thanks to The Writers' Cache, UPSSEFW, and the Clandestine Writers, plus Melanie Bateman, Karen Brooksby, Renee Erikson, Janeal Falor, Sue Fulmer, Rosario Gil, the Isert sisters, Jenny Lyman, Jocelyn McDaniel, and Michelle Stoddard for feedback and encouragement at various points in this process, and special thanks to Abigail Samoun for believing in this story. I also appreciate the many experts and reenactors who have shared their knowledge on everything from blackpowder firearms to Victorian fabrics. As always, thank you to my husband and kids: without your support, I couldn't do it.

About the Author

E.B. Wheeler attended BYU, majoring in history with an English minor, and earned graduate degrees in history and landscape architecture from Utah State University. She's the award-winning author of over a dozen books, including Whitney Award finalists *A Proper Dragon* and *Born to Treason*, as well as several short stories, magazine articles, and scripts for educational software programs. In addition to writing, she sometimes consults about historic preservation and teaches history, and she enjoys gardening, fiber arts, folk music, and exploring the West with her family.

Find more about her and her books at ebwheeler.com

www.ingramcontent.com/pod-product-compliance
Lightning Source LLC
Chambersburg PA
CBHW071645260626
47170CB00001B/239